MW00653835

COLD SPITE

COLD SPITE

COLD JUSTICE® - MOST WANTED

TONI ANDERSON

Cold Spite

Copyright © 2024 Toni Anderson

Cover design by Regina Wamba of ReginaWamba.com

Digital ISBN-13: 978-1-990721-77-9

Print ISBN-13: 978-1-990721-76-2

The characters and events portrayed in this book are purely fictitious. Any similarity to real persons, living or dead, is coincidental and not intended by the author. Any real organizations mentioned in this book are used in a completely fictitious manner and this story in no way reflects upon the reputation or actions of those entities.

All rights reserved.

No part of this book may be reproduced, scanned or distributed in any printed or electronic form without permission. Please do not participate in encouraging piracy of copyrighted materials in violation of the author's rights. Purchase only authorized editions.

Contact email: info@toniandersonauthor.com

For more information on Toni Anderson's books, sign up for her newsletter or check out her website or new store.

ALSO BY TONI ANDERSON

COLD JUSTICE® SERIES

A Cold Dark Place (Book #1)

Cold Pursuit (Book #2)

Cold Light of Day (Book #3)

Cold Fear (Book #4)

Cold in The Shadows (Book #5)

Cold Hearted (Book #6)

Cold Secrets (Book #7)

Cold Malice (Book #8)

A Cold Dark Promise (Book #9~A Wedding Novella)

Cold Blooded (Book #10)

COLD JUSTICE® – THE NEGOTIATORS

Cold & Deadly (Book #1)

Colder Than Sin (Book #2)

Cold Wicked Lies (Book #3)

Cold Cruel Kiss (Book #4)

Cold as Ice (Book #5)

COLD JUSTICE® – MOST WANTED

Cold Silence (Book #1)

Cold Deceit (Book #2)

Cold Snap (Book #3)

Cold Fury (Book #4)

Cold Spite (Book #5)

Cold Truth (Book #6) - Coming soon

For Alex McTavish

A bright, young soul. Gone too soon. Forever missed.

COLD SPITE
Cold Justice® – Most Wanted (Book #4)

When FBI Agent Delilah Quinn survives an attempt on her life, she pretends to be dead in order to outwit her attacker. There is only one person she can turn to for help—a man she never wanted to see again…a man who abandoned her five years ago and left her heartbroken. A man definitely on the killer's hit list.

FBI Hostage Rescue Operator Cas Demarco lives with the burning regret of choosing to join HRT and leaving Delilah behind. News of her death devastates him. Then she calls him out of the blue and he can't help but seize this one last chance to make things right.

With both Delilah and Cas targeted for death, a task force is set up to catch their would-be killer, who they believe is a disgraced former Navy SEAL they helped convict of drug trafficking. Out of prison and on a ruthless quest for retribution, the former SEAL is eliminating everyone who wronged him—without leaving a shred of evidence behind.

Can Delilah and Cas prove who's responsible for the attempts on their lives and have a second chance at a future together? Or will the rogue ex-SEAL double-down on his promise to destroy them both?

———

Cold Spite is the fifth book in the Cold Justice® – Most Wanted series, featuring agents from FBI's Hostage Rescue Team.

All books standalone.

Sign up for Toni Anderson's newsletter to receive new release alerts, bonus Cold Justice® stories, and a free copy of The Killing Game:

www.toniandersonauthor.com/newsletter-signup

Content Advisory: This book contains common tropes found in the Romantic Thriller/ Romantic Suspense genre, including violence, sex, and strong language. If you are sensitive or easily triggered, please take that into consideration and read responsibly. For more details, check out the book page on my website.

1

Five years earlier

Ricky Alonso removed his treasured bone-handled balisong —the only physical legacy he had from either of his unnamed and unknown biological parents—from his back pocket, flipped it open, and used it to slit the thick plastic wrap covering the off-white brick of prime Colombian cocaine. He closed the blade with a flick of his wrist and slipped the butterfly knife into his back pocket. Each brick was marked with a simple line drawing of an open hand, indicating exactly who was gonna kill you if you messed with their product. Ricky wet the end of his finger and lightly pressed it to the cut. He licked the tip of his finger and grimaced at the bitter taste on his tongue.

"*Es bueno, jefe.*" Pedro, barely eighteen and initiated into the gang by his older brother, Felipe, when he was fourteen years old, sampled the coke after he did, his dark eyes going wide.

Ricky liked him. Pedro was a nice kid.

This was the part of the job he hated.

"*No soy el jefe, chico.*" Ricky wasn't the boss. He was a *soldado*, a foot soldier, who had somehow, ironically, found himself in charge of this small cell of the Mexican cartel. The last *patrón*, or chief, had been a crazy asshole who'd gotten himself shot by the *La Guardia Nacional* four months ago after kidnapping a blonde tourist he'd taken a shine to. They'd both died in the shootout.

Ricky had managed to protect the rest of the men from the same fate, which had earned him kudos with them and their bosses.

Ricky took orders.

Followed rules.

Same as everyone else. Otherwise, you risked the wrath of the cartel leaders—amongst others. But here, in this small corner of hell, he supposed he was, theoretically, in charge.

Unless they discovered the truth.

Then he was dead.

It would all be over soon. He needed to get through the next few hours, and everything would be okay—except for the whole ripping-out-his-heart-and-letting-it-bleed-to-death thing.

That was a problem for later. First, they had to survive.

"You want to try?" Ricky offered the brick to the hulking man with sandy-brown hair who watched him with animus gleaming in his pale blue eyes.

The American shook his head.

"This is the only chance you get, *amigo*." Ricky smiled coldly and let the warning ring loudly through the sweltering heat of the mechanic's workshop from where they were currently running their operation. "The people we both work for don't like it if we help ourselves to the merchandise."

"I don't do coke. I'm not a junkie."

Probably scared of the random drug screenings conducted by the US military, although most active-duty personnel figured out a way to get around them if they needed to.

Those blue eyes were hard and distrustful even though the man's expression remained largely flat. "I'm just the delivery guy —as long as I get paid."

Ricky gave him a skeptical look. Two of the gang members narrowed their gazes to match his. No one trusted the man from

Louisiana. Even in a world of stone-cold killers there was something off about the guy. Something that made the hair on Ricky's nape lift in warning.

His gut twisted.

He fucking hated this plan.

"Pay him his money." He jerked his head at Pedro, who scrambled to get the cash, then turned away from the table where the boys were weighing the latest consignment of cocaine. *"Ponlo en su camióneta. Cuéntalo primero."*

He left the other gang members to skillfully stash as much coke as possible in the Cajun's bright shiny new truck that cartel money had probably paid for and headed into the office where Lacey waited.

He walked inside, shut the door, and sucked in his breath. Leaned against the glass as he took in the most beautiful woman he'd ever laid eyes on. She made it so he could barely breathe. She sat there wearing nothing more glamorous than cutoff jeans, a white tank, and strappy leather sandals, but the vision of her hurt his eyes.

The things he felt for her were strange and overwhelming. He didn't have a family. Had never had a family. Wasn't sure if this was what love always felt like but, if it was, no wonder wars had been fought over it. She was everything he'd ever wanted. Everything he could never have.

He cleared his throat, wished he didn't feel as if he was going to throw up. "You're sure you want to go through with this?"

She ran her fingers carefully through her short blonde hair. "I'm sure, baby." Her voice was soft as powdered sugar.

She stood and walked toward him, and it was like watching silk dance in the wind.

"I don't trust him with you." His voice was like gravel in his throat. His hands caught her hips as she stopped in front of him.

She ran her fingers down the front of his T-shirt and then hooked her thumbs into the waistband of his jeans.

"He wouldn't dare touch me." They were both conscious of the eyes watching them through the glass office windows and the fact people could be listening to them.

Hell, he *knew* people were listening to them.

"I don't like you being anywhere close to that *hijo de puta*."

Her expression tightened, at odds with her sotto voce. "I can take care of myself."

He cupped her jaw. "He's dangerous."

Her lips curved, and he ran his thumb over their warm pink softness. "I have plenty of weapons."

They were so close he could smell the mint of her toothpaste. He wanted to taste her. He needed to taste her. Everything about this woman consumed him even though he couldn't afford to be distracted.

She kissed him, and the feel of her mouth on his washed away all rational thought. He slid his hands over her butt and pulled her hips to his, her breasts pressed to his chest, her arms wrapped like vines around his neck.

Despite the oppressive heat, he wanted to feel her skin against his. Wanted to absorb the sweetness of her body, feel the lithe strength of her matching him perfectly in every way.

She opened her mouth and slid her tongue against his, and he wanted to press her against the wall and fuck her until they were both slick with sweat. And then lay her on the softest bed and make love to her until she couldn't move. He wanted all that, and the thought of letting her go was as unthinkable as cutting out his own tongue. And yet...

Whistles and lewd comments from the outer garage reminded him they weren't alone. It was too dangerous to drop his guard. One wrong move in this pit of vipers, and they'd both be dead.

He slipped the balisong out of his back pocket and into her shorts without the others being able to see. "If he touches you, kill the motherfucker." He pulled away and exited the office.

He strode up to the Cajun and didn't stop until he'd pushed the guy up against the door of his extended cab. All his men gathered around him, but despite what this *pendejo* mistakenly thought, Ricky didn't need their backup to hand him his ass.

"The woman is mine, ¿*entendido*? You make a move on her, you even breathe in her direction, I'll dice you up and feed you to the vultures myself."

The man's muscles tensed as if to fight back but then his eyes slowly took in the other men in the garage—all dangerous, most of them killers—and then rose over Ricky's shoulder to find Lacey, who Ricky could hear walking toward them.

Ricky didn't turn around or risk taking his eyes off this treacherous piece of shit.

"Don't worry, *amigo*." The Cajun sneered. "I wouldn't touch your whore even if she begged me." But his face said otherwise.

"Want me to kill him for you?" Pedro offered, eager to prove his devotion.

Rage and fear churned inside Ricky. He only had to say the word, and this scumbag would be dead. But he wanted this motherfucker ruined. He wanted him stripped of honor and exposed as the worthless *pedazo de mierda* he really was. Killing him wouldn't serve Ricky's purpose. So he left the rage banked deep inside and tried to tame the fear.

"No. Not today, *amigo*. He has a delivery to make."

"That's good to hear," Lacey said from behind him. "Because this whore has plans tonight. I have a date with my girlfriend and don't want to be late." She chewed gum impatiently. "Let's hit the road, *compadre*. Unless you've changed your mind about doing this, in which case Ricky here can give me a ride to the border, can't ya, baby?"

The air crackled with tension as the gang members looked at him for instruction.

It was his decision, who lived and died. It was a heady power, and he could see how easily it would corrupt.

"Whatever you want, baby."

Ricky stood back and crossed his arms over his chest, staring down the Cajun. The man straightened and then sneered at Lacey.

"Get in." He climbed into the driver's seat and started the engine with a roar.

Lacey reared up on tiptoe to brush her lips over Ricky's cheek. "See you soon."

He nodded brusquely. It took everything in him to let her go. A million things wanted to trip off his tongue. All of them began with "I love you. Be careful."

Lacey hoisted herself into the truck and waved to all the guys. They drove away with a blast of heat and fumes from the hot exhaust. Ricky had never felt more alone.

"*Lacey estará bien. Él no se atrevería a tocarla.*" Pedro patted his shoulder.

She'll be okay. He wouldn't dare touch her.

Ricky wanted to throw up.

Pedro looked at him uncertainly. Ricky wanted to warn this young man to get out of town. To leave now before it all went to shit and his life was destroyed forever.

Ricky looked around the garage as the cartel's many minions continued packing coke and money into heavy canvas bags. There were other deliveries to be made. Misery to disseminate. Money to collect. Lives to ruin and accounts to be tallied. Hours of work to be done in this evil trade to keep the top of the organization wealthy beyond belief.

Sweat beaded his temple and ran in a thin trickle over his jawline and down his neck. He hated the intensity of the heat—the cloying miasma of engine oil, casual violence, cocaine dust, and greed.

A text came through on his cell. A fucking tongue, eggplant, taco, and droplet emoji from "Leticia."

The last person he wanted to have sex with, of any variation, was CIA Intelligence Officer Patrick Killion.

But it was the signal.

"I need a drink." He walked into his office and picked up his wallet, keys, and a packet of cigarettes he didn't like to smoke but did anyway.

His heart felt heavy.

He headed over to his beat-up Camaro, paused. Looked at Pedro. "Wanna come?"

Pedro grinned, eyes shining with happiness at being singled out. "No, *patrón*, I'll keep watch. I'll let you know if there are any problems. Don't worry. Lacey will be fine. The *puto cabrón* wouldn't dare cross you."

Ricky wasn't convinced, but he could do nothing about it now. He slid inside. He had his orders. Time to get the hell out of Tijuana. His mouth went dry as he pulled away, watching his crew in the rearview, men he'd spent months befriending and getting to know.

Men with girlfriends and babies to support. Men with mothers and grandmothers who loved them. Some of them were pure evil. Others, simply trying to survive.

Pedro's smiling face and warm brown eyes followed his path like a Golden Retriever watching its owner leave for work.

But Ricky Alonso was dead now. He wasn't ever coming back.

2

FBI Special Agent Delilah Quinn slipped off her sandals and rested her bare feet on the dash as the big-ass truck hugged the curve of the road heading to Federal Highway 1.

The muscles in Navy SEAL Seaman Recruit Joseph Scanlon's lantern jaw flexed with annoyance. Pissed her dirty feet were touching his precious penis extension.

She hid her disgust under an artless expression. Betraying his rank, his fellow sailors, his country didn't bother him, but her putting her bare feet on his stinking new dash did.

Asshole.

His fate was already sealed. The Bureau was monitoring the operation from high altitude drones, not to mention the camera in her necklace and the audio recorder in her purse.

He was so fucked.

He reached out and clamped his big hand around her calf.

She froze. Gritted her teeth. "Get your hands off me."

He sent her a glance as he squeezed and then slid his hand up to her knee and then down her thigh. "Come on, *cher*. You can't be satisfied with that slick beaner."

Her eyes widened in horror at the slur. *The hell?* "He's twice the man your coonass will ever be."

He barked out a laugh that held zero humor. "Being called a coonass is a compliment where I come from."

She tried to pull away, but his grip tightened to bruising pressure.

"Ricky is my boyfriend." She tried to sound indignant, but she'd be lying if she wasn't a little disconcerted.

"You don't need a boyfriend, *cher*. You need a man." His fingers inched toward her crotch, and she jerked away and found herself wedged into the corner staring at this dickwad and breathing heavily.

"You heard what he'll do to you if he finds out you touched me."

"I'm not scared of *Ricky* fucking *Alonso*."

"I'm not a cheater." *Unlike you.* He had a wife and young kid at home. Not to mention the whole smuggling drugs and possibly other things across the border after pledging the oath of allegiance.

His grin was surprisingly attractive but didn't quite meet those cold eyes. "Come on, Lacey. A little fun can't hurt anyone."

She didn't say anything.

"I'm sorry for calling you a whore." His cheek pulled one side of his lips into a practiced smile. "I admit I was jealous. I hated seeing the greasy prick put his hands on you."

There was nothing greasy or sleazy about FBI Special Agent Casta Demarco, but perhaps she was playing this wrong. They needed to arrest Scanlon on the US side of the border. And a guy like Scanlon would appreciate having his ego stroked.

She bit her lip, let her expression turn uncertain. "Ricky doesn't like sharing."

He lowered his voice. "Ricky doesn't have to know, *cher*. This can be between you and me. Our little secret."

The idea turned her already sensitive stomach. The last week or so she hadn't been able to keep anything down. Nerves at the culmination of a six-month-long undercover operation where she'd played Ricky Alonso's flaky American girlfriend, crossing the border every weekend to visit a man who'd spent almost a year working his way up to a position of power inside the cartel.

"You think he isn't banging a local girl when you aren't in town?" Scanlon gave a loud whoop. "Funny, you don't look like a dumb blonde."

She hunched her shoulders and pouted. "He wouldn't do that to me. He loves me."

Scanlon shot her an incredulous look. "What does love have to do with anything? Men like to fuck beautiful women. It's the natural order of things."

She wondered if he cared how willing those women were. There was something predatory about Joseph Scanlon. The butterfly knife that Cas—*Ricky*—had slipped into her back pocket pressed into her glute muscle.

"So"—she caught her bottom lip—"you think I'm beautiful?"

His gaze slipped from the heavy traffic to run up her bare legs to settle on her breasts through the flimsy shirt she wore.

"Everyone thinks you're beautiful." He stroked a surprisingly gentle finger down the smooth skin of her shin. "So how about I come up for a while after I drop you off? You'll still have plenty of time to meet your girlfriend." His warm fist curled tightly around the bones of her ankles, like a manacle.

"What about the merchandise?" She glanced at the border guard booth they were slowly approaching.

"It'll be fine for half an hour."

"Half an hour? That's all you got in you?" She smiled coyly.

He shifted in his seat. "I need to drop the shipment off and get home."

"To your wife."

Scanlon grunted.

"She won't mind you *coming up* for half an hour?" She shifted in her seat and watched him eye her breasts.

"She won't mind what she doesn't know." He sounded so sure of that. "And ain't no one stupid enough to steal my truck, but I have a tracker on it, just in case."

Her eyes widened. "You have a tracker on your own vehicle?"

"Just in case anyone gets any stupid ideas." Scanlon's vehicle was next in line at the border control. "Now you keep jiggling those fine titties and smiling with that pretty smile of yours at the nice man, *cher*." He pulled on a ball cap that had NAVY in bold type across the front. And she noticed he leaned his elbow on the window, making sure his bone frog tattoo—an unofficial Navy SEAL insignia—was in the border agent's face.

The stern-faced guard checked their docs and, after a perfunctory couple of questions, let them through. She didn't have to jiggle a damned thing.

"Where's your apartment?"

"Ricky isn't going to like it."

"I got to drop you off, don't I? Anyway, you leave Ricky to me."

She gave him the address. She went quiet because that's how Lacey would react. Lacey Reed would absolutely let this asshole screw her to get him out of her hair. And then beg Ricky for forgiveness if he ever found out. It wasn't like she had much of a choice, a girl like that. She used her body to get what she wanted. Her power was in the men she manipulated. At least, that was Delilah's cover. That was Lacey's backstory. Always fucking the wrong guy. And being screwed over.

Scanlon reached Lacey's apartment and parked in the shadow of a dying palo verde tree. She went to get out, but he grabbed her arm and pulled her half over the console, mashing her breast with his meaty hand, exposing her nipple to whoever was watching. He kissed her roughly, forcing her to open her mouth. She made herself relax. Prayed no one overreacted.

He started to fumble with the button on her shorts. She jerked away, thinking she might have to pull that butterfly knife on him if she wasn't careful. Threaten to cut his dick off.

She wiped her throbbing lips and hid her disgust. "Let's go inside. We don't want to attract any undue attention, remember?"

Scanlon rolled his shoulders in an arrogant shrug.

She pushed open the door and looked around, the way she would if she was worried about anyone seeing Scanlon enter her apartment.

Her heart beat a little faster as she spotted a guy reclining in his car, wearing sunglasses as he listened to music.

The smell of garbage wafted from a nearby dumpster. She stood in the parking lot and fumbled in her bag for her keys. Scanlon got out of his truck and slammed the door shut.

He came around the back and she turned, dropping the bag and holding up her badge with one hand and Glock 23 with the other.

His wide-eyed surprise was gratifying.

"FBI. Hands on your head." Her heart was pounding, and acid sat under her breastbone, but her gaze didn't waver from the hulking Navy SEAL. "I repeat. FBI. Put your hands on the back of your head, Joseph Scanlon, and then down on your knees."

His lip curled in a sneer. "If you want me on my knees, you need to be on your back, *cher*." He lunged for her, and her hesitation to shoot the bastard cost her. He tackled her, knocking the weapon to one side. She dropped her badge and grabbed at the knife Cas had given her as Scanlon slammed her to the ground. The skin of her back grazed and burned against the rough asphalt. His weight crushed her ribs and winded her, but he wasn't expecting the blade that she pressed against the vulnerable flesh next to his carotid.

He drew his hand back as if to strike her.

"I gave you one free pass." She locked onto his gaze and let him see the contempt she felt for him as she pressed the steel close enough to sting his skin. "You won't get another."

He hesitated and then finally, the sound of footsteps running out of the nearby building assailed their ears.

The agent formerly reclining in his car, stood over them with his gun pointed at Scanlon. "Get off her, you sonofabitch."

Scanlon reared up onto his knees as members of the Hostage Rescue Team dragged him backwards off of her and cuffed his hands behind his back. She rolled onto her side and climbed unsteadily to her feet, closing the handles of the knife around the blade, and slipping it back into her pocket.

"Your boyfriend isn't going to be very happy with you, you traitorous bitch." Scanlon spat out. "Nor the cartel."

"Oh, that's rich." She gave him a feral smile as she picked up her badge and her gun off the ground. There was a scratch on the barrel now which pissed her off. "Break the law, pay the price. Can't wait to see the look on your wife's face when she hears how much your marriage vows mean to you."

His eyes changed then. Filled with a cold hatred that sent a shiver of fear down her spine. "Leave my wife out of this."

She tried moving her shoulders. The flesh burned, but she didn't think any bones were broken. "Pretty sure you're the one who brought her into this, not me. You came on to me, remember?"

She bent her head and leaned forward as one of the techs came to collect her necklace and purse for the camera and mic fitted inside. "I guess she can make up her own mind when she hears the tapes."

With a roar Scanlon broke free of the men detaining him and charged her again. The tech jumped aside. She feinted left at the last moment, and Scanlon crashed to the hot tarmac. A heavy-set operator placed his boot between the man's shoulder blades and shifted his weight to keep him there.

Delilah walked over and crouched so she could look directly into Scanlon's furious face. She shook her head. "I don't get it. You had everything. Why did you decide to betray your colleagues, your wife, your country?"

"I didn't betray anyone, bitch."

"Well, I guess bitch is a step up from whore. And a jury gets to decide the rest."

"I'm going to make you pay for this."

"Threatening a Federal Agent? Way to pile on the charges, pal."

"I'm going to rape you and kill you and laugh while I'm doing it. I'll smash your skull in so no one can recognize that pretty face of yours."

She straightened and hooked her hands into the back loops of her jean shorts. "Whatever gets you off in prison. Enjoy because it's the closest you're gonna get to touching a woman for the next ten years." She made light of it even though his threat curled inside her and unexpectedly made fear spurt. She stood back as two HRT operators hauled the disgraced Navy SEAL to his feet and handed him off to NCIS agents, who read him his rights. The FBI had agreed to hand him over to the Navy to prosecute.

She exhaled a long breath as she watched him being led away.

"You okay?" the FBI agent asked as Scanlon was loaded into the back of a black van.

She wiped her mouth with the back of her hand. "Nothing a shower and gallon of mouthwash won't cure."

Her eyes caught on a beaten-up red Camaro as it cruised into the parking lot. Her mouth watered as she watched Cas climb out, those long legs and lean frame looking oh so good. He stared at her for a heated moment with yellow eyes that shone like gold, scanning her for damage which he thankfully couldn't see. He exchanged a greeting with one of the Hostage Rescue Team operators who he slapped on the back like an old friend.

Her heart sank a little.

He'd applied for HRT and had been accepted into their prestigious trials which started next week. That was partly why they'd made the arrests today. But after nearly twelve long and dangerous months, it was time to pull Cas out from his undercover role. It was affecting him, giving him dark thoughts and self-doubts. Plus, the investigation had run its course.

And now she was going to have to resign herself to a long-distance relationship because there was no way Cas, himself a former Navy SEAL, wouldn't sail through HRT's selection process with flying colors.

Her heart clenched and that familiar nausea washed through

her because she loved this man so much she wasn't sure she could stand being so many thousand miles away from him.

She planned to put in for a transfer, but she hadn't told Cas that yet.

Her father was an Assistant Director in FBI HQ, and she would absolutely, for once, use her connections to get a position commuting distance to Quantico. She didn't have to see Cas every day or even every week, but as often as they could make it work with busy schedules.

Even if she took a step down on the career ladder it would be worth it. She needed this man in her life. She wanted to spend more than a few stolen weekends with him. She wanted time when they weren't pretending to be other people. When they weren't worried one wrong word would get them both killed.

"Agent Quinn."

She snapped her head to one side to look at the other agent. His tone suggested it wasn't the first time he'd said her name.

"Yes?"

"Let me give you a ride into the office to get an official statement regarding today's events and then you can go home and get some rest."

She nodded and then shot Cas a rueful look as she followed the agent to his car.

Cas would also need to be debriefed. But she'd see him later. They had all the time in the world now.

3

After a long day, Cas came out of the interview room. He wanted to find Delilah. Make sure she was okay. Instead, he bumped straight into the Special Agent in Charge of the San Diego Office, Peter Ridgeway. Ridgeway wasn't his favorite person, but then Cas preferred the people on the ground doing the grunt work rather than the pen pushers and administrators.

Cas was officially based out of the LA office, but he'd barely started work there before being fingered by the undercover division for this assignment. He'd met his own SAC a total of two times and doubted the guy would recognize him in a crowd. Ridgeway though, he liked to keep up with what was going on in the San Diego office and surrounding area.

Ridgeway held out his hand to shake Cas's. "I wanted to say congratulations. Great work today."

Cas's brows hiked. *Today*? He'd been undercover for nearly a year.

"Both the *Policía Federal* and *Policía Federal Ministerial* were very happy with the information we provided. They raided the garage shortly after you left."

Cas's mouth tasted of sand. "Did they catch everyone?"

Ridgeway nodded. "They got them all. Ten dead. Four injured.

Three arrests. No *members of la Guardia Nacional* or civilians were hurt. They found nearly three tons of cocaine on the premises and are hailing it as one of the biggest wins against the cartel in years…"

He kept talking, but Cas wasn't listening.

Sickened, he closed his eyes. *Ten* dead? And four casualties whose wounds would likely fester in jail until they died.

"Who? Who was wounded?" he interrupted.

Ridgeway blinked, clearly taken aback.

Cas cleared his throat. "I'd like to see a list of the victims from today. Sir," he added belatedly.

Ridgeway's lips pursed. "I'll have someone send it to you."

Cas nodded. "I appreciate that. Thank you."

Ridgeway placed his hand on Cas's left shoulder, and it took everything in him not to violently shake him off. "Anyway, I wanted to extend my personal congratulations on a job well done. There's a commendation in this for you, mark my words."

The man's eyes danced with delight. The deaths were barely a postscript on his conscience.

Cas watched the SAC stride away as if he had somewhere important to be, perhaps a press conference or a meeting with the FBI Director. Cas pulled out his personal cell. There was a missed call from Delilah, and he closed his eyes as more pain piled on.

What he was about to do would break her heart, but it was for the best. She'd find someone else. Someone better suited to the Assistant Director's daughter—as the man in question had been keen to point out to him before his interview to get into this year's round of the Hostage Rescue Team's selection process.

The threat had been explicit, although the man hadn't uttered the words. Keep seeing Delilah and Cas's chance of getting into HRT would be zero, zilch.

So, that was his "choice."

Be with the woman he loved knowing that it was only a matter of time before she realized for herself that their wildly differing backgrounds would never work in the real world. Or get a shot at

HRT selection, which had been his dream ever since he'd met a man named Kurt Montana attached to his SEAL team, in a dusty Afghan desert.

The fight for justice, even in a war zone, had appealed to Cas's innate sense of fairness, his sense of honor, and he'd applied for the FBI from his bunk in Kandahar. But his undercover role with the Mexican cartel hadn't felt particularly honorable. Even though he knew the evil of the drug trade, had seen friends from his days in the foster system succumb to the lure of chemical oblivion, the stories of hardship and violence of the men he'd met in Mexico resonated. He'd been one bad decision away from that being his life. Instead, he'd been fortunate. Joining the Navy, having the aptitude for the SEALs and then the Bureau. Not everyone was that lucky.

Funny, he'd always thought being lucky would feel good.

Hotness slithered through his gut.

He texted Killion asking for a breakdown of what had happened in Mexico and exactly who'd died. The thought of Pedro and a couple of the others being hurt cut deep. If they were injured, perhaps he could figure out a way to get them treatment, or possibly extradited to the US. Perhaps he could spin it so Pedro could turn state's evidence in exchange for more information on his brother's role in the cartel.

His hands shook as he read Killion's reply. A list of names and photos of the dead. Saliva flooded his mouth as an image of Pedro flashed onto the screen. Blood dribbled out of his mouth, and his eyes were closed.

Bile rose up his throat, but he forced it down. Tears burned at the back of his eyes, but he wouldn't let them fall, not when today still had more pain in store for him.

He needed to get it over with. Inflict all the punishment in one go and hope to survive the aftermath. He headed outside to the parking lot. He'd handed the Camaro back to the FBI's carpool and picked up his truck which had been dropped off here by one of his colleagues from the undercover division.

Keys were in the ignition.

Delilah texted him an address and a sense of numbness enveloped him.

He had to end this thing now. Before he hurt her even more than he already would.

He used his cell to direct him to the condo she'd bought a year ago when she'd first been assigned to the west coast.

The fact she could afford to buy anything around here on a single salary reaffirmed they came from polar opposite backgrounds.

There was a space on the road near her place, so he pulled in and turned off the engine.

He forced the emotion out of his head. No way would he be able to do this if he thought too much about it. He was an old pro at dissociation.

He checked the house number and then headed down the narrow path, eyeing the clear turquoise pool with envy, passing the tamed hibiscus bushes and beneath the jacaranda trees with their obscenely beautiful lavender-blue flowers.

He found the right block of condos and climbed the steps to Delilah's front door. He'd been dreaming about this moment since the day they'd first realized their pretend romance was actually the real deal.

She opened the door, her natural long dark hair wet from a recent shower and the familiar scent of her almost brought him to his knees.

She flung herself at him and entwined her arms tight around his neck. He wrapped his around her and held her tight. Sank his nose into the crook of her neck and inhaled. This was it. This was all he would allow himself.

He squeezed her tight and felt her wince. He pulled away. "Are you okay?"

"Fine." Her brown eyes were shining with joy as she pulled him inside.

Despite the guilt about what he intended to do, he looked

around with interest. It was the first time he'd been to her home, and even though he was torturing himself, he was curious about her space. Her couch and recliner were a soft brown leather that looked classy and expensive. The walls were painted off-white, and the floors were glossy hardwoods. There were paintings on the walls that looked to his uneducated eye to be originals.

"Want a drink?" She turned and headed toward the small kitchen.

"What the hell happened to your back?"

She looked over her shoulder and grimaced. "Scanlon jumped me when I arrested him, and I got a bit scraped up." She fished into the back pocket of her tight-fitting blue jeans, handed him his treasured balisong knife. He cradled it when he really wanted to cradle her.

"He almost peed his pants when he realized we had recordings. Wife's gonna be pissed when she hears him proposition me in the truck."

"That motherfucker." Rage heated his bones. "Did he hurt you?"

She shook her head.

"Delilah?"

Her head jerked up then. It was the first time he'd used her real name. He hadn't dared before, not when a mistake could mean her death.

"He didn't hurt me. He just wanted to take what belonged to you."

It was as if someone had scooped out his insides and dumped them in the ocean.

Those brown eyes softened in concern. "I heard about what happened back at the mechanic shop. Are you okay?"

He shook his head but didn't say anything else.

"What is it? Having trouble adjusting to our new reality?" She laughed softly as she handed him a bottle of his favorite beer.

"Want to go on a date?" Her eyes shone with love. What else would make her look at him like that? "We can hit a restaurant on the beach, catch a movie. Do something that normal people do."

Normal?

He'd never been normal.

He placed the beer carefully on the counter. She took a step toward him, but he held up his hand to ward her off.

She paused, and he saw the way her eyes started to change.

He cleared his throat. "Thanks for the beer, but I have to drive to LA tonight."

"Now?" She crossed her arms over her chest.

He nodded. "Yeah. I plan to be on the road to Quantico in the morning."

She blinked. "Oh. Well, I took off next week and thought I'd help you move. That way we get to spend a little time together before you start selection and we can maybe pop in to meet my parents. They're dying to meet you."

A bitter laugh escaped. He put his hand over his brow.

"Cas?"

His name on her lips sent a crack through the wall of his heart.

She took a step closer. "What is it? What's wrong?"

He thrust all the emotion away. The despair. The hurt. The insidious fucking hope. "I need to be honest with you about something."

Ironic, as she was the only person he'd ever been truly honest with and even she didn't know half of his dirty secrets.

"Sometimes things happen during an assignment that shouldn't happen. Emotions get amplified. People say things that in the cold light of day might not be true."

"Things?" She hiked a fine brow in obvious confusion.

"Yeah. They, er, say things and make promises in the heat of the moment."

"Are you telling me you don't want me to drive across the country with you?" A dent of confusion crinkled the skin between her brows. "I get that you need some time to process what happened over the past twelve months—"

"Not just that." His voice was sharper than he'd meant it to be.

"Oh, *oh.*" Her hand covered her mouth. "You mean things like 'I love you' and 'I want to spend time with you when we're not in danger of being sliced and diced by the cartel'? Those things."

He wanted to deny it all and tell her the truth, but then she'd never let him go. She'd convince herself that the feelings they shared would compensate for his lack of pedigree and breeding. It wouldn't. Not in the long run. He wasn't worth the sacrifices he knew she was willing to make.

"Look, we had great chemistry in bed, but it wasn't real, okay? It was a reaction to the danger we were in. The situation. The tension. The fact you look like sex on a fucking stick."

Her eyes swam with tears. Her voice grew thick. "I don't believe you."

He couldn't look at her. He had to cut the ties irrevocably. Kill the beauty of everything they'd had together and let her move on. He made his expression cold. "You were a good fuck, Delilah, but don't ruin things by getting clingy. I'm trying to do the right thing here. I'm going to be thousands of miles away. I'm not making any promises about fidelity, and I know women like you expect promises." He met her gaze then and let his expression open up. "I mean, if you're willing to keep things casual, then maybe we can hook up again next time we're on the same coast."

She flinched away from him and sorrow as sharp as his beloved blade sliced through his chest cavity and shredded the organ in his chest until it was bloody.

"Get out." She wrapped her arms around herself and curled over as if in pain. She screamed. "Get out. Get out. Get out!"

The sight of her hit him like a felled tree. This woman had faced down killers and drug dealers with an easy smile.

Nothing had dented her composure.

Nothing.

Except him.

Cas searched for numbness, but all he found was heartbreak and grief. So what if her beloved father hated him? So what if his own dreams were crushed? Didn't matter he was doing it for her own good, this felt like dying. He forced himself to get moving, to leave her in her small, neat kitchen before he fell to his knees and confessed it was all a lie and he'd take what he could get for as long as she wanted him.

Ultimately, it would destroy him, but as long as she was okay, what did it matter? He hesitated on the threshold of her home blinded by the late afternoon sun. He looked over his shoulder and she stood there with dry eyes and a blank expression on her pale, beautiful face.

He inhaled unsteadily and then turned away, stepping into the setting sun. Into a life of loneliness and wishful thinking.

4

FEBRUARY 8

Present Day

F BI Special Agent Delilah Quinn was tired and grouchy as she waited outside the office of the Special Agent in Charge of the San Diego Field Office. The door opened, and she stood quickly.

Peter Ridgeway's expression dropped at the sight of her. "Can it wait?"

She hesitated. Shook her head.

He released a sigh that ruffled his thinning bangs. "Come in. Be quick. I have a meeting downtown."

She strode inside as Ridgeway went around to the other side of his desk. He didn't sit.

"Joseph Scanlon was released from military prison three weeks ago." She crossed her arms and tried to make it a position of power rather than the self-hug she feared it actually was.

His expression didn't change.

"You already knew." Inside she deflated.

"Friend of mine at Coronado kept me updated."

But he hadn't thought to inform her. She didn't know whether to be pissed or take it as a compliment.

"Scanlon was an exemplary prisoner. He apparently planned to head back to his hometown in Louisiana to work in the family business." Ridgeway pushed his wireless glasses up his thin nose. Cleared his throat. "If he'd been staying in the area, I would have let you know, but I'm sure you agree that I can't be expected to keep track of every released felon and notify all the agents involved in their cases. That would be a full-time job in itself."

His tone aimed for humor but only managed patronizing.

"Of course not." Her tongue stalled as she opened her mouth to tell him of the unsettled sensation she'd experienced recently. The feeling of being watched. Ridgeway overtly checked his wristwatch, and she knew her time was up. Just as well. The idea of appearing paranoid with her boss was not high on her wish list.

"How's your father?"

She set her teeth. "Fine. Thank you."

As a former Assistant Director of the FBI, her father was well-known and respected throughout the Bureau. More so than Ridgeway.

"Give him my regards."

"Of course." Her father considered SAC Peter Ridgeway a bit of a toady, but Delilah wasn't about to tell him that. Thoughts of her father sank her mood even lower.

Ridgeway headed to the door and let her exit before him. "Scanlon's served his time."

Debatable.

"He's rehabilitated, found God, and hopefully learned the error of his ways."

She raised a skeptical brow. The disgraced former Navy SEAL she'd crossed paths with was a mean, angry, dangerous individual, but she had to hope the prison system had some positive effect on its inmates, even if it was simply the desire never to go back.

"Let's hope so, sir."

Ridgeway nodded vigorously as if they'd agreed on something and then strode away.

Delilah stood for a moment in the corridor and stared out of the huge glass windows across Vista Sorrento Parkway and I-805 to the green hills beyond. The sun was shining, but then this was Southern California. Even February was beautiful here.

Old memories side-swiped her. Thoughts of Scanlon and the op that had captured him always brought back painful reminders she preferred to ignore.

None of that mattered anymore.

Old history.

She should warn Scanlon's ex-wife, who'd taken their daughter and headed north to Washington State.

She should notify FBI HRT operator, Cas Demarco, but the sonofabitch could look after himself.

Even the thought of him made her grind her teeth. Last time she'd seen, or rather *heard* the rat bastard, he'd been in court, hidden behind a screen under a fake identity in order to protect both his undercover personas and his real identity.

Agent Z.

It suited the guy—all dark, brooding mystery and sexy swagger.

But the attempts at secrecy had been performative as far as Scanlon was concerned. Despite his illegal activities, Joseph Scanlon had enough friends back at Coronado that it wouldn't be difficult for him to track down the name of another former SEAL, now turned FBI agent, who'd been working with the DEA and CIA and posing as a cartel member across the border in Mexico. A man who had helped get him thrown off the teams and into Miramar.

She was pretty sure Demarco had been avoiding her as much as he'd been avoiding the media with the whole *Agent Z* thing. Avoiding the chance she might make a scene or embarrass him again.

Not in this lifetime.

Six years ago, the Bureau had been after Lorenzo Santiago—at the time an associate of Manuel Gómez, head of *El cartel de Mano de Dios* down in Colombia. But not long after the operation started, Gómez and most of his organization's leaders had been scooped up and arrested following an anonymous tipoff. The few remaining *Mano de Dios* members, and Santiago, had gone so deep underground that the FBI had almost folded up its investigation and gone home.

But then Demarco had heard a whisper about an active-duty Navy SEAL who was said to be transporting drugs across the border. No way could the FBI ignore that rumor because if a SEAL was willing to smuggle drugs, what else might he be willing to do?

So Demarco had gone even deeper undercover, and that's when Delilah had appeared on the scene. She'd been his FBI contact, his "handler"—if a man like Demarco was capable of being handled—posing as his drug-addicted girlfriend. She never met the major cartel players face-to-face, but she'd known they watched her undercover persona's apartment sometimes and searched it when she was in "rehab." Her identity had been back-stopped to the nth degree and her appearance easily disguised with a short blonde wig she still kept in the go-bag of her vehicle.

After the bust, the Bureau had decided Demarco was too much of a potential target and had taken him out of his undercover work and moved him far from the border.

And he'd been all too happy to leave.

The Hostage Rescue Team had been his dream all along and, as expected, he'd passed selection and made the cut.

Bitterness twisted in her stomach.

Nowadays most of those cartel members were dead or in prison. Santiago's organization had imploded spectacularly last month in the Arizona desert. It was doubtful there were many people who even remembered a young man named Ricky Alonso or his flaky girlfriend, Lacey Reed.

Even if Scanlon *was* looking for revenge it was doubtful he'd go after another former SEAL and active member of the Hostage Rescue Team. The cowardly asshole was much more likely to go after his ex-wife, and her, the rookie female agent who'd helped arrest the motherfucker—for using his esteemed status as one of the premier military operators in the world to earn money as a drug mule for the murderous cartel.

The hatred in his eyes as he'd lain on the asphalt was something that woke her up from her dreams sometimes. Not that she'd ever told anyone that.

Someone touched her arm.

She jumped.

"Hey, you okay?" Her partner, David Gonzales, had appeared at her side.

She glanced at him. They were assigned to the Public Corruption Unit, her undercover days long over. She didn't miss them. She just missed *him*. And that was something she'd deny to her grave.

"Fine." She shook it off. If she worried about every ex-con she'd helped put away, then she was going to have a very stressful life and would be better off quitting now.

She wasn't a quitter.

David didn't look convinced.

"Scanlon's out." She couldn't help smiling at her very handsome colleague as he sent her a heavy frown.

"That's early, right?"

"Nearly two years early." She shot him a look. "Good behavior, not to mention, he *found the Lord.*"

"Didn't know *He* was lost." David raised his chin on the inhale. "You think he'll come after you?"

She shook her head. No way was she about to share her paranoia with David. "But I figured Ridgeway would want to know."

David shot the empty office a look. "What'd he say?"

She barked out a laugh and started walking back down the corridor toward their squad room. "He already knew. Someone at Coronado felt it prudent to inform him."

"But he didn't tell you." David easily kept up. "Hmm."

"What's *hmm* mean?" She kept her voice light because David

was one of the smartest people she knew, and if he thought something was suspicious then so should she.

"It means that either Naval Command or SAC Ridgeway is wrong about the threat Scanlon might present."

She pulled a face. Neither of them thought that highly of their SAC. "I'm going to reach out to the ex-wife. Make sure she knows he's out."

"He'd be a fool to go after anyone," he eyed her pointedly, "especially a Fed."

She rubbed her arms. "Scanlon's an arrogant ass, but he's not stupid."

He nudged her elbow. "Want some good news?"

"What?"

"Clarence organized a meet with Gunther."

"Finally."

Clarence Carpenter was David's Confidential Informant who he'd flipped after Carpenter tried to bribe a city planner who was a close personal friend of David's. The planner hadn't taken kindly to the offer. Now the FBI hoped to use Carpenter against a local mayor rumored to be open to taking under the table payments in exchange for preferential treatment.

Delilah switched gears. It was stupid to be worried about Scanlon. He was probably back in the Louisiana swamp that had spit him out as a young man. Sipping brews and eating crawdads. She probably never even crossed his mind.

Time to get on with her job, the job she lived for. The job she loved. "When's the meet?"

"Tomorrow morning." He slanted her a glance. "Early."

That didn't give them a lot of time. "We have the recording equipment ready?"

"I have it. We'll meet him at 7:30 a.m. to wire him up. I booked a room in a nearby hotel so we can be close-by in case anything goes wrong." David sent her a smile that could have conquered Hollywood.

The memory of the heated golden eyes of another handsome FBI agent punched through her chest and made her heart clench.

Demarco had made his choice. She hadn't been worth it five years ago. She doubted he even remembered her nowadays—too busy making a mark for himself, making a name, clawing away at the need to prove himself a hero rather than a villain.

The love she'd once felt for him had morphed into contempt. She might not be the smartest person in the room, but Delilah had always been a straight A student. Because she was really, really good at learning her lessons and never made the same mistake twice.

———

Joseph Scanlon stared through the Steiner Military-Marine 10X50mm Tactical Binoculars and watched the whore leave work and get into her car. A surge of something that felt a lot like joy unfurled inside him.

She was right on time.

Right on schedule.

For years, he'd been planning this operation down to the last second.

She might not know what hit her, but he would. It was a pity there wouldn't be more time to catch up, but he was on a tight schedule and had no intention of going back to prison.

He slid backward through the dry brush as slowly and carefully as withdrawing from an enemy position. Once he was out of visual range, he checked his surroundings before stepping out onto a path.

He slipped the notepad into his back pocket and began hiking back to his vehicle, careful to keep up his cover as a birder, just in case someone was watching as the day turned to dusk.

He was going to make them all pay, one at a time, and then he was going to live out his life with no one ever being able to prove he'd done anything illegal.

Not this time.

Special Agent Delilah Quinn was first. She was going to get what was coming to her. He just wished he could hurt her enough to make up for the years he'd lost. But he couldn't. No one could. But he'd get the bitch. And then he could move on to the next target and finish this thing. No one got the better of him. No one. Especially not a lying bitch or a greasy two-faced loser.

5

Delilah pulled up outside her condo on Palmilla Drive. It was only a thousand square feet, but it had two bedrooms, AC, and two parking stall allocations, one beside the unit and another in a lot to the east of the complex, which came in handy between her Bucar and current lodger. There was also street parking, where her personal vehicle currently resided, somehow relegated to bottom place.

The townhouse wasn't as close to the ocean as she'd dreamed when she'd won the lottery and gotten the San Diego Field Office as her First Office Assignment, but it was an eleven-minute commute to work and a mere fifteen minutes from the Village of La Jolla with its pale gold beach, eclectic restaurants, and fancy shops. The complex had palm trees and a nice pool. The other residents were quiet and tended to mind their own business.

She'd grown up all over the country but spent most of her formative years in DC and Maryland after her father had been based at FBI HQ. So she didn't take the good weather for granted. Her parents lived in Virginia now.

She pressed her lips tight together as she thought of them. She needed to schedule a visit. Soon.

She jogged up the steps to her front door. She went to punch in the code, but the handle turned easily under her palm and the door swung open.

She grabbed her mail from the mailbox. "Val?"

"In here."

"You okay?" It was dim inside except for the TV screen.

"Dandy." Her best friend, Valerie Strauss, slumped in the armchair watching a rerun of *Love Island* while inhaling what looked like a gallon tub of potato chips. Delilah's black FBI ball cap was pulled over the other woman's long hair which had been dyed brown for a recent stage role. Valerie loved commandeering her stuff, but especially that cap.

The house was a mess, but it was hard to be irritated with her friend for long. Valerie was the person who'd stayed with her, looked after her, and picked up all the broken pieces five years ago.

"How'd it go?" Delilah winced as Valerie crammed another fistful of chips into an already bulging mouth. "That good, huh?"

"Their loss." Words were barely discernible between crumbs. Valerie had had an audition for a movie earlier that day. "But the good news is…" Valerie twisted in the recliner, covered her mouth with her hand and grinned, eyes sparkling. She chewed some more and wiped her hands and mouth on a piece of paper towel she had on her lap and then took a huge gulp of soda that she'd balanced precariously on the arm of the leather chair. "The *really* good news is that the flooring guy will be finished by end of day Wednesday and the painter can get in there Thursday. I can move back into my place on the weekend."

Three months ago, Valerie's LA apartment had been flooded by a cracked pipe in her upstairs neighbor's bathroom. As she'd planned to stay with Delilah for eight weeks anyway, during the run of a play she'd starred in here in San Diego, it had made sense for her to crash here. And it hadn't even been that difficult as Valerie worked evenings and weekends, while Delilah worked mostly dayshifts in the office and at home in the evenings. Not to mention, Valerie had spent the last two weeks on a cruise and had only returned this morning in time for this audition.

But despite the fact Delilah loved Valerie like a sister, she was looking forward to having her own space back.

Maybe that's why she was so on edge. Perhaps it had nothing to do with Scanlon. Perhaps it was simply the disorder of her usually neat, everything-in-its-place home that made her feel as if she was constantly grinding her teeth. Apparently, she'd grown used to being alone, and it was hard to go back to sharing space. Even on the rare occasions she dated, she rarely brought people into her home.

Delilah smiled. "As much as I've enjoyed hanging out with you, that *is* good news."

Valerie grinned. She was no fool. "I know. I mean I love you like crazy, but cohabiting is a lot harder now than it was when we were back in college. You're such a slob."

They both laughed. Delilah was a little obsessive about every-thing being in its place, and Valerie was messy as hell.

Valerie tossed a throw pillow straight at Delilah's chest.

Delilah caught it one handed and tossed it onto the couch because she didn't want to risk spilling the chips or soda over her favorite recliner.

Neat freak.

"Wanna go out to get dinner to celebrate the good news?" Delilah suggested.

"Sure. My treat. Do I need to change?"

The woman was wearing torn jeans and a white button-up shirt that managed to look both chic and elegant despite the crumbs.

"Maybe lose the cap."

"But I like the cap. You have the right to remain silent." Valerie waggled her index finger without looking away from the TV. "Lemme watch the end of this episode, and then I'm pretty much ready to go."

Delilah checked her watch. "No rush. I want to get in a quick run as I missed it this morning. Wanna join me?"

Valerie groaned and shook her head.

Delilah grinned. "How about we go to that restaurant on the beach? I think it's open on a Monday night. Should be quiet."

"I love that place."

Delilah went into her bedroom and put her weapons on the dresser, stripped off her suit, hanging it carefully before tossing the shirt, and underwear into a hamper in the corner. She needed to do laundry and visit the dry cleaners this week. She pulled on black leggings, running top, and her favorite lightweight gray camo moto jacket. Then she sat on the bed to lace her bright yellow/orange striped running shoes. She placed her smaller backup Glock 26 inside a sticky holster in one of the concealed pockets on the hip of her pants.

She slid creds and a slim card holder which contained a credit card, debit, her driver's license and an emergency hundred dollars in cash into her zippered jacket pocket. Her dad had taught her the value of being prepared from an early age, and it had served her well as an agent. Out of necessity, her work cell went into the other pocket but she decided to leave her personal cell behind beside her Glock 23. She headed back into the kitchen and noted it was full dark now. She debated taking a water bottle but decided against it. She wouldn't be gone long. Instead, she grabbed a large glass of cold water, chugged it down, and left the glass by the sink beside a dirty plate and mug.

Her fists curled but she resisted putting them in the dishwasher.

See.

She knew how to let things go.

"Back in thirty minutes." She snagged Valerie's pink ball cap off the hook by the door and dragged it over her head, drawing her hair through the notch in the back.

"I'll be here." Valerie leaned over the arm of the chair to wave goodbye. "Unemployed, old, fat, aspiring actress."

Delilah rolled her eyes and headed out into the evening. Valerie ate like a frat boy and never put on weight. She should hate her for that alone.

But being overly dramatic was part of Valerie's charm, especially when she didn't take herself too seriously. Delilah was convinced her friend was going to breakout in the role of a lifetime soon. And she would be cheering her on every step of the way.

Outside, the air was fresh with just the hint of incoming rain. Normally she'd head due south to Rose Canyon Open Space Park, but as it was already pitch black, she decided to stick to the lit sidewalks. She cut north along a path between the buildings.

She ran for five minutes but like everything else today, couldn't find her rhythm.

Her breath felt tight. Her gait was off.

As an FBI Special Agent, she was expected to maintain a certain level of fitness and running had always been something that came easily to her. Maybe *she* was getting old.

Frustrated, she stopped and stretched the way she should have before she set off. She did a series of side lunges followed by glute and piriformis stretches, and arm swings, feeling slightly ridiculous, but this was California, and runners littered the streets. After a few minutes, she began running again, finally hitting her stride.

She pounded the pavement and increased her speed, pushing herself because she only had time for a short run so she may as well make it count.

She dodged a large garbage bin that had been left out and glanced across at a dog who jumped up against the fence barking, setting off a neighborhood canine chorus which felt strangely reassuring.

The cool air felt crisp against her face and body as sweat pooled under her arms and between her breasts. She checked her watch, upping her pace again. That feeling that something wasn't right continued to plague her, and she patted her hand to her weapon to reassure herself, but there was nothing out there except the night.

Turning the corner, she headed for home.

6

The wail of sirens lit up the night. Nothing unusual there, but they snagged her awareness as she ran closer to home. She passed the elementary school before she realized fire trucks were pulled up in her complex. Flames visible over the roofs of the buildings.

Her heart pounded.

She pushed through the crowd, chest heaving as she caught her breath. Aghast, she stared as fire crews rolled out hoses toward her section of the condos. She turned the corner and horror rushed through her as she realized it was her unit and the one below it that was on fire. That lower unit had been empty for the last couple of weeks.

"Valerie!" she shouted and looked around, frantically searching for her friend. She couldn't see her.

What the heck had happened?

Flames were visible through her living room windows and licked the roof tiles. She pushed to the front of the crowd and headed toward one of the firefighters.

"There's someone inside!" she yelled.

His expression darkened. "You're sure?"

She hesitated. "Not a hundred percent, but she was home

when I left for a run thirty minutes ago." She swung around. "Maybe she got out?"

Of course she got out. It was a short walk to the front door. Unless the floor collapsed, or she'd been overcome by fumes…

Glass shattered in a small explosion, showering her Bucar with lethal shards.

Her hand went to her mouth.

"You need to step back." The firefighter's blue eyes met hers, sympathetic, but also determined. "I'll let the chief know the owner is possibly inside."

She opened her mouth to correct the record, but he'd already moved away. She could mention she was FBI, but it wouldn't make much difference right now. Her badge wasn't going to put out that fire.

She clenched her jaw and squeezed her hands into tight fists. What had happened in the short time she'd been gone? An electrical fault? Someone squatting in the ground floor apartment with a lit candle or unattended stove?

Her home was gone, but she refused to think about it. Possessions, even precious ones, were nothing compared to people's lives.

Her eyes smarted. Surely Valerie would have gotten out when the smoke alarms went off? Delilah replaced the batteries religiously every year.

Perhaps Valerie was in her car…

Delilah hurried back through the throng of onlookers. Valerie's old, battered Sebring convertible sat in her other assigned parking space.

Delilah tried the handle, unsurprised when it opened. Valerie rarely bothered to lock anything.

It was empty.

Delilah leaned against the side for a moment, trying to calm her panic, to think.

She used her work cell to call Valerie's phone. No reply.

Trepidation crawled up her spine and made her lips feel numb.

Sweat cooled on her skin and she started to shiver. There was a blanket on the back seat, and she dragged it out and huddled beneath it.

A terrible reality hit.

What if Valerie was still inside her apartment?

She closed her eyes for another minute, fighting not to break down. The scent of smoke coated the back of her throat and made her want to gag. Finally, she put the blanket back in the car and forced herself to head to her condo again. Careful not to trip over fire hoses and equipment, she arrived on the edge of the crowd. The fire looked under control now. She caught the eye of the firefighter she'd spoken to earlier and stepped to one side to talk to him.

"Do you know anything?" Her voice was rough with smoke and emotion.

"We haven't been able to enter yet but..." His voice trailed off filled with obvious compassion.

"What?"

"One of the guys on the ladder spotted someone on the chair inside. Looked like a female, but she wasn't moving. Then the beam collapsed."

Gore rose up in her throat as anguish assailed her. She covered her mouth with her right hand. Tears flooded her eyes.

"We're going to need a statement from you."

She nodded and her knees wobbled.

His hand gripped her arm and kept her upright. His eyes were kind. "Take your time. We're probably going to be here for hours yet, but we need to talk to you. Any idea how this started?"

She shook her head. She could barely see through the sudden onslaught of tears. She backed away. "I need to grab some water. I'll be back."

She hurried to her SUV parked along the street. She felt grimy and cold. Disoriented and numb. The world had shifted ninety degrees off-kilter. Her stomach threatened to rebel. She needed to find her center before she could talk to anyone. She needed to change clothes and get her shit together.

She climbed inside. Slumped as all energy left her. Her fingers tightened on the steering wheel. Tears ran down her face and dripped off her chin and down her neck. Snot clogged her nose and throat.

She needed to report the damage of her Bucar and tell her boss about the incident. But there was no point disturbing them until she had a few more facts.

Valerie's mom...

Oh, God.

Should she call her?

What if the victim by some miracle wasn't Valerie? What if the firefighter was mistaken and had just seen the cap and a sweatshirt? For the second time in her neat, orderly little life she didn't know what to do.

Last time, she'd called Valerie.

A sob ripped out of her throat, and she covered her mouth again as if trying to shove it back inside.

She knew she had to make a statement, but she desperately needed to talk to someone first. It wasn't like she was going to disappear.

She needed a friend. She texted David.

I'm coming over.

He didn't reply, but he'd know something major was up for her to invite herself over like this. Hopefully, he didn't have company.

David lived in a gorgeous five-bedroom house on a quiet cul-de-sac less than a five-minute drive from her own home. He had an outdoor barbecue, a kidney-shaped pool, and a hot tub complete with pool house. You could see the ocean from the balcony off the master bedroom—or so he'd told her. He'd bought it with money inherited from his grandmother, and she hoped he wouldn't mind putting her up for the night until she could figure out her next move with the insurers.

She pulled onto the driveway, parking in front of the three-car garage beside his Bucar. Her legs shook as she climbed out of her SUV. Even here streaks of gray were visible against the night sky. The smell of smoke tainted the air. She checked her cell. David still hadn't replied.

Maybe he was in the pool. Or out?

It felt presumptuous to grab her go-bag, so she left it in the trunk.

She went to the front door and rang the bell, noticed that the door wasn't latched properly. She pushed and it swung open. Unlike Valerie, this wasn't like the careful, competent agent she knew.

Even the thought of Valerie made tears flood her eyes.

"David?"

Her voice echoed disconcertingly off the Italian marble floors.

He could be in the pool. He could have a guest who had perhaps failed to shut the door properly. The beat of her pain-filled heart ratcheted up a notch.

Something didn't feel right.

She drew her backup Glock from the holster. Her service weapon was in her burned-out shell of a home along with her best friend from college.

The lump of grief wedged in her throat was so big it threatened to suffocate her.

"David?" she croaked.

She crept into the foyer, listening to the sixth sense that told her something was wrong.

She eased through the hallway and headed left toward the living room where David liked to relax and eat dinner in front of whatever sport was playing on TV.

A hockey game was muted on the screen, but David wasn't anywhere to be seen. She went to the kitchen. A pint glass like the ones she'd had in her home sat beside the sink. A wineglass beside it. She glanced out of the window at the incredible backyard that was lit with pool lights.

The feeling of unease increased. Where was he?

She walked over to the French doors, and her eyes widened in shock.

David lay face down, unmoving on the flagstones. She ran outside to his unmoving form. A pool of blood soaked the slabs beneath his head. She didn't want to move him, so she slipped her fingers into the collar of his shirt and searched for a pulse in his neck. His skin was warm but there was no pulse beneath his skin. No breath being drawn in and out of his lungs.

He was dead.

He'd been dead for a while.

It didn't make sense.

Another wave of grief slammed into her.

She sat back on her heels as her brain tried to compute the events of the evening. What on earth was going on?

Was this an attack on the FBI? Did she need to warn her fellow agents? She fumbled for her phone then spotted a Glock lying on the pool deck.

David's service weapon?

She went over and squatted beside it.

A Glock 23.

She frowned.

David carried a Glock 22 as his service weapon.

She noticed a familiar scratch on the barrel. Her blood stalled inside her veins, and the world started to spin.

That was *her* service weapon.

She placed her hands on the ground to combat the dizziness.

Absolutely nothing made sense.

Until it did.

Cold washed over her.

She stared at poor, beautiful David whose life had been stolen from him. Her friend. Her colleague.

Someone had used her service weapon—a weapon that had

been in her home when she'd left for her run—to murder her colleague and then left it here for the authorities to find. Presumably, that same someone had also set fire to her apartment? Had they murdered Valerie thinking she was Delilah? She flashed back to her friend wearing her FBI ball cap. They had similar hair and features and were enough of a similar size to raid each other's closets. Her living room had been in darkness except for the TV.

Her stomach churned, but she dared not puke.

Oh, God.

Had someone—Joseph Scanlon immediately sprang to mind— created some sort of murder-suicide scenario in an attempt to get away with killing her? Disgracing her—the way he'd disgraced himself and his uniform?

Assuming the killer had come straight here from her place after killing Valerie and setting the fire, it would be difficult for a Medical Examiner to distinguish whether Valerie or David had died first.

Bile rose up her throat at the thought of these two beautiful souls being murdered. No way this was a coincidence—not when she tied them together so neatly. She forced the nausea away and breathed deeply.

The terrible beauty of this plan was that once authorities figured out the body at her place was Valerie and not Delilah, investigators would likely believe she was involved with a double homicide.

Had she seen anyone who could alibi her in the last few hours? The firefighter? Maybe she'd luck out and be spotted running on someone's doorbell camera. Unfortunately, nothing said she couldn't have murdered Valerie before setting the fire and going for a run, then come over here to shoot David dead.

She'd even texted him her intention for goodness' sake.

Scanlon.

It had to be Scanlon.

No one else she'd put away would be this coldly vindictive. Or this dangerous.

The question was, what did she do about it?

Did she go to Ridgeway?

He was strictly by the book and would suspend her from duty until an investigation was completed, which would take months if not years. And it wouldn't take Scanlon long to discover she wasn't really dead, which would put a giant bullseye on her back.

She had no doubt he had an alibi all lined up for tonight.

She glanced at the gun. Scanlon wouldn't be sloppy enough to leave his own DNA or prints on the weapon. And, despite what they showed on TV, the chance of the lab being able to match what was left of the slug that had killed David back to her gun with any degree of certainty, was remote at best.

David deserved justice.

So did Valerie.

Delilah made a decision, one that would probably cost her her career. But no way would she leave the incriminating evidence behind and make herself the target of an investigation that would sideline her indefinitely when she knew she was innocent. She ran into the kitchen and used a dish cloth to open the drawer where she knew David kept his freezer bags. Pulled out two and hip-checked the drawer closed again. She froze as she noticed the dirty glass beside the sink again. It had an eagle carrying a barrel—from her favorite brewery.

It was hers.

She knew it was hers.

The son of a bitch had taken the used glass from her apartment after murdering her best friend, presumably mistaking Valerie for Delilah.

She put the glass in the sink and ran the water until it became hot. Used the dish towel to grab the detergent and squirted a big dollop of soap inside the glass. She washed it thoroughly then rinsed it inside and out with the searingly hot water.

That should get rid of any trace of her DNA and prints.

She left the glass in the sink.

Next, she went back outside to David. Wished she could go

back in time and save him. But wishes were pointless and did neither of them any good.

The most effective way to hunt Scanlon would be to pretend she was dead. She'd make some calls as soon as she got somewhere safe.

She had connections.

They'd help her.

She scooped up her service weapon using the large Ziplock bag. She checked the chamber and the magazine. Looked like one bullet had been fired. One was enough when it hit the right place.

Presumably, the killer had used a suppressor and had taken that with him. How had he murdered Val?

She flinched away from even thinking about it.

Hopefully, Val had died quickly. Scanlon was a former sniper and Navy SEAL. He knew a thousand ways to kill someone.

She crouched and looked around for the bullet casing.

Didn't see it.

Where would Scanlon have shot from?

She glanced at the house.

The shadows—where else?

She scooted toward the side of the house and, after a brief search, spotted the gleam of brass along the narrow pathway that edged the south side of the building.

She put the bagged weapon and the bullet casing into her large inside jacket pocket and then retraced her steps, wiping down anything she might have touched.

On a small, recessed, kitchen counter that David used to stash his mail, she spotted his old cell phone and forty dollars in cash. He'd dropped the cell a couple of weeks ago, and the screen had cracked, but she knew it still worked because she'd teased him about his need to have the best of everything.

The lump in her throat kept growing.

Why shouldn't he have the best?

He deserved it.

A tear dripped down her face, and she wiped her cheek impatiently on her arm. She took the money with the vow to pay it back, then slipped the cell into her pocket along with a charger. Then she powered down her work cell and popped the SIM card. Slid the phone into her pocket and the SIM into her wallet beside the hundred and forty dollars, which was all she had on her person.

Then she went back to her car, keeping her head down as she climbed inside, killing the dome light.

There was no reason now for the FBI to be chasing her in response to David's murder—unless she'd missed something else Scanlon had planted, but she doubted it. A murder weapon and a used glass were more than enough physical evidence to tie her to the crime scene—especially combined with the fire at her place.

Her fingers gripped the steering wheel as she tried not to panic. Maybe she was acting crazy. Maybe talking to Ridgeway was the most sensible move?

She realized she was physically shaking. If she went to Ridgeway, she'd be looking over her shoulder for the rest of her life even if he believed her. The former Navy SEAL was a talented marksman, and there were a million ways he could get to her without her even spotting him.

She refused to live like that.

There was no proof it even was Scanlon, not yet anyway.

She wouldn't let him get away with what he'd done. Even if it cost her the only job she'd ever wanted, she wouldn't let the killer walk calmly away and not face the consequences.

She drew in a deep breath. David would have applauded this plan. She knew he would.

Another tear tracked down her left cheek. She scrubbed it away.

It would be a couple of days before Valerie's body was formally identified, which gave Delilah time to make a solid game plan.

Grief hit her all over again that these two brilliant, vibrant human beings had been murdered. The fact it had been because of their association with her made the guilt pile high, but also increased her determination to find their killer while she held the upper hand. It wouldn't last for long.

She forced herself to move. To reverse her SUV and drive calmly away even though it went against everything she'd been trained for, everything she believed in.

It felt like a disservice to Valerie and to the friends, colleagues, and family members who would mourn both Delilah Quinn and David Gonzales. But by going off the grid, she could track down Scanlon before he realized anyone was onto him. Find their killer. And then she'd take great pleasure in taking him down and putting him away. Again.

Unfortunately, she couldn't do it alone, and she was going to have to ask for help from the one man she'd hoped never to talk to again. Her personal feelings had nothing to do with this anymore. He needed to know about the danger. And he had resources she wanted access to.

Plus, he owed her, even if he would never fully understand the depth of how much he'd hurt her. He owed her.

He might be a rat bastard, but he was an honorable rat bastard.

7

Mon., 10:00 p.m. Local Bar

Cas Demarco nursed his Dance of Days pale ale and glanced up at the hockey game on the TV screen in the corner of the bar. He had no skin in the game and found his attention wandering.

Gold Team had returned to Quantico from Boston on a commercial flight yesterday afternoon, and they'd spent today cleaning and checking their equipment.

Despite the successful outcome to the last mission, a thin pall of misery hung over the squad. The memorial service for the former team leader who'd lost his life in an air crash last month was being held the day after tomorrow, and Cas knew he wasn't the only one who wasn't yet ready to say goodbye. He wished to hell someone had a few answers as to why the plane had gone down.

Using the mirror behind the bar, he watched Jordan Krychek, who sat at a table by himself, nursing a beer. Krychek had been in Africa with Kurt Montana on a secret mission but had left the day before Montana—officially making him the luckiest bastard on the planet. He didn't look like he felt lucky though. He looked miserable.

Krychek had been closed-lipped since his return but was clearly suffering from survivor's guilt, which Cas understood all too well. He had the feeling there was more to this story. Classified stuff. He wanted to know everything, but he'd resigned himself to having to wait. For now.

He'd learned patience.

Slowly.

Torturously.

Beaten into him by Firearms Instructors who, combined, knew more about the fine art of sniping than he could ever hope to learn.

Patience was essential in his line of work—hunting people who didn't want to be found without them ever suspecting. Ironically, he'd never imagined he'd become a sniper when he'd joined HRT; he'd assumed he'd be knocking down doors. Not that the snipers weren't capable of knocking down doors when occasion required. And the assaulters could shoot their asses off too. But the emphasis on training and practice was key.

Marksmanship was a degradable skill.

It was not unusual for any member of HRT to shoot more than a thousand rounds in a week. Even today, he'd spent an hour in the Thunder Dome with his favorite Heckler & Koch MSG90 punching 7.62x51mm NATO rounds into a blacked-out silhouette.

He'd come a long way from the unwanted and unloved boy growing up in a foster home—and from his Navy SEAL and FBI undercover days.

Although sniping wasn't that different to working undercover. Snipers saw things others never noticed. They performed complex calculations in a split second, taking in everything from windage to the curvature of the earth's surface before making a shot. The same way an undercover agent judged facial expressions, voice tone, and every aspect of their surroundings to make sure they weren't blown. Snipers remained hidden and camouflaged from view, even when lying in plain sight. Same could be said of being embedded with killers and cartel members—they looked right at you and never saw who you truly were until it was too late.

If they penetrated the veil, you were dead.

He'd enjoyed it for a little while, the cat and mouse, shutting down bad guys who trafficked misery in all its various guises. But seeing the number of innocents who got caught up in the life, who became entangled whether they liked it or not...that had taken a toll.

It could have so easily have been him.

One flip.

Heads or tails.

Heaven or Hell.

One bad decision could have led him down a different path. He'd enlisted on his eighteenth birthday, a week after one of his friends had overdosed on opioids.

The idea that he, a pathetic, unwanted scrap of a human being could make it as far as he had was living proof that the American Dream was alive and well. He was one of the lucky ones—and if someone had said that to his bitter, sullen, eighteen-year-old self, he'd have spit in their eye.

He took a drink as the brown-eyed gaze of a woman who'd always seen straight to the heart of him flashed into his brain.

Delilah Quinn.

The smartest person he'd ever met. And the sexiest. And the most impetuous. That was saying something, given he'd been a SEAL and some of those guys were batshit.

Where was she now?

Still in San Diego last he'd heard. Probably married to some highflyer.

Moisture evaporated from his mouth, and he took another sip of beer to ease the dryness.

Regret was never far behind thoughts of Delilah. The sounds she'd made, the look of betrayal on her face when he'd told her it was over...it haunted him still.

In the end, she'd let him go without another word.

What had he expected?

That she'd ignore his callous words and shitty behavior and get herself reassigned to this side of the country so they would have some sort of chance together? That she'd beg for scraps? From an asshole like him?

Not Delilah.

After what he'd said to her, he was lucky she hadn't shot him. She was not the sort of woman to beg, or to follow a man at the cost of her own career.

Why should she?

He'd avoided her at trial. It had been easy. His identity had been protected—although he figured he probably shouldn't vacation in Mexico or Colombia any time soon.

Delilah though, she'd gotten up on that stand and testified like a badass, then headed back to work the next day, nothing but her gold shield and service weapon for protection.

She terrified him.

On every level.

Thankfully, the cartel tended to avoid direct confrontations with US Government officials—with the notable exception of last month's escapade in Arizona. But that had been a byproduct of one man's evil and another man's desperation, rather than company policy.

The cartel had come off worse during that exchange which would hopefully prove a further deterrent to others thinking about attacking US citizens. But nothing would really change. The void would be filled, and he could only pray the successors were less bloodthirsty than the Santiagos.

The bar door opened, and ten pairs of eyes swiveled to check out the potential danger.

A sweet-looking blonde with Shirley Temple curls came inside and looked around. She hit the bar, showed her driver's license, and ordered a beer. She stood nervously tapping her painted nails on the counter while the barkeep fulfilled her order.

She checked her phone, and for about five seconds, Cas contemplated saying something, but he was too damned tired. Out of the corner of his eye, he saw Ford Cadell eyeing the pretty, young woman with interest. Cadell was a good-looking mother-fucker. Thankfully, their other leading Lothario, Ryan Sullivan, was playing pool in the back room.

It was late.

He should go home because they had to be up early tomorrow, and he should make sure he had a clean, pressed shirt ready for Wednesday.

The blonde paid for her beer and looked around for some-where to sit. Cas watched her via the mirror as she chose the seat at a table next to Krychek. She tried to strike up a conversation with the taciturn operator.

Good luck with that.

Cas shared an amused look with Cadell. Cadell grinned and finished his drink, leaving the glass on the counter. He nodded to Cas and headed out the door.

Cas tipped his glass back, about to do the same as a news story on the TV caught his eye. The footage was of a house fire, but it was the ticker tape that grabbed his attention.

An FBI agent from the San Diego Field Office was missing, feared dead, following a fierce blaze.

His fingers started to tremble as he placed the empty glass back on the bar.

Cas recognized the townhouse complex. He'd gone there the day he'd walked away from Delilah, leaving the best part of himself in California. His heart started to pound, and he felt as if someone had ripped the stool from beneath him and he was free-falling.

It must be someone else.

Delilah couldn't be dead.

A fire?

No way.

The vision of her burning to death rushed at him in all its merciless, vicious glory.

He found his feet and knocked the glass over, which rolled across the bar and smashed on the other side of the counter. He stumbled, bumping into one of his sniper teammates, Sebastian Black, who'd also been playing pool. The operator grabbed his shoulders.

"Whoa, man. You okay?"

Blood drained from his head, and a wave of ice ran over his scalp. He shook off the other man and bolted outside, running halfway along the building to stand against the wall, hands braced wide as he heaved what little he'd had in his stomach into the dirt.

Footsteps followed him but the roaring in his ears drowned out everything, even his sense of self preservation.

The thought of Delilah being dead made him realize what a massive mistake he'd made five years ago. Made him realize the magnitude of everything he'd thrown away. So what if her father hated him? So what if he'd threatened to hinder Cas's attempts to get into HRT? From what he knew now, the management wouldn't have taken directions from an Assistant Director without solid evidence Cas wasn't right for the teams. They'd have made their own assessment.

And even though he loved this job, he *missed* her.

So much.

So fucking much.

They could have tried to make a long-distance relationship work. They could have figured out a way. But she'd deserved so much better than what he could offer her. Her father had been right about that.

He'd been nothing.

Nobody.

Suited to working with the dregs of society because that was where he'd fitted in best—or so he'd thought at the time.

Delilah was a damned good agent. Best he'd ever known. And

he could still see the devastation in her eyes when he'd dumped her.

A decision he'd regretted every day since.

She'd deserved better than him, but he was the one she'd wanted. He should have held on to her like a limpet clinging to an exposed rock during a storm—but he'd been too damned scared.

Scared her father was right.

Scared she'd come to her senses and dump him, and he'd once again be left with nothing. So he'd left her first and told himself it was her father's fault.

Coward.

"Are you sick or did you have too many beers?" Sebastian Black watched him from a short distance away.

Sweat coated Cas's forehead. Grief welled up through his pores like poison.

"Not alcohol." He forced the words out, his voice gruff. "I received some bad news. A...friend...died."

"Shit. I'm sorry, man. You look like a ghost. Want me to drive you home?"

Cas closed his eyes and leaned his face against the rough wall. "No. I can drive. Thanks." He pushed away, walked slowly to his truck, head down, feet scuffing the gravel of the parking lot. The sea breeze felt chilled against his skin, but he needed it to combat the sweaty, clammy feeling that made him want to throw up again.

Had anyone told her parents yet?

Of course they had. The FBI would be all over that shit. Stephen Quinn was still a legend in the Bureau even though he'd retired. The FBI Director herself would probably deliver the news. Despite his personal resentment, Cas's mouth went dry at the pain this would cause them. Delilah had loved them deeply. And they her.

No one would think to inform him...

He got to find out from a freaking news report.

Because their relationship had been a secret, and it had been over for five years. Of course, no one would think to tell him. He'd been a speck in her life. A temporary blip. And yet he felt as if he was being stabbed to death with regret and remorse.

Because she meant nothing to me. Because she'd been a good fuck but not to confuse that with more despite the words I gave her.

Ha.

The joke was on him.

He felt as if he was dying.

Sebastian shadowed him to his vehicle. "You sure you're okay?"

Cas turned. "I appreciate the concern. I need some space, okay?"

Sebastian held his gaze as if assessing his soberness and then nodded. Stepped away. "Call me if you need anything."

Cas somehow hauled himself into the driver's seat and sat there breathing heavily as Sebastian walked back into the bar. Tears filled his eyes at the thought of someone as incredible as Delilah being taken from this world.

All the mistakes he'd made bombarded him. The worst? That he'd hurt her. Because he was a coward, he'd hurt a woman who meant more to him than life itself. And now she was dead.

He wanted to fix it, but it was too late. And wasn't that just like him? Too-little-too-late. Should be his middle name.

Fuck!

He wasn't sure how much more loss he could take. First, two team members who'd been like family. And now Delilah...

Who'd been his moon and stars.

He hadn't seen her in nearly five years, but the loss felt like a gaping wound leaking his life's blood into the dirt.

Maybe life had been easier as a pathetic orphan with no connections and no one who gave a shit, but it wasn't the life he wanted. Not now he'd tasted more.

A sob burst out and he tried to smother it with both hands.

His personal cell rang and he fished it out of his pocket. He didn't recognize the number, so he declined the call. The phone rang again, and fury rose up inside him. He answered, effervescent from rage at the silence on the other end.

"If this is a spam call, you need to know I have the capability to track you down and kill you from a thousand yards. You'll never see me coming. You'll never know I'm watching you until there are two extra holes in your skull and the closest wall is wearing your brain. Think long and hard the next time you call someone with the intent of scamming them to steal their hard-earned cash because you're too stupid or lazy to earn your own."

"Well," came a husky voice from his best and most terrifying memories, "am I ever glad I'm not a scammer."

8

"Delilah?" His heart banged hard against his ribs. "What the actual fuck?"

"Look." She hesitated as if unsure of her welcome. "I know I shouldn't be calling you, but it's important."

Her words crushed him. She thought he was angry that she'd contacted him. She didn't know he'd seen the news or that he was sitting crying in his truck like a baby because of the foolish mistake he'd made all those years ago.

He'd been desperate to protect himself. To wrap his emaciated heart with barbed wire and warning lights to keep it safe. From what?

From happiness? From light and laughter and lust so brilliant he'd thought he'd die every time he looked at her?

He was such a fool.

Such a goddamned fool.

He could hear her breathing on the other end of the line. He gripped the phone tighter as if it were a physical connection to her. "Are you all right?"

"I guess." She gave a bitter laugh. "I've had a hell of a night."

The despair of fearing this woman was dead had reawakened something inside him. Knowledge—that he'd been an idiot, which was something he already knew. Realization—that he'd never get another chance. And hope—that maybe he still had time to win her back.

She cleared her throat. "Scanlon's out."

His eyes widened. He looked in the mirror and dragged his sleeve over his face to mop up the tears. She didn't need his pathetic weeping. She'd called him for help.

"I think he tried to kill me tonight, but instead murdered my friend, Valerie Strauss—I told you about her. She was staying with me." Her voice hitched. "He also shot and killed my partner, David Gonzales, at his home."

Partner?

His mood crashed.

Of course she had a partner.

"I don't have any proof it was him." Her voice sounded small and scared as if she thought he wouldn't believe her. Cas had never heard her sound cowed before. "It's only a feeling and, well, the fact he's out and suddenly both my friends are dead…"

"You always had good instincts, Delilah." His heart still beat too hard under his ribs, but it had settled a little. The fact that motherfucker had been released early shouldn't surprise him, and yet it did. Sometimes it was as if the prison service and law enforcement were on opposite sides in the fight against crime.

He forced himself to think clearly. "Are you safe?"

"I…" Her voice trembled. "For now."

He inhaled, searching for the breath he needed to calm himself. Searching for his sniper cool somewhere inside the seething mass of emotions that writhed inside him.

"I might have made a serious mistake," she admitted.

He could hear her gnawing her bottom lip, something that had always driven him mad with lust, but right now all he cared about was rescuing her from whatever predicament she was involved in.

Him.

Delilah's hero.

The idea was preposterous.

"Tell me exactly what happened."

She spoke quickly but haltingly. The words stumbled over one another as she talked him through the events of the evening.

"I should have left the gun and the brass at the scene." Her breathing was ragged. "I thought—"

"You did the right thing. In fact, you should get rid of this cell phone because that's the only thing that can tie you to the scene."

"Except the murder weapon." Her words were bitter.

"The slug will most likely be useless for ballistic comparison, and you know it. The only person who knows for certain you weren't carrying your service weapon when you went for your run this evening is the killer."

"You think I should lie about what happened?"

She sounded so horrified by the suggestion, and he decided not to point out the fact she'd started this ball rolling when she'd left the scene without calling the cops.

"What's to be gained from telling the truth? When the FBI or cops eventually ask you what happened, tell them that after the fire, you got into your car and drove."

"I texted David to say I was coming over."

David.

He shouldn't hate a dead man.

"He didn't reply, and now I know why." She sniffed.

"So you changed your mind about going over. You suffered a terrible shock. Lost your best friend and your home. You drove aimlessly, not thinking. Eventually you got to the beach and walked for hours."

There was a tick of silence. Her voice came low and intimate. "How did you know I'm at the beach?"

Because that was her happy place. The place where she liked to think. He said nothing.

"How am I going to explain my disappearing act?"

"Let's worry about that when we have to." Even though she was going through her worst nightmare, the words warmed him. The "we" made him feel as if they were allies again. The fact he'd happily take the scraps of anything she offered wasn't lost on him.

"Ridgeway is going to have my ass." Agitation shone through her voice. "I'm going to lose my job."

The way things stood, that was a decided possibility, but he had an idea. "Do you trust me, Delilah?"

She gave a bitter laugh. "I don't have a lot of choice right now."

The barb struck flesh.

He cleared his throat. "You were right to do what you did. If Scanlon is on a rampage, then he'll be moving onto the next target rather than trying for you again."

"That *doesn't* make me feel any better."

It made him feel a hell of a lot better. "It's the only advantage we have right now."

"If it's Scanlon doing this…"

"It's Scanlon." The guy had always been an arrogant sonofabitch. Joseph Scanlon had never once considered that Cas might have been a Navy SEAL who'd already hung up his trident. "I'm going to talk to a couple of people I know and see what I can—"

"No. No! I don't want you involved."

What the hell?

She thought she could go after Scanlon alone? It was so Delilah that for a moment he couldn't speak.

"I need Killion's cell number."

Killion? Shit. "Why?"

"He'll have an idea who to talk to in order to get an unofficial task force set up. The number I have for him isn't working."

"FBI isn't big on 'unofficial,' and Killion is CIA."

"I'm aware." An unfamiliar bite colored her tone. "Killion knows me, and he knows my dad. Hopefully, he will help me do what I need to do."

"You can't seriously think about going after Scanlon alone?"

"No. Only if I have to. That bastard murdered two people I care deeply about and wants me dead. I'm not averse to someone else making the arrest, but I want him watched. If we can put together enough evidence to arrest him for these crimes, he won't be able to hurt anyone else. Going to need phone records and to dig into surveillance cams in the area to see if we can pick him up. What's he driving nowadays? Any travel records? Maybe someone saw him at one of the scenes. What's his access to weapons? As an ex-con—"

"He'll have an alibi." Cas knew how to run an investigation even if that wasn't what he spent much of his time in the FBI doing. Members of the Hostage Rescue Team knew better than most how you had to be prepared to defend every decision made in the field, every bullet fired, in a court of law or on the Hill in front of politicians wanting to score points off one another.

"Which we'll have to break. Killion will know someone who can help me and maybe even allow me to keep my job when this is all over."

It stung that she'd rather ask the spook than him.

"I need to know where Scanlon is. I need to talk to the ex-wife and make sure she and the kid are protected, but right now I don't even have a laptop."

Cas shifted his focus. "Let me help. I can bring in officials from HRT—"

"No," she said sharply. "Not until I have some proof this is actually Scanlon. I don't want to be the laughingstock of the Bureau if I'm wrong. Right now, I have zero evidence."

Cas dragged his hand through his too long hair. He needed to stall her. "I can get you Killion's cell in the morning. It'll raise too many flags if I try to track it down tonight. You need money?"

The hesitation told him everything.

"Where are you?"

"Better if you don't know."

He resented the hell out of that. "Look. I'm going to book a room in that place where we used to meet. You still have that old ID?"

There was a long pause. "In my go-bag along with my wig. But—"

"I'll book it under the fake identity. If they query the ID, say that's all you have and you lost your wallet."

"Or my house burned down." Her laugh was bitter.

"Charge whatever you need to the room. You can pay me back when this is all over."

She didn't reply. Too many memories? He'd certainly never gone back. For a self-inflicted wound, it sure was painful to even think about that old grand hotel.

"I'll make arrangements for cash and a burner cell to be dropped off, in the meantime dump the cell you're on. I'll arrange some extra ammo too." Although, he had no desire for her to get into a firefight with Scanlon, who would be a formidable opponent even after years in prison. "Send me the room number as soon as you get set up there."

There was a long hesitation, and for a moment, he thought she was going to refuse his aid. To bolt.

"Okay. Thanks. I appreciate the help. Watch your back. Scanlon will probably come after you next."

"I can look after myself."

"Huh. Somehow, I knew you were going to say that."

She hung up on him before he could tell her to stay safe.

9

————————

D elilah stood in the gritty sand as the surf washed over her bare feet.

She'd done it. Spoken to the man who'd broken her into little pieces years ago and survived to tell the tale.

It was a new moon and pitch black. The whoosh of the waves along with the freshness of the air calmed her inner turmoil and solidified her determination.

She could do this.

She took out the SIM card and threw both it and David's old cell phone deep into the ocean. Then she retraced her steps back to her car and brushed off her sandy feet before slipping her sneakers back on.

She drove to long term parking at the airport, careful to avoid areas covered by surveillance cameras. She still wore Val's pink ball cap and stank like a thousand cigarettes. She took it off and tied back her long, dark hair, then got out and opened the trunk. She pulled the wig out of her go-bag and eased it over her skull, adjusted it so it looked natural and hid her own hair. She checked it in the compact mirror she kept in the bag.

It gave her a jolt to see Lacey Reed staring back at her.

Joseph Scanlon had dragged her back in time.

But she was a different person now.

She certainly wasn't the naive fool who'd believed every practiced lie Demarco had spun.

She pressed her lips together. Pulled out her go-bag, locked the SUV, and started walking to the terminal. There she used the restroom and freshened up a little, washing her face and hands, stuffing the pink cap into the bag and switching out the camo jacket for a black hoodie. She also switched her orange sneakers for a pair of black runners. Even though it was dark out, she pulled out dark glasses and slid them on her nose. Then she headed out of the terminal and walked out the main doors, hailing a cab. She had it drop her at the Marriott and walked through the lobby and out the side entrance.

The sea breeze was cool, and she shivered as she headed to the Hotel del Coronado. The old historic resort was where she and Demarco had met for stolen nights and weekends that were still seared into her mind.

She forced aside the memories.

She had no intention of reliving that illusion. The good times paled beside the bad.

The fact he'd offered to help her now didn't negate what had happened. Helping was professional courtesy—same as warning him he might be next.

She spent ten minutes in the shadows of the large shrubs, watching the entrance and any vehicles for activity that would signal he'd betrayed her. Deciding to take a risk, mainly because she didn't have much choice, she climbed the white painted steps. Inside the dark lobby with its impressive chandelier and heavy wooden columns, she glanced around, half expecting to hear shouts to get on the floor before being arrested for murder or leaving a crime scene or just being alive when she should have been dead. She wanted to believe Demarco wouldn't betray her, but he'd proven himself to be an excellent liar.

Blind trust was for suckers.

She refused to be that gullible ever again.

The reception desk clerk's expression didn't change as Delilah walked up to the marble-topped counter. Old keys on green tassels hung behind the desk, harking back to a different era. Delilah tried not to hold her breath as the woman examined the old ID, but the smile told her the plan had worked.

The woman handed over a card for a cabana room, and Delilah nodded and walked away. Still half expecting to be arrested, perhaps inside the room, away from other guests. But nothing happened.

In the room, she sagged with sudden exhaustion. Tears wanted to fill her eyes, but she pushed them away. She'd cry later. First, she was going to help prove Joseph Scanlon had committed these crimes and put him away for good this time, even if it was the last thing she ever did.

10

It was a two-hour drive to Camp Peary and the CIA's secret training facility known colloquially as "The Farm." Cas forced himself to stay calm even as his foot wanted to press ever harder on the accelerator. Delilah was smart enough to keep her head down, at least until they got a bead on Scanlon's location.

He'd sent her to the last place Scanlon would risk being spotted. After being Other Than Honorably discharged and stripped of his trident, Scanlon would be a fool to show his face anywhere near Coronado.

Ironically, Cas had spent more time in San Diego as an FBI agent than as a SEAL. As a frogman, he'd been based out of Little Creek, Virginia. Norfolk was a short drive south of Camp Peary.

Cas slowed as he came within sight of the first military checkpoint. He'd called ahead. To his surprise and despite the late hour, Patrick Killion walked past the guards and climbed into his truck.

They shook hands.

"Longtime no-see."

Cas pulled over to the side of the road. "I'd say the same, but I did spot you on TV last year. That wanted poster was a good look for you."

Killion's teeth flashed in a sharp grin. "The end of an exemplary career. It was time to hang up my boots anyway."

"Rumor has it you got married, but I find that even harder to believe."

Killion huffed out a laugh. "The world has been deprived of one of its great bachelors, *amigo*. Or so my wife likes to tell me." He gave a sudden frown. "I don't think it's the compliment I thought it was."

"She's a brave woman."

Killion grunted and scratched the back of his neck. "People who say that have never met Audrey."

Cas would like to meet her. One day.

"I'd invite you to the house, but she's sleeping. We're expecting a tadpole any day now."

"Tadpole?"

"Sorry. Inside joke." He cleared his throat. "Big tadpole. A baby. We're expecting a baby any day now."

Despite years of training, Cas couldn't disguise his surprise. "You're going to be a father?"

A wildness filled Killion's gaze. "Yeah." He laughed. "Crazy, huh? I'm terrified. I mean, give me a mad dash through the jungle at night avoiding armed hostiles any time—except, thinking about it, that's how we got into this situation in the first place."

"Your wife sounds like an interesting woman."

"She is." Killion's gaze filled with something Cas had never seen on the spook before. A tenderness that cut through the embedded cynicism and ingrained bitterness. Then his expression hardened into the operative Cas knew and trusted. "Something tells me you weren't suddenly overcome with the desire to catch up at zero dark thirty. What gives?"

"You see the news?"

"Not today. Until Audrey pops, I'm not only in charge of running the training programs here, I'm also dealing with a very grouchy pregnant woman—and I'll deny the grouchy comment even under enhanced interrogation. I haven't had a lot of spare time today, especially as I also had to collect batrachotoxin—"

"For an assassination attempt?" Cas joked and then realized he shouldn't have because who the hell knew what happened around here.

Killion eyed him. "For my wife. She's a frog biologist. She has some experiments she's running on freshly imported specimens, but I draw the line at her exposing herself and our baby to one of the deadliest neurotoxins on earth."

"Fair." Cas's lips twitched. "So you did it instead?"

"We're still working out the logistics of her taking on a student, although with recent developments south of the border, I'm thinking she could probably start applying for faculty positions again if she wanted." Killion shrugged. "It's not rocket science. All that's involved is poking a cute, but deadly, frog with a sterile swab and then putting the swab into a pre-labeled sample jar without letting it touch anything else. Like a high stakes game of *Operation*. The art is not scratching your nose while wearing those same gloves."

"You're still here so I guess it went okay."

"Audrey oversaw from a safe distance. She's bossy." His lips curled into a genuine smile.

"You obviously love it." Cas had never imagined Killion would settle down in domestic bliss, albeit surrounded with poison dart frogs and armed guards. It made something inside Cas twist uncomfortably.

"So what did I miss on the news?"

"Someone tried to kill Delilah in San Diego last night and set her up for another murder." Cas explained the situation. "She asked for your help." He cleared his throat. "And maybe you can get a message to her parents. They're going to be devastated by the news especially after already losing their son. Her father might be able to pull a few strings."

"Might be a risk." Killion grunted. "Her old man's suffering from dementia."

Demarco's brows hiked. "She didn't mention that." It cut him a little. Part of him still hated the guy for what he'd done five years ago, but it was becoming more and more obvious that Cas hadn't deserved his daughter. "You think he'll accidentally mention the truth to someone?"

"Who knows? It's a potential problem though." Killion scraped his teeth over his bottom lip, clearly thinking.

Cas had expected the former CIA Intelligence Officer to crack a joke, but his mouth tightened.

"How much do you think she wants to keep her job?"

Cas shot him a look. "As opposed to working for the Agency you mean?"

Killion shrugged. "She'd be good at it, and there's no better operative than someone who's already supposed to be dead."

Cas felt everything inside him contract. "I can't answer for her, but regardless, we still need to figure out who killed those people and tried to set her up."

Killion stared out of the windshield for a full minute. "Let me talk to a few friends in the Bureau. See what we can pull together to figure this out." He cracked the window. "But you need to bring her in."

"Bring her in?"

Killion shot him a look. "As competent as Delilah is, she can't handle this alone. The FBI is less forgiving than the Agency when it comes to breaking the rules. Not to mention, Joseph Scanlon might be a psychopath, but he's a competent motherfucker." Killion held his gaze. "If he figures out she's alive and gets his hands on her, she'll wish she'd never been born. I'm too old and selfish to deal with that."

The saliva in Cas's mouth evaporated. The thought of anyone hurting Delilah enraged him. He checked his watch. Conflict tearing him apart. "I don't know if I have time to go get her before Montana's memorial service on Wednesday." He realized it was after midnight and swore. "Tomorrow."

He hadn't had many father figures in his life or men he looked up to, but Kurt Montana had been one of them. "If I can persuade her to stay in a hotel room for the next couple of days, I can leave as soon as the service is over. Convince her this is the only way."

The idea of missing the service went against every grain of decency he possessed.

Killion's gaze flicked away. "Montana was a good man."

"He hated spooks."

Killion huffed out a laugh. "Everyone hates spooks. Even other spooks." He checked his own watch. "Look, I happen to know there's a flight out of Norfolk to San Diego leaving at zero-five hundred for a SEAL joint training exercise. Even better. It flies back without personnel onboard tonight. Nineteen-thirty Pacific Time. You might not get much sleep, but it'll get you back in time for the service."

"I'll need to clear it with my boss."

"Consider it cleared."

"It'll be better if I do it myself." HRT leadership did not like being dictated to by the CIA, and Cas knew better than to assume anything. "You're sure you can get us both on the return flight?"

Killion smiled, and Cas remembered all the crazy things they'd done while infiltrating gangs and cartels in places the FBI didn't usually venture. "Some idiot put me in charge of this place. I've discovered I can pretty much do anything I damned well please."

The cold wind ruffled Cas's hair through the open window.

"Anything I can provide you with for the journey?" asked Killion.

"Maybe a couple of burner cells? I have everything else I need in my go-bag."

Killion nodded. "Wanna come back to the house for a couple of hours' sleep? We have a spare room."

"I thought you said Audrey was asleep?" Cas was startled. Killion had always been notoriously guarded when it came to his private life.

He shrugged. "I wasn't expecting you to stick around. She

TONI ANDERSON

probably won't even wake up until after you've gone, so don't worry about it."

Cas nodded. "That would be good. Thanks."

"I might have some answers for you regarding a possible task force before you leave."

Cas reversed and headed toward the checkpoint and watched in surprise as the barrier was lifted without any ID checks or questions. The feeling of being watched crawled all over him.

He frowned.

"What?" Killion had a glint in his eye that Cas didn't completely trust.

"Security seems a little lax, considering."

"See that platform over there?" Killion nodded toward a wooden structure nestled in the trees.

Cas eyed it. "Looks like a deer hide." It was hard to make out in the near darkness.

"Yeah, but it ain't no deer they're scoping."

The idea of crosshairs on his skull made Cas sweat. He was usually the one holding the long gun.

"I have a signal I can give if I'm here under duress."

"Hopefully not something you might do by rote."

"No, but if I put an imaginary gun to my head you might want to duck."

Cas's hands instinctively tightened on the steering wheel.

"They're under strict instructions never to shoot Audrey and never to shoot me should she be the one to give the signal. She's not above trying to kill me on occasion."

"I remember the feeling." Cas laughed reluctantly. "You seem happy."

"I'm the luckiest man alive and smart enough to appreciate it." Killion's eyes shone in the darkness as he guided Cas past the sniper position and down a narrow track between the trees. "I always thought you and Delilah—"

"Don't." Cas's tone was firm.

"Just saying. I thought you were—"

72

"Patrick," he warned.

"Ah." Killion nodded sagely. "Figured."

Cas's throat lurched on a hard swallow. He hadn't realized anyone suspected. "I messed up."

"Goes without saying."

They came upon a pretty Cape Cod style house complete with a white picket fence and the Stars and Stripes, lit up and fluttering in the brisk wind off the York River. Cas pulled to a stop and grabbed his go-bag out of the back seat. Decided to leave his rifle where it was.

"Any other safety measures I need to know about around here?"

Killion shook his head. "But I advise against going for a walk in the woods or picking up any stray amphibians while you're on site. Come on. You can grab some sleep while I wake up a few people who might be able to help us figure this out."

"Delilah will be pissed that I'm bringing her in."

"Better than her getting arrested, or dead."

"Yeah." Those alternatives were unbearable.

Killion opened the door and waved him inside. His voice dropped to a low whisper. "Delilah's a good person—for an FBI agent."

And Cas was the dead-last person on earth from whom she'd want help.

11

Despite the cool outside temperature, Clarence Carpenter was sweating through his favorite Hawaiian shirt. He debated whether or not to take a jacket as it didn't really go with his outfit, but he was going to the mayor's office so he probably should, plus, who knew what this wire thing the Feds planned to attach to him looked like.

He gulped down the protein shake he'd grabbed out of the fridge for breakfast and then put his hand on his stomach as he belched. He tossed the empty container into the recycling bin and wiped his sweaty forehead.

If his boss found out he was working for the Feds, he was going to end up inhaling concrete. Hopefully, if he could give the FBI the mayor, both the FBI and his boss would be happy and leave him the hell alone.

He'd told that prick Gonzales that he was working under his own initiative and that his boss didn't have a clue why he was so successful at getting so many lucrative contracts. He wasn't sure the agent had believed him, but no way was he implicating Frank Bannon in anything illegal—the guy wasn't known for his patience or understanding.

If this meet worked out, he'd tell Frank what had gone down

and why, and then they'd use the situation and make sure the Feds only learned what they wanted them to learn.

A tangle of anxiety wound around his chest. He grabbed the keys to his SUV and tossed them into the air. Caught them with a determined flourish.

I can do this.

He repeated the mantra as he picked up his cell from the charger and slipped it into his back pocket. Grabbed his sports jacket off the back of the kitchen stool, just in case.

He headed out the front door to where his car sat on the drive beside the tall hedge of bougainvillea that his neighbors kept asking him to trim.

Did he look like a gardener?

He shook his head and then shimmied down the narrow gap and conceded that perhaps they had a point. Maybe he'd ask his brother to give him a hand on the weekend or perhaps hire one of the local kids who lived nearby. Get them off the street, where they shot hoops, and doing something useful for a change.

He checked his watch which glowed in the pre-dawn light. He'd organized this meet early so his boss wouldn't wonder where he was this morning.

He scowled as he climbed into the driver's seat. The Feds better not fuck up his career.

Frank was a good boss. But a scary son of a gun.

He put the key in the ignition and jolted as Kendrick Lamar blared out of the sound system. He winced and turned it down because the last thing he needed was to draw attention to himself.

He shifted forward to drag the phone out of his back pocket and toss it on the center console. Then he yawned and rubbed his eyes before twisting to pull on his seatbelt.

He sat back and, let out a little squeal as a meaty forearm came around from the backseat and grabbed him around the neck.

"What the—" The words were cut off along with his ability to draw in air.

His fingernails dug into the man's arm and tried to pry him off as his feet scrambled. He couldn't breathe and whoever this guy was, he was far too strong for Clarence to dislodge him. He felt his vision start to gray and slapped his hand toward the horn to get someone's attention.

"Oh, no, you don't." The accent was thick and guttural.

Clarence found himself jerked violently back between the gap in the seats. He didn't know what the hell was going on, but he flung his fisted hand back toward his assailant and connected with what felt like a beard. Had Frank heard about the meet with the Feds and sent someone to get rid of him?

I can explain!

He tried to get the words out, but the guy had him in an unbreakable headlock and Clarence's lungs were burning with panic and the fierce need for oxygen.

His knees banged the steering wheel as he tried to escape but the seatbelt locked him into place. He reached back again, and this time grabbed a handful of hair and pulled as hard as he could, tearing some out.

Weakness began invading his limbs, pins and needles throbbed in his fingers which suddenly felt numb. His legs gave out. The blackness that had been creeping around his vision suddenly rushed in. He lost consciousness not knowing why this was happening or if he was ever gonna wake up.

12

Delilah woke to a knock on the door and sat bolt upright as all the events from last night bombarded her with startling reality. A glance at the clock told her she'd slept in. It was almost eight.

She and David should have been downtown listening in on Clarence Carpenter's meeting with the mayor by now. Immediately, she wanted to update someone on the case, but being supposedly dead made that difficult.

Her throat closed.

David...

Had someone found him yet?

Her stomach churned at the idea they hadn't, that he was still lying in his own blood in his backyard.

The knock on the door came again.

Damn.

She grabbed her Glock off the bedside table and stood behind the bathroom wall. If it was Scanlon, he'd probably shoot her through the door. If it was her colleagues come to lead her away in handcuffs, she didn't want them to see her armed. She wouldn't risk a firefight.

"Who is it?" she called out.

"Room service."

The deep timbre of the voice caught her by surprise and sent a shiver of recognition along every nerve fiber of her being like a fuse had been lit.

Suddenly, she felt sick. Nervous. Panicked. Talking to him on the phone was one thing. She should have known he wouldn't keep his word. She should have known he'd turn up like a bad penny, mistakenly believing he was her White Knight.

In her fairytale, he was the villain.

She walked to the door and checked the peephole.

There he stood all tousled blue-black hair that still had a curl he could never quite tame. Casta Demarco. Teller of Lies. Destroyer of Hearts.

She quickly opened the door, not wanting to draw attention or notice, no matter how much she'd rather avoid this man for eternity.

He slipped inside and she caught the scent of him, leather and rain, things that reminded her of the East Coast rather than him. When she'd known him he'd been sunshine and clean male sweat, heat and the musky essence of danger. He lowered his heavy-looking bag carefully to the floor. She closed the door softly and flicked the security latch back into place. Steeled herself against the effect he'd always had on her.

"What are you doing here?"

A smile curled those full lips. "Not glad to see me, Delilah?" He wore all black and looked like the rugged operator he was rather than the daredevil undercover agent he'd once been. He crossed his arms, clearly uncomfortable to be in the same room as she was.

Ditto.

She felt woefully unprepared for this reckoning in only an oversized T-shirt and panties. Her clothes from yesterday were hanging in the shower after she'd walked in there fully dressed last night. The tinge of smoke still clung to her nostrils, but maybe it was her imagination, her senses unable to fully let go of the horror of last night.

"Want some coffee?" Determined to pretend he didn't affect her, she went over to the hotel's machine and put in a pod.

"Sure." He yawned widely.

Maybe she wasn't the only one pretending.

"Did you get any sleep last night?"

He jogged one shoulder in a tense shrug. She tried to ignore the way his muscles bunched in his arms. He'd aged sickeningly well.

"A few hours on the flight. You?"

"A surprising amount in the end." Once sleep had claimed her, it had been reluctant to let go. Dreams were so much better than reality. "How d'you get here so fast?"

She handed him the mug, careful not to touch him. She had no intention of doing anything that might make him think she still had feelings for him. She would rather take a bullet than go through that nightmare again.

"Military flight."

"You here to arrest me?" she asked through gritted teeth.

"Not yet."

She turned and made her own coffee, desperate for a hit of caffeine to kickstart her brain. The presence of two queen-size beds made her remember the other times they'd been together in this iconic hotel. They'd once spent two whole days completely naked, never once leaving the room.

Bitterness seared her tongue. "I told you I didn't want your help."

"Why don't we discuss this when you're dressed?"

Her brows hiked and fury rolled through her. His tone suggested she might be trying to deliberately seduce him or something—like he was unable to control himself around her and like that might be *her* fault.

How very *male*.

"You woke me, Demarco. When you arrive uninvited, this is what you get. I wasn't expecting company." She let her anger and outrage show even though she kept the volume low. She looked down at her bare feet and resisted the desire to tug the T-shirt lower.

His eyes glittered like amber. "I only thought you'd be more comfortable if you had some pants on—"

"Save it for someone who still believes your bullshit." She put her hands on her hips. "Rest assured, I am not trying to tempt you with my irresistible body. Trust me when I say I wouldn't hook up with you again if you were the last man on the planet, with the exception perhaps of Joseph Scanlon. So don't worry about your reputation or your honor on my account. Your body is safe from me."

She strode over to her bag which she'd placed on the armchair in the corner and picked it up. She grabbed her coffee mug with the other hand and headed into the bathroom, closing the heavy door behind her with her heel.

She dressed quickly and brushed her teeth. Washed her face. She wished she had a little makeup, lipstick or mascara, but she hadn't considered it enough of a necessity to put in her go-bag. It would have been useful armor against this man, her former lover, a person who'd seduced her, gutted her, and left her to drown in grief—not that he knew the details.

She needed every weapon she could gather against this man.

Tears filled her eyes because it had been Valerie who'd helped her through the terrible nightmare that had happened after Cas had dumped her. The loss of her friend hit her anew and she wanted to break down and weep. For David too. Two good people murdered for no good reason.

She forced the tears back past the lump in her throat. She'd cry when they arrested their killer.

She stared in the mirror and wondered how her world had been so easily tipped on its head. This time yesterday, she'd been blissfully unaware of what was to come. She thrust the thoughts and self-pity aside. Valerie and David were dead and knowing Scanlon, he wasn't finished yet.

No rest for the wicked. There was work to do.

She got dressed in dark navy jeans and a navy shirt with white buttons. She pulled on old leather boots, feeling a little more like herself.

She stuffed all her things into the bag, using a plastic garbage liner for her wet clothes. She slipped her weapon into a pancake holster at the small of her back, brushed the tangles out of her hair and went back outside. Cas was pacing the room, drinking his coffee. She watched his eyes flicker down her length before he looked away.

Was that *attraction* she saw in his yellow eyes?

Fury bubbled.

He had no damned right.

"What's the plan?" she bit out. "I assume you have one?"

"There's a military plane headed back to Naval Base Norfolk at nineteen-thirty tonight. We're both going to be on it."

She bristled. *Really.*

"Killion's idea, not mine." He correctly read her response. "We'll set up a center of operations somewhere in Virginia. Killion is making calls. He wants to set up a task force."

She stiffened.

"On the down low, but if Scanlon is involved, we have to prove it, and to prove it we need to know where the sonofabitch is, where he's been, where he's going and who he's communicating with. We can't do that with just you and me."

"I told you," she gritted out, "I don't want *your* help."

"Hey, I'm a target too. We may as well work together, but I can't simply go AWOL from work."

Of course not. Nothing got between Cas Demarco and his job.

She placed the bitterness next to the grief and pushed it aside. For now.

"SAC Ridgeway said Scanlon was planning to head back to

Louisiana after his release, so I figured he'd presumably have to meet with a parole officer there at regular intervals."

"You spoke to Ridgeway?" Surprise hiked his brows.

"Yesterday. Before everything went down. I got a phone call from a San Diego Police Department detective friend of mine telling me Scanlon was released from Miramar as of three weeks ago."

"What did Ridgeway say?"

"He knew already. Said Scanlon was a reformed man and had found God."

"Well, he certainly embraced the Hellfire."

She rubbed her arms. "I'd had a feeling of being watched at times recently. When I was in La Jolla and a couple of times when I was out and about on the job."

"Presumably, that's where he realized you had a partner?"

"Presumably." She bit her lip to keep from crying. "David Gonzales. He was going to go far in the Bureau." Intelligent. Handsome. Kind. "I ignored the feeling when I should have listened to my instincts. Wrote it off to my routine being thrown by Valerie staying with me. I should have paid attention. I should have moved Valerie to a hotel or..."

Demarco said nothing as she trailed off.

She crossed her arms. "Anyway, I found out his parole officer is a guy named Jim Jenkins in Thibodaux. It's a thirty-minute drive from Scanlon's father's home, where his dad and twin brother still live."

She'd done some research yesterday, checking up on the guy.

"I remember them from the trial."

They exchanged a quick look at that.

Scanlon's people were from the bayous of Louisiana. Joseph Scanlon had grown up creeping around that swamp with the same ease as the alligators who inhabited the place. They needed to avoid confronting him on home ground if at all possible.

"So even if we can't find the guy before then, we should be

able to discover when he has an appointment and track him after that."

He'd be unarmed too. Only a man eager to go back to prison visited a parole officer while armed.

Demarco stared at her, but she couldn't read his expression. She wished he'd say something. She turned away. "Ideally, we need to collect enough evidence to have him arrested at that next appointment."

"Which we can amass in Virginia." Demarco was dogged in his determination to get her out of California.

She narrowed her eyes. "What *exactly* did Killion say to you?"

"That if you want to stay dead, he can get you a gig at the Agency."

"Great." She didn't want to work for the CIA. She loved her job as a Special Agent. "What else did he say?"

"That you can't do this alone and hope to stay in the FBI."

She tapped her foot. She hated that he was probably right. "So now what? We have nine hours to kill before we catch the flight out of here."

His eyes flickered to the bed.

She sneered. "Yeah. Not happening."

"I'm not a fool, Delilah." He looked affronted.

God. That hurt.

He crossed his arms. "Look, I have a friend from my old SEAL team who's now a BUD/S instructor. I figured I'd use the opportunity to go talk to him. See if there are any rumors running around the teams regarding Scanlon. See if I can determine who his friends are."

"How do you know you can trust this friend of yours?"

Gold eyes flashed to hers. "We did three tours together."

Whatever the two of them had had together apparently held no comparison to the SEAL brotherhood, no matter how dangerous their undercover work had felt at times. She hated him all over again. "And what about the men from Scanlon's platoon? They served together too."

Cas nodded. "During the trial, they were split regarding their opinion on Scanlon."

"You mean half of his platoon believed him and the other half believed the Bureau."

"The evidence against him was overwhelming, especially with the video. That's why Naval Command stripped him of his trident."

She bit the inside of her cheek. "Do you think any of his SEAL buddies would help him get revenge for what happened?"

"Honestly? No. But that's one of the things I'm hoping Senior Chief Tommy Whalen will help me ascertain."

She held her hand out to the balcony and blue pool beyond. "And I get to sit around here all day?"

He stared at her with that flat-eyed stare that had enabled him to hold his own with some of the deadliest killers in the world. "If you promise to come with me to Virginia tonight without any trouble, I'll buy you some sunglasses and a hat. You can sit in the vehicle and guard the gear while I ask Tommy some questions. We'll come back here for something to eat afterwards and head to the base airfield around six."

She chewed her lip. Leaving San Diego felt like running away. Like she was abandoning Val and David. "Why do we have to run the task force out of Virginia? The murders happened in California."

"Well, for one, your official FBI photo will be on every news station around here for the foreseeable future and, secondly, because I have to be back in Virginia tomorrow for a personal commitment."

Her lip curled. "So I have to fly across the country because you have a dental appointment?"

"It's a memorial service for a fellow HRT operative."

Remorse stabbed at her. "Damn. Sorry." She rubbed her brow. Then she asked the question she'd been avoiding. "Do you know if they informed my parents yet?"

"Probably."

Delilah looked away. She wasn't sure what the best decision would be regarding her parents. With her dad's illness and delicate mental state, it might be better not to tell him anything. He might forget that someone had told him she'd died—the way he sometimes forgot that her brother was dead.

Her throat closed as she thought of Christian. He'd been in college and had died from an accidental opioid overdose eight years ago.

And her father had been overprotective of her ever since and had been furious when she joined the Bureau—not that he'd stopped her, for which she was grateful. He'd had the power.

When Demarco was still pretending to be in love with her, he'd claimed he'd wanted to meet her parents.

She was grateful she hadn't introduced them. Once they'd got to know one another, her father would have loved this guy, and he'd have been devastated when Demarco dumped her. Stephen Quinn was petty enough to have taken it out on Demarco's FBI career, and Delilah would not have wanted to be responsible for that. It was obvious he was a dedicated agent.

Demarco went over to his heavy kitbag and pulled out a burner cell. "Here." He tossed it to her.

She caught it.

"Call your mom. Maybe your dad has enough friends to pull a few strings in DC." Demarco had always been slightly cynical about her powerful connections.

But nowadays he didn't get to judge her.

She stuffed the cell into her pocket, dug into her bag and pulled out the blonde wig. "I'll call from the vehicle when you're talking to this Tommy guy." She wound her own hair into a pony, pinned it tight to her nape. She slid the wig carefully into place and added a couple of clips to secure it.

Demarco's expression went carefully blank as she faced him. Pretending he didn't remember that they'd once fucked frantically against a wall in this very hotel with her wearing only this wig and nothing else.

Something in her chest tightened, as if there suddenly wasn't enough oxygen in the room. She couldn't stand to be confined to this space with this man for a second longer. She pulled oversized dark glasses from the go-bag and slid them on.

"Let's go."

13

C as felt ill as he looked up at the white-painted, wooden exterior of the iconic Victorian Hotel del Coronado that rose up in front of him. The American flag planted on its red-roofed rotunda snapped briskly in the ocean breeze.

In any other circumstances, he'd go down to the beach and walk barefoot in the sand, feel the heat of the sun on his skin after months of cold, damp weather. But not these circumstances.

Delilah obviously detested him, and that was no surprise. He'd earned every ounce of animosity she threw at him. What he wanted to earn next was her forgiveness, and if that wasn't possible, then the least he could do would be to protect her from this dangerous threat.

He strode over to the valet and handed the guy his ticket. He didn't miss the man giving Delilah the once-over as she moved to a nearby bench to wait. She had no idea what she did to men, even Scanlon who'd almost tripped over his tongue when he'd met Lacey Reed—Ricky Alonso's pretty, junky girlfriend who regularly came to visit him across the border to get high and to get fucked.

The FBI's plan for her to catch a ride back across the border with the SEAL as he transported a large shipment of coke in his nice, shiny new truck had worked brilliantly. She'd caught him on camera doing the deed, not to mention propositioning her and then assaulting her during the arrest.

Cas had hated that plan, hated the danger it put her in, but he was a small cog in the wheel of justice, and orders were orders.

He still hated the plan, even all these years later.

Cas had no doubt the bastard would have pulled over to the side of the road and raped her if she hadn't pretended to go along with the idea of having sex with him. The fact she'd "belonged" to him—to Ricky Alonso—had been a big part of the attraction for Scanlon.

The guy liked flirting with death.

Scanlon certainly hadn't liked taking orders from Ricky, but he'd had little choice after taking money from the cartel. They'd *owned* him. Until the FBI had shut it all down.

The defense had implied Delilah had led the guy on and entrapped him, but the video and audio were the final nail in that coffin—the jury of other military personnel had clearly seen that suggestion for the ruse it had been.

Cas snapped back to the present as his car arrived, a gray Jeep that Killion had arranged. He placed their bags in the back seat. Delilah strode to the passenger side, that roll of her hips as enticing now as it had been almost six years ago when he'd first met her.

His mouth went dry as he got behind the wheel. He had to force what they'd once been from his mind. She'd told him what she thought of him. He had zero chance of winning her back, and that was for the best.

His mood bottomed out.

But if he could help her then, perhaps, he could redeem himself for the wrongs he'd done to her. The pain he'd caused. And there was no way he'd ever leave her in danger. No way.

Tommy's home wasn't far, but they'd arranged to meet at a café on Orange Ave and Tenth.

Cas pulled around the back of the coffeeshop. "Want anything?"

"Besides my life back?" She looked at him over her glasses. "No, thanks."

He hitched his chin toward the backseat. "I have weapons in the bag."

"I'll watch them."

He hesitated. Handed her the keys but held on to them for a moment. It was the closest he'd come to touching her in five years. "Don't run out on me, Delilah. I'm here to help."

She shot him a glare and looked away, her throat rippling. Neither of them mentioned he was the one who'd run out on them both.

They didn't have to.

He headed inside the busy café. He was early but then so was Tommy. They smacked each other on the back, ordered drinks and food, and then found a table near the window.

"What's it feel like to be part of the old guard?" Cas asked with a wry smile as he sat down.

The instructors had been demons during their induction and BUD/S, but once they'd earned their tridents *most* of the instructors had turned out to be good guys—with a few exceptions.

"Not gonna lie. The power is heady." Tommy leaned back in a chair that looked too small for the giant out of Arkansas.

You didn't need to be big to be a SEAL. In fact, it could be a detriment when you were trying to complete the requisite number of chin ups after another grueling timed swim. But size helped when you were lugging around heavy equipment and munitions that weighed more than a full-grown Rottweiler.

"Have you screamed anyone into quitting yet?"

Tommy smirked. "A couple. Almost lost my voice with one guy." He leaned forward so no one could overhear. "Maybe I'm sick, but it's fun. And the ones who quit? I'm doing them a favor. They would never have made it through BUDS let alone any actual real-world deployments."

Cas nodded. He knew. It wasn't simply about physical strength. It was about mental fortitude. Grim determination to prove to the instructors that they were a bunch of assholes and wrong about you. This was how team spirit was built. Push everyone to the limit, beyond the limit, reduce them to the basic components of human beings just trying to survive, and see how they reacted.

Did they fold? Or did they stand back up and finish the job?

"How's the FBI treating you? Bored out of your skull yet?"

Cas smirked as he thought about the missions abroad, the serial killers, old Russian KGB agents, and deadly nerve gas he'd faced recently. "It keeps me busy. Hoping to keep at it for a few more years yet."

The guy's eyes crinkled in amusement. "Guys like you and me. They'll have to carry us out on our backs."

Cas took a bite of his croissant to hide the truth of that statement. He was nothing without his job. It was what he drew all his self-worth from. His pride. His arrogance.

What else did he have?

Certainly, no pedigree or over-inflated bank account. His job defined him, and he wasn't about to fuck it up. He wiped his mouth.

"You heard Joseph Scanlon got early release?"

Tommy took a sip of his coffee and smacked his lips at the flavor. "I figured that's why you suddenly decided to visit."

Cas shrugged a shoulder. "I had a spare day, thought I'd come check out whether or not you think he might become a problem for me."

"Hard to say." Tommy used his tongue to clean the pastry off his teeth. "I hear he was a model prisoner at Miramar. But—" He shook his head. "He always had a look in his eyes I never trusted, you know?"

Cas nodded. It had been a glint of maliciousness and evil.

"Most people think he's a waste of space and the Navy in general have washed their hands of him."

Most? "He have *any* friends left in the Teams?"

"A couple of guys he deployed with on Team seven."

"Names?"

Tommy's eyes shuttered. "I'm not looking to mess up my fellow sailors, Cas."

Cas wiped a napkin over his mouth, still hungry. "I don't intend to mess with them. I just want to know who to watch out for."

"Scanlon won't come after you. He'd be crazy to do that."

"The female FBI agent? The one who arrested him? They believe she died in a house fire last night."

"That was her?" Tommy's brows crunched together in a worried frown. "You think it was Scanlon?"

"Hell of a coincidence if it wasn't."

Tommy held his gaze for a long moment and then wrote two names on a clean napkin. "You didn't get those from me." He checked his watch. "I gotta go, man."

"Involved in a joint training exercise by any chance?"

Tommy looked surprised. "How'd you know about that?"

He tapped his nose. "Friends in low places." Killion's intel, plus the fact the flight over here had been full of active-duty SEALs and equipment.

"That, and the fact Admiral Sagal is retiring. We're having the ceremony this afternoon with so many active-duty SEALs being here."

Sagal had been in charge of the SEAL teams for more than a decade. He was also the man who'd ordered Scanlon stripped of his Trident.

"It might be wise to review security measures—just in case." Cas gave him a pointed look.

Tommy nodded thoughtfully. "Security is tight but always worth reviewing it from a SEAL point of view."

Because you never expected an attack to come from someone on the inside.

The two men stood and shook hands. "It was good seeing you, man. Don't leave it so damned long next time."

Cas squeezed Tommy's hand. "I won't."

He didn't need to ask him to listen out for any rumors or news regarding Scanlon. Tommy would make discreet inquiries and contact him if anything came up.

Cas went back up to the counter and ordered two more coffees and four pastries to go. Delilah had always had a weak spot for sugary treats and maybe he'd earn himself some brownie points.

If not, he could eat them himself in a fit of despondency.

He walked down the avenue and cut back through the lane behind the buildings, checking his six to make sure he wasn't being followed. No matter how much he trusted his old friend, Tommy, now was not the time to drop his guard. He had too much to lose to make a mistake.

He hoped Delilah was where he'd left her. The look in her eyes had said how little she trusted him or wanted his help.

Lucky for him, she didn't have much choice.

14

Delilah sat in the warm Jeep working up the courage to make the phone call. Her fingers shook as she typed in her mom's cell number.

"Hello?" The voice was wary.

"Mom, don't say anything, okay?" A choked sob on the other end of the line twisted Delilah's heart in a knot. "Are you alone?"

"Give me a moment."

Delilah waited while her mother moved somewhere where she could talk in private.

"I'm in the upstairs en suite bathroom. What's going on? I had the FBI Director on the doorstep first thing this morning offering me her condolences."

Shoot. Of course, the director would take a personal interest. How would she react to the knowledge Delilah was still alive? Probably not well.

"I'm so sorry. I didn't have any way of contacting you last night." Not without being sure she couldn't be tracked. "I'm gonna need you to carry on pretending I'm dead for a little while."

"Are you in danger?"

She thought about the look in Joseph Scanlon's eyes the day she'd arrested him. The threats he'd uttered. Had he acted on them? The thought of what he might have done to Val haunted her.

"I think I might be." She tried to lighten the mood. "How are your acting skills?"

"When the life of my child is at risk? Darling, I'm worthy of an Academy Award."

Delilah smiled even though what she really wanted to do was cry at the reassuring sound of her mother's voice.

"Your father…"

She could hear her mother making herself say the words.

"As you can imagine, he's very upset."

Delilah wanted to curl into a ball and sob.

"Tell me what's going on," her mom insisted.

"It's complicated."

"I am not the one who's lost their faculties, young lady. Tell me."

"Okay. Fine. I went for a run last night and when I came home my condo was on fire and Valerie…" Her voice stumbled. "I think Valerie was inside, dead."

"Oh, my goodness." Horror was reflected in her mother's tone.

Her parents knew Valerie well. Delilah had often dragged her friend home to family gatherings.

"I spoke to a firefighter who said there was someone inside the apartment—I assume it was Val. It hit me hard, so I went over to David Gonzales' place, my partner at the Bureau, because he lives close by and we're friends. I found him shot dead."

It sounded fantastical.

If this was her case, she wouldn't believe her version of events. She'd exchange a knowing look with fellow agents and work to put her at ease and then break her story.

"Why didn't you tell anyone?" Her mother's hushed whisper was confused. "Your coworkers?"

"I believe I know the person responsible, and he's trying to frame me for the murders even in death. I don't want him going to ground if he thinks I'm on to him, and he won't think I'm onto him if he believes I'm in the morgue."

"Delilah, you can't go running around chasing dangerous killers on your own. You know better than that." Her mother's words were a forceful whisper.

"I'm not alone. I have a CIA friend helping me figure this out." No way would she implicate Demarco.

"A CIA officer? How do you even know him—"

"I worked with him on the Scanlon case."

Her mother went quiet. She was the wife of a former top FBI official and knew when not to ask questions.

"Look, I'm not going rogue. I'm simply going dark until I can get this guy—me along with a task force of other officials." That was her hope anyway. "I don't have all the details figured out yet."

"I don't know how I'm going to tell your father you're not dead. He was devastated earlier. This is going to confuse him even further. Make him really feel like he's losing his mind because that's how I feel."

"Then don't tell him."

The silence suggested her mother was thinking about the merits of that.

"It has to be this way, Mom. If we don't get this guy, I'm going to be looking over my shoulder for the rest of my life." She heard the sniffle of tears. Delilah's mouth went dry. "I'm sorry, Mom. Truly. I'll come home as soon as I can. To visit and help out. Help look after Dad."

"I know he made mistakes. He struggled to cope after losing Christian…"

She'd struggled with the loss too. They all had.

"If you'd seen him earlier today…"

"I don't mean to hurt him. Or you."

"I know, honey. I know."

Delilah could tell her mother was crying and that made her feel wretched.

"I better get back downstairs. The caregiver is here, but Stephen's upset, so I need to be there. I'm going to tell him the truth and hope he can hold it together and keep it a secret. The way he's progressing, he may have forgotten everything in a few days anyway."

Delilah squeezed her fingers into a tight fist. She hadn't realized he was deteriorating so rapidly. Her father would have been a useful ally to have, but she couldn't ask anything of him. Not in his condition. Few people knew of his cognitive decline because he was a proud man and that's how he'd wanted it. She wouldn't betray him.

"I love you, Mom. Give him a kiss from me."

She hung up and turned on the radio to listen to the news. Her supposed death and David's murder were the main headlines. Which was good, she reminded herself, steeling her heart against the emotions that wanted to wreck it. The coverage was exactly what Scanlon would expect.

She heard footsteps and glanced around as paranoia raised its ugly head. The Jeep was in shadow, and no one would expect her to be sitting there, disguised as a blonde, in a back alley in Coronado, but she needed to keep up her guard.

Demarco arrived carrying goodies from the coffee shop. He went to the passenger side and Delilah slowly buzzed down the window.

The look of him made her insides ache.

He handed her the tray with a smile. "In case you changed your mind about being hungry."

Ignoring the effect his presence had on her, she took the tray, her stomach rumbling despite her earlier refusal.

He went around and climbed into the driver's seat and grabbed one of the coffees and a donut.

Something on the radio caught her attention. She frowned and turned up the volume.

"A third person was discovered dead in his car early this

morning. The FBI are refusing to confirm reports that he was a Confidential Informant linked to the two dead FBI agents."

She sat frozen, staring at the radio in alarm. Had she misjudged this whole situation?

"Who's that?" Demarco noted her reaction.

She swallowed. Hard. "It could be David's CI. We were supposed to meet him this morning."

"Are you saying this whole thing *might* be related to an active case? Not Scanlon?" Demarco's golden eyes were laser focused on her face.

Delilah shook her head. "It makes no sense. Clarence Carpenter was a low-level player. He scheduled a meeting with the mayor of La Mesa City. Rumor has it the guy is taking bribes. It's a Public Corruption case but hardly Watergate and hardly worthy of a triple homicide."

"Might be to someone who feels threatened. Who knew you were meeting with him?"

She pursed her lips together. What if she was wrong about all of this? "I only found out myself yesterday afternoon. David arranged it all."

Demarco tapped his fingers on the steering wheel in a habit she'd forgotten he had. "So, either you're mistaken, and this situation is related to one of your current cases, or…"—he held up a finger and she wanted to bite it off—"Scanlon has gone to a lot of trouble to throw investigators off his scent. Why didn't he anticipate your friend, Valerie, being in the apartment if she's been staying with you?"

Delilah stared through the window. Forced the emotions into a dark pit. Grasped at logic. "She was gone the last two weeks on a cruise. Only got back yesterday morning for an audition downtown."

"That timing makes sense. He's been out of prison for three weeks. Presumably, he'd wait a week before beginning recon on revenge plans that would put him right back inside."

Demarco believed her...but she'd been wrong before where this man was concerned.

She ignored the protest of her stomach, thrust her croissant into the brown paper bag, and put her coffee in the cup holder. Doubts assailed her. "What if I am wrong?" She grabbed her head between her hands. "What if someone discovered Clarence was talking to us and killed him to prevent him passing on anything incriminating and then went after us?"

"That would suggest some major-league corruption." Those rich yellow eyes watched her. "Even if that's the case, why frame you for your partner's murder? If this was related to a Public Corruption case, why murder you and try to make it look as if you killed your lover?"

Lover?

He thought she and David had been lovers? She opened her mouth to correct him and then changed her mind. Perhaps if he thought she'd been involved with someone else, it would help keep a wedge between them. She knew how charming he could be. How charismatic. How susceptible she was to him despite everything she knew to be true. Fighting that attraction, despite what he'd done to her, would be difficult, which was humbling to admit even to herself.

"To discredit me?"

Demarco shook his head. "Once he added this Clarence guy to the mix, he stirred things up a little too much... Unless he somehow incriminated you in that murder too?"

"How? I was already supposed to be dead."

"We don't know when Clarence died."

True.

"Did you have any kind of personal relationship with this Clarence guy?"

She shook her head. "He was David's CI. He flipped and culti- vated him. I'd seen Clarence in passing, but today was the first time I was going to be directly involved with him."

"I think that by killing the CI, Scanlon overplayed his hand."

"I don't think the FBI will see it that way."

"How could Scanlon have found out about the CI or the meet?"

She chewed her lip. "David met with Clarence yesterday morning. He didn't say where but probably some parking garage somewhere. Someone could have followed him, but David would have noticed."

Cas shook his head. "Scanlon is a former Navy SEAL sniper. He might be rusty, but he knows how to surveil without being spotted. But easier to put a tracker on his vehicle."

Her breath hitched. "David often parked his Bucar outside his garage. The killer could have stuck a transmitter inside. Picked up the conversation and knew the location before I did."

Cas nodded. "That would be my bet." He tapped the steering with his thumb. "I want to take a look at the bodies."

She reared back. "Why?"

"Because. Scanlon was a sniper and a damned good shot, but SEALs know how to snap a neck or use a knife. I want to know how each victim died."

She was breathing heavily, and she forced herself to calm down. She'd seen dead bodies before, but it was different this time. Two of these people were dear friends.

"How are you going to get in there?"

He flashed her a grin. The one that had made him so irresistible to the foolish young woman she'd been.

"I'll change into a suit and show my very bright shiny shield and tell them I'm a friend of the family who's come to confirm your identity."

She hunched her shoulders. She bet he'd charmed his way into many situations and beds in the past five years. "What am I supposed to do? Wait in the parking lot with every Sheriff's Department Deputy walking by?"

"I'll drop you back at the hotel. Get something to eat. Try to sleep. The military transport does not offer in-flight meals."

"Fine." She knew too many people who might frequent the San

Diego County Medical Examiner's Office to risk hanging around the parking lot. She hesitated. Forced her bitterness aside. "Thank you. Thank you for helping me."

He took her hand and squeezed. She jolted in shock at the familiar heat and strength of his fingers.

"There are very few things in this world that I have absolute faith in, Delilah, but I have always believed in you. Always."

As much as she wanted to treasure the words, she knew them for lies. She pulled her fingers away and nursed her hand in her lap as if she'd been stung.

His eyes shuttered, and he turned away to start the engine. Perhaps he believed what he said. Perhaps he'd forgotten the other words he'd said to her five years ago. But she hadn't. And she hadn't forgiven.

No matter what happened, she didn't think she'd ever forgive Cas Demarco. Maybe one day she'd tell him why.

15

Demarco dropped her off at the main entrance of the hotel with some cash and one of his credit cards.

She needed to stock up on a few things, starting with a change of clothes to take with her to Virginia. She had to replace everything anyway, so she may as well get started. She had money. She'd pay him back when she could safely access her accounts. Or she could borrow it from her mom in a pinch.

She headed down to the boutiques beneath the hotel and picked up a couple of nice shirts and T-shirts, black pants, jeans, plus a pair of black work shoes. She hesitated over a dark navy wool blazer and then decided what the hell. She was going to Virginia, hopefully to begin work on an FBI task force. She needed to look like a professional.

She added a roll neck sweater, socks, panties, bras from another boutique and saw a cute grass-green sundress with a ruffled neckline and deep V at the front.

Screw it.

She tried it on and wore it out, along with a new, broad sun hat. Not even her own mother would recognize the blonde woman Delilah had become. Certainly, she didn't look like her usual over-serious FBI self.

She dropped her purchases back in the room and then headed outside through the hotel complex and found the footpath that ran along the beach, heading south. She felt naked without her weapon, but there was nowhere to hide it in this girly ensemble, and her greatest chance of success was living the disguise—the way she'd inhabited Lacey Reed.

And look how that had turned out.

Her mood dropped.

But, damn, she'd been convincing. Scanlon had certainly believed she was just some stupid girl.

He'd underestimated her then. She wouldn't make the same mistake with him.

Gradually, the sound of the waves crashing along the beach filled her with a deep sense of peace and soothed the agitation within her. This was her happy place. The day was overcast, and there was a slight chill on the breeze, but the sun still buzzed her cheeks.

Head high, she threaded her way through milling tourists and locals, people walking dogs and pushing strollers. The red flags were out to stop people swimming in the dangerous riptide, but it didn't stop the surfers who queued up to ride the breakers.

In the distance, she could see small Mexican islands that dotted the horizon. She kept walking. It was high tide, so the wreck of the SS Monte Carlo was hidden by the surf.

Last time she'd walked this path, she'd been holding hands with Cas Demarco, and her heart had been whole, her future almost as bright as the glare off the ocean.

Seagulls squawked overhead, and birds she couldn't identify bobbed just beyond the violent surf. A massive tanker sat offshore.

She kept going, watching the crashing waves swirl around the storm drains and splash up against the rocks, spraying everyone with salt water. She dashed through a gap in the onslaught and narrowly avoided getting soaked.

She reached the Naval Base. The sun's reflection off the argent sand made her eyes smart. She stared thoughtfully at the fortified base that turned men into SEALs.

How could one program produce men as diverse as Cas Demarco and Joseph Scanlon? Both were skilled warriors, and the ability to kill was presumably a plus for anyone going to war. But one was a cold-blooded psychopath and the other was the most passionate man she'd ever met.

After a few moments, she turned her gaze back to the ocean, not wanting to get on anyone's radar for being overly interested in this small slice of a sand barrier island that produced some of the world's toughest Special Forces.

Abruptly, she turned and headed back to the hotel, detouring to the taco shack for some food.

Hunger had finally hit her, along with the feeling of exhaustion from everything that had happened yesterday. She grabbed a table and stared out at the ocean. Sipped a Coke and ate fish tacos while trying and failing to ignore memories of the man who'd once shared every moment of these experiences with her.

She'd fallen so hard, so fast.

Had the constant danger heightened her response to him? Had danger been the alchemy that had transformed lust into something deeper, something cosmic? She'd never been in love before, and she'd felt like such a fool when it had ended. Special Agent Delilah Quinn who'd spent her life proving to her father and coworkers that she was competent at the job and not just a nepo-baby, completely suckered by the person she'd trusted the most.

And then even that pain had been eclipsed by what had come after, and Val had held her hand through it all.

Poor Val.

Tears rolled down her cheeks, but there was no one close enough to notice, and she was adept at hiding her misery beneath a neutral expression.

She couldn't afford to drop her guard.

It had nothing to do with Scanlon.

Cas Demarco was the real threat to her, and she couldn't forget it. Last time, he'd almost destroyed her. She refused to go through that again.

Next time, she might not survive.

16

The San Diego County Medical Examiner's Office sprawled between County Services and the Sheriff's Office.

Cas parked front and center of the main reception and headed inside the large, pale yellow and glass building. He'd changed into a suit and tie in the Jeep, which had to be one of the most uncomfortable experiences of his life—and he'd had many.

He strode up to the receptionist and said quietly, "I'm a representative of the Quinn family. I'm here to officially identify the body of their daughter, Delilah Quinn."

She took his driver's license. "Okay, sir. Take a seat while I verify the information and we prepare a viewing room."

"No need for a viewing room." He didn't need accommodations. "I'm law enforcement, although I'm not here in an official capacity." He pulled out his FBI creds. "I don't want to delay the Medical Examiner who must be extremely busy, but I promised the parents I'd take care of this for them, ASAP. They live in Virginia and the trip would be hard on them." He held the woman's blue eyes and wondered why lying had always come so easily to him even though it went against his inherent code of honor. Maybe his parents had been actors? "They want to know for sure if their daughter is lying back there."

She assessed him for a moment. "I'll go through and ask if it's okay for you to join them. They're doing the posts now."

Cas nodded. He didn't particularly want to bump into any of Delilah's coworkers, but perhaps he'd learn something if he did.

The receptionist came back and waved him through a secure door. He followed her along the corridor. The AC was set cold enough that a shiver skipped across his shoulders and down his spine. Still not cold enough to mask the smell of disinfectant and something else, something slightly foul and pungent that tainted the air.

They came to an area outside the main autopsy suites.

"You'll need to gown up." The woman indicated a small changing area off to one side. "Once you're ready, press the red button and someone will come to collect you."

Cas nodded and hastily donned a gown, booties, gloves, and hair cover. It wasn't his sexiest look, but he wasn't trying to impress anyone.

Except Delilah.

Which he had no hope of doing, so what difference did it make how he looked?

He slapped the red button.

A few seconds later, a young woman with freckles, wearing frameless spectacles and blue scrubs, came to the glass double doors and pressed the button to allow him entry.

"Agent Demarco?"

Hostage Rescue Team members were operators not agents, but he didn't correct her. The less impact he made the better.

"Dr. Richards just finished the second autopsy and is taking a break. I'm closing FBI Special Agent Gonzales. Special Agent Quinn is in the same suite along with another cadaver. If you're okay with that?"

"Yes." Had this really been Delilah, he wouldn't have been able to see for the tears, but as far as these people were concerned, he was a fellow professional making a formal identification for the family—not identifying the only woman he'd ever loved.

"Fire victims..." She trailed off.

"It's okay. I've seen fire victims before." He'd once seen an entire houseful. The cartel had picked up as many of the competition as they could find. Bound them. Locked them in a house in the desert outside of El Paso and torched the lot of them.

Grim didn't begin to describe it, but he doubted he'd seen more than this young medical professional.

"Yes." Her expression looked wise and pensive. "But it's different if you knew them when they were alive. Were you close?"

The question made him ache. "Not really," he lied. "We worked a case together five, six years ago." He pushed the memories aside. "I guess you could say that back then we were close."

Until he'd blown it all to smithereens.

"Prepare yourself. It's bad."

They entered a large bright room where three metal tables were arranged parallel, each occupied by a naked corpse. Cas was immediately hit with the acrid stench of burnt flesh, coupled with the scent of decomposition despite the relatively fresh nature of the bodies. He raised his hand in instinctive protest.

Perhaps the smell was left over from other cadavers, but the ventilation system was forceful enough he could feel it lifting his gown.

He'd puked his guts up during his first autopsy for the Bureau. A humiliating experience for the cocky former SEAL. Working for the FBI had brought him to his knees in ways his Navy SEAL career never had. Probably because he had been solving crimes that directly impacted individuals. In the Navy, he'd been following orders and having the time of his life even during deployments into active war zones. But eventually even that hadn't been enough. He'd needed to do more, and he'd found his calling thanks to a chance meeting with a Hostage Rescue Team member. He thanked God for his blessings, which were many, even if they didn't include having someone to share his life with.

But maybe that was the price he'd had to pay for having a job he loved.

At least, that was the bullshit he'd believed until recently. Maybe he still believed it, deep down where that lonely, abandoned kid lingered. That he didn't deserve to be happy.

He shook off the thoughts.

This wasn't about him.

He tried to hold his breath because this part of the job stank. Literally and figuratively.

The young doctor took pity on him and handed him some Vicks VapoRub to smear beneath his nostrils.

"The smell is actually a mix of Cadaverine, Putrescine, Indole, and Skatole, plus a few hundred other nasty compounds that build up during decomposition." The young physician rolled a trolley containing what were presumably David Gonzales' clothes and belongings to the side of the room. His gold shield lay on the top of the pile, and it hadn't protected him one iota. A timely reminder.

She blushed slightly as he stared at her. "I find it helps me deal with it better if I understand the science behind it."

He realized belatedly that they were the only people in the room, the only ones breathing anyway. "Just you and Dr. Richards for three autopsies?"

"Yep. Today anyway. We already completed a homeless guy and a fentanyl overdose. Dr. Richards is an early riser." She pulled on fresh surgical gloves with a snap. She went back to the table and removed a threaded needle and poked it through the skin of Gonzales' chest, the thick black thread closing the Y-incision like a zipper, hiding the internal organs that had been weighed, measured, and sampled, inside.

When he didn't speak, she filled the silence. "Looks like Dr. Richards took the FBI agent with him on his break. Perhaps you know him?" She gave him a name, but he didn't recognize it.

"I'm based out of Quantico these days." He'd assumed there

would be someone local in attendance. "The agents in the field office here must be devastated."

"Sounds like it. They're forming a task force to look into the murders."

He wondered what they'd found out so far and if they could transfer the investigation to the task force Patrick Killion was hopefully assembling.

Finally, Cas forced himself to stare at the blackened corpse who looked as if she was struggling to fight off an attacker. He knew it was an illusion, but it still tore at him.

The doctor looked up. "She has the classic pugilistic attitude where the ligaments and muscles contract due to the heat." The young woman pressed her lips together. "Fire victims always look angry in my experience. Pissed." She put another black stitch into Gonzales's pale chest. "But perhaps that's my overactive imagination."

"I can see why they'd be pissed." Cas took a reluctant step forward and stared at the woman who'd been Delilah's best friend. The long dark hair hid it, but the back of her skull looked shattered, which further distorted her blackened features. There was no way he could identify this woman based on facial features but that should work in his favor.

Lying about the identity of the victim went against the grain, but if it kept Delilah safe, he'd do it. And he was pretty sure her friend, Valerie Strauss, would forgive him if it meant finding her killer.

He cleared his throat before asking, "Did she suffer?"

The doctor hesitated. Then seemed to decide that she could talk to him. He *was* a federal agent. "We're not yet sure how she died."

He angled his head toward her in question.

"There's no soot in her trachea."

His eyes widened. "She was dead before the fire started?"

She nodded.

How? "Doctor..."

"Deuck. Linda Deuck." Her cheeks flamed.

"Dr. Deuck. Linda. Was there any other sign of trauma?"

The woman nodded. "When we removed the ball cap she was wearing, we discovered massive injury to the skull. Unfortunately, that trauma meant that most of the brain matter cooked in the fire."

His stomach wanted to repel the earlier baked goods. He forced it down. "She was hit on the back of the head?"

Linda pursed her lips. "Perhaps. But not necessarily. It's possible when the fire was being extinguished something smashed into her skull. The roof collapsed."

Hmm. "So how do you think she died?"

"Evidence is inconclusive. It's possible she was unconscious when the fire started. Drunk or drugged. Or asleep. Toxicology is being run. We're going to ask a forensic anthropologist on staff to reconstruct the skull to see if we can discover a specific injury, but she's currently out in the Pacific doing some work for DPAA for the next two weeks."

The "Defense POW/MIA Accountancy Agency" identified and repatriated the remains of US war dead. It was a noble undertaking.

Cas frowned. "I honestly can't tell if this is Delilah or not." No one possibly could by looking at what remained.

"I don't suppose Agent Quinn had any distinguishing marks? Tattoos?"

And this was the moment he put his career on the line. Or maybe he'd done that the moment he walked in the door. Delilah had told him she and Valerie had matching tattoos at the base of their spines. He'd traced his tongue over Delilah's whenever he'd had the opportunity.

"She apparently had an infinity tattoo low on her back."

Linda's features fell. "We found one exactly like that. A simple infinity loop. I'm very sorry for your and her parents' loss. We can also run DNA, but there's a backlog, and this won't be a priority now…"

He closed his eyes and nodded, grief dragging at him for this young woman and the pain Delilah would forever bear at the loss of her friend. When he opened his eyes, he saw what remained of Valerie's clothing hanging in a drying cabinet. The remains of an FBI ball cap, almost unrecognizable, sat on a tray. It cemented in his mind that this was a case of mistaken identity. The killer had assumed the victim was Delilah as she'd sat in the semi darkness of Delilah's living room wearing Delilah's ball cap. Cas would keep that misconception alive for as long as humanly possible until the killer was caught—and hope it didn't cost him his career.

"Any idea how the fire started?"

"Well, obviously that isn't part of my job." Her eyes shot to the door. "But I overheard the other agent say the fire appears to have started in the downstairs apartment."

He pressed his lips together. He hadn't found as many answers as he'd hoped for.

He turned and looked at poor David Gonzales. He'd been a good-looking guy until someone had pointed a gun at the back of his head and pulled the trigger. The exit wound had taken out his right temple.

Had he and Delilah loved one another? Or had it been more casual? Any jealousy he felt was misplaced. And he would rather Gonzales, and Valerie, still be alive and for him to forever be out of Delilah's life, than the current circumstances.

Delilah deserved to be happy.

"You find the bullet?"

"Fragments only. Nothing definitive. Agent Gonzales died instantly."

He hid his relief.

"What about the other guy?" Cas turned to stare at the body on the third table. A man in his early thirties. "He connected?"

The overhead lighting emphasized the dark circles under Linda's eyes. "Apparently, he was an informer for the FBI, for these agents actually. Clarence Carpenter. He was found in his car in his driveway this morning. Died of asphyxiation." She finished one line of the Y and started down the torso. "It's possible Agent Quinn was asphyxiated prior to death also, but we haven't found the usual markers. The fire could have masked them."

Cas frowned and went to look closer at Clarence Carpenter. Even basic recruits were taught various chokeholds to subdue attackers. By applying pressure to the carotid artery in the neck, the blood supply to the brain was cut off. If you held a chokehold for long enough, the recipient died.

The marks on the dead man's neck were reminiscent of a chokehold from behind. Had the attacker hidden in the back of Clarence's vehicle?

"Seems suspicious."

"Highly." Linda agreed.

"You have his TOD?"

"Between five and seven a.m. this morning. Roughly."

"So after the two FBI agents died." Voices could be heard coming down the corridor. It was time to leave. "I'll get out of your way." He headed toward the exit. "Thank you for your help. I will call Delilah's parents and inform them of the sad news."

"I'm very sorry for their loss."

"Thank you." He nodded slowly. If that'd been Delilah's body on that gurney, he'd be in a fetal position on the floor, weeping like a babe, and this woman wouldn't be able to move him for a week.

And this had to be how Delilah felt, he realized suddenly. She'd lost her best friend and her partner. He'd been so relieved she was alive, he'd forgotten she was dealing with so much trauma. Not only the loss of two people she cared about, but also her home and possibly her career.

It was a wonder she could function at all.

He hadn't been there for her before.

He knew that.

But this time.

This time.

He'd be there for her.

Scanlon wasn't getting anywhere near her. Not on his watch.

17

Delilah had changed out of the sundress into something a little more work appropriate. Now she sipped another coffee while she paced the hotel room with the burner pressed to her ear. She'd managed to track down a landline number for Nicole Zimmerman, Scanlon's ex-wife, who'd remarried and now lived in the Seattle area.

She'd done a few web searches, but without access to FBI and law enforcement databases, she had no idea if anything untoward had already happened to the woman. She desperately wanted those resources.

It was a risk, but she couldn't not warn her about the possible danger.

"Hello?" A young high-pitched voice answered.

Delilah cleared her throat. "Hello, I'm looking for Nicole Zimmerman. Is she there?"

"Mommy! It's for you."

Delilah pulled away at the piercing volume. At least the kid and mother were still alive. That was good news. She waited patiently while sipping her coffee and wearing a groove in the floor.

"Hello?" The voice was tentative.

"Nicole Zimmerman? I'm with the FBI."

"Yes?"

The tone turned frosty. Nicole hadn't been a fan of her or the FBI. In fact, she'd been a constant pain in the ass online until the video and audio tapes had been released during the trial. That had been too much evidence for her to overlook then.

"My boss requested that I connect to make sure you were aware that your ex-husband was released from prison three weeks ago."

"Yes. He wrote to me from Miramar to let me know and to apologize for everything that happened. He wanted to reestablish a relationship with Melody, our daughter."

An apology?

Didn't sound like Scanlon.

"Forgive me for being curious, but are you going to let him see her?"

Nicole gave a bitter laugh. "Well, technically he has legal rights. And my new husband, Preston, said every man deserves a second chance. We both think Melody should spend time with her father, supervised, of course."

"Of course."

The idea of Scanlon being suitable father material for a young girl seemed preposterous, but maybe Delilah was wrong about the guy. She'd only seen the nasty side of Scanlon—the drug mule, the liar, the betrayer of his unit and his country, the wannabe rapist. Maybe he was a great dad.

"As it happens, they're meeting up for the first time this afternoon."

That jolted her. "In Seattle?"

"Yeah. He practically begged me to make it happen. I'm pregnant, and the doctor has told me to get plenty of rest," she added as if excusing her decision.

Delilah felt that familiar stab of hurt but pushed it away. "It's important you take care of yourself…"

What was she supposed to say now? That she thought Scanlon

had attempted to kill her last night and murdered three other people in an elaborate frame? To be careful? Maybe she was completely off the mark about the guy.

She covered her face with her hand. She wasn't sure anymore.

Anger could calm over time and five years was plenty. Perhaps this situation *was* related to one of her current cases. Maybe she was closer to a big public corruption scandal than she'd realized. Something huge. Someone with a lot to lose? The governor or some tech bro who thought he was God and beyond the law?

Maybe she was simply paranoid. Which left her where?

Absolutely fucked.

The Agency might not be such a bad option after all.

She gripped the back of her neck. "Okay. I just wanted to make sure you were aware."

"Thanks. Agent—"

"Have a great day." Delilah spoke over her and then hung up without leaving her name. She wasn't a complete idiot, although the risk she'd taken suggested otherwise.

There was a knock on the door and she pulled her weapon and moved behind the wall to the bathroom. "Who is it?"

"It's me."

Cas.

Demarco, she corrected herself.

Using his first name was too intimate, and she needed distance.

She walked over and checked the peephole. He stood there wearing a dark suit and carrying that large, heavy bag of his. She'd rarely seen him in business clothes. She hated that he looked even better in a suit than dressed in jeans and a T-shirt.

She opened the door. Let him inside. Put her gun in the holster at the back of her dark jeans as the door closed with a firm bang.

He glanced at the bags on the bed. "You went shopping?"

She winced. "I hope you don't mind." She went and grabbed his credit card. "I have receipts and will pay you back as soon—"

"Delilah." He held up his hand. "It's fine. I can afford a shopping spree for a friend."

"I'll pay you back," she repeated firmly. She had expensive tastes and paid her own way. Then she frowned. "Is that what you think we are now? Friends?"

It sounded so mediocre and tepid, like warm milk.

It sounded *wrong*.

He stared down at the cream marble floor. "I guess that depends on you. I had hoped to earn back your friendship, but I also know I treated you abominably."

"Abominably." She crossed her arms over her middle. "That's a good word for it."

"I'll understand if you can't forgive me."

"Will you? How very generous." Her eyes watered, and she looked at the ceiling, blinking rapidly. "It's actually not that easy to forgive you, even after all this time. The things you said…"

Misery washed over his features. "I'll never forgive myself for the way I treated you that day and afterwards." He opened his mouth, but she spoke over him.

"That I was a good fuck but not to make the mistake of thinking you were emotionally invested? And that the high stress of undercover work made people say things they didn't mean—like 'I love you'?"

Suddenly the weight of her secrets was too much to bear. And why should she bear them alone? What sort of self-destructive bullshit was that?

"I didn't know it at the time, but I was pregnant with our baby. That day at the condo."

Demarco went sheet white.

"The day you scraped me off your boots like dog crap." Tears came now. This had been her silent wound for years, and he deserved to know it all. All the reasons she would never be his *friend*.

"After you dumped me, I went to bed and cried. Not long after, I started to cramp and bleed."

He took a step toward her. "Delilah—"

"Don't." Her glare was forceful enough he took a step back. "Do not touch me. I lost the baby—that's the first I'd known I was pregnant, so the pain of losing it was unexpectedly acute." Her laugh came out ugly. "And I don't blame you for the miscarriage, don't think that. Ten to twenty percent of known pregnancies end in miscarriage." She blinked rapidly, trying to stem the tears. "But the fact I went through that alone… I blame you for that."

He collapsed down to the bed as if his legs could no longer support him.

She clenched her fists determined to tell it all, to spare him nothing.

"Unfortunately, I wouldn't stop bleeding. The doctors tried various medical procedures, but nothing worked. I had to undergo an emergency hysterectomy—it was that or die."

She didn't tell him that she hadn't been mentally strong enough to make the choice. Between Cas leaving her and losing a baby she hadn't even known she was carrying, she'd zoned out and been incapable of making a decision. Or perhaps it had been blood loss and the threat of ischemia to the brain. The doctors had made the choice for her. She still mourned her lost fertility but was grateful for her life.

He looked aghast. "Why didn't you call me?"

"Are you fucking kidding me?" Her voice was as brittle as shattered glass, but she was proud she wasn't shouting.

He opened his mouth as if to argue.

"Don't. Don't you dare. Don't you *fucking* dare." She paced the room, barely able to stop herself from slamming out the door. This truth was something she could never outrun, and he deserved to know why she couldn't forgive him, why they couldn't be something as insipid as friends. "You had no right to know anything. Not about the fetus who died in the womb or the fact I almost died, too, or about whether or not I have a uterus. You told me exactly what I meant to you, and I owed you nothing after that."

Demarco looked as if he might vomit.

"Val..." A shiver stole over her. "She's the one who got me through it. Val—who is now dead because some bastard thought she was me. While you packed your bags and headed merrily off to the Hostage Rescue Team, she held my hand." She bared her teeth in a snarl proving exactly how much she wasn't over this. "You had your path, and I had mine. I'm grateful you ripped the blinders off before I did something stupid like request a transfer."

His olive skin looked ashen.

"So, regardless of your coming here, uninvited, to help me out of the shit show my life has become, do not mistake that for friendship. We are colleagues at best. You are here because you insisted on helping me. That's all. It's all we will ever be."

Her heart pounded, and she wanted to whirl away and run down to the sea. She didn't have the luxury. She pushed the emotions back down so she could function the way she needed to if she hoped to make it through this mess with her career intact. "Do you want to shower and eat before we leave for the air base? I'm not hungry. I had tacos at the shack."

The shack where they'd used to hand feed each other like besotted fools. Demarco stared at her mutely, as if she'd poleaxed him.

Yeah.

She probably had.

She checked her watch. Nervous energy crawling through her. No way could she stay here with him looking at her like that. As if *she'd* hurt *him*.

"If not, let's head out and be ready to catch that flight out of here."

She pulled her long brown hair into a tight pony and dragged the blond wig over her forehead and back, adjusting the fit.

"I need to change." His voice sounded scratchy and suspiciously deep.

"Fine." She slipped on her sunglasses. "I'll wait on the balcony."

18

S canlon stood beside a little bird of a social worker whose neck he could snap with his fingers. The woman who'd vowed to love him until death-did-them-part pushed through the doors and walked towards him, fat with another man's bastard.

The fucker, *Preston*, stopped twenty feet away, arms crossed over his polo-shirt-clad chest, pretending he wasn't shitting his pants.

Scanlon moved his lips into a smile as his daughter looked up at him with big blue eyes that were eerily similar to the ones he saw in the mirror every day. If it weren't for the fact she looked so much like him, he might have questioned the kid's legitimacy, given he'd been deployed for most of his wife's pregnancy. As it was, there was no doubt as to her parentage.

"Melody." He held out his arms and frowned when the girl pressed back against her mother's legs. She'd been two the last time he'd seen her, but he was her father. She shouldn't be scared of her own blood. He had no reason to hurt her.

Nicole squeezed her daughter's shoulders. "It's okay, honey. This is your father. You remember him, don't you?"

The little girl shook her head from side to side so fast her hair got caught in her eyes. She held her mother's hand and twisted to press her face into Nicole's groin, a place he'd spent a lot of time in back in the day. He bet *Preston* didn't go down on Nicole nearly often enough for her liking.

Nicole frowned at him. "What happened to your face?"

He touched the healed scar. "Someone tried to knife me in prison."

"You look just like Virgil." She shuddered.

His twin had always unnerved Nicole. He unnerved most people. "Yeah, he thinks it's pretty funny."

The kid tried to pull away back toward the door, but Nicole held onto her and scolded her. "Enough of this nonsense, Melody. You know who this is." This new prim version of Nicole looked embarrassed by her daughter's behavior. "She has a picture of you in your dress whites in her room." Which was hardly the same as seeing her daddy in the flesh. He'd repeatedly asked Nicole to bring her to visit him, but she'd refused, saying prison was no place for a child.

More likely it was too much trouble to make the journey.

He understood. It was a choice. Everyone got to make choices, even people who were incarcerated.

Nicole crouched down and gave Melody a quick hug and then turned the kid back around to face him.

"Sorry. She's a bit out of sorts. We sprang this on her on the way over. I didn't want to give her too much time to object."

Melody's bottom jaw thrust out in mutiny.

Oh, yeah, she was a Scanlon all right.

"We'll be back in a couple of hours, honey." She looked at the social worker, who nodded, and then pried Melody's hand from her own.

"Be good, baby." Nicole's eyes begged. "Your father just wants to spend a little time with you."

Preston uncrossed his arms and shifted impatiently.

"Sorry." Nicole backed away.

God, she was pathetic.

His wife had ditched his ass as soon as he'd been found guilty.

She'd told him after he'd been sentenced that she'd barely gotten through deployments. There was no way she could wait seven years for him to get out of prison. So much for honoring. So much for obeying.

She'd moved back to her hometown to be closer to her bitch mother, and then she'd met "*Preston.*"

He'd never beaten her. Never given her a slap even though she'd sometimes deserved one. He might not have been completely faithful, but that was a man's nature. Spread his genes far and wide.

If he'd wanted her back, he figured it wouldn't take much. Nicole liked sex. A bit of flattery, some practiced charm, the right timing, she'd be flat on her back, begging for his cock to plow her like the good ol' days.

But he didn't want her no more.

She repulsed him.

Even if she hadn't been carrying someone else's bastard, she'd lost all her appeal. The day she'd left him, she'd ceased to be anything except for an insult to his pride and caretaker of his child.

He watched the couple push out through the doors and climb into a silver Lexus. They drove away.

He lowered his gaze back to the girl who looked resentful and a little scared.

He held out a huge pink teddy bear, and she took it tentatively.

He turned to the social worker. "Can I take her for ice cream?"

"It's February."

"I want ice cream," Melody stated, sticking her bottom lip out to match her jaw.

The woman shook her head. "Visitation has to be here—"

"I thought it just had to be supervised."

The woman's lips compressed like she'd sucked on a lemon.

"You could join us. I'm buying." He gave her a smile, careful to crinkle the corners of his eyes.

The social worker looked uncertain. "We have a room assigned for you and your daughter to get reacquainted."

He tilted his head. "You know this isn't a mandatory supervision order, correct?"

She looked startled by that. "Yes."

"I volunteered for this to speed up the process because I am keen to get to know my daughter again."

Melody looked at him sharply.

"I'm aware of the circumstances, Mr. Scanlon," the social worker said quietly.

He waited.

Finally, she relented. "We can go to an ice cream parlor a couple of blocks away, but after that we need to come back to the center. Let me tell the receptionist and grab my coat."

The woman left him and Melody in the foyer staring at one another uncertainly. Then Melody smiled.

19

C as drove the borrowed Jeep the short distance back to the airbase with his brain on fire from all the things Delilah had told him.

Her words had robbed him of the power to breathe, of the power to think. That she'd gone through so much—that she'd lost a baby, that she'd almost died—and he'd been piously telling himself he was doing the right thing by walking away. That she'd be better off without him. And all the while she was suffering in pain and misery.

Alone.

No wonder she was bitter and angry. She must have hated him so much. She still hated him, and he couldn't blame her. He'd let her down in the worst way.

The fact he was a fool was not news, but the chances of him redeeming himself in any way seemed elusive at best now that he knew the full story. But he owed her. He owed her more than he'd ever realized and even if he hadn't screwed up so badly five years ago, he was desperate to help her now. He had no intention of letting her down again.

He glanced across at her in the passenger seat. She had her head tilted back against the headrest. They'd agreed it best she keep up her disguise while on this side of the country. Killion had worked out a cover story that hopefully reduced the risks of her being identified.

Cas didn't know if he'd be part of the team actively trying to figure this out or not. Gold Team might get called out on an op at any moment. But he hoped he was. He really hoped so. First though, he had to get through Montana's memorial service tomorrow morning.

He dug into his pocket and tossed her his handcuffs. "Put those on."

She gave him a look, then slipped one of the metal bracelets around her narrow wrist. She twisted and gave him her back, so he could click the second cuff into place.

He wondered if she, like so many former military or law enforcement people, carried spare handcuff keys or a shim secreted about her person. Not that it mattered, as this was only temporary. An act. He'd let her go if she asked.

"I forgot to tell you…" She closed her eyes again as if enjoying the warmth of the sun on her face.

He waited patiently. The windows were all rolled down and the scent of the beach filled him with memories of their doomed romance. Funny how the Virginia coastline didn't wield the same power over him. Or perhaps it was the fact everything here was soaked in memories of her.

"I called Scanlon's ex."

That dragged his attention back to the reason he was here. Not to reminisce. Not for forgiveness. Not for a second chance. Men like him didn't get second chances with women like Delilah Quinn.

He turned his attention back to the road and pulled up in a short queue at the guard house. "She know who you were?"

Her lips pinched. "I didn't give her a name. I informed her that her ex was out." She shifted in her seat as they approached the guards. "She already knew. Apparently, Scanlon wrote to her from prison. Told her he was getting out and asked if he could spend some time with the kid. The wife is pregnant with her second husband's baby, and I got the feeling he'd be happy if Melody wasn't around."

The fact she'd been talking to a pregnant woman must have brought all her agony to the surface again.

That, and seeing him.

And having her friend and boyfriend murdered and her house burned down.

The weight of everything that had happened to her clad his bones with sorrow.

"Scanlon's not exactly ideal father material." He winced as he said it. The same could be said of him. He'd never thought about being a dad until about an hour ago, and the lash of hurt he'd felt in the aftermath had hit him unexpectedly. He put that pain where he put all the rest. In a closed box deep inside that he'd deal with later.

Much later.

"She said she was planning to let him have supervised visitation rights and he was meeting with them today. I didn't push for more details. But if we can find out when and where, we'll have another data point for tracking his location."

He nodded. Said nothing.

She eyed him over her large sunglasses, but they were at the barrier now so she kept quiet.

Cas flashed his creds. After a silent sweep of the vehicle for explosives, the guards waved him through with only a cursory check of Delilah's ID.

Killion had arranged a prisoner transport and pulled in a few favors to make sure no questions were asked on this trip. The joy of being high up in the Agency.

Cas swung the Jeep over to the hangar where the plane he'd caught that morning still sat amid activity as various supplies, from armored vehicles to crates of equipment, were loaded onboard. It was a rare moment of military efficiency to make sure the hold wasn't empty on the return trip.

Cas turned off the engine, left the keys in the ignition for the Jeep's true owner. The motor ticked in the sudden quiet. He wanted to apologize to her. For everything. But she probably didn't want that from him, and it wasn't enough. "Ready?"

"I'm more than ready."

Cas got out. Walked around and opened Delilah's door for her. "Can you manage?"

"Yes." She hesitated. "Thanks."

He nodded and left her to it. Went to retrieve their gear out of the rear compartment. "Where did you leave your vehicle?"

"Airport. Long term parking. Got a cab to the island and walked the rest of the way."

Smart.

He swept his hand in front on him to indicate she lead the way. She headed up the ramp into the belly of the beast. All around, men watched her hips sway. It was an old trick. If they were watching her ass, they weren't noticing her face. Which would be great if he wasn't also ensnared.

She'd been a great undercover agent, but he'd been a thousand times more scared for her than he'd ever been for himself.

One more thing that had sent him running. Her father had simply been the excuse he'd needed to persuade himself he didn't really have a choice. In reality, there was always a choice, and he'd made the wrong one.

Inside the plane, they dodged cargo until they reached the front of the aircraft. He released her cuffs. "Do me a favor and don't make a run for it. Anyone comes by, pretend you're secured to the netting."

She sat heavily in one of the red plastic pullout seats. "It's a mistake not going after him right now."

"We need more information."

"Which we get by following him."

Cas shrugged.

She cocked a brow in question.

"Blame Killion, not me."

"Fine."

He almost shared with her that Killion was going to be a father and how insane was that—but it seemed wrong to talk about other people having kids after she'd told him she couldn't. They'd never even discussed having children...

"I'll go talk to the captain and double check the time of departure." The last thing he wanted was to be late for the service tomorrow. But Delilah's safety topped even that. Especially now.

There were some debts that could never be repaid.

Montana would understand. It was the choice he'd want Cas to make.

"I'm not going anywhere. Hey, one thing."

He jerked his chin in question.

"I don't like other people knowing my medical history." She couldn't hold his gaze and looked away.

His heart gave a thump, and he laughed a little incredulously. "Who exactly do you think I would tell?"

She shrugged one nonchalant shoulder. "I have no clue. Your buddies? Your latest squeeze? For all I know, you're married with kids—" She cut herself off and blinked rapidly.

"No." He sat beside her and leaned close. "There's no one. No wife, no kids, not even an ex worth the mention, except you." He met those warm brown eyes of hers and gave her the truth. "There was only ever you, Delilah, and I screwed it up. I knew it the moment I lied to you and walked away." He couldn't tell her about her father's interference, not when the man had dementia and she loved him. He wouldn't do that to her. "I was scared of the enormity of my feelings for you and feared I'd be destroyed if you ever changed your mind and decided you were better off without me. I was a coward, and I'm sorry for it. I've always been sorry for it."

Tears spiked her lashes. Her jaw looked like it would break it was so tightly clenched.

"I know I'll never get that back. I'm not saying this in some foolish attempt to, to...I don't know, rekindle what we had." His throat worked as he fought for the words she deserved. "I'm glad you found someone else." He wanted to touch her but didn't dare. "I'm sorry you lost him on top of everything else that happened."

He climbed to his feet and was about to walk away when she spoke, her voice deep and gruff with emotion.

"David and I were never lovers. We were work partners, but you somehow decided that meant more, which is freaking insulting, by the way."

He paused as his heart pounded.

"I don't have anyone significant in my life right now." Her eyes narrowed when he looked back at her, some sort of hope building in his chest. "But that doesn't mean I've been in love with you all these years. Because I haven't." She glared at him.

Yet, for the first time since he'd seen that news broadcast in the bar last night, for the first time since he'd left her staring after him like a wounded doe in the building that had burned to the ground, he thought he might have the sliver of a chance with this woman.

And he could work with a sliver. A sliver gave him hope. Something he hadn't had in years.

There was no way he could act on that or reveal his feelings because she was the one who was scared of getting attached now. She was the one scared of rejection. And he'd done that to her the way life had done it to him.

So he kept his thoughts hidden. He was an expert at that kind of deception.

He nodded. "Understood."

20

Delilah stretched her aching limbs and yawned widely. It was 3:15 a.m. East Coast time, and her eyes were scratchy with fatigue. The flight was loud, cold, and uncomfortable. Thankfully they'd begun their descent. They were near their destination.

Cas—*Demarco*—was stretched out on the floor, head on his kit bag covered with a thin blanket. He'd gone to sleep soon after takeoff. He looked as peaceful there as if he were sleeping in one of the comfortable beds at the Del. She guessed he had a lot of experience doing this, from his SEAL days and with the Hostage Rescue Team, who were always racing all over the US and the world, being the quiet heroes, saving the day.

It had been his dream to get into HRT.

He'd once told her he'd set his eyes on it as a young SEAL deployed to Afghanistan. His platoon had had an HRT operator embedded with it, collecting evidence on a high-value target the FBI agent had then arrested and escorted back to the US for trial.

He'd told her he hadn't liked how many innocents were caught up in urban warfare. Didn't enjoy the bloodlust some of his peers had developed over time. But he liked the idea of taking down specific targets and prosecuting actual crimes. That's what he'd told her anyway, when they'd lain naked in bed, side by side, both reluctant to sleep when their time together was always short.

And he'd done it. Passed selection into the most elite tactical law enforcement unit in the US, if not the world.

She'd known he would.

Had it made him happy?

Happy in a way she hadn't been able to?

She watched him now, taking advantage of the fact he couldn't see her staring. He was still unfairly beautiful, like some fallen angel. All that thick, silky, sinfully black hair and eyes that shone like polished gold. His face was a little older, more mature, less boyish. The groove between his dark brows carved deep, as if a frown was his default expression nowadays.

His confession that he'd lied filled her with mixed emotions. Gratitude because she hadn't been wrong about their feelings for one another. Sadness that he hadn't had the faith to believe in what they'd had—that it hadn't been enough for him to take a risk on. Anger because he'd caused her so much pain with his lack of courage.

What a classic alpha male. Tough on the outside. A seething wreck of scarred emotional turmoil on the inside.

It was done now.

She was glad they'd cleared the air.

No more secrets.

There'd be no repeat of mistakes from the past. She was going to be too busy clearing her name before she became wanted for murder to have time to fall into that emotional quagmire again.

Suddenly, he opened his eyes and stared straight into hers. She blinked and looked away and hoped he didn't realize she'd been ogling him for some time.

He climbed slowly to his feet and stretched out his arms above his head, showing off the breadth of his shoulders before taking a seat two down from her. The noise from the engine changed and the wheels dropped. They were about to land.

As soon as the plane stopped taxiing, they picked up their

belongings and walked to the rear of the aircraft to deplane via the ramp.

Demarco's cell dinged, his personal cell, which he pressed awkwardly to his ear as he juggled the kit bag that was heavy enough to contain a small arsenal. Whatever he was listening to didn't make him happy.

They started down the ramp before it was even fully down. Thankfully, he didn't bother with the handcuffs this time.

He slid the cell back into his pocket. "Killion sent a friend of his to meet us." He scanned the area and pointed. "Alex Parker. Runs a cybersecurity firm and consults heavily with the BAU. Wife's an agent." He lowered his voice. "Rumor has it he's a former spook."

She eyed the man standing a short distance away beside a large black SUV as they strode across the tarmac toward him. Parker opened the rear for their luggage.

They all shook hands.

"Agent Quinn? Nice to meet you. Sorry to hear about your friend and colleague." Parker turned to Demarco. "Operator Demarco. I recognize you, of course, but we haven't been formally introduced. Alex Parker. You can put your stuff in the back here too."

Demarco hung onto his belongings. "My truck is here. I'll need it in the morning."

Delilah felt a sudden pang that they'd be separated, but what had she expected? Nobody thought Demarco was dead. He didn't have to keep a low profile. He was expected to report for duty tomorrow.

Funny that it hit her so hard. She should be used to saying goodbye to Cas Demarco by now.

"Killion had your truck driven back to your apartment complex." Alex Parker smiled and transformed an average-looking face into devastatingly attractive.

Wow. He'd have been a very useful spook.

Demarco's brows rose. "Seems like Killion thought of everything." He sounded resentful rather than grateful.

"Get in. We'll talk on the way."

"We appreciate the help," said Demarco, as if he and she were a team. And maybe they were in this. Scanlon, if it was Scanlon, wouldn't be satisfied just with her. He'd want Demarco too. But Demarco was HRT and his whereabouts were more protected than most.

He wouldn't be so easy to attack.

For that, she was grateful.

Delilah took the back seat and fought another yawn.

"What can you tell us?" she asked once they were underway. Parker drove fast but handled the vehicle in a manner that suggested he knew what he was doing.

"Not that much. I was only brought onboard this afternoon to check what my team and I can find out about Joseph Scanlon since his release and to see if we could pick him up in the La Jolla area last night."

Delilah sagged a little to know it was only about 30 hours since her friends had been murdered and her life had been upended. "Thanks for helping us. I can pay for your services as soon as I can access my accounts. Did you find anything to place him at the scene?"

"Nothing yet." He caught her gaze in the mirror. "We can discuss payment when this is all over. I admit I kind of like Killion owing me a favor."

She huffed out a laugh. "This is a heck of a big favor."

"Even better."

She suddenly remembered she was wearing the wig and began removing the pins and dragged it off her head, shaking out her own long dark hair and scratching her scalp. She breathed out a long sigh.

She caught Parker's glance in the mirror again, but it wasn't the perusal of a man who found her dazzlingly attractive. Her mood dropped. "You aren't sure if you can trust me."

Demarco bristled like her own personal attack dog.

"I'm very careful about the people I invite into my home, Agent Quinn. I have a wife and a baby I love beyond reason. When I say I'll do anything to protect them, I mean *anything*."

Demarco stiffened.

Delilah was amused but grateful the HRT operator kept his mouth shut. Despite recent evidence to the contrary, she did not need him to fight her battles.

"Let me know when you make a decision. In the meantime, you can drop me at a hotel—as long as someone lends me money to pay for it." She laughed self-consciously. As much as she wanted to be independent, she wasn't. Not right now. She wanted to visit her parents but even that wasn't safe. She wouldn't place them in Scanlon's target zone.

"You can stay at my place," Demarco told her. "I have a spare room."

Delilah opened her mouth to argue, because spending too much time with Cas Demarco would be a mistake of epic proportions. At the same time, she'd already spent a lot of his money and didn't want to bankrupt the guy when he was doing her a favor.

"That's not necessary," Parker interrupted. "You are welcome to stay with us if you'd like to, but I want you to know it's only because I *do* trust you. We have a spare room that's soundproofed —you never know when you'll need to stash a kidnap victim."

At their combined looks of surprise, he grinned. "And it's particularly useful as we have a six-month-old baby who is teething and has the lungs of a future opera singer."

Demarco glanced back at her anxiously as if he thought she'd crumble at the thought of being close to a baby.

She stopped herself from rolling her eyes. The fact that he cared shouldn't be something she held against him, but over the past five years she'd had plenty of time to inure herself against the pain of being infertile. Didn't mean she didn't ache with want sometimes, but she wasn't a fragile flower. And there were plenty of advantages to not having kids.

"Maybe I'll redesign my spare room because that sounds useful." Her mouth went dry. "Except I don't have a spare room anymore."

"Let's deal with catching the killer and keeping you safe before we worry about that aspect of things," Demarco told her.

She refrained from telling Demarco he didn't have to worry about a damned thing when it came to her former home.

"Operationally, it would be easiest if you stay with us until after the memorial service tomorrow. My wife and I plan to attend, as does Killion. Georgie will be at the FBI's daycare, but we have a dog who'll keep you company. Afterwards, we can meet with a few other interested parties who've been read into the situation."

"What people?" This was her life. She didn't want to be in the dark about who was getting added to the circle—not that she had a say now she'd asked for help.

"People Killion trusts. Tonight, we all need some sleep and tomorrow, we have to take a moment to pay our respects to a good man."

She pressed her palms together at the need to honor the dead. "I really should call Valerie's mother."

"Again, you can do that. I'm not in the FBI, and I'm not your superior. But if you do, you risk negating everything you've done up until this point to hide the fact you survived. Valerie Strauss will still be deceased—that won't change. But it might harm our chances of finding her killer."

Delilah hunched over. "How do you know it wasn't me? Really?"

He gave her a long look in the mirror. "I dug a little. As far as your story goes, I found you running past several door cams around the time the fire started." He cocked a brow. "It's generally advisable to stretch *before* you start running, by the way."

She laughed unexpectedly. "Believe me, I know."

That was fast work. And presumably illegal without a warrant.

"And you *could* have killed your friend. Set a fire in the apartment downstairs. But then when you came back, you hung around for far too long if you were the killer. In fact, why go for a run at all? Seems like a weird thing to do when you could have just disappeared and faked your own death. Plus, I checked your background," he was staring straight ahead now, "nothing there but integrity and character. Someone who has dedicated her life to service and upholding the family tradition within the Bureau."

She drew in a deep breath, grateful to this stranger for making her feel respected and believed, despite the circumstances. "Thank you. I appreciate that. I hope the FBI feels the same way when this is all over."

"The FBI is overrated," Alex joked.

Demarco grunted.

She smiled. Alex Parker was doing his best to reassure her that everything was okay, but for some reason Demarco's nose was out of joint.

"I set up some searches for Scanlon's cell phone location and for his presence on any flight manifests. Unfortunately, it shows he was at his family's home in La Croix, Louisiana, all day Monday, but travelled from New Orleans to Seattle today."

Delilah felt deflated.

"Could he have flown under a false identity and left his cell behind?" suggested Demarco.

"Yep. For sure," Alex agreed. "I'll set up facial recognition programs tomorrow to scour the internet in case he appeared in the background of anyone's social media posts, or in any malls or street cams that are online in the San Diego area."

She was impressed. "He has a twin brother, Virgil. Monozygotic twin so identical in every way, except Virgil has a scar down one side of his face. He was a little heavier than Joseph the last time I saw him, but who knows what shape he's in now."

Parker passed the few cars on the road and left them quickly behind. "I'll add Virgil to the searches tomorrow. Anything from the autopsies?"

Demarco cracked the window for some fresh air. "Time of

death of Clarence Carpenter was between 5 and 7 a.m., so after Delilah's house burned down."

"Which could make me look guilty once they find out I am actually alive," Delilah muttered.

Demarco glanced over his shoulder. "I didn't falsely identify Valerie's remains as yours because the fire damage was so extensive it was implausible. But I remembered that you told me years ago how you and Valerie had matching tattoos at the base of your spine. When the Assistant Medical Examiner asked for any identifying marks, I mentioned that tattoo, and she drew her own conclusions."

Delilah flinched.

"That won't protect you if it comes to light you'd seen Delilah alive and well," Parker commented.

"I'm aware." Demarco's deep voice rolled over her, and she tried to ignore the magnetic pull he always seemed to have on her. "Obviously, I'm hoping that doesn't happen before we are ready to reveal the truth about Delilah's survival. But no one saw us together that I'm aware of, and when we were together, she wore the wig. I did speak to a friend of mine this morning, a Senior Chief at Coronado. He came up with two names of friends of Scanlon's who are still on the teams. Mark Johnson and Kevin Holtz."

Delilah recognized the names from the investigation. Despite being close friends of Scanlon's, they'd had no discernible links to his criminal activities, but they'd been potential witnesses.

"I'll see if one of my people can find any recent electronic links between them and Scanlon. Anything else?" asked Parker.

They were getting close to Quantico now.

"One thing." Demarco swung to face her with a look of disquiet on his features. "I didn't tell you earlier, but Valerie suffered significant skull trauma." He indicated the back of his head. "Here."

Delilah covered her mouth. "He hit her with something?"

"The assistant ME wasn't sure. A beam fell during the fire and struck the body which could either account for or help obscure the damage. Their forensic anthropologist will be back in a couple of weeks, and she'll attempt to piece it together. But Valerie was dead before the fire started. There was no smoke inside her lungs."

"Scanlon was a Navy SEAL sniper. Bashing someone's head in seems uncharacteristically brutish." Parker turned off the interstate.

"It gets the job done." Demarco frowned. "What if he shot her through the window first? Set a timer to set off a fire."

Alex Parker mulled it over. "What about the lack of a visible entrance wound?"

Demarco gave her a look, his features shadowed by the darkness. "Bullet could have gone through her eye socket. The fire burned away most of the soft tissue."

"Could he have made that shot?" Parker asked. "Because he couldn't rely on the fire burning the evidence before the emergency services arrived and perhaps pulled her out of there."

"Before he went to prison, he could have made the shot." Demarco crossed his arms. "Now?" He shrugged. "He had three weeks where he could have practiced every day. With the right weapon, he could have made the shot from the opposite roof."

"But he took my service weapon from my bedroom. He more likely crept inside shortly after I left. Mistakenly thought it was me in the chair, hit me from behind like the coward he is. The only light was from the TV and the one under the microwave. I doubt he'd have been able to tell me and Val apart." She drew in a breath but ignored the sharp pain that cut into her ribs at the thought of her friend's suffering.

"In and out in sixty seconds," Demarco agreed. "Start the fire as soon as he believed you were dead. Makes sense."

"Was that your usual evening routine? The run? Watching TV?" Parker asked.

She shook her head. "I usually run early in the morning, three times a week, but I missed that morning because I had court and had to meet with the prosecutor first thing. But the TV? Sure.

Sometimes, I'll sit and watch TV while I eat dinner." Then she'd do more work, assuming she wasn't called out for something.

"So he kills Valerie thinking it's you, steals your weapon, and then heads over to David Gonzales's place and shoots him." Demarco laid it out.

She flinched.

"The CI, Clarence Carpenter? He was choked, which is much more Scanlon's speed. But he died between 5 and 7 a.m., so that addition to the plan had a few flaws—assuming it's connected." Demarco gave a half shake of his head. "He had five years to plan it. He could have had his brother or one of his friends go map out the area of Delilah's complex and follow her routine. He could have practiced his ass off with Glocks and whatever as soon as he got home. But for some reason he decided to improvise and kill the CI and try to inadvertently link it to the deaths of two FBI agents?"

"Perhaps he always planned to kill someone involved in one of their cases to throw investigators off his trail. Perhaps it was a matter of finding the right someone, anyone, on the day to target," Alex mused. "Clarence Carpenter put himself on the top of the list when he contacted Gonzales for a meet that day."

"We have to assume he bugged David's Bucar." Agitation rushed along her nerves along with growing fatigue, whereas Demarco looked wide awake and fully refreshed after his uncomfortable nap. "In which case, he presumably removed the bug after he murdered David."

"Which still leaves us with no proof." Demarco sounded despondent.

"We have some starting points. Let's see where they lead us and, in the meantime, let's all get some rest." Parker pulled up outside a tall apartment building and got out of the SUV to open the trunk.

Demarco put his hand on the door handle. "You'll be all right without me?"

She held his gaze as memories of her absolute devastation

bombarded her. "I'll be fine. The same way I've been fine for the past five years."

Dammit. She hadn't meant to say that last bit out loud.

His expression darkened.

"Good night, Demarco," she said firmly. She refused to feel guilty.

"Good night, Delilah." His eyes were unreadable in the shadows. "I'll see you tomorrow after the service. Call me if you need me. Anytime. You know the number."

She nodded. She wished it wasn't etched onto her brain.

"I won't let you down again."

He closed the door before she could react to that statement.

Just as well.

He'd apologized. It was over five years ago, and she needed to move past the anger and grief. But it didn't mean she had to forgive him, and it didn't mean she wanted him thinking he was some medieval knight riding to her rescue. She didn't need that bullshit. She needed help to catch Scanlon and put him away, but professional assistance only.

She slid over the console into the passenger seat and looked up at Demarco's building as Alex Parker climbed back into the driver's seat.

Weird to see where he lived after years of trying not to wonder.

Alex put on his seatbelt while reversing out of the lot. "You two have a history. Will that make it difficult for you?"

She eyed him. "Exactly how deep did you delve?"

"Deep enough." He stopped the car before putting it back into drive. His eyes met hers and it was the sympathy in them that told her he knew everything there was to know that had been recorded —and had guessed some of the rest.

"Demarco is involved in this whether I like it or not. I'll deal with it."

Parker pulled away. "We aren't far now."

She shivered under her new wool blazer. "I'm grateful for your help with this." She swallowed. "And for trusting me. Your wife is a lucky woman."

"I'm the lucky one." His eyes were sad when he looked at her. "We'll figure it out, Agent Quinn."

"Call me Delilah—although it has the same number of syllables, so it's up to you."

"Delilah it is."

Five minutes later, Alex drove through tall automatic gates monitored by cameras and slid smoothly into the attached garage.

"Home, sweet home," he said softly. "This way."

He led her through a secure metal door, and they were greeted by a soft woof.

Alex patted a golden retriever on the head as the dog wagged its tail.

"This is Rex," he said softly. "Valiant guard dog."

She slid her fingers into Rex's soft coat and petted him while he wagged his tail some more.

They turned right and into a huge dream kitchen, down a corridor and into a small, open-plan sitting room and bedroom with an attached bath.

He put her bags on the bed.

This was a pretty fancy spare room. "Is this for a housekeeper?"

"More for my in-laws when they occasionally come to visit. But it is, more or less, soundproofed, and the windows are bullet resistant. Plus, there's no way of anyone finding a clear vantage point for any of the windows at the back of the house without me knowing an intruder is on the grounds."

"You take your security seriously," she noted.

He tilted his head to one side as he appeared to consider her words. "I take my family's safety very seriously. Security is my business."

She nodded.

"Mallory put a few basics in the drawers, and the bathroom is fully stocked. Relax. Get some sleep. I promise that things are in motion even if it seems we aren't doing much of anything. We might be gone in the morning for this memorial when you wake up, especially as you're on West Coast time. We're dropping Georgie at the daycare first thing, so take your time. Make yourself at home, and help yourself to anything to eat or drink."

"Thank you. I've already put you to a lot of trouble for which I'm sorry." She hugged herself.

"Nothing I'm not used to."

She laughed at that. "You must have a very understanding wife."

"You have no idea. You'll get to meet her tomorrow. Anything else I can get you?"

"Do you have a computer I could use? I want to do a little research—I'll be careful."

His gray eyes held hers. "I can do that…"

A shiver of apprehension washed over her at the expression in his eyes. "What?"

"If this isn't Scanlon, if we discover that this is actually, instead, related to Clarence Carpenter and one of your public corruption cases, it might be harder to justify disappearing the way you did."

She bit her lip. "I know. Cas, *Demarco*," she corrected, "told me to lie about going to David Gonzales's home and taking my service weapon. Without the weapon or witnesses, no one can link me to David's death despite the fact I texted him." The lump in her throat was solid stone. "But if there's no proof to connect me to the murder then there's no evidence to convict the real killer either." She blinked away the grit of fatigue. "And I think the same might be true for Valerie's murder. If the ME can't rule it a homicide, Scanlon—or whoever—might get away with it." She clutched her hands together wishing she could get a grip on herself and her grief but knowing that while the killer was walking around free, she never would. "And if he can get away with killing two FBI agents, then perhaps the system doesn't work quite as well as it should."

Alex looked down at his feet. "Can I ask why you haven't called your father for help?"

She rubbed her temple and decided Alex Parker had earned the truth. "Dad has early onset dementia." She forced down the knot in her throat. "We've kept it quiet at his insistence, but I don't even know if he'll recognize me when I next see him, let alone whether he'll have a coherent conversation with someone who has the power to act about something this complex." She met Parker's clear gray eyes. "When I saw him at Christmas, he mostly knew who I was, but there were a couple of times... Anyway, I'm not saying I won't contact or leverage his cronies if I have to, but if I can keep him out of it, I will."

"I'm sorry."

She nodded in acknowledgment. "My mother had all firearms removed from the house for everyone's safety and has put alarms on the doors so she can hear if he leaves the house. She's preparing really, for if things get worse."

Parker pressed his lips together. "I can imagine how hard it must be to see someone you love lose themselves that way." He put his hand on her shoulder and then moved away. "Try not to worry. We'll figure it out."

He softly closed the door, taking the dog with him. Drained and exhausted, she sat on the edge of the bed and held her head in her hands as thoughts from the last two days bombarded her. Val, David, Clarence, Scanlon, her job, her home, *Demarco.*

How could they possibly figure this out when the evidence was on the other side of the country?

Her eyes threatened to close she was so tired. She dragged off her clothes, found an oversized T-shirt in a drawer, curled up under the covers, and tried to sleep.

21

Despite the late night, Cas was up early the next morning. He'd just finished ironing his best white dress shirt when someone began to pound on his door.

He shook the shirt out and then slid his arms into the still hot material, buttoning it up as he headed to the door. He checked the peephole and, as he'd expected, a shirtless Ryan Sullivan stood there in black dress pants and shiny black shoes.

He opened up, and Ryan stepped inside.

"Can I borrow your iron? Mine broke."

"It was broke last time you needed it too."

Ryan looked at him like he was an idiot. "It's still broke."

"There's this thing they invented called the internet. You can go online and order a new iron." Demarco snapped his fingers together. "And it appears on your doorstep, like magic."

Ryan grinned. "Why bother when I can use yours?" He indicated the spare room. "You mind?"

"Go ahead." With a heavy sigh that had nothing to do with Ryan, Cas headed over to the fancy espresso machine he'd won at a fundraiser last year.

"I'll take a coffee, too, if it's not too much trouble."

Cas shook his head as he added a second mug. "Want me to whip up some breakfast while I'm at it?"

"Nah. I figured if I was hungry we'd stop at the drive-through on the way to the service."

Classic Ryan.

"Where'd you disappear to yesterday anyway?"

"I had a little personal business to take care of."

"Was she pretty?"

Cas shook his head as he made another beverage.

"Oh, come on, Grandpa. Lighten up. One of these days you might actually wanna get laid."

"I'm younger than you are, motherfucker."

"Only in age."

Cas held out the mug of coffee as Ryan came back into the room while slipping his arms into the sleeves of his hastily pressed shirt. Ryan took the mug while Cas went to unplug the iron before he joined his buddy back in the living room.

"Where'd you go?" Ryan blew on the dark roast.

"I can't tell you. Not yet."

Ryan's eyes narrowed. "You in trouble?"

"Not me." He could look after himself. "Someone who used to be close to me."

Ryan was serious now. "If you need help…"

"I know." Cas nodded.

Ryan might be a pain in the neck, but he and their fellow operators on Gold Team would help Cas bury a body if necessary, no questions asked. But he wasn't sure what they could do right now, and he didn't want to have to lie to any of them about Delilah. He couldn't risk exposing the fact that she was still alive. Even though he trusted them implicitly, the more people who knew, the more chance of it accidentally slipping out to the wrong person that she'd survived the fire.

"Let's get the memorial over with, and maybe we can start to get back to normal around here." Although the reintroduction of Delilah into his life—a woman he loved with his whole being—

had knocked normal out of the window. But he couldn't think about her like that. Not anymore. He had to think of her as a fellow professional—not even a friend. She had made that more than clear yesterday. She needed his help with no strings attached.

Didn't mean he couldn't remind her of his incredible charm though, and then maybe…

He cut himself off. No maybes.

This was work.

And possibly his last chance of redemption.

Ryan was uncharacteristically quiet as he stared out of the window at the view across the town with the Potomac beyond. As a sniper, Cas liked this place from an overwatch position perspective, but the main reason he stayed here was that a few of the other single guys from HRT did too. Made for a nice sense of community.

He finished his coffee and put the mug in the dishwasher. Then he grabbed his black suit jacket and found a black tie. He handed Ryan one too. Easier to do that than wait for Ryan to find his own. "I'll meet you in the parking lot."

"Want me to drive?"

"Nope. I need my truck after the service. I can drop you off at work."

"Ackers is planning drinks and canapés at his place afterward, but Shane has to take Grace to the hospital for a scan. I figured I'd watch Grace's kids."

Grace Monteith was the widow of one of their teammates who'd been murdered by a sadistic serial killer on the first day of the year. She had two young children and was seven months pregnant with the third. The team were doing their best to help her through what had to be the worst time of her life. And, although they'd never replace Scotty, they could at least help ease the burden of being a single mom.

Cas grunted with annoyance. "I meant to paint the nursery last weekend." They'd been in Boston for most of it.

"There's time yet before the baby arrives, and they don't care what color the walls are."

Cas nodded. Talk of babies and nurseries reminded him of Delilah —although it had been hard to think of anything else since Monday night. She'd always had that effect on him. Another excuse he'd used to destroy what they'd had. He wouldn't allow anything to interfere with his goal of getting into HRT, so he'd eliminated her from his life.

Her father's threat had probably been a bluff and even if it hadn't been, Cas could have gone through selection and then got back in touch with Delilah and let the HRT brass duke it out with the Assistant Director.

Kurt Montana would have gone to bat for him.

Delilah would have waited.

She'd have still been on the other side of the country, but he knew now, they could have made it work.

He'd been so scared of the rejection he'd believed was sure to come that he'd left her alone to deal with what had been one of the worst times of her life. He'd been a coward and a fool.

If he were her, he'd never forgive him either.

"I'll show my face at Acker's place." Cas needed to ask for some time off and that would be the best place to catch his superiors feeling sentimental and in a "there's more to life than work" frame of mind.

Or not.

Cas fixed his tie and collar in the mirror by the door, squinting at his reflection.

What did Delilah think when she looked at him now? Had he aged horribly compared to his foolish 27-year-old self? He'd caught her staring at him on the plane, but her expression hadn't exactly been full of lust. More like regret and what-the-hell-was-I-thinking.

Ryan stood behind him fixing his own tie. "I hate funerals."

"It's not a funeral." There was no body to bury.

Ryan pulled a face. "Same difference."

Cas ran his hand through his hair. He didn't remember ever worrying about his appearance before and rolled his eyes at himself. She'd told him she wasn't interested in starting anything back up, and he had to respect that. She had to hate him for what she'd been forced to go through. But he couldn't douse the tiny kernel of hope that kept springing to life inside him, along with the knowledge that this might be his last chance to find any kind of happiness outside his job. His last chance with the only woman he'd ever cared about.

"Okay, Cinderella." Ryan stared at him. "You look good, not that Montana will give a shit, but I'd definitely do you."

"As if I would lower myself to a cowboy as fickle as you." Cas smiled as he opened the door. "After you, amigo."

Ryan high-fived him. "See you in the parking lot."

Cas headed down the stairs rather than use the elevator. It was good exercise, and he wasn't a fan of confined spaces—something he'd had to overcome during SEAL training. He checked his cell, but neither Killion nor Delilah had contacted him. He was impatient to know what was going on, and man enough to admit he'd been a little jealous of Alex Parker last night, sweeping in to save the day with his good looks and his fancy car and access to information. Considering the guy was happily married, it was not Cas's finest moment.

Sebastian Black leaned against Cas's truck, checking his phone screen. He looked relieved to see Cas but didn't say anything about what had happened on Monday night.

Damian Crow, aka Birdman, strolled over and climbed in the backseat without a word. Cas had arranged to give the others a ride before this thing with Delilah had kicked off. He was glad he was able to keep his promise. These men were the closest thing to family he'd ever had.

He wasn't sure what he'd shared with Delilah. Nothing familial. More like finding the missing parts of himself. Their relationship had been a mix of euphoria and astonishment, adrenaline and paralytic fear, wrapped up within a supernova's worth of lust.

And he'd killed it.

Dead.

They drove to St. Francis of Assisi Catholic Church in silence. The parking lot was already almost full even though they'd arrived early.

They found a space in the far corner. Ryan tossed the FBI ball cap he'd been wearing onto the dash and smoothed his hair.

Cas spotted Shane Livingstone, Will Griffin pulling up with Yael Brooks, and the heavily pregnant Grace. Payne Novak, Charlotte Blood, Dominic Sheridan, and Ava Kanas piled out of Novak's truck.

Quentin Savage and Haley Cramer, Eban Winters and the pretty redhead they'd help rescue from a volcanic island in Indonesia climbed out of Savage's SUV. The redhead reached for Eban's hand, and he took it, pulling her close.

Lincoln Frazer drove up in his Lexus with Aaron Nash riding shotgun. Cas's eyes widened as the principal from their last mission, Assistant District Attorney Hope Harper, climbed out of the back seat and took Aaron's hand as they walked to the church. Obviously, they were not hiding the fact they'd become involved during an op even with the higher ups in attendance, but that was classic Nash—Mr. Integrity.

Frazer wrapped his arm around a tall blonde who had a nononsense set to her chin. It was the first time Cas had seen the legendary profiler with anyone.

It was good that people had their support systems in place. This was a difficult time for everyone, even professionals who knew the risks when they signed up for the job.

His throat went tight as loneliness crowded him.

Montana had been more than their boss. He'd also been a father figure to many of them. A hard man, a competitive man, but someone who had your back. He was the reason Cas had left the SEALs early and joined the FBI. He was the reason Cas was able to hold his head high when he looked in the mirror—at least he had been able to, until Delilah had told him what had happened after he'd dumped her.

Alex Parker arrived in an Audi sportscar with a pretty brunette Cas knew worked at the BAU. No sign of Delilah.

The two of them exchanged a look.

"What was that about?" Ryan asked suspiciously.

Cas shrugged.

"Since when do you know Alex Parker?"

Cas shot him a look. "I don't."

Ryan's eyes narrowed thoughtfully then Donnelly walked up, and she and Ryan started bickering like a couple of kids.

Cas glanced around through the trees that surrounded the church, an uncomfortable itch forming between his shoulder blades. "Let's go inside and find a seat. It's gonna be packed."

Without waiting, he strode inside and slid into the pew behind Novak.

He leaned forward to murmur to his team leader. "Looks like half of CIRG are here." The FBI's Critical Incident Response Group encompassed the national tactical, investigative and operational support groups including HRT, the Crisis Negotiation Unit, and the Behavioral Analysis Unit. "Better hope no bad guys attack anything in the next couple of hours."

"Unfortunately, I would not take that bet," Novak whispered back, "but Red and Blue teams are on notice. Other people can hold the line today."

Cas scanned the pews, surprised to see the blonde from the bar Monday night sitting up front beside the new FBI Director, plus Daniel Ackers, director of HRT, and another woman.

He leaned forward to speak to Novak again. "Who's that in the front?"

"Montana's ex-wife and daughter."

Daughter?

Cas had known the man had a kid he didn't see very often, but for some reason he'd imagined she was around twelve. He turned and spotted Jordan Krychek crossing himself as he walked down the center aisle. The operator slipped into a pew on the opposite side of the church. Dinah Cohen, on loan from the Israelis, sat behind him.

Cas wondered what her deal was and if she knew anything about the plane crash that had killed his friend and mentor. If so, she wasn't talking, instead spending most of her time observing their training methods and acting as a liaison—although between whom was beyond him.

The church pews were full now, and people ranged along the side of the walls. Donnelly walked in late and squeezed in at the other end of their line, jamming in like a wedge beside Ryan, who wriggled like an infant with a wet diaper. The music started, and they all quieted. The priest began the ceremony.

Cas's gaze was drawn to the depiction of Christ being crucified above the altar. The sunlight glowed softly through the stained glass. The scene was calm and peaceful, totally at odds with how he felt inside.

Novak stood and gave a powerful eulogy about exactly what Kurt Montana had meant to them all. Despite the tough exterior, tears streamed down Novak's face, and he wasn't alone. Cas's throat was so tight he thought he might choke.

When Novak sat back down, Cas saw Charlotte reach for his hand. Novak held on like he was in free-fall.

They stood to sing a hymn, and the room filled with the sound of voices. But not Cas. He couldn't make a sound.

Emotion roared inside him as eulogy after eulogy honored a man who'd served his country for more than two decades. Cas had loved him more than the father he'd never known. And if it hurt this much to lose Montana, how would it feel to actually lose Delilah?

He'd had a solid preview on Monday night, and it had felt as if he were being eviscerated.

Scanlon was the antithesis of Montana. What would Joseph's next move be?

He'd come after him.

Cas knew it as surely as he knew the color of his own eyes.

Maybe they could set a trap. Use him to lure the motherfucker to his own doom.

Cas silently apologized for cursing inside a place of worship, not that Montana had been particularly religious.

Cas stared at the official FBI portrait of the guy in front of the Stars and Stripes. The fact that Montana was dead and never coming back hit him all over again like an RPG.

What a waste. What a tragic waste. Just like Scotty.

And Delilah...she'd missed death by minutes.

Any other night, and it would have been her in her apartment, and while she wouldn't have been so easy to creep up on, Scanlon was a big guy who'd once been among the fittest and deadliest operators in the world. Maybe he'd lost his edge in prison—or maybe he'd honed it against the rough walls of his cell and the hard nature of his peers.

Cas remembered the way Joseph Scanlon had watched Delilah when she'd been posing as Lacey Reed. He'd lusted after her like a dog after a bitch in heat. As far as they could tell, Scanlon hadn't assaulted Valerie. Maybe there hadn't been time. Perhaps Scanlon had reason to know David Gonzales wouldn't be home for long. Or perhaps crushing the woman's skull had cooled his lust.

Scanlon wasn't necessarily academically brilliant, but he was crafty as hell. Once he discovered Delilah was still alive...

The thought of her being at that guy's mercy made Cas feel physically ill. The memory of the twisted, battered, blackened corpse filled his mind so completely he could even taste the toxic air of that autopsy suite.

His heart started to pound as his mouth went bone dry.

He clenched his jaws as the walls closed in on him. He loosened his tie, which was suddenly strangling him. The skin on his shoulders felt as if a thousand ants were doing a jig. The need to get out of the building became overwhelming.

He tried to remember all the lessons in calm that had been

drilled into him over the years and breathed deep and slow, but it didn't help. Nothing helped. Sweat beaded on his forehead, and a headache started to build. He stood, ignoring the concerned looks of his teammates, and pushed his way through the crowd that rippled around him like water. At the entrance, he took in a lungful of cold, clean air and wiped the sweat from his brow.

He fucking hated funerals.

Not wanting his colleagues to see him like this, he headed toward his truck, past the white marble statue of St. Francis, and around the side of the small adjacent school.

He was parked in the far corner of the lot, near the trees. He dialed Delilah's burner as he went.

She picked up almost immediately. "Any update?"

He cleared his throat. "No. I just got out of the memorial service. I wanted to check up on you. Are you okay?"

"Yeah. I'm fine. I'm eating toast and drinking coffee at Parker's place and desperate to make some progress. What's up?"

"Nothing. I was, er, worried…" He closed his eyes. "Shit. Sorry. I know I'm probably annoying the hell out of you, but I…" He laughed self-consciously. "I guess I can't help myself."

"Try harder." Thankfully her tone held a little humor.

He opened the driver's door and noticed a glint of light reflecting off something deep in the trees.

He frowned. In the same moment, he realized that the ball cap Ryan had tossed onto the dash was missing.

Someone had been in his truck.

That same someone was currently watching him from the woods.

A thousand things ran through Cas's mind, the main one being Scanlon was a former sniper in the teams, but also that all SEALs were demolition experts.

Bomb or bullet?

The thoughts bombarded him in the space of a heartbeat. Rather than get into his truck, Cas left the door open, ducked low, pivoted, and sprinted behind the row of vehicles as fast as he could run. The blast wave ripped through the air, caught him mid-stride and flipped him forward, scraping him across the asphalt like he was sliding into home plate.

22

Delilah stared at the screen of the cell phone in confusion. At first, she thought there was something wrong with the device, that it was malfunctioning, but the connection was still live. Slowly, the roar of noise faded away, and the hair-raising sound of a human scream pierced the line.

A bomb.

That was a bomb.

She sucked in a gasp.

"Cas. Cas!" The horrifying reality of what had happened had her shouting into the phone, desperate to know if he was alive.

How could he be? The bomb had sounded catastrophic.

Even if he was, he could be terribly injured or maimed...

She heard movement, crashing sounds, and heavy breathing.

"Cas?" She wanted to go to him, to hold him, to help, but she didn't even know where he was.

She heard him make a noise. A grunt of pain.

"Are you okay? Please answer me. Are you hurt? Where are you?"

What if he was dying?

"I forgive you. It wasn't your fault. Losing the baby and my medical problems were never your fault. We both know I'd have

155

probably pushed you away after the miscarriage. The same way you pushed me away. We're a lot alike. Stubborn. Stupid. Please, don't die on me now. Not now we've—"

"I'm okay." His voice cut off her words and she slapped her hand over her mouth as joy and horror filled her. Joy that he was alive. Horror that he might still be seriously injured.

"There was a bomb, but I'm okay. Unhurt. I have to hangup because I can't hear for shit. I need to warn people in the church."

A lump filled her throat. It was so *Cas*. Thinking of others. Being the hero. He had always considered himself part villain, but he'd never understood that was the part of him she'd loved the most.

He hung up on her and she lowered herself, shaking, to the floor. Tears came then. Tears she'd been holding onto since she'd found David's body.

And wasn't it humiliating that, even after all these years, after everything that had happened, it was the thought of Cas Demarco being hurt that truly had the power to bring her to her knees?

23

It was a miracle he'd managed to hold onto the cell phone. He couldn't hear whether or not Delilah was still on the other end of the line because his head felt as if he were underwater but hopefully, she'd heard him and knew he was okay. Last thing she needed was to worry he'd met the same fate as her friends.

He didn't know if Scanlon—it had to be Scanlon—was now waiting in the woods planning to pick off anyone who came outside the church or if he'd already run away like the coward he was. Cas crawled around the nearest vehicle and sat behind a massive truck wheel, using it as a shield.

He called Novak.

"Car bomb. Keep everyone inside. I'm okay but deafened, so don't bother with instructions. I'm worried there's a shooter in the woods. I'm gonna take a look."

He hung up and stuffed the cell in the pocket of his ruined suit.

Suddenly, there was someone crouching beside him. Alex Parker. He must have followed him out of the church.

"Are you okay?"

Cas read his lips and pointed to his own ears. "Yes, but I can't hear anything yet." He was probably yelling. "Spotted a possible scope or binoculars in the woods." He got into a low squat and pointed in the direction. "I want to check it out before anyone else exits that church."

Other operators would be checking the area for secondary devices.

Parker nodded. Mouthed, "Together."

Cas nodded. They both shifted position and spent a moment sheltering behind the engine while the fire a few vehicles over burned out of control. Parker popped up and down quickly, to offer a target. No one took the bait, but it wasn't Parker that Scanlon was after.

"I'll go left and try to flank him." Parker made sure Cas could read his lips. "You go right after we hit the trees."

Cas drew his weapon. Parker counted down with his fingers. On zero, they both sprinted across to the woods and paused for a second behind the trunk of a mature oak.

Nothing happened. No shots fired.

With a nod, Alex cut away while Cas worked his way, tree trunk by tree trunk, toward where he'd seen that flash of reflected light.

As a trained sniper, Scanlon could be lying completely camouflaged waiting for a clear shot. They both knew the tricks of the trade. It had been sloppy to let the glass catch the sun, and Cas knew with certainty it was the only reason he was alive right now.

Scanlon was making mistakes, but he had spent the past five years in prison—which had clearly blunted the man's skills.

Cas's ears finally began to clear a little, and he could hear himself breathing hard. He forced himself to calm down. Use his training which he'd worked on non-stop the whole time Scanlon had been locked up. He crept forward, presenting as little of a target as possible while at the same time providing Parker the opportunity to circle around. They arrived at the location at around the same time. Cas spotted tracks through the wet rotten leaves. Pointed.

"That way."

They started to haul ass. Almost immediately, they hit a park with a bunch of baseball fields. Thankfully, there were no games going on. In the distance, just cutting into another stand of trees, was a figure wearing a black ball cap.

They both broke into a full-out sprint across the grass between baseball diamonds, ignoring the fact they were wearing slippery-as-fuck dress shoes.

Was it Scanlon?

The guy was white. Right height and build for the former SEAL as of five years ago.

He disappeared from sight.

They ran through someone's backyard and there, about thirty yards ahead, the guy climbed into a white van. He must have spotted them because his tires spit gravel as he screeched away.

Cas and Parker both bent double to catch their breath. "You get a plate?"

Parker shook his head. "Covered in mud."

Cas got on his cell to Novak. "We need a roadblock. White male. White van. Heading north on Old Triangle Road."

"Million different ways he could go from there. Roadblock is going to arrive too late. It's pointless," Novak argued.

Cas swore. Novak was right. "We need an Evidence Recovery Team on the area in the woods where I believe the bomber was watching from."

"Affirmative."

"Perhaps they'll get something off the device."

"Doubt it. I'm standing looking at what is left of your truck and wondering how the fuck I am even talking to you. You wanna fill me in on what's going on?"

Cas caught Parker's quiet gaze. "Heading back now."

They began walking to the church, Cas suddenly registering aches and pains from the blast. The sting of the palm of his left hand where the skin had scraped off on the asphalt. The bang on his right knee.

He expelled a deep breath. "What do I tell them about Delilah?"

"You don't have to tell them anything."

Cas shook his head. "I can't lie to them. Not now there's been a direct attack on HRT. It has to be Scanlon. If Delilah truly wants to keep her job, she has to come forward now." Even though he didn't want her to. "Where's Killion?"

"He was delayed. Audrey had some contractions in the middle of the night."

"She okay?"

"Yeah. They stopped. Probably Braxton-Hicks. He was on his way here when I last spoke to him."

"Shit." Cas rolled his stiff shoulders. "I mean, that's great she's okay. But I wish he was here to deal with the higher-ups, so I don't have to."

"You trust him."

Cas eyed the other man. "Yeah. I trust him. For a spook," he said pointedly.

They stood in the woods looking down at the burning wreckage. The explosion had totaled both vehicles either side of his truck and damaged a lot more.

Hell.

"It's a miracle no one was hurt." Cas looked at the men and women milling around. His friends, his teammates. Wives. Children. Innocents. "Scanlon would have happily killed or maimed any number of people to get to me."

Parker nodded. "Disguise it as a mass casualty event—especially as the FBI Director was in attendance. If it weren't for Delilah surviving the attempt on her life, we would never have put the pieces together so quickly."

Dammit.

He couldn't risk her.

He couldn't let her down.

Not again.

But he couldn't lie to his teammates, either.

It was an impossible situation. "Who else knows Delilah is alive?"

"That I'm aware of? Lincoln Frazer from BAU. Mallory. Killion. We can trust them to understand the significance of this situation and the delicate nature of what we need to do in order to catch the bastard. Plus, they have enough clout to get Delilah's actions retroactively sanctioned. There's an issue though."

"What?"

Alex rubbed the back of his neck. "It's one of my best friends' wedding this Sunday, and we have a rehearsal dinner on Saturday night. Frazer, Mal, Killion are all supposed to be going, along with most of the negotiators. After that, I'm supposed to be spending the week in the Caribbean."

Cas met the man's gaze. "The FBI and HRT can take care of this motherfucker. He planted a car bomb at Kurt Montana's memorial service. He won't know what hit him."

Parker frowned. "Which is all well and good, but first we have to prove it was him. And where does that leave Delilah in the meantime?"

Cas didn't know, but he had no intention of letting her get in the line of fire.

An ambulance arrived, closely followed by Patrick Killion who climbed out of his Jeep and stared up into the woods to where Cas and Parker stood in the shadows.

"You better get yourself checked over." Parker scanned Cas to assess his injuries.

"I'm fine."

Parker rolled his eyes. "You took a hit. You know bombs can cause internal damage. You can't save the girl if you up and die on her."

Cas snorted. "The girl doesn't want me to save her. Plus, Delilah would flay both our asses for calling her a 'girl.'"

Parker huffed out a reluctant laugh. "True. Go see a medic."

They started toward the others and Cas wondered what the hell he was going to say to his teammates and exactly how he was going to keep Delilah safe while at the same time hunting down the man who'd tried, and nearly succeeded, in killing him.

He pulled out his cell, wincing as his hands started to bleed. "I need to call her. I was talking to her when the bomb went off."

Killion started walking in their direction.

"I'll do it," Alex said. "Put her mind at rest you're in one piece. You deal with all the people who are going to want to know what happened."

It made sense, but Cas resented it. But with his fellow HRT operators busy checking every vehicle for more explosives and police patrol units arriving on scene, he didn't have a lot of choice.

He doubted Scanlon would have gone beyond planting something beneath his truck, but no one would be willing to take a risk.

Scanlon must have been watching him, or he'd figured out what Cas drove and the fact he'd be at this memorial service today.

Cas needed to reverse engineer all those details and figure out how Scanlon had got here and where the hell the bastard was right now.

24

Scanlon slammed the palm of his hand against the steering wheel, heading south on I-95. He couldn't believe the motherfucker had managed to survive the blast. Whatever sixth sense Demarco possessed had just saved his life.

Scanlon glanced at the FBI cap on the passenger seat. A mistake. He needed to get rid of it, but he'd liked the idea of a souvenir especially as that bitch Quinn had been wearing one when she'd died.

He checked the wing mirrors. No one was following. No cops. No Feds. He eased off the gas. He couldn't afford to get caught.

No one was after him. Too many white vans to count on the roads. They had no reason to suspect he'd left Louisiana again after going to visit his daughter in Washington State yesterday.

He wore a latex mask which was hot and stuffy, but he didn't want to be spotted on any traffic cams or placed anywhere close to Virginia. He was not going back to prison.

His heart pounded though his breathing remained even. He'd stayed fit as he was able to while incarcerated, but adrenaline was pumping through his veins like liquid fire. Nothing revved an engine like a live fire exercise, and he hadn't had the benefit of constant training to dampen his body's natural responses.

Even though the bomb had failed to kill Demarco, this had been way more fun than killing Delilah Quinn. He'd only meant to stun and disorientate the FBI agent, but her skull had shattered like an eggshell.

It had changed his plans, but as he'd been on a tight schedule it had been just as well.

He yawned. He hadn't had a lot of sleep the last couple of days, and he had a long way still to go tonight.

He'd sleep later.

When they were all dead. Every last one of them who'd come after him and humiliated him and taken what was rightfully his. And he'd live out the rest of his years, sitting on the dock watching the sun set over the bayou with a pole in the water and a beer in his hand. Fuck the military. Fuck the government.

He needed to readjust his plans and figure out how to get that prick Demarco, but there were a thousand ways to kill a man. A thousand ways to die. Although none quite as emotionally satisfying as blowing him into a million pieces while he watched from the sidelines.

25

They left the bomb scene to the Evidence Recovery Techs, and Killion insisted on a meeting with Ackers back at Quantico. Which was how Cas found himself entering a room in Building 64 that the FBI sometimes used to run special operations they didn't want anyone else to know about.

The bombing meant the canapés were on hold. Cas was pissed that Kurt Montana's memorial service had been disrupted, but there wasn't a lot he could do about it. The incident had to be investigated, and they needed everyone looking for the perpetrator, for Scanlon, before anyone else got hurt.

Cas had been cleared by a medic and had changed out of his ruined suit at the HRT compound. The guys were all angry, shaken. They wanted to know what the hell was going on. He couldn't share his suspicions, not until after he'd spoken to Killion and Ackers, and the other higher-ups who had the power to make decisions—decisions that could affect Delilah's career, and possibly her very survival.

If the FBI fired Delilah for leaving the scene of a crime, he had no doubt she'd go after the former SEAL herself. And he wouldn't allow that.

The guys on Gold Team were his brothers, but he wouldn't risk Delilah. Not again. Never again.

"Okay, so I've updated the FBI Director with information that might be pertinent to this investigation." Killion sat on the front desk, swinging his left leg like some cool high school geography teacher. The innocuous demeanor was deceptive. "She agreed we needed to form a task force to investigate events of the last few days."

"We?" Ackers asked sharply. "What's an attack on the FBI got to do with the CIA?"

Everyone in the room knew the CIA was not legally allowed to act on US soil or against US persons.

Killion held up his hands in mock defense. "I'm here only to get the task force up to speed with what I know and maybe push through the usual bureaucratic bullshit so we can speed this investigation along. May I continue, or would you like me to recite the Constitution first?"

Ackers scowled angrily and sat down with a disgruntled expression in a plastic chair. The Director of the Hostage Rescue Team was upset by this morning's events and not used to being talked to with anything but deference. Killion wasn't exactly known for his tact or for being intimidated by rank or titles of so-called authority figures. This was a man who'd faced off with some of the world's most dangerous criminals and terrorists on their home turf and knew practically everyone in the intelligence community. An angry FBI agent, of any rank, wasn't likely to make much of an impact on the former intelligence officer's Kevlar hide.

Killion flicked him a glance that might have been an apology. Cas didn't have Killion's immunity from the pecking order. He had to abide by the rules. So did Delilah.

"Who's going to be in charge of the task force?" Cas wanted to know how they'd deal with Delilah.

"ASAC Greg Trainer is on his way." Killion checked his watch.

"Twenty minutes out. I'm not familiar with him, but I believe he has a decent rep."

Cas's mood sank.

"While we wait for him why don't you fill everyone in on the events of the day, Operator Demarco?" Ackers instructed. "We all want to get to the bottom of this as quickly as possible. Kurt Montana deserves better."

"He does." *He really does.* Something an asshole like Scanlon wouldn't give a shit about.

Where to start?

Cas didn't want to betray Delilah, but at some point, her role in the story would need to come out. It had to if she wanted to remain an agent with the Bureau.

"Two days ago, I became aware of the fact a man who I'd first encountered as an undercover FBI agent had been released from the brig in Miramar. He's a former Navy SEAL, and we caught him smuggling drugs and weapons across the border for the Mexican cartel during a combined CIA/DEA/FBI operation. Myself and another Special Agent out of the San Diego Field Office gathered the evidence, and she arrested him when he was back in the States."

Cas had been busy extricating himself from Mexico and his undercover role. He stretched his neck that was still stiff from his earlier rendezvous with the pavement.

"We both testified in court, although my identity was concealed. Scanlon was convicted and sentenced to seven years." Cas met Novak's gaze. "He was released two years early three weeks ago for good behavior."

The intensity of the stares of his two HRT compatriots reminded him of cartel captains looking for a reason to gut you.

"Monday night, I became aware that the other undercover agent in that operation, Special Agent Delilah Quinn, was believed dead in a house fire in San Diego."

"Wasn't there another agent who died in San Diego also?" Novak leaned forward, eyes brimming with suppressed anger.

Cas nodded. "Agent Quinn's partner on the Public Corruption Unit, David Gonzales, was shot and killed at his home." The death of two agents had shaken the FBI community. Now this bombing incident had put everyone on high alert. "One of David Gonzales's Confidential Informants was also found dead that morning. I don't know the status of that investigation."

"And you suspect this former Navy SEAL?" asked Novak.

Cas nodded.

"Why?"

"He threatened us during his arrest, which isn't unusual. It also fits with his character despite what the prison service might believe." Cas hated lying, even by omission, to a man who was a friend as well as his team leader. "Today, when I left the service to get some fresh air, I spotted a glint of reflection off a lens in the woods. At the same moment, I noticed an FBI ball cap that Ryan Sullivan had left on my dashboard was gone." He looked up and met Novak's piercing gaze. "I didn't think. I ran. A second later, the bomb went off." He held out his grazed hands. "Could have been a hell of a lot worse."

"You're damned lucky to be alive," Novak growled.

"Where do you come into this?" Ackers asked Killion with ill-concealed contempt.

"I was involved in the operation six years ago—on the other side of the border. Behind the scenes, mainly, but I was able to feed Demarco enough information to keep him safe and also make him look like an asset to the cartel."

"He saved my ass more times than I can count." Cas still regretted being unable to warn some of the younger members of the cartel before the shit had gone down, but it hadn't been possible without getting a bullet between the eyes or having to fight his way to the border. The young men who'd died in the shootout with the Mexican police haunted him. It had been another reason to get out of undercover work. Sometimes he liked the bad guys too much.

Novak's and Ackers' expressions both relaxed a little at the realization Killion had actually helped Cas and that his involvement in this was likely in the past and not the present. That wasn't always the case with the CIA.

"Are you a target?" Novak asked the spook.

Killion pulled a face. "Doubtful. My role was never publicly revealed. I spent most of my time in a dark apartment in Tijuana with a DEA analyst who looked like Fidel Castro and smelled so strongly of hashish I was high every night."

Ackers clasped his hands together. "Do you have any proof that it was this Navy SEAL who planted the bomb or killed these agents in San Diego?"

"No, sir, but attacks on myself and Agent Quinn just a few weeks after his release certainly begs the question."

"What about the cartel? Could they be after revenge?" Ackers directed the question at the spook.

Killion pulled a face. "I doubt it."

Cas explained. "Most of the people from back then are dead or in prison. The ones who aren't? You know as well as I do they tend to avoid tangling with Feds on this side of the border. Plus, it seems odd to have waited all this time if they'd wanted their revenge—especially as Agent Quinn was right across the border in San Diego the whole time. Would have been easy enough to snatch her years ago."

His stomach clenched at the thought. Delilah had dismissed his concerns. Told him she could look after herself. And he'd been so freaked out at even the thought of losing her he'd cut and run.

Like that would make it hurt any less.

Imbecile.

He heard people enter the building and then watched as a tall, thin guy who must be ASAC Greg Trainer walked in, followed by Lincoln Frazer, Alex Parker, Mallory Rooney and, to his surprise, Delilah.

She shot him a concerned look.

The fact she was worried about him sent a small thrill of satisfaction through him.

Novak's gaze narrowed as he noticed the exchange.

Shit.

Killion moved to lean against the wall. Trainer introduced himself to Ackers and the others and then introduced everyone else, pausing as he indicated Delilah step forward. "And *this* is Special Agent Delilah Quinn."

Acker's eyes widened, and his mustache stretched over his tightened lips. "Aren't you supposed to be dead?"

She smiled faintly. "Hopefully, the person who tried to kill me on Monday night thinks so."

"Who did they pull out of that fire?" Novak asked sharply.

Delilah folded her arms, and Cas saw her bottom lip quiver before she firmed it. "My best friend from college, Valerie Strauss."

There was a moment of quiet to acknowledge the loss.

"You believe it's this Scanlon fellow?" said Ackers.

"I do." She held his boss's gaze. "Now we just have to prove it."

26

Delilah took a seat on the opposite side of the room from Demarco as ASAC Trainer outlined what was happening regarding the investigation into the explosion that had blown Cas's truck into a thousand different component pieces.

She was so grateful to Alex Parker and Mallory Rooney who'd come to get her from the house. Otherwise, she'd have lost her mind.

There was a scrape on Demarco's chin, and he winced as he stretched out his neck, but he looked surprisingly unscathed, considering. Considering someone had tried to blow him up.

She shivered as the knowledge rolled around inside her that by rights, they should both be dead.

Instead, he was startlingly and vividly alive.

He looked ridiculously good in a ubiquitous black T-shirt and black tactical pants. Black hair tousled. Mouth pressed into a habitual faint smile that always made him look like he knew something you didn't. He was more heavily muscled than he used to be, and she didn't like the fact her body still responded to him like a compass needle seeking magnetic north.

She forced her attention away from him. She was glad to take this on record and for a task force to be set up. She just hoped they let her work the case. And mooning over an ex-boyfriend who'd dumped her five years ago was not gonna help her achieve her goals. It never had.

"Does Scanlon know you survived?"

"Oh, yeah, he knows." Demarco leaned back in his chair. "Parker and I gave chase through the woods, but the sonofabitch had enough of a head start to get away."

How would that effect the ex-con's plans? What would his Plan B involve?

"Evidence Recovery Teams are working the crime scene. TEDAC agents are already en route from Alabama." Experts from the government's Terrorist Explosive Device Analytical Center knew everything there was to know about IEDs.

"You might want to have a demolition expert from the SEAL teams take a look," Demarco suggested. "Especially if you can find who specifically trained Scanlon in his craft."

That a man the US Navy had trained was now running around killing people would not be a good look for anyone.

ASAC Trainer continued without acknowledging Demarco's comment. "We believe at this point that the detonator was probably a cell phone. Correct?" Trainer looked at Gold Team leader, Payne Novak, who sat next to Demarco. Trainer's expression was decidedly unfriendly whenever he looked in her direction.

Great.

Maybe it was time to launch the Delilah Quinn fan club. Only her mother would join.

Novak nodded. "It's much more complicated and time consuming to set up a pressure trigger or something connected to the ignition or transmission. Considering how many Hostage Rescue Team members were in close proximity to Demarco's truck this morning, I doubt the bomber would risk spending longer than absolutely necessary to set up the bomb."

"Plus, he wanted to press that button and blow me up himself," Cas said confidently. "He'd want to personally obliterate me."

Delilah had to physically hold herself still at the imagery his words evoked and the memory of hearing the explosion over the phone.

"Why not plant it on your truck outside your apartment?" Trainer stroked his chin. "Surely less Feds around there?"

Demarco rolled his shoulders in a nonchalant shrug. "Either he didn't know where I lived or he knew that my building is full of FBI and US Marines, many of whom have windows overlooking the parking lot." He shifted in his seat.

Delilah spotted the wince he tried to hide. He was hurt more than he was letting on.

"If I had to guess, I'd say the former. I'm not that easy to find, and the chances of anyone following me or planting a tracker without me or one of the base guards noticing are slim to none."

It hit Delilah all over again. How close Demarco had come to being killed today. If she'd died on Monday night, there was a very good chance he wouldn't have known about Scanlon's release and wouldn't have been on guard. He'd be dead too. Contacting him had saved his life, and as much as he'd hurt her all those years ago, the idea of anything bad happening to him tore her up inside.

"But I suspect he had help. A guy just out of prison would struggle to pull off two attempted assassinations on opposite sides of the country without assistance," Demarco said.

"*If* it's him," Novak argued. "Two disparate incidents using different weapons and tactics? The only reason we suspect they are related is the tenuous connection to an old op."

"If it's so unlikely, why are we even here?" Delilah demanded hotly.

"Because," Greg Trainer sliced through the sudden tension, "the director insisted. And she also insisted we keep your role in this and the fact you're not dead as believed by your colleagues, quiet. Must be nice to have friends in high places."

"Why would she do that?" Delilah asked in confusion. "I don't know the new director."

"But your father does, doesn't he?"

Her eyes widened. No way had her father pulled any strings.

"I may have, hmm." Killion cleared his throat enough to get everyone's attention. "Chatted with the director on the phone earlier—before the service actually. Turns out Delilah's father and her father—who happened to be my station chief when I was in Islamabad—are good friends. I also happened to speak with him yesterday."

Delilah felt her eyes bug as the others refused to meet her gaze. Killion had used his and her connections to get this team put together. It was what she'd hoped for, but inwardly she reviled the nepotism. The other part of her was extremely grateful she wasn't in handcuffs and out of a career—yet.

"We need to figure out if Scanlon has help and if so, who else is involved," Demarco interrupted the awkward silence and pulled the attention away from her, "and if there are any other targets this man is likely to go after. Who were the judges or lawyers involved in the case, the superior officers who had him thrown out of the Navy—"

"He has a kid and an ex-wife, don't forget. I think he'll go after the wife." She cleared her throat. "I spoke with her yesterday to make sure she knew he was out of prison. She said Scanlon requested supervised visitation rights and she'd agreed. He was supposed to meet his kid yesterday afternoon, but I don't know any of the details."

Greg Trainer stared at her silently for a long moment. She clenched her hands in her lap and prayed he didn't throw her off the investigation. Regardless of what the director said, Trainer could sideline her to duties so meaningless she may as well be on a beach in Florida. As appealing as a vacation sounded, she needed to help catch this bastard before he hurt anyone else.

"The first thing we need to establish is whether or not Demarco was the target of the bomb or if this was an attack on HRT or the FBI in general. Given his statement, it seems likely that Operator Demarco was the target, but we need to confirm."

Trainer held up his hand when she opened her mouth to speak. "However, if we assume Demarco was the target we need to figure out how *the bomber* knew what Demarco was driving and how *the bomber* knew he'd be at this memorial service today." Trainer emphasized using the term "bomber" rather than using Scanlon's name.

Which was the correct way to run an investigation. Establish the facts via evidence not blindly follow an eyewitness's possibly biased opinion.

But she knew what she knew.

She opened her mouth to say something but promptly shut it when Trainer shot her another look.

"In the meantime, I'll reach out to the San Diego Field Office and see where they're at. See if I can bring in one of their case agents onto our team and have them sworn to secrecy to protect the fact Agent Quinn is alive."

She blew out a breath. "Thank you."

"Don't thank me. I have my orders." Trainer's lip curled. No one liked to be manipulated. "And, with his permission, we'll use Mr. Parker's company to see if he or his team can come up with anything that suggests Joseph Scanlon was anywhere near either crime when they occurred—or if we can rule him out as a dead end in our investigation."

"Scanlon's only been out for three weeks, and during that time he presumably had to set up his new civilian life." The older senior HRT operator with a thick mustache pointed out. "It's a pretty complex plan you two are suggesting he came up with in a short amount of time."

"He might have only just gotten out of prison, but he's had years to plan this." Delilah straightened the cuffs of her jacket, thankful for her shopping trip yesterday. At least she looked the part. "He has enough connections that they could have been doing some basic reconnaissance ahead of time. Like keeping tabs on where we lived and where the ex-wife moved to."

"I have the name of two of his friends still on the SEAL teams,"

Demarco offered. "Might be worth finding out whether or not they are OCONUS."

Trainer frowned. "We have to be very careful to find enough evidence to justifiably investigate active-duty military personnel. NCIS are gonna want in on that. So far, we have nothing more substantial than a hunch that Scanlon is involved."

"I don't know anyone else who wants to blow me up." Demarco's tone was dry.

Trainer sent Demarco a look. "Be that as it may, we have to prove it. And we have to prove it quickly enough to prevent more attacks on potential victims and not miss any leads that point in other directions, while providing clear motivation as to why we took the investigative decisions we did—especially when news of Agent Quinn's deception comes to light."

"We can surely find evidence Scanlon was in the vicinity, here today and in San Diego Monday night," Delilah pushed.

"Unfortunately..." Alex Parker glanced up from his laptop on the desk. "That's going to be hard to do when we have him on record as meeting with his child under the supervision of a social worker yesterday in Washington State, and there's no record of him on any commercial flights except to and from Washington State."

Demarco swore.

Trainer raised his brows in fake surprise.

"Well, I was in San Diego last night and look at me sitting here today," Delilah argued. "There are no records of me being on a commercial flight either."

"Scanlon doesn't have your connections." Trainer put his hands on his hips.

"He has plenty of connections." Delilah was done biting her tongue. "And I didn't ask anyone to pull strings for me, sir."

Trainer tilted his head to one side. "So you'll be fine with sitting this out while we investigate your attempted murder?"

She scowled. "What's the point in me sitting around doing

nothing while that bastard waltzes around plotting more death and destruction?"

"That's a no then?" Trainer looked smug.

"Give her a break. It's been a rough few days." Demarco was on his feet.

"Said the man who was blown up a couple of hours ago," Novak put in.

Trainer pursed his lips. "Agent Quinn left not one, but two crime scenes. Then let her colleagues in her field office believe she's dead. Forgive me if I'm not convinced she's going to be a solid team player on this."

"It's the only way I could think of to give myself some advantage over the person who tried to kill me." Tears welled in her eyes at the thought of Val and David, but she blinked them away. No way would she be anything less than professional in this room full of her peers. "I needed time to think."

Which didn't prove her innocence.

"You know procedure better than that. Even if he did try to kill you, why would this Scanlon fellow kill Agent Gonzales and this CI of his?" Trainer pushed.

Dammit.

She hadn't told them about the gun.

"I believe he was trying to set me up for David's murder. I think he decided to complicate the investigation and send the investigative team off in the wrong direction by also murdering Clarence Carpenter, but I have no proof of that."

"So more speculation. How exactly did he set you up for Agent Gonzales' murder?" Trainer looked skeptical.

Delilah glanced at Demarco as she made her decision. His gaze narrowed. Jaw tightened. She reached into her bag and pulled out the plastic bag containing her Glock 23 and the spent bullet casing and placed it on the table. "Because I found this at Agent Gonzales' house near his body." She tried to suppress the emotions that went with the words.

Trainer lifted the bag.

"It's my service weapon. I left it in my house when I went out for my run Monday night."

"You took it from the murder scene?" Trainer's expression was incredulous.

"I... *collected* it," she hedged carefully. "It hasn't left my possession since."

"You know better than that," Trainer pushed.

She dug her fingernails into the tabletop. "I knew that if the gun was found and identified as mine then I'd be the top suspect in David's murder, and I *knew* I hadn't done it. The killer made it look like a murder/suicide except he killed the wrong person at my house. He killed my best friend."

"How do we know *you* didn't kill them both?" asked Trainer.

"You don't." She held his gaze. This was a test. "But why would I be here if that were the case? If I went to all the trouble of murdering Agent Gonzales and Val, why am I sitting here in a room full of people who have the power to arrest me, rather than head to Montenegro and disappear forever? It will be weeks if not months before Val's DNA is tested. Enough time for me to confuse the trail, have plastic surgery, establish a fake identity."

Trainer shook his head. "With this in mind," he raised the gun, "you can't seriously expect to stay on this task force."

"Why not?"

"Conflict of interest?" Novak coughed into his closed fist.

"Then what about me?" Demarco glared.

"You didn't tamper with evidence," Novak snapped.

"You think Scanlon is stupid enough to have left fingerprints or DNA on that thing?" Demarco's voice was low and pissed. "Agent Quinn could have gotten rid of the gun and not mentioned it to anyone. No one would be any the wiser. I don't think Agent Quinn should be berated for making an executive decision when we are obviously dealing with a clever and ruthless individual."

"There really is a job for you at the CIA if you can't stand working for the Bureau anymore," Killion offered. "These are the scenarios we train for, what to do when there are no good options."

He was trying to divert attention onto himself. It wasn't working.

"Operator Demarco, what exactly is your relationship with Agent Quinn?" Trainer demanded.

Delilah sucked in a shocked gasp that he'd dare to ask that question in front of an audience.

Demarco looked equally stunned. Then he spoke quietly. "Before last Monday, we hadn't spoken with one another since before Scanlon was sentenced in court." His voice went gruff. "We have no relationship."

The words scraped the scab off the wound even if it was exactly what she'd told him yesterday.

"And during the undercover operation?" Trainer pushed further.

Bastard.

"We were friendly colleagues who worked well together and trusted one another implicitly."

He'd been her sun and her stars.

"So you were never personally involved?"

She noticed Killion examining his nails. Maybe the Agency was the way to go.

"We had to act as if we were in love for the undercover roles we were playing. We had to sell it to the cartel or die, and we were very good at selling it." Demarco looked Trainer in the eye as he avoided directly answering the question.

Delilah was reminded what an excellent actor Cas Demarco was and how she shouldn't believe a word that came out of those sinful lips. But she kept her expression carefully blank. They both had a lot to lose.

"Hmm." Trainer looked unconvinced.

"Well, now we've got all that settled," Lincoln Frazer spoke up. Delilah had met the FBI's legendary profiler for the first time outside a few minutes ago. "How about we move on to making a plan to catch the person who just bombed the memorial service of a fine FBI agent and good friend of mine?"

"You're okay with this?" Trainer waved his hand at where she sat. Delilah tried not to shrink with shame in her seat.

"There's nothing but positives in Agent Quinn's record, and in case you didn't notice, *she* didn't ask her father to pull in any favors on her behalf, which he could easily have done."

She stared down at the table in front of her. Would she have asked him if he hadn't been suffering from dementia? Maybe. She wasn't sure and didn't like what that said about her.

"I suggest we let her assist. Parker can use her insights to help figure out the man's movements over at his office while others on the task force"—he looked around the almost empty room—"I assume there will be others?"

Trainer's lip curled. "Supposed to be on their way from HQ, although why we can't run the investigation out of SIOC is beyond me."

"That's something you'll have to take up with the director. But let those others coordinate with the investigation into the San Diego crimes, including the Clarence Carpenter murder because that was more spur of the moment than the other two killings, and I bet that's where the killer made a mistake. Another team works the bombing from this side of the country. That way we can keep Agent Quinn at arm's length from the evidentiary part of the investigation and avoid any suggestion of impropriety should this go to court."

Trainer pressed his lips together. "Fine."

Delilah zeroed in on the profiler's words. "'*Should* this go to court'? Why wouldn't it?"

Frazer rested his unsettling pale blue gaze on her. "Because I very much doubt Joseph Scanlon plans to go back to prison. I pulled his files from the prison psychologists and his evaluations from the Navy before that. He showed definite signs of psychopathy and narcissistic tendencies."

"But they let him out?" Demarco's tone was incredulous.

Frazer steepled his fingers on the desk. "Severe psychopathy affects about one percent of the population but, believe it or not, not all psychopaths break the law, and not all criminals are psychopaths. You probably deployed with multiple psychopaths and trusted them completely."

Demarco grunted, and the sound was so disgruntled Delilah had to hide a smile.

"Joseph Scanlon is probably an extreme case exacerbated by what happened to him. He was very good at being a Navy SEAL and loved the attention that brought him, but somewhere along the way he decided he wanted more. He *deserved* more. So he figured out a way to get it and started making that short drive across the border—where he knew he wasn't even supposed to go without written permission—and began earning a nice little side income to pay for the fancy toys he and his wife enjoyed. He never expected to get caught. He especially didn't expect to get caught by some rookie female FBI agent." Frazer dragged this hand through his hair that still managed to look perfect. "And, frankly, I'm glad you pretended to be dead because from what I can see in his profile, that man is never going to stop coming for you. Not so long as he has breath in his body."

"Fuck." Demarco swore, but it was Frazer who held her attention.

"More importantly, I'm worried about what he might do, how he might lash out if he does discover you're still alive. I certainly wouldn't want to be the person standing next to him if that happens."

"So you think she should continue to pretend to be dead?" Demarco pushed.

"I'm saying if she doesn't pretend to be dead, there's a high probability she will be dead in the very near future."

"If he's that obsessed, we might be able to use it against him at some point," Trainer mused.

It was Delilah's turn to shoot Trainer a glare. She was not just a sacrificial lamb to be used without consent, although she'd happily lure Scanlon back to prison.

"I'd like permission to work on the task force too." Demarco stared at his bosses.

Novak shook his head, but Ackers appeared to be considering the idea.

"You can take the next few days. We'll decide later with regards to next week."

"What if we're called out on an op?" Novak's expression was pissed.

"Then Demarco will join his team and be deployed."

"Thank you, sir. I'd like the chance to find out who attacked us this morning."

"That's a priority for everyone in the FBI." Ackers stroked his mustache. "Operator Demarco can liaise between Mr. Parker's team, the task force, and HRT. I want twice daily updates. More if there's a break in the case."

The meeting ended, but small groups formed to discuss various actionable items. Parched, she grabbed a cup of coffee out of a vending machine. The narrow-eyed stares from Trainer and the head of HRT kept her away from their particular huddle.

"You okay?" Demarco came over to where she stood alone.

"Sure." She put the brew to her lips and then blew on the scorching liquid that resembled a dirty puddle rather than something humans should consume. "Just made to feel like something Trainer scraped off the bottom of his shoe, but whatever."

"He was way out of line."

"Was he?" She wasn't so sure.

"Yeah, he was. He had no right to question your integrity. You're a solid agent."

Emotion hit her in the throat that this man would defend her this way. It was as if he'd forgotten the role he'd played in her heartbreak. The words he'd given her in the plane came back, that he'd walked away out of fear of getting hurt. She'd known it. Of course she'd known it. He'd apologized, and perhaps she needed to put it behind her for now so the two of them could work together to catch Scanlon and then go their separate ways.

"I understand Trainer's point of view. I'd feel the same way if I were in charge," she admitted. "I wouldn't want me anywhere near this case."

"The two of you have way too many scruples." He leaned against the wall, crossing his feet at the ankles.

"Whereas you have none?"

He smiled. "Just enough to pass the polygraph."

His smile made her insides quiver, and her heart gave a crazy flip.

Dammit.

Something in her connected with him physically. It always had. It was an unconscious link she was unable to control on the cellular level, but on the organism level? She absolutely could control it. She knew better than to fall for the charm.

"You sure you want to drink that?" He looked concerned.

She sipped the coffee and grimaced. "It's disgusting."

They both laughed, and she felt herself slipping back into their old ways. The easy camaraderie, the almost psychic ability to know what the other was thinking.

And look how well that had turned out.

27

C as suddenly sensed Delilah pulling away and putting up shields, which made him clench his jaw in frustration.

He'd go slow.

Persuade her he'd changed...expect nothing in return.

He needed to concentrate on the danger they both faced and help her however she needed it. Build rapport with her again. Over time make her realize that, despite everything, she could trust him. He'd always have her back.

He cleared his throat feeling like a teen asking a girl on a date. It was how he'd always felt around Delilah. Tongue-tied and inadequate, which he'd hidden under the quiet, tough-guy persona that, unlike most people of his acquaintance, she'd seen through immediately.

"Is it okay if I call or text you at Parker's house tonight? To keep apprised of the case," he added quickly.

She shrugged like she didn't care, and her indifference pierced him like a needle through the heart. "Yeah, but I'm gonna need to find somewhere else to stay."

He frowned. Was there something wrong with Parker's place? "You don't like him?"

"I like him fine and his house is everything you'd expect from a multi-millionaire security expert—"

"Is it the baby?" The jab of pain was unexpected. He'd never expected to be a father, wouldn't have had the first clue about being one—but to realize what he'd lost, what she'd lost, hit him in a way it hadn't yesterday when she'd first told him. It felt permanent. Irrevocable. He grieved for what they might have had.

"It is the baby. But not how you think."

Her brown eyes met his.

"How then?"

She raised those fine brows and almost brought him to his knees. She was the one woman in the world for him. He had no clue how he'd found the strength to leave her behind.

Except, it hadn't been strength.

It had been cowardice.

And cowardice was easy.

She turned toward him a little, as if they shared a secret. "I'm not putting a baby at risk. I don't care how many security features Parker has, not when the FBI's top profiler stated Scanlon won't stop trying to kill me if he finds out I'm alive."

Fair point.

He examined the raw scrape on his palm.

Her gaze flew to his when she spotted the shredded skin.

He crossed his arms. He didn't want her to worry about him. "I'd offer you a room at my place but HRT plans to put cameras around my apartment and on the approach in case Scanlon tries again." He straightened up. "Hey, maybe we should find a hotel somewhere nearby. Watch each other's backs?"

She leaned close enough he could smell her shampoo and whispered, "I'm never sleeping with you again, *remember*?"

He flinched. "This isn't about that."

Although he really wanted to sleep with her. To hold her. Now was not the time. "I know you hate me. I understand why. But we used to work well together, before—"

"Yeah, *before*." She turned and put the disgusting-looking coffee on a nearby table.

"Look, can we call a truce? That isn't about forgiveness or friendship. It's not even the end of the hostilities because I know I earned them. It's just a temporary cessation of fire until we've caught this sonofabitch and put him back behind bars."

"I know what a truce is." She sounded irritable and tired.

"How about it?"

Before she could answer Killion came over.

"I have to get back to Camp Peary." Killion reached out to shake first Delilah's and then Cas's hand. "If you need somewhere to regroup or hide out give me a call." He handed them both a card blank except for a phone number. "I'll keep in touch with Parker and Frazer, but call me if you need anything in the meantime."

Delilah put her hands on her hips. "Actually, I'm going to need to figure out some cashflow and my own transportation and somewhere to stay that doesn't have an infant in the house."

Killion's gaze sharpened.

She crossed her arms, looking fierce and beautiful. "The idea of putting anyone else in danger, especially a child..."

"Parker can protect his family," Killion assured her.

"He shouldn't have to."

Alex Parker joined them. He sent her a concerned look. "I heard my name mentioned."

"Agent Quinn is reluctant to bring trouble to your doorstep." A smile tugged at Killion's lips.

Parker's gray eyes stared at Delilah. Cas couldn't read the man's expression which was disconcerting for someone who'd grown up surviving on his wits.

"This isn't up for discussion." Delilah held up her hand. "I'm grateful. You've been amazingly generous, but I will not bring danger to the home of a couple who have an infant."

Alex's gaze narrowed. "While I'm confident I can protect you and my family, I'm also happy not to expose them to risks that can be avoided. I think I may have a solution." He looked at Killion. "Quentin Savage planned to head to DC and stay at Haley's place this week before the wedding. He headed up to FBI HQ immediately after the bombing. He's putting the place on the market soon, but I doubt he'd mind if we borrow it for a few days."

"That's a great idea if he'll go for it," Killion agreed. "The way Audrey is going I doubt we'll make the wedding."

"I'll get Haley to ask him. She can talk him into almost anything even though he's the negotiator. I'll tell him it relates to protecting a potential witness from the bombing."

Cas rubbed the back of his neck. "I don't like the idea of Agent Quinn staying there without backup."

"He has a point." Killion stared blandly at Delilah.

"Things are tight. I could probably spare a bodyguard from the company, but I'd need to check with Haley first."

"I can do it." Cas wasn't about to let someone else protect Delilah, not when he was trained, willing, and able to do so. "Makes sense to stay together given we are both potential targets."

The three men stared at Delilah expectantly.

He knew he'd positioned himself back into her life without her consent, but he wouldn't push, and she had called him first, a fact that had probably saved his life. He wanted the chance to pay her back. To make up for some of the misery he'd caused her.

Delilah's mouth tightened. "Fine."

It was hardly a ringing endorsement, but it wasn't a "no."

"I'll arrange the delivery of cash, fake ID, vehicle, and anything else you can think of." Killion pulled on his jacket. "Should be dropped off this evening. Someone text me to confirm Savage's address." His phone buzzed. He checked the screen. "Gotta go."

They watched Killion leave.

"I'm heading to my office. Need a ride?" Alex offered. "I can show you the setup while I wait to hear back from Haley regarding accommodations."

Mallory Rooney had left already.

"And we should probably get out of here before Trainer's entourage arrives."

Cas checked his watch as they headed to the door. "I'm going to borrow a vehicle and go pick up some supplies from my place. I doubt Scanlon is foolish enough to attempt anything else today, but I'll take some HRT operators with me, just in case." To prove he was a team player and not about to go rogue.

He frowned at Delilah. "We need to figure out some way to disguise your appearance from the casual observer."

She touched her hair self-consciously. "I have the blonde wig."

He shook his head. "Scanlon knows that look."

"We should have something at the office." Parker headed down the path to the parking lot. "Come on. Let's see what my best analyst has found out about your friend Scanlon in the meantime."

28

"What the hell is going on?" Ryan Sullivan drove a work truck back to their apartment building.

Cas was keeping his head down in the back of the vehicle. Sebastian Black and JJ Hersh bookended him in the backseat, and Seth Hopper took shotgun. It was overkill, especially as Novak had even insisted on sending drones fitted with thermal cameras over the nearby buildings to check for snipers—in case Scanlon was lying in wait to finish the mission.

The guys needed to know what was happening for their own protection. "I'm pretty sure the bomber is a drug smuggler I helped put away five years ago following an undercover op down on the Mexican border."

Seth Hopper glanced around sharply at that.

They'd all gone a few rounds with the cartel last month.

"I doubt he has any connections left in the cartel given the turnover rate, but, unfortunately, he was also a Navy SEAL."

"Joseph Scanlon? You think that motherfucker blew up your truck?" Hopper was also a former SEAL, as was another sniper on HRT. But none had gone through BUD/S or been on the same team as Scanlon—SEAL Team One.

"Yep."

"If you know it's him, why isn't he arrested already?"

"Because there's this little thing called proof." Cas tried to sit up, but Sebastian shoved him back down.

Cas gritted his teeth against a lash of pain. "Hey, watch the injuries. One of us was almost blown up today."

"Sorry, man."

Ryan twisted around. "Thought you said you weren't injured?"

"I said," Cas gritted out, "that I wasn't *seriously* hurt. Doesn't mean I didn't lose some skin when I hit the ground. I'm fine. Just sore."

Ryan huffed and turned his attention back to driving.

"This have to do with why you ran out of the bar Monday night?" Sebastian asked.

"And disappeared all of yesterday?" Ryan sounded how a parent must.

"Perhaps."

"So, the friend who died..." Sebastian asked gently.

Cas shared the story, keeping the details to a minimum.

"He killed her partner?" asked Sebastian.

"Yeah. Then she called me because she decided the best thing to do was play dead, which Frazer told her was a smart move as Scanlon's a motherfucking psychopath."

"How do you know you can trust her?"

Cas felt a little sick going over a bump. There was only one way to make these guys truly understand. "I know because she's the love of my damned life, and I blew it. I broke it off and left her behind when I applied for HRT. I didn't do it kindly. I burnt it down to the ground and regretted it ever since."

There was a long moment of silence while they absorbed that information.

"That explains a lot," said Ryan.

Yeah. It did. "You can't share this information that she's alive or that we were together. And if the higher ups discover we were personally involved they'll take us both off the task force." Separate them—like her father had done years ago.

"Not even the other guys on Gold Team?" Hopper pressed.

"No. It'll get back to Novak, and he's duty bound to tell Ackers." Cas ached all over, but they'd arrived in the underground parking area of the apartment building, and he sat up and winced as his damaged skin protested.

"Novak is gonna be pissed." Sebastian scanned the underground parking lot.

As much as Cas respected his team leader, he wasn't budging on this. "I need to be part of this investigation. I need a chance to make it up to her. Promise."

Ryan raised his little finger and held it up between them. "Pinky swear."

The others all hooked their pinkies together in a tangled mess. "Pinky swear."

Cas shook his head and placed his grazed palm over their hands. "Thank you."

Emotion crowded the back of his throat. He might not have grown up with a family, but he had one now. And now he was going to track down and neutralize the motherfucker who'd put everything he held dear at risk.

29

Delilah stared, frowning, at a timeline on a whiteboard.
Alex Parker's team at the Cramer, Parker & Gray satellite office consisted only of a woman called Yael Brooks and a young man named Tim Theriault who looked like he should still be in high school. Apparently, most of the company's employees were in DC or were busy on jobs.

She was impressed by the amount of tracking they'd done of Scanlon's movements using his cell phone, but not what it showed. So far, the only time the man had left the great state of Louisiana had been on Tuesday when he'd gone to Washington State to visit his kid.

"This timeline doesn't add up." Parker watched her with a concerned expression on his face. "Even ignoring the cell data, it would be nigh-on impossible to go from California on Monday night to catching a commercial flight to Washington State on Tuesday morning from NOLA. And back to NOLA this morning. It's almost impossible for him to have committed both crimes and to have also visited his daughter."

Dammit.

She knew it was Scanlon, but how had he pulled it off?

"Do we have him on camera seeing his kid in Washington State?"

"Sure do." Yael pulled up a video feed.

In a cramped room full of toys sat an incongruous-looking Scanlon licking an ice-cream cone as he sat directly opposite the camera. A little girl sat on the floor a few feet away also eating an ice cream. They appeared to be talking, although no sound was available from the feed. An unknown female sat in another chair, observing, presumably some sort of social worker. Every so often Scanlon smiled up at the camera as if he knew someone would be reviewing the footage for this exact purpose.

Delilah leaned closer. "Is that a scar on his face?"

Yael zoomed in and sure enough there was a two-inch scar beside his left eye.

"That's his brother, Virgil," Delilah exclaimed.

"You're sure?" Parker sounded excited.

"Yes. His brother had a scar like that. The guy must have lost a few pounds and started pumping iron, enough to pass for his brother. They are identical twins." Excitement cruised through her veins. He was making mistakes. They could do this. They could catch him.

"I hate to burst your bubble." Yael rolled her chair away from her screen. "But check out this video I found of Joseph Scanlon leaving Miramar three weeks ago."

Delilah watched a black-and-white footage of Joseph Scanlon walking out of the brig into the parking lot and being met by what looked like his father and his brother.

She didn't get what the other woman was referring to until Yael enlarged him and she leaned closer at the screen.

"Dammit."

The man leaving the prison had the exact same scar.

"So, either Joseph pulled the trick of the century and got his brother to serve his sentence, or..."

She exhaled. "Or Joseph deliberately cut himself, so he and his brother are more or less indistinguishable to the camera. I wonder if Virgil got a matching tattoo?"

"I'd bet on it." Parker didn't look happy.

"Which begs the question," Yael voiced her thoughts, "which Scanlon showed up in Washington State?"

Delilah stared at the screen where the man had finished eating his ice cream and was now playing checkers with the little girl. "And how the heck do we prove it?"

30

Delilah arrived at Unit Chief Quentin Savage's modest townhouse wearing a red woolen hat over a long blonde wig, dark sunglasses, blue jeans, and a red parka that Alex said belonged to his friend Haley Cramer.

She stepped out of a Porsche 911 that also belonged to the other woman—a vehicle she'd left in Cramer, Parker and Gray's secure parking facility while she would be away for her wedding and honeymoon.

Alex insisted Haley wouldn't mind her using it, but Delilah was a little nervous.

It was a *really* nice car.

Delilah had never owned anything quite so expensive. Her family drove practical vehicles that blended into the DC burbs—a habit she'd taken to the West Coast even if she'd graduated to an SUV. The Porsche was sleek and attractive and gained attention even in the short drive over from the compound.

Alex's theory was that at a quick glance, most people would mistake Delilah for Savage's fiancée, who was a regular here. People saw what they expected to see. She grabbed the designer leather duffle bag that Alex had lent her and locked the car. Walked confidently to the black painted door of No. 12. She let herself inside, placing the bag in the hallway, and stood there looking around with some trepidation. The place was neat and tidy. Nicely furnished but little clutter. Definitely a bachelor pad. The couple were moving into a new house after the wedding. Somehow that made it feel a little less like an invasion of privacy to stay here now.

She went over and drew the shades. Parker had shadowed her back here, checking that no one followed her before he headed home to spend the evening with his family. Everything looked fine and, as a precaution, they'd checked for listening and tracking devices on her and her stuff at the compound. As Scanlon wasn't psychic, there was no way for him to predict where she was going to be and therefore no reason to believe she'd be in any danger at Savage's condo.

She slipped out of the heavy parka and hung it on a coat rack, removing the dark glasses and putting them on a side table. She removed the hat and wig too, leaving them beside the glasses.

Her phone buzzed, and a jolt of excitement moved through her.

But it was Alex saying good night and to text him if there were any issues.

She sent him a thumbs up emoji and found herself gulping in a breath.

It hit her how horribly alone she was right now. Val was dead. David was dead. There was no one in her life to share this time with except the man who'd hurt her so badly in the past, a man she'd never be able to trust emotionally again. The desire to go visit her mom and dad was almost overwhelming as each day brought a deterioration in her father's condition. But the idea of putting them in danger made that impossible. If Scanlon hurt them, she would never forgive herself.

Tears crowded her eyes, and she blinked furiously.

Suddenly, there was the sound of a key in the lock, and the door opened. Demarco stood there, staring down the barrel of her Glock 26.

He paused and then lines gathered between his eyes. "I wouldn't blame you one bit, sweetheart, but maybe let me come inside first to make it easier to dispose of the body."

He eased through the door, closed, locked it, and her heart thumped violently inside her chest.

She lowered the weapon.

"I brought sushi. I seem to remember you liking—" He cut himself off. "Are you crying?"

She slid the weapon back into the holster at the back of her pants. "No."

"Delilah," he admonished.

She wiped her face with both hands. "I was feeling sorry for myself, that's all. I know I've no right to. At least I'm alive." She headed into a small but well-stocked kitchen to search for plates. Demarco followed her and put the food on the counter in the center of the room, unpacking the bag. He looked like he wanted to say something else about her breaking down but thankfully dropped the subject.

He unpacked the sushi, and her stomach grumbled.

He added a couple of beers, and she got napkins as they immediately fell into a natural easy rhythm. And the loss of him, the enormity of how much she'd missed him all these years struck her all over again.

Goddammit.

He'd dumped her like a piece of garbage. So what if he'd admitted it had been a mistake? She'd been *eviscerated*.

She found a tissue and blew her nose, then washed her hands. She had every right to be emotional. She didn't need to apologize to anyone. Oddly, she knew the only person she needed to convince was herself.

She dragged a stool a little further away and joined him at the breakfast nook.

He'd uncapped the beers and held his up for a toast. She reluctantly tapped his bottle with hers knowing she was being drawn back into the enticing web that was Cas Demarco.

"To new beginnings and putting that sonofabitch back where he belongs."

She found herself nodding, although the new beginnings was a bit of a stretch.

He divided the sushi evenly onto each plate and split the wasabi and pickled ginger down the middle. She wondered if he was trying to tell her something, but she already knew she was his equal.

"Any updates?" He swallowed a piece of gyoza and closed his eyes like he'd gone to heaven. The guy had always appreciated good food.

"Discovered that Joseph now sports a matching scar to the one Virgil has on his face. The two of them are practically clones nowadays."

Demarco frowned. "That complicates things."

"No kidding. We'll have to track both of them all the time without knowing which is which." She used chopsticks to eat the first bite. The saltiness of the sauce burst on her tongue. God, she was hungry. She washed the food down with a mouthful of Chinese beer. "This is delicious."

She wiped her mouth and saw Demarco was smiling but not looking at her. He was trying to win her over with food. Not a bad tactic.

"What about you? Any updates?"

"Not really. Early days on the investigation into the bomb itself, although TEDAC were on scene and took the evidence to the National Lab here at Quantico rather than Alabama—at least initially because it might be possible to get touch DNA from the explosives and it is closer. Unfortunately, it will take time to process, but it's a priority." He pulled a face. "I had to confide in a couple of my teammates what was going on or risk getting water-boarded, but I also swore them to secrecy."

She gave a little shrug even though she dreaded the news getting back to Ridgeway even more than the thought of Scanlon figuring out the truth. "The cat is out of the bag, so I guess it doesn't matter."

"Not about us."

"Hmm."

"They won't tell anyone."

She ate another piece of sushi roll, not sure she believed him. "What about Trainer and all his cronies?"

"The director wants Trainer to keep it confidential, they'll keep it confidential."

She smacked her lips together thoughtfully. "Not that it matters."

Demarco's brows furrowed in anger. "It matters that Scanlon doesn't figure out you're alive, Lilah."

They both froze at the use of the nickname he used to call her in the heat of passion.

Her pulse raced and she held her breath.

Crimson stained his cheeks, and he looked away. Grabbed another piece of dynamite roll.

Appropriate.

She cleared her throat. "Scanlon will find out eventually."

"Yeah, but hopefully by then he'll be back in leg irons."

"From your lips to God's ear." She raised her bottle again, and he clinked it.

They ate in companionable silence for a few moments, and she felt remarkably at peace considering how much her life had blown up and how vehemently she'd hated Demarco right up until...

She couldn't pinpoint exactly when she'd truly forgiven him, but it was probably the moment that bomb had gone off and scared her to her bones.

Life really could be cut short in an instant and regrets were something she'd rather not have to live with. She already had too many to count.

She gripped the bottle tighter. "I'm glad you weren't killed this morning."

His yellow eyes locked on hers. Then he smiled. "Makes two of us. I spotted a flash of sunlight in the woods, and the egotistical fuck had taken an FBI ball cap off my dash."

He looked thoughtful. "I should thank you. If you hadn't called me up on Monday night, I wouldn't have been on guard. I wouldn't have been suspicious, especially in my grief...I owe you my life." He let the words sink in before asking. "Why did you? Call me, that is?"

Her throat tightened. "Because as much as I hated you, I didn't want that bastard to murder you too."

He nodded, acknowledging the truth. Then let the quiet stretch.

He'd always been able to hold his silence when anyone else would have filled the void with noise or movement. It was another thing she'd liked about him—the peacefulness of his company when they hadn't been fucking like bunnies. She hadn't remembered that until now.

She watched him maneuver his chopsticks with those long, clever fingers and recalled how his touch had made her body ignite. That was something she'd never forget.

She looked away. It had been so long for her. She'd dated a little, at Val's insistence, after a few years of being a virtual social recluse, but no one had come close to replicating the feelings she and Cas had once shared. She could count the number of times she'd had sex with anyone else in the past five years on the fingers of one hand—with digits to spare—but she'd bet money he couldn't say the same thing.

He'd told her there'd been no one else significant in his life— and for some foolish reason she believed him. Although she knew he was a very good liar.

But what if...

What if they were doomed to have been "the one" for each other? Only for Cas to burn them down as surely as her apartment had gone up in flames?

And perhaps, given his upbringing, she shouldn't be surprised. He hadn't had a loving role model the way she did.

He'd had a series of foster placements but nothing that had worked out long term.

What did that do to a child?

She watched his Adam's apple slide up and down his throat as he tipped back his beer. Just the look of him sent a shiver through her body. He reached across the butcher's block for some more food, and she noticed a dark stain on the back of his T-shirt.

"Are you bleeding?" Her voice came out sharp.

He twisted to look over his shoulder. "It's nothing. Some burning shrapnel fell out of the sky, and it keeps opening up." He turned his palms up toward her. "This is the worst of it. Oh, and I banged up my right knee, which hurts like a bitch now that I think about it, but it's just bruised. I feel most resentful about losing my truck. She was a beauty, and I'd had her for nearly a decade."

"Wow, hard to imagine you had the truck before we even met." She picked at the label on the beer. "That feels like a lifetime ago."

"It does." His voice dropped. "And yet, other times it seems like yesterday."

For a moment she couldn't breathe, the moment as fragile as a spiderweb.

Those golden eyes looked as if he felt it too, but then he looked away, breaking the spell. "Reminds me. I have all the things Killion promised, including an F150 with government plates." He hitched his head toward the front door. "It's in the bag by the front door."

The government tag would prove useful in terms of not getting stopped by other law enforcement personnel but meant Killion could probably track her movements. "What will you be driving?"

His expression was rueful. "I think Killion assumed we'd share, but I can have a teammate pick me up or you could drop me at the gates of Quantico. Tomorrow I'll borrow a vehicle from work."

"I kind of like the Porsche I'm driving, but I'll need to drop it back at the company lot tomorrow."

"Suits you. Sleek. Classy."

She glanced at his lips as he smiled that sad smile of his.

Dammit.

She had to get out of here before she did something stupid. But what difference would it make at this point? Her heart couldn't be broken again—it had never recovered. She knew this wouldn't go anywhere. She wouldn't get drawn into the same emotional entanglements that had scared him off last time. But laying him flat on the bed and having her wicked way with him?

The idea of that was tempting.

Her body buzzed.

"Any word on Johnson or Holtz?" She finished her beer and tried not to look like she was thinking about sex because it was truly a bad idea.

"Johnson is on the West Coast. Holtz transferred to SEAL Team Ten a couple of years ago, so he's based out of Virginia Beach. Apparently, SAC Ridgeway ordered an examination of the prison logs regarding anyone who visited Scanlon in prison after you voiced your concerns to him on Monday afternoon and then died. Trainer got a copy of that report and both the SEALs' names turned up on it."

She was surprised Ridgeway had followed up. Presumably her colleagues in San Diego would be examining all her and David's old cases to see who might hold a grudge. She hated to waste their time this way. She hated that her friends would be grieving her death. She hated hiding, but at the same time what Alex Parker said last night was correct. Catching Scanlon would make it worthwhile.

"I'd like to see that list of visitors. See if I recognize anyone."

"I can probably arrange that. Trainer might ask Parker for help tracking down all Scanlon's communications from prison anyway. Will take a while as a lot of journalists and groupies hooked onto his story about being set up by the government, and as far as I can tell Scanlon spoke to anyone who'd listen to his crazy conspiracy theories that were designed to somehow get him out on appeal."

"Good thing we got him on tape committing his crime then," she said pointedly.

"Yeah, well, I hated that plan from start to finish, and I hate the memory of it now." He stared down into his empty beer bottle. "We could have rigged his truck."

"Not without someone from the cartel potentially spotting the cameras when they loaded the cocaine. Plus, the conversation we had on our trip across the border showed he knew exactly what he was doing. My evidence nailed his case shut."

"Which is probably why he went for you first."

She shivered and wished he hadn't reminded her.

Then she yawned, covering her mouth in surprise. It was early, but she hadn't slept much last night. "I guess I'm more tired than I realized. There goes my plan to find out where Kevin Holtz lives and stake out his ass overnight."

"These are Navy SEALs, not some developer caught taking bribes." Cas's gaze was molten hot. "They'll spot a surveillance tail from two hundred feet."

She rolled her eyes and climbed to her feet.

"Plus, if they are involved and they see you—"

"Yeah, yeah, I know. I know. And I want Scanlon to believe I'm dead too, but doing nothing while he runs around the country attacking people without any consequence is beyond frustrating."

"There'll be consequences. You can bet on it."

She grimaced because she knew that likely meant HRT being deployed, which put Cas and his team in danger. She hated the thought of that more than she hated the idea of confronting the sonofabitch herself. But she wasn't stupid. She wouldn't go rogue or try to bring Scanlon down alone. If that was her plan, she'd have just stayed dead.

And Demarco would have been blown to smithereens this morning...

Her mouth went dry as the terrible realities of this week pressed down on her. It had been a difficult few days, and she hoped to hell Scanlon was taking a break too so they could all get some rest.

Alex and Yael had set up various programs looking for Scanlon's face in thousands of online places. Malls. Traffic cams. Airports. Transit. It was scary how much surveillance went on in this country, and that wasn't even counting any government programs.

Right now, she could barely keep her eyes open. "You finished?"

She cleared the leftovers into the fridge, surprised when he went outside and returned with more supplies, which he put away.

She turned when he was wiping down the counter. His T-shirt had stuck to the dried blood on his back.

"I'm pretty sure the only shower is in the en suite. Why don't you take one now, and we'll make sure your back is bandaged afterward so you don't bleed all over Quentin Savage's spare bed. I'll go after you."

His eyes were dark gold when they met hers. Was he remembering all the times they'd showered together? Or was that just her? He nodded without a word and headed off to gather his belongings.

She crossed her arms and wondered if the lust was all one way. Despite the odd sparks of heat between them, she wasn't a hundred percent sure he still found her attractive. She didn't want to care, but for some reason she did.

Which was messed up.

She pressed her lips together. She didn't need this right now.

And yet, that old adage crept into her mind. *No guarantee of tomorrow.*

Didn't matter. She had no intention of humiliating herself again.

Been there. Done that. Had the scars to prove it.

31

Cas stood under the hot spray and gritted his teeth as the water washed the dried blood out of the scrapes and gashes he'd picked up today. His hands stung, and his knee had blown up to twice the normal size.

And yet all he really wanted was to make slow passionate love to Delilah Quinn.

It was ridiculous.

He was a grown man. An elite tactical operator. The man who'd broken her heart. To think for a minute she'd be interested in starting something up with him again was nonsense.

But he'd sensed a softening in her attitude to him. In direct opposition to the hardening of his dick—even now as pain rained down on his flesh. The thought of the two of them together was enough to make all his good intentions evaporate.

Except he refused to mess this up.

He grabbed the shampoo off the shelf and hoped Quentin Savage didn't mind him using his stuff because in his distracted state he'd left his wash kit in the bedroom.

He knew Savage from various ops and liked him and most of the negotiators. He'd hung out with Max Hawthorne, a former British Special Forces guy, a few times. Eban Winters was an old friend of Ryan Sullivan's from childhood days. And Charlotte Blood was now a regular part of their HRT family since she'd started dating Novak. There were fundamental differences in each unit's ethos and tactics, but the bottom line was they all wanted to resolve any crisis with as little fuss and injury as possible. If the negotiators could talk someone into giving up their weapons and hostages great. If they couldn't, HRT was the last resort in the form of a physical assault.

Tip of the spear.

Protecting innocents was what mattered. *Servare vitas*—"to save lives" was their motto. Sometimes that meant standing down. And sometimes it meant fast-roping onto a building full of armed terrorists who were actively shooting back.

He rinsed the shampoo from his hair and then stared at the pristine white towels on the rack.

Shit.

He'd also forgotten to grab the towel out of his bag. Putting on wet clothes before applying salve and bandages defeated the point of getting cleaned up.

Dammit.

He couldn't even pat his front down because his palms had opened up again and he didn't want to stain anything.

He grabbed his dirty T-shirt as a modesty shield and opened the door into the bedroom where his go-bag sat on the bed.

Dripping wet, he breathed out a sigh of relief that the room was empty and then opened the bag wide to search for his dark gray sports towel.

A knock on the door had him whipping that sucker out and wrapping it around his hips like a whiplash as Delilah opened the door an inch.

"You decent?"

He cleared his throat. "Not exactly, but nothing you haven't seen before." He kept his hands low over his dick, which had a mind of its own when it came to this woman.

She opened the door wider, and her gaze ran up and down his body. "You couldn't find a bigger towel?"

Her tone was scathing, but the flush in her cheeks told a different story. Then her eyes lowered. "Damn, Demarco, you need an icepack on that."

It took him a moment to realize she was referring to his knee. "It's fine."

She rolled her eyes. "I'll go see if they have one in the freezer."

He used her absence to quickly drag on a pair of underwear. She was back before he could do anything else.

"Sit."

He shook his head. Raised his weeping hands. "I don't want to get blood on the sheets."

Lines formed between her fine brown brows. "Turn around."

He did so reluctantly and heard her sharp inhale.

"Let's go into the kitchen. I'll get you bandaged up there."

He felt a little stupid walking into the kitchen in his underwear, but if she could be blasé about the situation then so could he.

She pulled out the stool and waited until he'd sat down. "Here."

She pressed the cold pack into his hand, so he rested it on his knee.

She dragged another stool closer. "Prop your leg up here for a minute."

He needed both hands to raise his leg, which told him the injury was possibly worse than he'd initially thought. He hadn't really noticed the pain until now. He'd been too busy worrying about Delilah and catching Scanlon and being part of the investigation into the bombing. He winced as he pressed the cold pack hard against the swelling.

She went behind him, and he held his breath in anticipation of her touching him. The soft drift of cotton balls floated over his skin as she cleaned him up.

He shivered.

"Are you cold? I can turn up the heating—"

"I'm not cold." His voice came out low and rough.

Her touch paused for a second before the cotton ball came back, wet and cold this time and sharply painful as she disinfected the wounds.

He straightened in discomfort.

"Sorry."

"Nothing to be sorry about."

The delicate touch of her finger wiped antibiotic cream over the wounds. "It's stopped bleeding, but I'll put some gauze and Band-Aids over them. You should probably sleep on your front, but you'll need to keep the knee raised so it might not be possible."

She paused. "I, um, discovered that the second bedroom has been turned into an office. There's only one bed. So I'll sleep on the couch."

He twisted around and their eyes met. "You are *not* sleeping on the couch. I'll sleep on the couch."

"Don't be ridiculous. You can't sleep on a couch with all these injuries."

They were minor. "Then I'll sleep on the floor."

"Not happening."

He was probably going to hell, so he decided to make it worth his while.

"So we'll both take the bed. We're adults. I promise I won't invade your space." He laughed, bitterness leaking out. "It's not as if you'd be interested in anything I have to offer anyway, so what's the issue?"

The idea of just sleeping beside her made him ache, not sexually, although that was a given when she was around, but the plain old-fashioned need to be close to someone who meant more to him than anyone else in the world.

A sobering thought.

She looked away, clearly unwilling to acknowledge the truth of his words. She pressed a small pad against his back and then carefully taped the edges flat. He could feel her breath on his skin as she placed large band aids on other cuts.

He thought they were done, but then she took his hands in hers and cleaned and tended each one like he was precious to her.

Emotion lodged in his throat.

He didn't deserve her kindness.

The fact he'd never stopped loving her reared up so large it was like a flashing neon light exploding around his head.

She expertly bandaged each palm. Tied them off.

"Fine. We'll share the bed. You're in no condition to do anything anyway."

His dick decided to manfully protest but thankfully, she'd turned away to clean up the mess.

"Leave that. I'll clean up while you shower. Then we'll both get some sleep." His voice was gruff. He was getting to share a bed with Delilah again, something he'd thought would never happen.

He told himself it didn't mean anything, but maybe his plan for redemption was working. All it had taken was a massive explosion and a busted knee.

She slipped away without saying anything. Cas concentrated on clearing away the blood-soaked swabs and not thinking about the night ahead. One thing for sure. He was feeling no pain.

32

Joseph watched the sickle moon reflect off the bayou. He'd missed this in prison. Missed the scents and flavor of Cajun country, the uniqueness of the French triangle of Louisiana— the swamp, the food, the women, the music, the language. He intended to enjoy all of it in its entirety just as soon as he finished what he needed to do. He didn't plan on going back inside. He'd spent a lot of time figuring out exactly how to do what he needed without getting caught. Sure, they might suspect him, but proving it was another thing entirely.

He'd never confess.

Confessing was for *couyons*.

He was tired. He was pissed that the bomb hadn't killed or even maimed Casta Demarco.

Today had been a bust. A lot of effort for nothing. Still, it had been fun to make that motherfucker fly through the air.

He smirked.

Perhaps it wasn't a waste. Demarco wouldn't know who was to blame, and even if he did suspect, he couldn't prove nothing.

"Call Nicole." Virgil's gruff words nudged him into action.

Now wasn't the time to veer from the plan. Cas Demarco's survival was a minor detail. Temporary. No point rushing things.

He knew where Demarco worked. He relished a challenge. And he wasn't the only one who wanted a piece of that bastard. He and his associate had a deal. Something that would get them both what they wanted without either of them going to prison—assuming they didn't screw up.

He wasn't sure he trusted his associate not to give him up should they get caught so he made sure his alibi was watertight.

He pulled his cell out of the glovebox where it had spent the day. Dialed Nicole's number.

"Joseph?" Her voice was wary.

"Apologies for calling this late." He happened to know that Preston attended a Rotary meeting on Wednesday nights. "I was wondering if I'd be able to see Melody again soon?"

"Oh. Yes." She laughed. "Yes. She had a good time. I'm glad you two got along. When were you thinking?"

"I was wondering if I could take her overnight this time—if it's okay with you." *You fat cunt.* "I could fly up Friday night. Take her to the movies, then the zoo or something on Saturday. Bring her back Saturday evening."

"We have dinner plans on Saturday night…"

"Even better. I'll bring her back before church on Sunday morning, and you can save money on a sitter."

"Oh." She cleared her throat. "I suppose that would be okay. I need to ask Preston first."

"*I'm* Melody's father, not Preston." The words were sharper than he'd intended, and Virgil shot him a warning look.

"I know." God, she was such a weak fool. "I just want to make sure that fits with our plans. I doubt he'll object."

Preston could shove his objections up his skinny ass.

"You do that, *cher*, but soon, huh?" The endearment tasted sour on his tongue. "Good chance I may get a job on the rigs. If so, it'll be a couple of weeks before I'll be able to come up to Seattle again. But if Melody wants, maybe she could come down here sometime. Meet her grandpa. See where her ancestors come from."

His family had a big old house in LaCroix that had come down from his mother's side of the family. His father owned and ran the only decent mechanic's shop in town. They also had a camp out on Lake Fortuna where they spent as much time as possible hunting and fishing.

He'd missed the camp when he'd left to join the Navy.

He'd always been good at hunting—not that he was allowed access to weapons nowadays. He rolled his eyes at the ridiculousness of that rule.

"I guess she should know more about the other side of her family." Nicole had always liked the grand old house. The occupants, less so. "Will Virgil be there?"

"Virg's got himself a girl who he's more or less living with." That was a lie, but she'd never know. "But I'd like Melody to meet him. He is my brother."

Virgil pulled a simpering face.

Nicole hesitated for all of two seconds. "As long as you're there to watch her." Another long, considering pause. "You know, she actually has Winter Break all next week."

Really? What a surprise? He could hear her mentally planning an impromptu vacation with her slimeball husband.

That's right, you selfish bitch.

"Maybe you could start your new job later? I'll talk to Preston about you taking her for the whole week. Would be good for the two of you to spend some quality time together."

"*C'est vrais*. It would."

Virgil grinned beside him and raised his hand to high-five him. Joseph gave him a quiet slap.

"You check with that new husband of yours, *cher*, and get back to me ASAP. Then I'll know what tickets to book and whether or not to take that job on the rigs. You'll have to give me written permission to fly commercial with her. Or put her on a flight direct to New Orleans and I'll meet her at the other end."

"Oh. Of course. I'll text you back at this number tonight or tomorrow morning when I've spoken to Preston."

"*Ça c'est bon, cher.*" Joseph hung up and dropped the smile that had strained his mouth.

Virgil shot him a glance. "That bitch is gonna get what's coming to her."

"Amen, brother." Joseph stared at the dark water lazily lapping the edge of the bayou. "Amen."

33

C as woke early and blinked in the darkness, transfixed by the scent of Delilah. It hadn't been a dream. She was here. Beside him. He lay on his back with his one leg raised on a pillow, the covers thrown off because he ran hot and always had. He hoped to hell he hadn't snored.

He tested out his knee, and the swelling had gone down. It was stiff but not too sore.

He rolled carefully onto his side so he could watch Delilah as she slept. The streetlight outside provided enough illumination to make out her features. She looked like an angel. She'd always exuded a deceptive, almost childlike innocence but she'd toughened up these last few years. He wished he hadn't been at least partly to blame for that.

In sleep her beauty was on full display. Her long dark hair tangled on the pillows, full lips slightly parted, cheeks soft, brow unlined. She'd put on a little weight since they'd been together. She'd needed to. He dreaded to think how close to death she'd come following the miscarriage and emergency hysterectomy. She was lucky to have survived.

A bad taste lingered at the back of his throat that he'd had a part in that too.

He would never have left her if he'd known.

Fuck her father.

Fuck his dreams.

But that was the problem. He'd made a decision without consulting her. Without treating her like an equal. He'd run away like the scared little boy he'd always been deep down inside.

Her eyes fluttered, and she moaned. Turned over toward him. "What time is it?" Her words were muffled.

"Early. Go back to sleep."

He could watch her for hours.

She cracked a lid. "Are you staring at me?"

"Yeah."

"Why?"

"Same reason you were staring at me on the plane yesterday."

Her eyes opened slowly. "How do you know why I was staring at you on the plane?"

He said nothing, just listened to her breath in the darkness.

She mumbled something unintelligible. "I was thinking that if there really was a God you'd have gotten old and wrinkled, gone bald, and developed a generous paunch." Her laugh was soft. Low. "Obviously there is no God."

He reached out and smoothed the hair away from her cheek. "I figured that out before I was eight."

She caught his fingers, and he wondered if she was still asleep. "What happened before you were eight?"

"Things I don't want to talk about."

Her eyes opened wider then, but he didn't look away.

He'd never told anyone what had happened in one of his foster homes. He thought she'd pry deeper, but she simply lay there holding his hand.

After a few minutes, he thought she'd fallen asleep, but then she surprised him by murmuring, "I'm going to adopt one day. I'm going to find a kid like you and bring them home."

"May as well bring home a feral cat."

"Uh-uh." She shook her head slightly. "I'll find a kid where I still have a hope of making a difference."

His heart ached. If someone like Delilah had come along and chosen him out of all of the kids in the foster care system maybe, he wouldn't have spent so many years trying to prove them all wrong. All the people who'd picked the other kids. All the people who'd never even known he'd existed.

As if it was their fault?

How stupid to have lived his life like he was in competition with someone else when the only person who he'd really needed to convince was himself. And he still wasn't fully there. Not one hundred percent. He still didn't really believe he was worthy of a woman like Delilah Quinn.

"Did you tell your parents about the miscarriage or hysterectomy?"

She made a noise that could have meant anything. Then. "No."

He released the sense of anger that had swelled inside him at the idea her father had known Delilah was suffering alone and had not told him.

"I didn't want to have to explain about everything."

Him.

And now the old bastard had dementia so there was no way Cas could tell Delilah the truth. She probably wouldn't believe him anyway.

"Go back to sleep," he urged.

She made another noise, and he could tell she was drifting off.

She still held his hand.

He watched her.

34

R ear Admiral Lawrence Sagal sat on his porch of his home on the forty-acre property with a large mug of coffee in his hand, watching the sun come up, and wondered what the hell he was going to do with himself after nearly fifty years in the Navy.

His wife was in the kitchen baking something for a dinner party they were hosting tonight. His kids and grandkids were all coming over to celebrate with them, but he honestly felt more like sniveling than throwing a party.

Yesterday he'd cleaned out his office and "enjoyed" an official retirement ceremony where he'd felt like a horse being led to slaughter. Afterwards, he'd spoken with the men on the teams, then shared a few drinks in the mess. Eaten a cake that his aide, Darleen, had ordered which had way too much frosting for his liking. But Darleen had a sweet tooth and didn't care what he thought about cake anymore. Then his former underlings had carried his boxes out to his vehicle and waved him on his way.

And once he'd passed through those hallowed gates—with what looked like the entire community lining the way, holding parade-worthy salutes—he'd had to fight the desire the slam on the brakes and put his vehicle in reverse.

Goddammit.

He was only 66 years old. Fit as a string quartet. More competent than ten of his junior officers put together.

Ageism was a thing, right? Maybe he'd sue the damned bureaucrats in the government.

And perhaps his hearing was going a little, but he could learn to wear his damned hearing aids, and it wouldn't be a problem.

He gazed out at the land, most of which was rented to local organic farmers. Rental fees covered the taxes, and the fact they were organic meant they weren't exposed to God knew what chemicals—his wife's thinking. As a military man he'd long since stopped worrying about such things but Heather was determined they were going to have a long healthy retirement. The idea sounded like torture right about now, but presumably he'd get used to it.

Presumably.

He and his wife had bought this place four years ago and, as it was only two hours outside San Diego, they'd been able to spend many of their weekends out here. But living here full-time? He wasn't so sure anymore.

She wanted chickens.

He rolled his eyes and tapped his fingers on the arm of the chair. Chickens? Heather was way too soft-hearted to be a farmer.

They still had their place in the city...

No real reason to sell it despite Heather's rumblings. At least he could see the ocean from there. Feel the wind blowing what little hair he had left.

He stared at his cell phone and wished someone would call him and tell him how the latest naval exercises were going. Or maybe the president would contact him and request another two years' service.

Well, Mr. President. I was all set to enjoy retirement with my wife and her chickens, but since you asked so nicely...

He'd jump at the chance even though he didn't agree with the man's politics.

He sipped his coffee and squinted at the rising sun. There was a trail of dust coming along the road as a car barreled along. Probably someone headed to the horse ranch up on the hill. He was thinking about getting a couple horses. Might be nice to pretend to be a cowboy even though he'd never ridden a day in his life. Nothing said he couldn't start now.

He coughed a little. Conditions were so dry he worried 'bout the upcoming fire season. Nothing new there. World was going to hell. California was leading the way.

A crashing sound came from inside the house.

"Heather?" He pushed to his feet and hurried inside. Spotted a broken piece of crockery on the kitchen floor. Unbaked quiche filling spread in a thick yellow puddle. "Heather?"

He hurried around the large island and spotted his wife of forty-eight years sprawled on the ground with blood dripping from a gash at the side of her head.

He sank to his knees. Touched her shoulder and realized how frail this powerhouse of a woman suddenly seemed. Did she fall and hit her head? Had she had a stroke or some other medical emergency? Another goddamned reason to wish they were in the city.

"Heather?"

He searched for a pulse in her neck. The relief he felt at that strong beat against his fingers dissolved as someone stepped silently into view holding a gray 1911 pistol.

Larry's mouth went dry as rage grew. They'd done this to his wife? Hit her with the gun? Cowardly bastards.

His mind spun frantically for options. He'd left his weapon in the bedroom, locked up in case the grandkids found it. There was a shotgun over the backdoor. Cartridges in the credenza.

"What do you want?" he demanded. "You want money? It's in my wallet in the bedroom. I can get it for you."

The eyes were pitiless. "I don't want your money."

Larry hid his fear.

His wife was bleeding on the floor. She needed medical attention. But he had the horrible feeling this wasn't going to end well for either of them.

All these years protecting his country, and he'd failed to protect his own home.

"What then? What do you want?"

"I'm righting a wrong, Admiral. Taking back what should never have been stolen."

Was this about the land? He opened his mouth to argue but saw the attacker's finger squeeze the trigger and knew it was too late. He launched himself forward desperate to knock the gun out of their hands.

The bullet punched through his chest wall and dropped him like a stone.

He landed across Heather and felt her wince.

At least she was alive.

The assailant walked away, and Larry crawled forward, dragging himself inch by inch across the hard, wooden floor, gripping the edges of the boards with his fingernails. Finally, he was clear of poor Heather.

Christ, he didn't know how badly she was injured. She'd never hurt anyone. She'd waited patiently all these years, raised their kids pretty much single-handedly. All she wanted was some fucking chickens? How hard was that?

The bullet wound felt like a burning fire through his insides, and every breath felt shallower than the last. He needed to get to a phone and call 911. Get some help out here.

Vibrations rather than noise warned him that the attacker was still in the house and coming back this way. He tried to quiet his breathing but jolted in surprise when strong hands gripped his side and flipped him onto his back.

He blinked, breathing heavily. He didn't think he was going to have worry about retirement anymore.

The buttons of his shirt scattered as his attacker ripped it open.

Mouth agape in confusion, Larry stared down at his bare chest with its sparse covering of gray hair.

The scumbag held up his Defense Superior Service Medal with its pretty yellow, sky blue, white, and red ribbon.

He still didn't understand.

They wanted his medals?

The grin was evil. The eyes hard. Larry was straddled, arms locked against his sides as fear finally penetrated.

One by one the motherfucker pinned his medals to his chest, and Larry clenched his jaw in agony. Sweat coated his brow as he fought not to scream. The pain every time the pin went through his flesh was staggering. Tears leaked from the corners of his eyes.

His arms felt numb from where knees pressed relentlessly into him just above his elbows. He tried to move his lower arm, perhaps reach the gun tucked in the bastard's waistband, but he had no strength left.

Pins and needles gradually worked their way up his arms, and dizziness began to overwhelm him. He couldn't look at the bloody mess of his chest. He cursed the medals he'd once been so proud of.

The weight shifted, and Larry squinted up at his killer. He wanted to rear up. To punch and hit. To reclaim his home. To save his wife.

He couldn't even lift his head as his assailant held a shiny gold pin in front of his face.

"You see this one? I think I'll keep this one."

Larry's eyes slowly focused on his SEAL trident. He curled his lip. Remembered the effort it had taken to earn that bit of metal. He wasn't ready to ring the damned bell yet. "You can wear it, but you'll never be worthy."

He reached up and caught hold of his attacker's arms and gripped hard, digging in his fingernails, and gouging the bastard. They'd find this fucker's DNA. They'd know he fought back. They'd know he hadn't quit.

The attacker jerked away and ran out of the house.

Larry rolled his head to the side. Heather slowly lifted one terrified eyelid. He reached toward her. "Use your watch. Call 911."

Her eyes flared as she remembered the fancy smart watch their daughter had bought for her last Christmas. She mainly used it for setting timers.

She raised her wrist over her face and frantically pressed at the buttons. Then she met his gaze. Reached out to hold his hand as they both lay there bleeding onto their pristine kitchen floor.

Larry stared at the wooden ceiling and suddenly realized he should have spent more time enjoying the moment. Enjoying his family. His friends. His wife.

Her fingers tightened on his. He was pretty sure the criminal had left this time.

He risked making noise while he still had the chance. "I love you, Heather. Do me a favor. If you survive, enjoy our retirement for both of us, will you?"

She sobbed and rolled and crawled toward him. She grabbed a towel off the oven and pressed it to his side where the blood still oozed from his veins.

He covered her hand. "You deserved better than a miserable old goat like me."

She smiled at him. Eyes filled with tears. "I loved you from the day we met, Lawrence Sagal. I wouldn't change a thing—except maybe this."

He nodded, feeling himself fading. "I don't want to die. I don't want to leave you." *I don't want to ring that damned bell.*

"Then don't." She sniffled. "I waited too damned long to get you all to myself to die now."

Larry nodded but he was losing what little strength remained. Her cell phone started ringing. But she didn't respond. Neither of them did.

35

Delilah sat next to Yael Brooks as the talented woman typed hieroglyphs onto the screen. She tried not to remember waking up to a fragrant cup of coffee by her bedside and a sinfully attractive man smiling at her like she was the best goddamn thing he'd ever seen.

It had required every ounce of self-restraint not to reach out and drag Cas Demarco back into bed with her.

How long had it taken for him to undermine her defenses? One day? Two?

She was such an idiot.

"Are you okay?" Yael shot her a glance.

Delilah looked at her quizzically.

"Because you're grinding your teeth."

"Oh." Delilah felt her cheeks heat. "I was thinking about something."

Yael's lips pressed together as if holding words back. Then, "Would that something be Cas Demarco?"

Delilah blinked at her in surprise. "What are you? A mind reader?"

Yael bit her lip, clearly worried she'd overstepped and said the wrong thing. "I only figured it out because Shane—my boyfriend"—she blushed—"is also on Gold Team, and he mentioned something about Demarco being the target of the bombing yesterday, and he's worried about what that means for both Cas and the team. And then when Alex put me on this project, I did a little digging into the Scanlon case, and I know you were on it, and it didn't take long to figure out Demarco was Agent Z at trial."

Delilah read the pity in the woman's eyes and pressure built in her chest. "You did some more digging on me too, didn't you?"

Yael bit her lip. "Habit I'm afraid."

Delilah looked away, uncomfortable with people knowing a secret that only she, Val, and her physicians had known for so many years.

"I didn't tell anyone," Yael assured her. "Shane will try to get it out of me later, but given the circumstances, I won't tell him any details that don't pertain to the investigation or aren't his business. He's nosey but, trust me, I know how to keep a secret."

Delilah didn't know what to say to that. "The fact you and Alex figured it out so quickly makes me wonder if I shouldn't take out a full-page ad—or maybe update my dating profile"—which she never used—"Dumped. Barren. Armed. Difficult. Dubious sense of humor. Swipe right if you dare."

Yael's eyes narrowed in a glare. "*He* dumped *you*? What an ass. I thought he was a nice guy."

Delilah laughed, grateful for the show of female unity. "In fairness, he didn't know about the pregnancy. Just wanted to go off and join HRT without some long-distance relationship hanging around his neck."

"Asshole," Yael repeated. "Pity Laura isn't here to commiserate. Her last guy turned out to be a serial killer, so she'd have a lot of opinions."

Delilah wasn't sure what to say to that.

Yael shifted uncomfortably and then winced. "Sorry. I need to get up and move. I was shot last month. Nothing serious." She held up her hand at Delilah's obvious concern. "But I'm still healing. Alex was shot, too, but I swear he's a freaking cyborg he healed so quickly."

"I remember you now from the news." Delilah's eyes widened as she recalled other details of the case and the background of this woman. Her brother had murdered their parents and shot up their high school. Yael had been vilified and accused of being complicit in the murders.

Yael held her gaze and nodded. "Like I said, I know how to keep a secret. Anything not pertinent to the case will never leave my mouth. You can trust both me and Alex on that."

The woman looked uncertain as to Delilah's reaction though. Delilah knew the media had been vicious in their attacks on Yael. Delilah could only imagine what they were going to say about her when the truth came out that she wasn't dead.

"Thank you. I appreciate that." She stood too. "I'm going to grab a coffee. Want me to get you one?"

"I'd take a tea if you don't mind?" Yael rolled out a yoga mat and started doing a series of moves. "The office isn't usually this quiet by the way, but no one minds me doing my physical therapy exercises." She indicated the mat with her head. "In fact, if I forget, they remind me." She rolled her eyes. "We're kind of like a family —only better." She shot Delilah a shy grin.

"So where is everyone?"

She'd seen Alex Parker briefly, but he'd been called up to DC to deal with a high-level cyber intrusion that demanded his personal attention.

"Either on assignments or up in DC for the wedding. As all of the company are wedding guests, Haley hired another firm to provide security during the ceremony and reception."

Security?

"They are making sure the other group is up to snuff, which would be fun to watch as a fly on the wall because alpha males never like being told how to do their jobs. Plus, they have to liaise with the Secret Service as there are a lot of highflyers who may attend, including the president and various other politicians, not to mention a few random billionaires and the odd member of the royal family. Haley is pretty badass." She eyed her then. "I think the two of you would get on actually."

Delilah didn't feel very badass. "I'd rather elope than endure all that fuss."

"No kidding. If I ever get married, I'm going for a location wedding. Somewhere very remote and extremely expensive to get to."

"Is that imminent?" Delilah was being nosey but what the hell. Yael obviously had an inquisitive streak too.

Yael looked at her from a downward dog position. "Shane has been hinting but nothing concrete yet. We haven't been dating that long, and he's been crazy busy."

"But you'll say yes?"

"If he ever actually proposes, I'll definitely say yes. He's bossy and infuriating and sweet and considerate. Definitely the one for me, even if he isn't a fan of me riding a scooter to work." Yael's brown eyes shone with happiness, but it was quickly doused. "I'm still getting used to having someone in my life, you know? I'm more familiar with being alone, which is way easier. Getting out of my comfort zone has been a challenge. The fact he's interested in someone like me…"

"What do you mean?"

"Well, even aside from my family history," Yael performed a leg stretch. "I'm a geek. Used to spending my nights alone wearing sweats, munching potato chips, and surfing the dark web. I'm not exactly a social butterfly."

That image hit a little close to home. "Finding someone can be difficult for a lot of people."

"Not those guys, with all their manly confidence and badass tactical skills."

"Oh, I don't know." Delilah stirred her coffee and dumped Yael's tea bag into a composting bin. "Demarco grew up in the foster care system after he was abandoned as a baby. I know he struggles to figure out how he fits in and uses that brooding persona as a shield."

"Faking it until he makes it? I got news for him. He made it. HRT is a family. They love him, even if I now have my doubts as to his character."

Delilah laughed as she carried the brimming mugs across the room. "I'm not sure he knows that. Or maybe he does now, but he didn't used to feel that way." Or maybe he did, and she'd somehow been duped into feeling sorry for the guy which, under the circumstances, was a stretch.

"I'm still reserving judgment," Yael muttered.

Delilah noticed an alert pop up on one of Yael's screens.

"Hey, you have a hit."

Yael came back to her desk and sat in her very expensive-looking office chair.

"Facial rec. Oh," she sounded disappointed. "It's just the airport footage again. I watched that earlier."

"Can we watch it together?"

"Sure." She checked her watch. "I should be able to splice this all together now." She hesitated. "Alex asked us to go through the prison visitor logs together to see if you recognized anyone, but we can do this first." Yael started the video.

The images played in sequence dependent on the real time they were captured. On the monitor they watched Joseph Scanlon arrive at Louis Armstrong New Orleans International Airport early Tuesday morning in a cab. He wore a red ball cap, dropped off his baggage, maneuvered through security and headed to the gate.

Yael typed a few commands, and they picked him up getting off the flight in Seattle. He walked through the terminal, picked up a Coke from a vending machine, and then bought a big pink teddy bear, which he stuffed under his arm. Then he picked up his luggage, went outside, and hailed a cab.

"Lot of luggage for an overnight stay. Let's skip straight to the hotel. I can check the taxi records later in case there were any detours." Yael tapped a few keys, and they were outside the hotel and then inside the lobby. A few moments later, he had his keycard and was headed to the elevator.

Yael jumped onto the elevator camera, but the guy kept his head lowered and face indiscernible.

"Any cameras on the guest floors?"

"Not in the part of the hotel where his room is." Yael squished her lips. "You really think he went from San Diego to New Orleans on Monday night then from New Orleans to Seattle on a seven-fifteen a.m. flight Tuesday morning? There is a flight back at seven p.m., which he could have theoretically made and then somehow got to Quantico early yesterday morning to plant the bomb. But we have him booked and flying on the first flight back from Seattle to NOLA Wednesday morning." Yael tapped her fingers quickly on the desk. "His alibi for the bombing is he was literally in the air on a commercial flight at the time."

"It's a pretty good alibi." Delilah exhaled an unsteady breath. "But I know he's the culprit. It's just figuring out the how."

Yael replayed the sequence. Delilah stared at the footage and tried to figure out what it was that bothered her about it. Scanlon got out of the cab and walked through the hotel lobby. Glanced around as if looking for surveillance cameras and then stopped at the front desk.

"Hey, he didn't bother showing his ID to the desk clerk." Delilah watched him lean over the counter to talk to the person there, but he didn't reach for his wallet.

Yael nodded slowly and replayed the moment again. "Yes. He's showing up at the desk just so someone watching the footage would see him arrive from the airport and assume that was him checking in. Probably told the clerk he left the keycard in the room or something while he went to fetch his luggage. You think someone already checked in as him?"

"I'd bet on it, and it helps to have an identical twin brother when you want to pull off this sort of disappearing act. Can you look at the hotel footage and see if we can see the other Scanlon arriving earlier?"

Yael cracked her knuckles. "Yep. Let's do this."

Delilah spotted an intricate tattoo of a snake on the other woman's inner wrist. She thought about the tattoo she and Val had got together in college.

The knowledge that her friend had died because someone had thought she was Delilah filled her with renewed remorse.

She stood. "Another drink?"

Yael shook her head. "I'm working on getting a better sleep pattern, so I'm avoiding caffeine after 11 a.m. Which sucks." Her expression looked as if she'd eaten something sour. "I'll take a water though." She leaned back in her chair and tapped her short, painted nails on the desk. "This could take some time. I want to do the checks manually because some people know how to fool facial recognition software, and I'm guessing this guy might be one of them."

"Yeah." Delilah crossed her arms. "Something tells me good old Joe has been keeping up to date with security technologies."

"Well, I have an idea for speeding up the process that you are not going to approve of and are therefore not allowed to see." Yael leaned over, brought another screen to life, and clicked a few buttons. "So, in the meantime, you check out this list of prison visitors and see if any names jump out at you."

———

It would have taken hours of screening footage to narrow down potential targets who could have been Joseph Scanlon checking into the hotel if they'd used traffic cams or other legally available means. Instead, Yael hacked the hotel database and discovered the first Scanlon had checked in at 11:17 a.m.

It was theoretically possible that Scanlon No. 1 could have been on the flight from New Orleans and checked in then. And super simple for Scanlon No. 2 to turn up shortly after and claim he'd forgotten his key—or some such excuse. Yael printed out the best image she had of each Scanlon brother in Seattle, and Delilah placed them side by side onto a whiteboard.

They both wore ball caps, jeans, Nike trainers, navy T-shirt, and had the distinctive bone frog tattoo on their upper left arm that was partially visible. They both had a two-inch scar next to their left eye.

"No way I could tell you which of these men is Joseph from these images," Delilah admitted. She wasn't sure she'd know if she stood facing them in person.

Yael regarded them thoughtfully. "We know the guy on the flight carried Joseph's cell. Virgil's cell sat at his mechanic's workshop and then back to the house overnight, presumably in the father's vehicle."

"I'm sure his father will swear up and down Virgil was with him all day." Delilah pointed at the images. "But we have proof they were both in Seattle." She swore. "Except it won't be definitive unless we can get them both in the same shot."

Yael's lips pinched. "Something tells me they are not going to be that sloppy when they went to so much trouble to set this up."

"So they aren't likely to both walk out the front door when it comes time to leave?" Delilah let the wryness shine in her voice. "Any cameras at the rear of the hotel?"

"One but the angle isn't great. If someone knows it's there, it's easy to avoid it."

"Which we presume they did."

"Which we presume they did," Yael agreed.

Delilah pulled up a map of the hotel. "I know you have scans running looking for Scanlon in the background of any images, but can you narrow that search down to certain streets?"

"Sure. But do we assume that it was Joseph who met his kid then came back to the hotel where he and Virgil spent the night before Virgil flew home to New Orleans the next morning pretending to be Joseph—thus providing Joseph with what appears, at first glance, a rock-solid alibi for the bombing? In which case I'd guess the real Joseph left prior to that in order to get to the east coast in time to plant the bomb at Montana's memorial—probably Tuesday evening. Let me search for any security cams along that street, and we'll see where that leads us." Yael typed as she spoke, fingers blurring like the computer whiz kid she was.

Delilah felt old. And surplus to requirements.

"Any luck with the prison log?" Yael prompted.

Delilah shook her head. "I recognized a few names of SEALs and Joseph's family as regular visitors. A famous author and a podcaster who also tried to get an interview with me on several occasions. The other names mean nothing, but if I could see the photo IDs, perhaps that would spark something."

Yael pressed a couple of buttons and pulled up her email. "Sending now. I can get deeper background checks on anyone you want to follow up on."

"Thanks." Delilah wondered what Cas was doing and immediately made herself focus on the task at hand. She knew better than to get distracted by the handsome operator.

36

E arlier that morning, Cas had walked into Building 64 with a stupid grin on his face because he'd spent the night in bed with Delilah and had managed to not completely mess it up. He'd bumped straight into Greg Trainer, who'd narrowed his gaze thoughtfully and wiped the smile right off Cas's mouth.

"You trained in Virginia Beach, correct?" Trainer had snapped.

"Yeah. And?"

And that's how, three hours later, he found himself at his old stomping ground at the Joint Expeditionary Base Little Creek–Fort Story, Virginia.

He'd been coached relentlessly on the drive down by a ball-cracking agent named Makimi. For some reason known only to Trainer, the ASAC wanted *Cas* to take the lead on questioning. Makimi was to observe.

He walked into the interview room at the NCIS facility with Makimi one step behind him and pulled out the seat opposite Petty Officer First Class Kevin Holtz, who'd been picked up late last night on a DUI. The Feds had stepped in this morning and asked for the SEAL to be held until they could question him on suspicion of being connected to yesterday's blast.

In a rare courtesy from one government entity to another, the request had been granted.

Holtz took one look at him and groaned. His hair stuck up in untidy tufts, and the capillaries in one of his blue eyes had burst—common in divers—giving it a sinister red haze. "What the fuck do *you* want?"

Holtz obviously recognized him.

Cas had probably seen Holtz around, but he couldn't quite place where. The trial maybe? Cas had watched the TV coverage avidly in a pathetic bid to see Delilah and then howl at the moon and yearn for her like some lonesome voiceless desert wolf.

Cas sat down and placed the folder in front of him. Waited for Makimi to settle herself beside him. She was small in stature but fierce in personality. He didn't think she liked him.

"So," Cas began. "You know who I am."

Holtz's eyes narrowed realizing he'd already made a mistake. "I recognize a Fed when I see one."

His look of distaste was worthy of a sixteen-year-old girl.

Cas introduced himself and Agent Makimi. "I hear you were out celebrating last night, Petty Officer Holtz."

Holtz's gaze turned assessing. "Is that a crime?"

"It is when you drive home drunk," Cas countered.

"I had a few beers with the guys. Base is quiet, so we tied one on. I made a mistake getting into my truck to drive home. I apologized and will make any restitution the MPs feel is appropriate. It won't happen again."

"What were you celebrating?"

A sly grin spread over the man's face. "Being alive. Do I need another reason?"

"No, sir. No better reason." There was something in the SEAL's tone that suggested he knew exactly how close to death Cas had come yesterday, and he could only know that if he was in contact with the person who'd tried to kill him.

But perhaps Cas was projecting.

A heightened sense of awareness rolled over him, that survival reflex that had saved his ass on too many occasions to count. He wasn't in immediate danger, not unless the SEAL attacked him, but he felt like prey, and he'd been prey before. He didn't like it.

The guy had both wrists cuffed to the metal bar in the center of the table, but Cas knew he was mentally figuring out how easy it would be to attack him or grab his gun.

Cas was not so easy to ambush. Not anymore.

He found himself relaxing. He might not be used to interrogating suspects compared to more seasoned case agents, but he was this man's equal. He'd been a hell of a SEAL and a fucking awesome drug cartel captain. None of his people had ever dared to lie to him. The gang members hadn't been Navy SEALs, but they'd grown up on the mean streets, fighting for survival every damned day. That honed a person to the sharpness of a stainless-steel scalpel.

Pedro's shining eyes flashed into his mind. Some people were innocents regardless of the tattoos they sported or people they worked for.

It was an unpopular position, but he'd been in the trenches with those guys. Pedro wouldn't have squashed a bug, let alone physically harmed anyone. Bitterness filled his heart at all the things that op had cost him.

He brought his mind back to the seaman in front of him. Straightened his papers. "We're investigating the explosion that occurred yesterday morning. You may have heard about it?"

Holtz's bloodshot eyes flicked to Makimi. "I saw something on the news."

Outrage built that someone had attacked him at Kurt Montana's memorial, where other people could have been hurt, where his friends could have been caught in the blast. He had no doubt whoever had set that bomb off wouldn't have given a rat's ass if he was alone in the truck or not. Attacking him was one thing. Attacking his friends was something else entirely. Cas kept his features impassive, something he'd perfected from an early age to avoid blowback from temperamental foster parents, SEAL instructors, and cartel bosses.

This asshole was probably in on at least part of Scanlon's plan because how else could the ex-con hope to pull off something with so many working parts? Wasn't like he could walk into Walmart and pick up C4 and a couple of detonators.

"Evidence has come to light to suggest some of the explosives came from the ordinance kept here at JEB."

Surprise flickered across Holtz's features. Then he raised his chin and stared back at Cas. It looked like he was deliberately stopping himself from saying something that might be incriminating.

It was always the people who had something to hide who had to think more carefully about their words. Unlike the FBI agents conducting an investigation, an interviewee couldn't lie to the FBI without committing a felony. And maybe that stacked the deck in the Justice Department's favor, but if you had nothing to hide then why risk it? People did though. All the damned time.

After a few pregnant moments, Holtz leaned back as far as he was able in his chair. "What's that got to do with me?"

"We got a report of missing C4 from an area you had access to."

His shoulder rolled in a lazy shrug. "Stuff goes missing in the military every day. Surely even you remember that."

So he was no longer pretending he didn't know who Cas was. "Oh, I remember a lot of things, my friend."

That got Holtz's hackles up. "You ain't no friend of mine."

Cas raised a laconic brow. "Because I joined the FBI to help catch bad people doing bad things?"

Holtz sneered. "I bet you were too much of a pussy to stick it out in the Navy."

Cas had been to pretty much every active war zone on the planet and a lot of other places on missions that were still Top

Secret. Being called a pussy didn't so much as dent his armor, but some guys on the teams had a hair-trigger, and that would be enough to push them over the edge.

Scanlon was one of those guys.

Was Holtz too?

"Instead, you destroyed a good man." Holtz was preaching now. "Took his career away from him. The Navy took his damned Budweiser for fuck's sake. Something he *earned*. I know because I was with him every step of the way." He stabbed his finger at the table. "He earned that thing twenty times over." He shook his head. "And Naval Command took it away like some cheap service medal."

Budweiser was the nickname the SEALs gave the gold pin that featured an eagle clutching a trident, anchor, and flintlock pistol that they received on passing BUD/S. It was the pin won by sweat, endurance, and pure grit. The one Scanlon had dishonored with his conduct.

Scanlon, Holtz, and Johnson had gone through BUD/S together, so it was no wonder they were tight. Cas was still close with his cohort—Tommy Whalen being one of them. But if any of them did what Scanlon had done, he'd be the first to condemn them.

"He earned the right to *wear* the Budweiser," Cas corrected. "He lost that right when he began trafficking illegal goods across the border. Naval Command didn't take his pin, they just removed his right to wear it in any official capacity."

"All over transporting a bit of coke." Holtz leaned forward and slapped the desk hard.

The guy looked disappointed when neither Cas nor Makimi reacted.

"It started with coke." And a hell of a lot more than a *bit*. "You think the cartel would have let it end there? Before long it would have been weapons and then even possibly people, terrorists, criminals—the very people SEALs are sent overseas to deal with. Once the cartel had proof Scanlon was dirty, they wouldn't hesitate to use that information to force him to do other things."

"No one forces Joseph to do anything he doesn't want to do. Not the cartel. Not you."

Cas leaned back and gave the guy an easy-going smile. "And that's what I testified in court. Joseph Scanlon was never forced to transport cocaine across the border. He chose to work for the cartel of his own free will."

"Testified from behind a screen," Holtz sneered. "You were too chicken even to show your face."

That was a direct hit, but Cas refused to react. The only person whose opinion he cared about was the same person this scumbag's buddy had tried to kill.

Holtz yawned widely, but he looked far from sleepy. Possibly a stress response. From his scruffy jaw and messy hair, it looked like a few days since he'd seen a brush or a razor.

"You about to be deployed?" Or was there another reason for his sloppy appearance?

"Can't talk about that outside of my platoon I'm afraid."

Cas liked this game. "That's okay. I'll ask your Senior Chief. We went through BUD/S together."

The man's mouth thinned.

That's right, pal. There might be consequences you hadn't thought about — like being dropped from the teams or losing that promotion you were hoping for.

"Where were you yesterday morning?"

"I don't have to tell you a damned thing without a lawyer."

Cas stared right into his eyes. "We are quite happy to wait for your counsel to arrive. In the meantime, you stay top of our suspect list for the attempted murder of federal agents, and we get to tear your life apart, bit by bit until you provide us with an alibi that proves otherwise."

"You don't have any reason to suspect me aside from spite."

"Spite?" Cas didn't bother to hide his astonishment. "I didn't even know your name until this morning." That was a lie, but he let Holtz think it was something to do with the bomb itself that had led the FBI to his door. "We traced the explosives placed in my truck yesterday to munitions that have been reported missing from this base. Munitions you had access to. That's not spite. That's fact."

The stare was less cocky now. Holtz wet his lips. "A lot of people have access to that storage facility."

Cas held his stare. "I doubt that."

"I can give you the names of ten guys off the top of my head."

Holtz would rat out his colleagues to deflect attention. That didn't surprise him.

Cas examined his fingernails. Bored. "Senior Chief Lopez promised to look into that for me."

Cas took a moment to enjoy the slight flicker of dismay that crossed the man's expression. He was trying to make Holtz realize he might not have all the power when it came to relying on the military brotherhood. He couldn't know where everyone's allegiance lay. He wouldn't know whom to trust. Not now. Not anymore. Not with the sort of secrets that ended careers and came with long prison sentences.

Holtz shook his head. "Why do you hate Joseph Scanlon so much that you're trying to pin this on him? He's only been out a few weeks. Why can't you let him live his life? He's paid his debt to society. You have no right to persecute him this way."

Cas gave his best surprised face. "I am not questioning Mr. Scanlon." The use of his civilian title was deliberate. "I'm questioning you in relation to missing C4."

Holtz exhaled roughly. "Like I told you. I don't know anything about it."

"You ever been to Quantico, Kevin?"

The man's gaze flashed and then shot away. He shrugged and scratched his arm. "Sure. Did my basic there for the Marine Corps."

"What about more recently? You been there in the past six months?"

Holtz held his silence and his stare.

"You try to run some surveillance on me, Kevin?"

Holtz's eyes narrowed to thin slits.

"You know that makes you an accessory before the fact, right? Even if you didn't build a bomb with that C4, you'll be charged as an accessory to attempted murder of federal agents. Maybe even conspiracy to murder. You think the authorities are going to go lightly on you because you didn't press the button? Or maybe you did press the button." Cas tilted his head to the side as if considering. "We have some eyewitness reports of a man fitting your basic description detonating the bomb. Joseph Scanlon has an airtight alibi, so he didn't press the button. Maybe he got one of his few remaining friends to help him? Do him a solid?"

Holtz was too short and heavyset for the man he and Alex Parker had chased out of the woods yesterday, but Holtz didn't know that.

"You are not going to pin this on me." Agitation started to crack the bullish exterior. "I was on base yesterday. I have witnesses."

"I'll need the names of those witnesses. I'll be questioning them and will require sworn statements from each of them." Cas looked at Makimi. It was time to start piling on a little pressure. "Let's cut the bullshit, shall we? We know you took the explosives. We know that C4 was used to bomb the memorial service of a decorated former soldier. A man who deserved better. A man who was working with DEVGRU on assignment when he died. How's that gonna go down with your fellow SEALs when it comes out?"

Holtz's throat worked.

DEVGRU was the Naval Special Warfare Development Group (NSWDG), more commonly referred to as SEAL Team Six.

"Did you tell Scanlon about the memorial service and guess I was going to be there?" Cas kept his voice steady, though inside he was shaking with rage. "Did you overhear it somewhere?"—like the bar where HRT liked to drink?—"Maybe from another SEAL?"

Sweat coated the man's brow, although the room was cool. "I don't know what you're talking about. I haven't seen Joseph since before Christmas."

Cas pulled his lips to one side. "I forgot to mention we have your buddy Johnson in another interview room on the other side of the country." Cas was bluffing, but Holtz was getting nervous now. The idea of serving twenty-five years in a small cell would do that to a person. "First seaman to crack gets the deal, but here's the catch. There is only one prize." It was the wrong tactic to try to dare a SEAL, so he flipped it. "I bet it's not gonna be you, though, Kevin. Oh, no. You're going to go down in flames with your integrity intact. Your code of honor is worth a lifetime in prison and the loss of a job you so obviously love. Johnson's got two kids and a pretty wife to think about. He's gonna cave like a dam breaking." Cas smiled a cold smile. "You however? Nope. You're gonna keep your secrets and take your punishment like a real man."

Cas examined the scabbed over scrapes on the heels of his hands. "You know we can get touch DNA off devices now? We have your DNA in the database. And Scanlon's. All it's gonna take is one epithelial cell left on that bomb. Presumably you wore gloves, but did you wipe away the sweat on your brow and then pick up the C4 and detonator? Or scratch your ear? You think we won't find the packaging you put it in when we track down the vehicle the bomber used? You really think good ol' Joe remembered to get rid of it? He's been in prison for so long it would be hard for him to remember every detail of such a complex plan or know what we're capable of nowadays. Then there's the fact he's been hopping from coast to coast since last Monday. Guy must be running on fumes. Of course, he made mistakes."

A bead of sweat rolled down the side of Holtz's face.

"But I still don't think you'll give up Joe before Johnson caves. My colleagues out in San Diego are working him hard because they are pretty damned motivated." Cas dropped the impassive cloak back over his features as he drew out an image of Val's blackened corpse and slid it under the SEAL's nose. "That's their colleague Special Agent Delilah Quinn. Monday night her house burned down with her in it. And then less than 48 hours later, someone tried to blow me to smithereens. All just three weeks after Joseph Scanlon was released early for good behavior." Cas leaned forward over the table. "A coincidence the FBI can't afford to ignore. And we know he had help. They'll get Johnson to flip. I guarantee it."

Holtz's face lost its smirk, and his jaw tightened. "I don't know nothing about that."

"Murdering women is a new low, don't you think?"

Cas could see Holtz eyeing him, as if considering making a lunge even though he was cuffed to the table. Cas didn't fancy his chances, but SEALs were nothing if not determined.

"You really going to throw away an honorable career for some loser who was running drugs that could have killed your fellow Americans while you were working your ass off back in Coronado?"

The man had clamped his lips shut and glared.

"You drive a white van, Petty Officer Holtz? Or have access to one?"

Those blue eyes drilled into Cas now, and he knew he'd lost him even before the guy opened his mouth. He'd pushed too hard. "I want a lawyer."

Cas placed the photos back into the folder. "That can be arranged. In the meantime, if you'd write down that list of people who saw you on base yesterday morning—"

"Fuck you, asshole." He turned to Makimi. "And fuck you too."

Makimi stood abruptly. "I'm done here. We're wasting our time. Let's go." She opened the door and waited impatiently for Cas to join her.

Kevin Holtz knew something. If they let him out, he was going to contact Johnson and then he'd know Cas had lied to him—

unless he could get Trainer to tell the San Diego office to pick the other SEAL up.

"Demarco," Makimi snapped.

He stood and leaned over the table practically daring the SEAL to take a swipe and earn himself some extra time behind bars. Unfortunately, the guy didn't fall for it.

"We'll be in touch." He turned away.

"Hey, Demarco."

Cas paused and looked back.

The cocky smirk was back. "It's a shame about your girlfriend. She was hot. Even hotter now she's a crispy critter."

Demarco forced himself not to react even though he wanted to smash his fist through the other man's face. He was smarter than that. At least he was smarter than that in a room full of cameras.

"Think about the deal, Kevin. As soon as we get that DNA back, we won't need to sweeten the deal." He walked away without another word.

Outside, Makimi walked across the asphalt and climbed into her small silver sedan Bucar that they'd driven down here in.

She turned on the tracking app to make sure it was working.

"You know he'll check for a bug as soon as he gets out of here," Demarco commented.

"This one is newly developed. Voice activated. Transmits in bursts at a higher frequency than most detectors scan for. When the vehicle is stationary it only sends a signal after ten minutes. Piggybacks off the nearest cell signal. Invisible to most people searching for electronic surveillance, even Navy SEALs." Her dry tone lightened the mood. "Fraction of the size of a conventional tracker and is monitored via satellite."

She handed him a second one to look at. It was the size of a computer chip, so small he was worried he was going to crush it or lose it. He placed it back in the shielded case and put the box in the console.

"A team of agents from the Richmond field office have been tasked with monitoring him. They'll stay close enough they can pick up the trail and stop him destroying evidence should he happen across a white van."

Cas wasn't sure they'd be good enough to catch a SEAL who knew he might be being followed. "It lasts less time than conventional ones?"

"Not that much less given the reduced frequency of signals. With luck it won't matter." She checked the time on her cell then paused to read a message. "Trainer wants us back at Quantico, ASAP. He says there's been some sort of break in the case."

"A break in the case meaning we have Scanlon in custody and whoever he conspired with? Or a break in the case meaning we are one step forward in the investigation that could take months?"

She side-eyed him. "Not sure, but sounded more like the latter."

"So how about questioning Holtz's colleagues as to his whereabouts yesterday morning before we head back? Save us six hours in the car tomorrow if Trainer decides we have to come back to do exactly that."

She narrowed her gaze, weighing his request.

Technically Cas was a higher rank, but Trainer seemed to listen to the other agent. Cas didn't want her persuading the task force leader that he was more trouble than he was worth. He wanted to be as close to the case as he was able to get. As close to Delilah as humanly possible.

"You said yourself we want Holtz to know we're serious. We may be bluffing about some aspects, but we know he might be involved, and we need to verify his alibi. Plus, he might head straight to the van as soon as he's released, in which case we're still here and ready to follow up."

Her mouth curled into a sudden smile. "Funny, you don't look like a screaming optimist, but the words coming out of your mouth prove otherwise." She started the engine. "Fine. We'll take a couple hours on the base, talk to his colleagues. Check out what explosives he might have had access to—to send him a message that we are not playing games."

Cas grinned.

"Let's hope your old friends don't decide they like him more than they like you."

He pressed his hand to his heart. "You wound me."

"Yeah, yeah." She rolled her eyes. "Save it for someone who cares."

But he could tell he was growing on her.

37

Delilah was working her way through the visitor log. Kevin Holtz appeared to visit every time he was on the West Coast. Mark Johnson had gone almost weekly when he wasn't deployed.

Delilah's brows raised at that. The guy visited more often than Scanlon's own family, although making the trip from Louisiana couldn't have been easy. Perhaps Joseph should have thought about that before he started his side hustle for the cartel.

She came across images of women. More than she could have ever imagined. Were they personal friends or groupies attracted by the publicity? She printed out their images and basic information.

Nicole and the kid never visited.

Her lawyer did though, presumably to deliver divorce papers.

Delilah bet that had made him cranky.

She dug her fingers into her scalp. No one jumped out aside from the SEALs. She was going to have to dig deeper into each of the visitors to see if any of them were likely to have assisted Joseph on his murderous quest.

Alerts dinged on one of the monitors like an old-fashioned bicycle bell.

Yael rolled over to the machine and hurriedly opened a feed. "And we have a hit! Across the street from the hotel from an ATM. He's wearing a ball cap—which I actually added to the possible variables given the ones he and his brother wore earlier—but I'd say there's a good chance that *this* is Joseph Scanlon leaving the hotel at 7:04 p.m., Tuesday night."

So he could have made it to the East Coast in time to try to kill Demarco.

Delilah stared at the image. As much as she wanted to get excited, the picture was grainy and indistinct. "It looks like him, but I'm not sure it would pass for an ID in court. Can we clean it up?"

"It's never going to be great quality," Yael warned.

Delilah considered. Right now, it proved nothing. The guy could argue he just went out to dinner or for a walk around the neighborhood. "Can we see if there was any activity in the room? Room service order being placed? Calls received? Movies rented? Anything that puts someone else in the room while this guy is on the street?"

Yael nodded, but Delilah wasn't finished. "And can we follow this individual and see where he goes? We might get lucky. Presumably, if it's Joseph, he's headed to SeaTac."

Twin creases scored the skin between Yael's eyes. "We can. None of the other facial rec programs have had any hits in SeaTac though, except for the recorded flights we know he was booked on, to and from New Orleans."

"Could he have used prosthetics? A disguise? Facial recognition tricking clothes?"

Yael watched her patiently until she ran out of steam. "Yes, to all of those things. And if he changes disguises again before catching a flight then we might lose him completely. Or he could drive to a different airport and fly from there."

Delilah wanted to bitch and moan with frustration, but it wasn't Yael's fault. Yael wasn't her technician, and she was doing a hell of a job, a job that would normally take a lot longer. Delilah scrubbed her face. "I'm sorry for pushing so hard."

Yael gave a soft smile. "Trust me, I've worked with the FBI before—where do you think I met Shane?"

Frustration had her clenching her jaw. "I worry he's out there planning to hurt others." While her friends lay dead in the San Diego morgue.

Yael reached out and squeezed her shoulder. "We'll get him."

"I'm worried about his ex-wife," she confessed. "I think he'll go after her next. I mean she hated me before the trial and spouted all sorts of lies about me entrapping her husband. But she changed her tune as soon as the videos were shown in court, and she began divorce proceedings the moment Joseph was found guilty."

"She ever apologize to you?"

Delilah snorted. "No."

"But you care about her wellbeing."

Delilah shrugged. "It's my job."

"That's not why you care about her." Yael leaned back in that fancy chair of hers and quirked a shy grin. "You're a good person, Special Agent Delilah Quinn."

The comment hit her unexpectedly and made emotion lodge in her throat. She crossed her arms over her chest. "I'm a good agent."

"That too."

"I hate being side-lined," she grumbled.

"Hey, this isn't sidelined." Yael raised her arms and indicated the many monitors. "This is the cutting edge of the investigation."

"I wish I knew what was going on with the task force."

"We could hack into the task force database if it makes you feel better."

Delilah's mouth dropped open. "You couldn't."

Yael's blinked innocently. "I'm literally paid to try."

Delilah clenched her fists. "You might get away with it, but somehow, I think if we were caught, I'd be off the case and out of a job before I could blink." The temptation was there though. She liked to have all the information. She was used to being in charge.

She was also part of a large organization she believed in. One she trusted would keep working to get to the bottom of what had happened. But the wheels of justice ground excruciatingly slowly and Delilah was impatient to catch this sonofabitch.

She wanted her life back.

She wanted her friends avenged.

Most of all she wanted the danger that Scanlon represented back behind bars where he deserved to be. Where he couldn't hurt anyone else.

38

Senior Chief Terry Lopez stopped them before they'd even gotten out of their car. "Great to see you, Cas, but I'm afraid we're going to have to reschedule this for another time." He caught Makimi's eye and nodded. "Ma'am."

Cas didn't bother to hide his annoyance. They'd known each other too long and too well for him to worry about the other man taking offense. "Good to see you too, but this isn't a social call. We're in the middle of a murder investigation. We don't have time to wait around on the Navy's timetable."

The Senior Chief had ink-black hair and skin as swarthy as Cas's. Unlike Cas he was on the short side, but it had never held him back. Terry put his hands on top of the sedan and leaned down. "Sorry, man. I don't have a choice. Everyone's been called in for a TOC huddle."

Tactical Operation Center huddle was shorthand for a panic stations team meeting.

"They raised the threat level to FPCON CHARLIE and all non-military visitors are being asked to exit the base until we get a handle on the possible threat."

Force Protection Condition (FPCON) CHARLIE meant something had happened or intelligence indicated there was some form of terrorist threat against personnel or facilities.

Cas's spine tingled.

The sky was overcast. The temperature in the low fifties—about normal for February. The sound of a helicopter thrummed in the near distance. The wind whipped the flags that were all set at half-mast.

Shit.

"Who died?"

Lopez leaned closer and lowered his voice. "Rear Admiral Lawrence Sagal and his wife were found murdered in their home about an hour ago by their son who's a captain at Coronado. The admiral only retired yesterday."

Sagal had been a hard man but a fair one. A good leader. This would hit the Special Forces community hard.

"Command is worried someone tortured information out of the guy, so we're all locking down until we can figure this out and doublecheck protocols."

Thoughts raced through Cas's mind. NCIS would be leading in the murder investigation, given the Admiral's knowledge of Naval facilities and operations.

Cas gripped Lopez's wrist to stop him moving away. The guy leaned closer with a question in his eyes.

"We need to verify Kevin Holtz's movements for all of yesterday. It's urgent."

Lopez looked impatient. "I don't know what the fuck is gonna happen in the next twelve hours. I suspect at minimum we're gonna have a thorough review of security after this briefing. I'm gonna be lucky to get home at all tonight, and my wife is not going to be happy with me."

"Terry, I wouldn't ask if it wasn't important."

Lopez looked to the sky. "Oh, man. No. Not today. You're not calling in that favor for saving my life all those years ago. Not today."

"If that's what it takes... Hey—" He lowered his voice as

personnel scurried about. "This could be related to your threat. Sagal stripped Scanlon of his Trident. Holtz was just going on to us about the unfairness of the whole thing, and now the guy is dead? Don't forget someone tried to blow me up yesterday, and we all know who the number one suspect is."

Lopez pressed his lips together.

Cas pushed his advantage. "You know they're friends."

Lopez pulled a face. "They went through BUD/S together. You know how that goes. Holtz keeps his nose clean and does his job."

"He had access to bomb materials. I'm not saying it was him, but someone has to be helping Scanlon, and he hasn't been out long enough to make that many new friends who have access to C4 and detonators on this side of the country."

Lopez heaved out a sigh. "Fine, but I doubt I can verify his movements without him finding out. People are going to want to know why I'm asking questions."

"I don't care if he finds out."

Lopez's brows beetled.

"I want him to sweat, Terry. I want him to wonder who the fuck to trust and be looking over his shoulder. I want him to be curious what evidence the FBI got off that bomb. If he's innocent, he'll be pissed. If he was where he said he was, then you'll be helping verify his alibi. If he's lying, then he has a problem. But if lying is his only crime, then maybe I'll cut him a break." Cas shrugged and watched the wheels spin in Lopez's eyes as the installation went into lockdown all around them.

Lopez looked off into the distance. "I don't like doing this to one of my men, but fine. If Holtz was involved with yesterday's bombing the Navy needs to know."

"Thank you, Senior Chief. Any idea how Sagal died?"

Lopez shook his head. "But I hear it wasn't pretty." His gaze sharpened. "You really think Scanlon could be complicit?"

Cas gave an exaggerated shrug. "Another person involved in Scanlon's downfall dies in unexpected circumstances...? That's a hell of a coincidence if he isn't involved."

Lopez's nostrils flared. "You need to watch your back. If you're right, you have one of the most dangerous men in the country gunning for you."

Worse—gunning for Delilah.

"Don't worry, my friend. I'm operating on FPCON DELTA."

Lopez held out his hand and squeezed Cas's. "Don't underestimate him. And make time for a social call soon, huh? We may be a step down from your HRT buddies—"

"You know that isn't true." Cas hated that Lopez might think that.

Lopez let go of his hand and rapped the top of the car. "Time to head out. I'll be in touch."

Makimi put the car in gear and joined the long line of vehicles leaving the base.

39

J oseph was under the hood of a tricked-out banana-yellow
Ford Bronco when he heard footsteps approaching. He
peered out under his arm.

"Hi, there, LaCroix Police here. Deputy Herbert. Looking for
Joseph Scanlon." The deputy who nodded at him had full cheeks
that were shiny and red and didn't look as if they'd ever felt the
scrape of a razor.

Joseph straightened and wiped his hands on a dirty rag. The
scent of motor oil and feel of grit on his fingers was familiar but
not what he'd wanted out of life. That's why he'd joined the Navy.

And look how well that turned out for you, couyon?

"Well, you found him."

The deputy reached out to shake his hand. The young officer's
hand felt clammy in his despite the fact the temperature was only
in the fifties today.

Joseph mentally calculated the quickest way to put him down.

"Police Chief wanted me to come by and say 'Hi.'"

I bet he did. "Hi."

"Nice vehicle." Deputy Herbert nodded to the Bronco.

Piece of shit. "Needs a new carburetor and the timing fixed."

The deputy put his hands on his hips. The guy was barely out of diapers. He was already carrying a little extra weight. Give him five years of Miss Sunny's world-famous beignets, and he was gonna struggle to fit behind the wheel.

"You got your parole officer sorted out?" The deputy used his serious face, as if now they'd done the introductions they were done with pleasantries.

"Yes, sir, I sure do." Joseph crossed his arms and noticed the man's eyes lock onto the tattoo on his biceps. He half expected an audible gulp. "Jim Jenkins in Thibodaux. Got an appointment with him tomorrow afternoon. Four thirty. I better get back to working on this vehicle so the owner can get it back for the weekend."

Jim Jenkins was a slimy son of a gun who was a parole officer probably because he was too fat and lazy to become a cop. Considering the look of this one, it was a low bar.

The deputy cleared his throat. "I have to ask. Have you left the parish at all this week?"

Joseph blinked and raised his brows. Cocked his head to one side.

Oh, yes. It was happening.

"Tuesday, I went up to Seattle to visit my kid. I didn't see her when I was in prison." *'Cos her bitch of a mother had refused to let her come.* "I had permission. Got back Wednesday morning." He smiled and hoped he didn't look as angry as he felt. That he needed permission from an asshole like Jenkins to travel out of state when he had once traveled the globe to fight for his country. Look at how that country had treated him? Like he was nothing but a common criminal. *"C'est tout."*

The deputy nodded slowly, then rubbed at the corner of his eye like he had allergies. "I don't suppose your brother is around here anywhere, is he?"

"You want to speak to Virgil? He done something wrong?"

Deputy Herbert cleared his throat. Found his balls. "I don't know, has he?"

Joseph smiled at that. "He's probably in the back there." He indicated the small office at the back of the crammed workshop. "My daddy is out on a breakdown. Some young lady stuck on Bayou Road."

The deputy nodded. "I'll drive out that way after I leave here. Could you ask Virgil to step out, please?"

Joseph didn't know whether to be impressed that the cop had any self-preservation instincts at all, or disgusted he wasn't brave enough to walk inside a mechanics workshop in his own town. Imagine the guy off home soil. Imagine how brave he'd be if the other guys actually fought back. What was the Police Chief thinking sending a wet-behind-the-ears grunt like this to his home? That he was too pathetic for Joseph to bother to hurt?

He calmed himself. The mission was the only thing that mattered. Local cops were a mild hindrance at worst.

"Virgil!" His voice rang off the metal roof. "We done got company."

There was a mutter and a curse.

Virgil walked out the office holding his cell phone to his ear. They both wore identical jeans and T-shirts.

"What you want with me? You think you can harass me the same way you get to harass my brother, you got another think coming."

The deputy held up his palms in surrender. "No, sir. Trying to verify your brother's whereabouts."

"Why?" Virgil barked and Joseph was surprised the cop didn't piss his pants.

The deputy slowly backed toward the large garage doors, obviously rattled. "Someone killed that SEAL commander, the one who stripped you of your military rank after you were convicted."

Joseph feigned surprise. "Which one?" Because in truth there were a whole bunch he'd like to gut and mount on the wall.

"Rear Admiral Sagal. Someone attacked him and his wife in their home this morning."

"Ah, that's too bad. About the wife that is." He bared his teeth in a smile.

"You weren't a fan?" the young deputy asked.

Joseph raised his arms in a full body shrug. "Isn't that why you're here, Deputy Herbert?"

The deputy pressed his lips together and puffed out his cheeks. "*C'est vrai.*"

"Anything else we can do for you, deputy?" he asked. "Coffee, beignet?"

Regret twisted the young man's features. "No, sir. Thank you. I apologize for interrupting your morning. I'll go take a run out Bayou Road. See if your pa managed to start that lady's vehicle."

"Mighty good of you." Joseph nodded approvingly.

Virgil clapped him on the back as the cop climbed into his cruiser. "They send nothing but the best for you, brother. Ain't no way they're going to figure this out."

They were idiots, and the justice system was there to be manipulated. You just needed to know how to play the game. That first trial had taught Joseph a lot about that game. Mainly, don't get caught, but also, always create doubt. Make them have to prove everything beyond all reasonable doubt.

The justice system, it was a beautiful thing.

40

Delilah sat in a room in the small building on the outskirts of the FBI National Academy where she'd completed her training seven years ago. She'd always known what she wanted to do in life. Be like her daddy and stop bad people doing bad things.

Put them in jail.

Keep innocents safe.

Except that hadn't worked with Scanlon. Not in the long run. Secretly, she wished she'd shot him, back when he'd tackled her during the fumbled arrest. As shocking as it was, she wished she'd pulled the trigger and removed the stain on society that was Joseph Scanlon.

Val would still be alive. David too. Clarence. The admiral and his wife, Heather.

Delilah jolted at the sound of gunfire that penetrated the double-paned windows making it sound as if they were under assault. It was agents on the gun ranges and NATs—New Agents in Training—being put through their paces, being taught how to make an arrest without getting rugby tackled to the ground.

You got used to the noise after a while, but today it made Delilah twitchy.

Assembled in the room was a small group of people who

looked like they were in detention—although a lot less teenage cool than *The Breakfast Club*. Greg Trainer, Lincoln Frazer, Yael, and herself. Thinking about it, Yael was pretty cool. Delilah felt obsolete beside the brilliant, younger woman.

Maybe it was the lack of a uterus or maybe it was the fact someone had actively tried to kill her, but she felt old. Old and unwanted and on edge.

Trainer had succeeded in getting the task force moved to FBI Headquarters, closer to where he lived. He'd hung around Quantico because he wanted to see what Alex Parker's team—which today was Yael—had uncovered, and what Cas and Makimi had discovered at JEB Little Creek–Fort Story.

The two agents were on their way back from Virginia Beach right now, and Trainer apparently trusted the other female agent enough to let her into the secret of Delilah's survival.

Delilah was pissed about the move because it effectively pushed her out of the investigative loop, because the FBI Director had made it clear she still expected Delilah to stay dead until Scanlon—or whoever the hell had attempted to kill her—was arrested. She didn't think FBI security would be happy with her donning a disguise to try to go into work every day.

Whatever.

No one gave a damn about her feelings even though she was one of the targets.

Boo-hoo.

At least she wasn't dead.

She didn't know if that meant Demarco would be heading to DC, too, and that thought draped her in sadness.

She picked at the dry cuticle on her thumbnail. Why couldn't she simply move on and find someone else? Someone who wouldn't destroy her when he left again. Someone nice. Someone boring. Someone reliable, she corrected herself. Someone she could count on not just when things were difficult, but in the minutiae of the day to day.

Demarco excelled at crises. He'd spent his entire working life training for crises. It was the ordinary she wasn't sure about.

Frazer was on the phone, advising someone out west about a serial killer stalking the highways across the country. Trainer read the report she'd quickly put together outlining Yael's findings.

The clock ticked, and Delilah swore her sanity was getting stretched thinner and thinner by each auditory movement of the second hand.

Finally, Cas and Makimi swept inside with a cold wind and raindrops dripping off their coats. His eyes swept the room until they found her. Locked on and held.

Emotion filled her.

The things he made her feel…

A fine quiver moved through her that had nothing to do with stress or fear.

It was electricity.

It was *life*.

She hated that she felt this way again. Knew that he'd break her heart in the end no matter what he might say in the meantime.

Perhaps it would be worth it.

Perhaps it didn't matter.

Being fatalistic about her doomed relationship with Cas Demarco but unable or unwilling to stop falling ever deeper into the mire was a new low.

He frowned at whatever he saw on her face and then took a seat beside the agent he'd spent the day with. Makimi laughed at something he said, and he turned to respond.

Delilah looked away.

Was she really going to be jealous of a professional woman doing her job—over a man who had never believed she was enough?

Hell, no.

Makimi was not the issue here.

If Makimi, too, was naive enough to fall for the guy, Delilah would give her her number so they could hold each other's hands in the aftermath.

"Update," Trainer demanded from Cas first.

"Holtz was pretty shaken when I suggested Johnson was being offered a deal to flip. We planted the bug on his car, but I have my doubts as to him not finding it or taking evasion tactics—be it borrowing a friend's vehicle or employing a signal jammer. He was recalled to base after he was released from custody. He dialed Mark Johnson. The guy didn't pick up, but maybe the call itself is a signal to check however they really communicate."

Like a draft email that was never sent or a chat box on their favorite video game.

"Unfortunately, the increased risk assessment at both military installations means Holtz didn't lead us anywhere, but I was thinking that perhaps we could look into where he's spent any time recently using his cell phone data."

"Guy wouldn't be communicating with Scanlon on his normal cell if he is involved with conspiracy to commit murder of federal agents," Trainer argued. "He's a SEAL. He understands technology."

"Even so, knowing where he goes might give us some clues as to where to start looking for that vehicle."

"Or like you said, maybe he borrowed it from a friend, or stole it. That's what I'd do if I'd planned this crime." Trainer scratched his neck.

It's what Delilah would have done too.

"You get the list of people with access to explosives at JEB?"

Cas checked his cell. "Yes. I can send it to you or print it out. Holtz is on it. Lopez is looking into Holtz's whereabouts on base yesterday. Even if he has an alibi, the fact he knows we are investigating might force him to make a mistake or request a deal."

"Email me what you have," Trainer instructed.

Yael raised a finger. "One suggestion. Perhaps you could look for a pattern of other unassigned phone numbers that ping off cell towers alongside Holtz's personal cell? Maybe you'll get lucky and figure out the burner cell number and be able to cross reference it to one making calls to numbers in Louisiana or Coronado."

"Good idea." Trainer's expression brightened. "I'll get our techs at SIOC on that."

"Did you have the San Diego agents bring Johnson in?" Cas asked.

"No. Not yet." Trainer looked annoyed.

Delilah thought it might be his default expression. "Where was Johnson when Admiral Sagal was murdered?"

"On exercise off the coast. Unless he has an identical twin too, he didn't do it." Trainer's biting comment made Delilah cross her arms defensively.

She'd told him her theory that Virgil Scanlon was the man who'd flown to and from Seattle on Joseph's ID and met Joseph in a hotel room there. As expected, until they had solid evidence that both men were in Seattle at the same time, Trainer wasn't convinced enough and nor would a jury be. It wasn't enough that the twins *could* have done this. The FBI had to prove they *had* done it. Then they had to prove which one of them committed the crimes.

"Where was Joseph Scanlon today?" It was another cross-country hike to the admiral's house but possible. Maybe he had access to a plane or something. Some light aircraft. She wrote the idea down in a note to herself.

"He was at his mechanics shop all day today."

"Are you sure?" She didn't bother to hide her skepticism.

"Yes." Trainer's blue eyes blazed. "Deputy went down there and verified."

She opened her mouth to say something, but he wasn't finished.

"*Both* brothers were there, in the flesh. Unless there's a third we didn't know about, then Joseph Scanlon did not kill Larry and Heather Sagal."

She stared down at the table. The guy was acting as if her suspicions were paranoia rather than justified.

"How'd the admiral die?" Cas asked.

Trainer tapped a few keys on his laptop and turned the screen so they could all see.

Delilah winced.

"Mrs. Sagal received a blow to the back of the head."

Delilah exchanged a look with Cas. Val had also died from a blow to the back of the head.

"The admiral..." Trainer swiped the photos, and a gruesome sight filled the screen. A bullet punctured Sagal's lower ribcage, but that wasn't the detail that stole the show. Each of the Admirals considerable number of medals was pinned to his bare chest.

Nausea stirred in Delilah's stomach.

"I'm assuming from all the blood the admiral was alive when this was done to him?" Cas asked.

"That seems to be the pre-postmortem consensus," Trainer said.

AKA the ME's best guess.

"Sagal just retired. Maybe someone with a long-held grudge decided it was time to get his or her revenge?" Agent Makimi suggested.

"I'm sure the admiral had a long list of enemies. With Joseph Scanlon having an alibi that has been verified by law enforcement personnel, he is not a suspect—"

"Any chance this police officer knows the family?" Delilah cut in. "Might he have lied—"

"Are you suggesting some sort of giant conspiracy in the great state of Louisiana now, Agent Quinn?"

She was thinking just within Joseph's local parish.

"It's his hometown. Good chance he went to school with most of the cops in the police department and Sheriff's Office. It's not impossible." Cas backed her up.

Trainer looked impatient. "Don't you two think we should open our minds to the idea Joseph Scanlon might *not* be responsible for all of the crimes committed this week?"

"Not really," Cas shot back. "You see what isn't pinned to his chest?" He pointed at the admiral's bloody torso.

Trainer stared hard at the photo, but Delilah got there first. "His trident."

Trainer's eyes widened.

"That's right. His gold trident. His Budweiser, as we call it on the teams. You know who was harping on and on about Naval Command stripping Scanlon of his Budweiser today?"

Makimi looked up and met Trainer's stare. "Holtz. He did make a big deal of it."

"Fine." Trainer sat back in his chair. "But the fact remains we have nothing to place Joseph Scanlon in San Diego on Monday nor today. We have no evidence placing him in Virginia on Wednesday or planting a bomb—in fact, as of right now his alibi is he was on a flight when that bomb was detonated."

"We don't have proof *yet*." Delilah spoke quietly and tried not to sound resentful.

"Then get me the proof it was his brother on that flight. *That's* how it works, Agent Quinn." Trainer twisted his head around as if relieving tension. "San Diego agents are investigating leads that involve Clarence Carpenter's boss in the building trade who is believed to have mob ties. They're also chasing the links with the mayor's office, but as you know it's hard to do without tipping off the press or the person of interest, so it's taking time."

The murder of Clarence Carpenter made so much more sense now. How to slow down and tangle up an investigation. Throw in a random murder and watch the suspect pool bloom.

"Did we get the DNA back from the Carpenter murder yet?" Frazer looked up from whatever he was reading on his phone.

Trainer shot him a look. "That murder occurred Tuesday morning. It's Thursday."

Frazer shrugged. "Technically possible to have the results by now. You should follow up on that."

Trainer assessed the profiler like the other guy was trying to pick a fight. He visibly calmed himself. "I'll call them on the drive back to HQ." He collected his papers and shut his laptop. "As of now the admiral's murder has not been connected to the attempted murders of both Agent Quinn and Operator Demarco and is not under the remit of this task force."

Delilah's temper spiked. "It's obviously related."

"Oh, yeah? So why can't anyone point me to a single shred of evidence?"

She ran her hand over her face. Because Scanlon was a clever sonofabitch. "What about the ex-wife and kid?"

Everyone looked at Lincoln Frazer.

"The wife is a possible target. He'd see her betrayal as unforgivable. I don't believe he'd harm his own child. Mainly because he'd consider her his property. Narcissists like spreading their genes around even though they rarely make good parents."

A wave of distaste flowed over Delilah at the thought of being someone's property. She'd been so lucky with her own parents, even if her dad was a little overprotective sometimes, especially since her brother had died.

"I'll have a local agent go out and interview the wife. See if she's seen or heard anything suspicious. Scanlon's in Louisiana right now, and even if he is the mastermind of all this, I doubt he's about to get on another flight tonight."

"She's pregnant. Can they at least warn her she might be in danger?" Delilah pushed.

"On the basis of what exactly? Three separate incidents that, as things stand, Scanlon is alibied for?"

Frustration rose up inside her. "Perhaps I could go talk to her—"

"No. Unequivocally, not," Trainer said firmly.

Delilah opened her mouth to argue.

Cas interrupted. "It seems likely that if Scanlon was orchestrating this, then he had help. We're looking into Johnson and Holtz. What about the people he was locked up with? Anyone recently released who might share his point of view?"

"Good idea. We need to check." Trainer nodded. Makimi and Yael both made notes. "What happened with the visitor logs?"

Yael answered. "We're still checking them. He was remarkably popular."

"For a psychopath," Delilah muttered grimly.

Frazer smiled.

"Keep working on it, and keep me informed." With that he stood up, waving Makimi ahead of him through the doorway.

Yael leaned over. "I'm gonna catch a ride with Shane. See you in the morning?"

"Sure."

"I've got a bunch of searches running." She touched her arm. "We'll get that proof. It just takes time because of the size of the data pool."

It felt as if they were trawling the Atlantic with a tea strainer.

Delilah pressed her lips together and nodded. "I'll look through what we have on his prison visitors again tonight. See if I can find anything that might hint at an accomplice."

Emotions crowded her. Frustration that Trainer wouldn't let her do anything useful. Fear that Scanlon would defy Frazer's profile and kill a little girl because if he couldn't have her, no one could. Grief. Isolation. With a sucker punch of what felt a lot like unrequited love.

Tears pricked her eyes, and she didn't want anyone to see. Especially not Demarco. She stood, pulled on sunglasses despite the heavy cloud cover, slipped into her jacket and quietly left.

41

"**D**elilah. Hey, Delilah, wait up!" Cas jogged along the badly lit path to the parking lot. He'd exchanged a few words with Yael, who was waiting on Shane to give her a ride home. She seemed pissed with him, and he'd asked her if he'd done something to upset her. She had looked around the room only for them both to realize Delilah had slipped away.

The woman in question paused and turned around. "Wanna shout that a little louder?"

Cas winced as he realized his mistake. Delilah wasn't exactly a common name.

"Sorry. I was worried you were going to ditch me, and I was hoping for a ride back to the house." He tried to diffuse the tension by injecting humor into his voice.

She carried on walking, obviously upset with him. The rain had stopped, but water dripped off the branches of the nearby trees.

Apparently, he'd lost what little charm he usually possessed. Everyone seemed upset with him today.

He lengthened his stride to keep up with her. She wore sunglasses, but it was dark, and no one was around. Something was wrong.

"I guess it proves I'm too old for undercover work."

She grunted. "You'd never have made that slip if we were in danger of being overheard by anyone else. You were always brilliant at playing a role." Disgust laced every word.

She whipped off her sunglasses and gripped her head as if in pain. "Dammit, I don't mean to make every word a jab at you." Her expression was naked and vulnerable. "I'm just still so bitter that you left me."

"Delilah—"

"No, let me get it out. Let me get it out, and maybe I can finally let it go." Her lips were pinched and her skin so pale. But it was those dark eyes that haunted him. "You told me we could carry on hooking up but that you couldn't promise to be monogamous when I was going to be on the other side of the country—as if I was something interchangeable, like a blow-up doll."

He flinched.

"As if I wouldn't have moved heaven and earth to be assigned to an office near enough for us to make it work…"

"It was a mistake."

She shook her head slowly from side to side. "That's the thing. It wasn't a mistake. Everything you said was carefully calculated to drive me permanently away, and it was good. Damned good. Even without everything that happened to me afterward, it was the best script you could have written, designed to make me not call your bluff or chase after you. You hooked into my pride and my self-confidence, and you shredded them both to the point I was emotionally destroyed. I barely survived. I tried to move on, but it was never the same. Never as good. Never something I could trust. I've barely dated since. You stole my ability to love."

His heart shriveled, but she wasn't finished making him die inside from the pain of hurting her.

"We could have had *everything*, but instead you stamped on it like it was a cockroach. And you didn't just break *us*, you broke *me*." Her hair was wild in the damp breeze, but she didn't seem to care. She was shivering, but he didn't know if it was from cold or the feelings that were ripping through her. "You walked away, and I wanted to die. But you didn't care."

He opened his mouth to speak, but how could he defend himself when everything she said was true?

"But the worst thing is…"

He wasn't sure he could cope with anything worse than that. He'd persuaded himself at the time that he'd done it for her, but he'd been lying. Part of him wanted to shut down, bury himself in the emotional wasteland he'd so often used to get through the hard times.

He steeled his spine for the worst.

"Now I see you again, and already I can feel myself forgiving you. Forgiving everything you did. And I still don't really understand one hundred percent why you pressed the destruct button."

They reached the truck that Killion had lent them. Forgiveness didn't feel like the gift he'd hoped it would be. She opened the door, but he hesitated to get in. At the same time, no way would he leave her unprotected.

He climbed in. Handed her the blonde wig that lay across his seat. She stuffed it beside the gear stick.

"I'm not ready to go back to the condo yet, but I can drop you off." Tears glittered in her eyes.

He shook his head. He wasn't leaving her alone. "Are you okay to drive?"

She sniffed and wiped her nose with a tissue she had tucked into her sleeve. "I guess we'll find out."

She put the vehicle in drive. It was dark out. The moon and stars obliterated by heavy clouds that rolled overhead. The campus lights shone in the distance along with the lab and HRT and the Thunderdome. They headed off base, and she drove aimlessly down rural road after rural road, heading deeper into the boonies, turning onto land belonging to the Department of Natural Resources.

Cas wished he could think of something to say that might make her feel better. "It was never you."

She guffawed, but he leaned forward and tried to show her the truth in his eyes.

"It was always me." He had nothing left to lose by telling her the truth. Or most of it. The worst of it. "You know I grew up in the foster care system, but it's hard to explain how deeply that affects your psyche."

She was quiet now, and he could sense her listening to every word. He never talked about this. Not even to his friends. Not even to Seth Hopper, who'd also grown up an orphan and understood better than most. But Seth had been adopted into a loving family, and Cas never had. It made it worse somehow. To be the one not chosen. Like everyone was better than he was. Like he was defective.

He looked out into the dark void of the surrounding forest. Couldn't look at her as he spoke his truth. "I believed from a young age that there was something wrong with me and that was why my parents abandoned me. I believed that I didn't deserve to be loved. I wasn't good enough to be loved."

Her eyes shot to his, and he wasn't sure this was the best place to have this conversation when she was driving down a gravel road. But what the hell? He was ready to grab the wheel if he had to. The last thing he wanted was for her to be hurt.

"But I was smart and had really good grades, and I realized from a young age I got noticed when I did well in class. Noticed and praised and that was the closest feeling to love I'd ever experienced. That was the only time I received positive attention from adults, who expected a kid like me to be a dumbass useless piece of shit. You better believe I was the best goddamned student in Texas after that."

Anguish twisted her mouth, but that wasn't the sad part of his story.

"Eventually, I was placed with a foster family that believed in education and had gifted kids. I was finally able to stretch and grow."

He rubbed his hands together, the scrapes from yesterday now forming brown scabs that had begun to itch.

"When I was eight, my foster family had a relative come to live with them. The father's sister. She was probably mid-forties. She seemed nice at first, and she gave the family I lived with a break. They had three kids of their own and fostered me and another little girl called Fern. I was probably the happiest I'd ever been in my young life at this point."

He could see the dawning of what might have happened to a little boy who had had no one to look out for him. No one to protect him.

"Turns out she was a sexual predator. Of course, I didn't understand any of that back then. I was just a kid who lived to please the adults around him and who was too terrified to tell his foster parents what was being done to him when they weren't around. I started to withdraw into myself, and my grades began to slip."

He could see the sheen of cartilage beneath the skin of Delilah's knuckles as she gripped the wheel.

"One day Fern caught the woman on the bed with me and saw everything. She started screaming which woke the other kids. The woman"—he refused to say her name though it was etched like black rot on his soul—"she slapped Fern and called her a liar. Said that she'd misinterpreted her giving me an innocent kiss good-night. But she was already packing her bags and walking out the door by the time the parents arrived home. They were horrified. Devastated even. They reported it. They had to. Cops turned up. Social services. They questioned me, but I refused to talk. Fern and I were both removed from the home, but charges were never laid." Trees whizzed past but he wasn't seeing them, or the road, or Delilah. He was remembering the absolute sense of loss and abandonment of that time. "I learned later they adopted Fern back into their home."

The unfairness of it, all these years later hit him anew.

Delilah pulled over on the side of the road with a spray of grit.

He had no idea where they were, but there was no sign of anyone else nearby.

She reached out to grip his hand, and he held on tight.

Tears flooded his own eyes—a grown man of nearly 34, an elite tactical operator, bawling his eyes out because of something that had happened to him as a child.

"I decided fuck them. Fuck them all. I was in it for me only at this point. I changed schools. My grades went back up. I made friends but I didn't let anyone get real close, you know?" No one except her. "Then one day in eighth grade, we had a field trip to a Naval Base in Fort Worth. I saw a poster for the SEALs—an operator, geared up and sitting on the outside rails of a helicopter, looking like the coolest thing I'd ever seen—and this guy, some dumb fuck recruiting asshole who sat behind a desk all day, looked at me and said, SEALs were elite. Only a small number of men even got accepted into SEAL training let alone passed BUD/S and not to get my hopes up." Cas huffed out a watery breath and wiped his eyes. "'Not get my hopes up.' Man, what a thing to say to an abandoned, abused child." He shook his head and gave a humorless smile. "Well, I showed him. I couldn't control who loved me or wanted me, but I could control how hard I studied, and I could control my physical fitness, and I could apply to the fucking Navy if I wanted. I could be a goddamn Navy SEAL if I wanted. So that's how I ended up a straight-A student and star athlete of my high school. Focused on being the best at everything I could possibly master in an effort to prove everyone was wrong about me."

It sounded so pathetic and cliché to say it out loud.

"And I think when I met you everything between us was so perfect..." He closed his eyes at the memory of how good it had been to fully connect with someone possibly for the first time in his life. He opened his eyes and stared straight into hers. He touched her face. Cupped her cheek. "I loved you more than I'd ever loved anything—even more than I'd loved being part of that pseudo family who'd pretended to want me."

She sobbed then. Grabbed his wrist.

"Delilah, what we had was so very perfect I was absolutely terrified down to my marrow that it was going to crash around me in flames and you were going to leave me. Maybe not immediately, but eventually—or you were gonna die on me because you were so fucking fearless, and that would be my fault too. My bad luck would become your bad luck, and I couldn't face that either."

Her eyes shone like diamonds.

"I didn't believe someone as incredible as you would want someone as damaged as me. So I didn't tell you. I didn't tell anyone. I shut it down. I shut *us* down," he corrected, "so I didn't have to deal with the loss of you at some point in the future."

"Cas." Her voice cracked.

His throat squeezed tight. "The smartest kid in the class, dumb as a fucking rock. I was that little boy terrified of losing it all again. I'm so sorry I hurt you. I convinced myself you'd get over me pretty quick and move on. I had no idea about the miscarriage or the fact you almost died. I would have come to you if I'd known either of those things. I'd have thrown away my chance to get into HRT and come no matter what or who—"

She unclipped her seatbelt and tucked her legs under her as she turned toward him. It was dark, but he could see her features in the dashboard lights. Her eyes were bloodshot. Her hair was windblown and wild. She had never looked more heartbreakingly beautiful.

He turned away.

"Cas?"

His hands were fists on his knees. He braced himself for her sympathy. For her acknowledgment that he'd been right all along or that it was too late and none of it mattered anymore. They could move on now. At least he'd told her the truth. He wouldn't tell her about her father's stupid threats. He'd been a fool to let the man come between them, but that was the least of it.

She touched his shoulder.

"I don't want your pity. I never stopped loving you, but I was too much of a coward to tell you. Too much of a coward to stay. You're right that I deliberately used tactics I knew would keep you from coming after me." He smiled down at his lap then angled his head to look at her. "Pride is a deadly sin, you know."

"Oh, I know."

The grief in her voice shook him. That he'd joked about such a thing. "I'm sorry, Delilah. If I could go back and change things, I would. I'd—"

"Shut up and kiss me, you idiot." She took his hand and tugged.

His eyes went wide in surprise. "What?"

She grabbed the lapel of his suit jacket. "I said shut up and kiss me."

42

Delilah knew she was probably making a huge mistake, but she could no more stop than she could turn back time.

She had missed him. Missed his face, his smile, his touch. The way he'd tried to protect her even though he'd turned out to be the biggest danger she'd ever faced.

He released his seatbelt and knelt on the seat opposite, bending his head because he didn't fit in the cab. She raised her hand and ran her palm over the rough stubble of his jaw all the way up to his ear, sinking her fingers into his silky hair.

What that woman had done to him. What the family had done. It made her so angry on so many levels.

"Are you sure?" He sounded so uncertain.

Like it wasn't obvious she wanted, needed, him to kiss her. "Do I have to beg nowadays?"

His gold eyes flared in the dim light. "I'm the one who needs to beg. For a kiss, for scraps."

He rested his hand on her hip, and his fingers tightened, pulling her toward him. He lowered his mouth slowly, their eyes locked as if they were both terrified that if they looked away this would prove to be a dream.

But the scent of him. The feel of his firm lips against hers. The touch of those strong fingers gripping her to him as if he were afraid to let go. It all felt achingly familiar.

He was warm when she hadn't felt warm in years. She opened her mouth and invited him in. Tangling tongues, reawakening senses. Deepening the kiss, feeling her blood heat, her skin tingle, and her body flare to life.

She reached up and undid the top button of his shirt, then the next. He'd removed the tie earlier. She slid her hand inside the material and over the smooth muscles of his chest. Felt his heart pounding wildly beneath her palm.

Her fingers slipped to his belt buckle. He stopped her with his hand on hers and she stilled.

"You're sure about this?" His voice was a low growl and she could feel the emotions vibrating through him.

She held his gaze. Nodded. She was very sure. Because maybe the memories were wrong? Maybe what she thought it had been like was all in her imagination. But more than that, she just wanted to be with him again.

"Then let's take this to the back seat where we have a little more space."

Part of her wanted to make a joke to release the tension, but she couldn't speak, and she didn't want to ruin it. She climbed between the seats. Cas quickly drove the truck farther into the woods, then turned off the headlights and followed her into the shadows. They were deep in the forest. Hopefully alone.

He took off his jacket and hung it on the headrest of the front seat. She did the same and suddenly felt weirdly like she didn't know what to do anymore.

Maybe this was a mistake. Maybe—

"You're so beautiful." She heard him swallow.

She turned to make him out in the shadows. "You can't see me."

"I don't need to see you. You're seared on my brain like sunlight."

They were pretty words. He'd always been good with pretty words.

"I don't feel beautiful." She confessed. "I haven't felt beautiful since you left me."

He shifted. "I'll never forgive myself for what I did to you."

She found his eyes in the darkness. "I'll never forgive you either."

He froze.

"But I understand it better now. You were wrong to do what you did. You were totally wrong, but I understand a little more. I just wished you'd trusted me enough to have a conversation. This conversation."

He caught her hand and kissed her fingers one by one. "I do too. I was a coward."

Still, he didn't move toward her, and she bit her lip.

In the past he wouldn't have given her the breath to speak. When they'd been alone, they'd devoured each other without thought to the consequences. But he made no move to kiss her again, and she realized that perhaps he was here, doing this out of some sense of guilt or obligation...and that thought was unbearable.

A person could be beautiful without invoking passion.

"It's okay if you don't want me anymore, Cas." It would hurt, but it needed to be said. "It's okay if you no longer find me sexually attractive or just want—"

"Not find you sexually attractive?" His voice was a heavy rasp. "I think you are the most divine creature to have ever walked the earth. I think that one day God up in heaven looked down at this small, sniveling creature named Casta Demarco and thought, what else can I do to try to bring this human to his knees? Oh, yes, a woman. I will create someone he can barely look at without getting tongue-tied and aroused even when surrounded by people who will judge him for it. I will create someone who steals the very oxygen from any room she walks into. Who makes his mouth water and his hands shake with desire. Who makes him weak and vulnerable in every circumstance. I'll create this vision and let him fuck it up and make him think of her, regret the loss of her, every single day of his life. That should do it. That should finally be enough of a punishment for existing." His voice was thick with fear rather than sugar-coated with charm. "Now I'm too terrified to touch you because I don't want to hurt you. What if I screw it up again?"

"We can't screw this up more than we already did." She laughed a little. "There are no guarantees in life, Cas. Not for any of us. And us being here together now doesn't guarantee us a future. But, perhaps, we could enjoy the moment. Life is short. We were both supposed to die this week, remember?"

Her eyes had adjusted to the dark, and he looked terrified by the reminder.

"I want what we used to have. I want the passion. The fire. I'm not some fragile creature."

He shifted. "Lilah, you are the strongest person I ever met. I want you more with every breath and that doesn't seem possible."

The fact he called her Lilah, something he'd only ever done when they were intimate, gave her the courage he thought she possessed. She started undoing the buttons of her shirt. "Then prove it."

His eyes changed then. Gaze sharpening on hers. "You want me to prove how much I want you?"

"Yes. No. God, it sounds so stupid when you say it like that." She covered her face with her hands. "I'm no good at seduction. You have all the fancy words, and I just have these feelings inside, screaming to get out. I used to have words…" She'd lost her voice when she'd lost him.

"You don't need any words." He grabbed her hands in his. "I did this to you, Delilah—me, someone who knows how easily breakable we all are beneath the surface. I'm so sorry I hurt you, baby. You want me to show you how you make me feel? I can do that, but you must tell me if you change your mind or if I am too rough. Because I'm not sure I can go slow or be gentle."

"I don't need slow or gentle."

"I do." He moved her hands aside and began to undo the remaining buttons of her shirt, taking his time to slip each carefully free of its buttonhole. When he reached the last one, he spread the shirt wide and took her in. He traced a finger over the curve of her breast encased in a simple cotton bra.

"I have dreamed about these breasts."

Her nipples peaked against the fabric and he grazed his thumbnail gently over the tip of one.

"And these nipples. So pretty and pink." He pushed the cup down and moved his thumb back and forth over the tight flesh.

She shuddered.

He leaned back to remove his shirt and weapon and holster as she tugged off her shirt, her gun, and toed off her shoes.

She went to undo her pants but his hands stopped hers. "Let me."

She let him take over again, but it was awkward and cramped in the back seat, but that somehow seemed right. Being easy would be wrong. He pulled the material down her legs and over her ankles. Then he dragged her toward him so she was half lying down.

He pinned her hands and pressed them against her thighs as he eased her legs apart. She was still in her underwear but barely. She felt exposed. Vulnerable. Something she didn't allow herself to be with anyone else. Ever.

He kissed her stomach, her hip bones, and then lower, sliding his tongue down the side of her panties at the crease of her leg before letting go of her hands to pull the material aside.

He found her clit first, unerringly settling his mouth on that nub of flesh that sent wildfire blazing through her body.

Her head went back and a cry came out of her mouth. He put his hands under her ass and shifted her bodily toward him, pushing her thighs wider and sinking his tongue into her core.

She bucked and throbbed and couldn't breathe.

He jerked the material of her panties impatiently, and they

gave way with a ripping sound. His tongue worked her agonizingly slowly, cruising the folds of her vulva, devouring her until she shook. His hand pushed the cup of her bra up, his fingers finding her hard nipple and rolling it with the exact amount of pressure that sent waves shooting from her breast to her sex. His mouth sucked on her clit, never letting up, and then she was flying, trembling, flinging herself up and out into the darkness—and it was just like she remembered. The pleasure, the *euphoria*.

She wanted more. Her hands reached for his belt, and she quickly unbuckled it. He leaned back to get rid of his pants, and she unhooked her bra and tossed it into the front seat.

She sat up and straddled him, placing her hands on his shoulders.

"Oh, I have definitely dreamed about this." His hands skimmed her body, touching her breasts, her face, bringing her close enough to kiss her deeply, thoroughly.

His hands settled on the cheeks of her ass. "This ass might be my favorite part of you."

"You're an ass guy?" She chuckled. She hadn't expected that.

He squeezed and brought her forward so the center of her brushed against his erection. "Only this ass." He nuzzled her ear. "I don't have any protection on me, but I had the all-clear at my last physical. I haven't been with anyone since."

She nipped his jaw, grateful that he still thought to ask. It was a risk, but as she hadn't been with anyone in too many years to mention, it was a slim one. Cas wouldn't lie to her about this.

"We don't need a condom." Her body ached for him, and she didn't want to wait. If she waited, she might lose her nerve. She slid her hand down his hard length, skin as soft as silk over rigid flesh.

He groaned then squeezed her ass and brought her closer to him. "Don't tease me. Lilah. I can't take it."

His thighs widened and forced hers farther apart, bringing her down so her opening kissed the tip of his erection.

His fingers dug into her flesh, and she could feel a fine tremor moving through his entire body. Those unusual yellow eyes held hers. Then he gripped her knees and eased them slowly toward him, and she sank down, biting her lip at the exquisite sensation of being filled.

She started moving, watching him as she did so. Watching what she did to him.

He took her nipple into his mouth, shooting another wave that sparked through her body to her core. He started speaking to her in Spanish then, and she didn't know what he said, but it was sexy as hell.

He grabbed her hips, and he was thrusting up into her and hitting that spot that made her cry out again as another orgasm shot through her and exploded like fireworks inside her body. Cascade after cascade of pleasure rushed through her. And then he went taut beneath her, and he held her so tightly as he came inside her that she swore she'd have bruises tomorrow.

He exhaled and his muscles lost all their tension. He stared up at her, and she stared back.

The sex had been incredible—just as she'd remembered—but she wasn't sure it solved anything. Perhaps it didn't have to.

He hooked her hair behind her ear. "I'd like to do that again in a bed sometime soon."

She inhaled sharply as he rocked inside her. "How soon?"

43

Cas closed the door of Quentin Savage's townhouse and grabbed Delilah when she would have walked into the kitchen to find food. He pushed her against the wall. The only thing he was hungry for was her.

She wanted to know he still desired her.

How could she ever doubt it?

He pushed the blazer down over her shoulders but trapped her arms there. He ran his unshaven jaw over her neck and ear, feeling her tremble.

He tugged her shirt out of her waistband and undid the buttons one handed, still restraining her with the other hand. Then he unsnapped her jeans and slid the zipper down, easing his hand inside and between her legs to find her sweet heat.

Her head went back, and she bit her lip. He kept the rhythm, pressing the heel of his hand against her clit with every stroke, watching her face, searching for exactly what worked for her.

She started to cry out, but he didn't stop until she closed her eyes, head thrown back, breathing hard, her flesh spasming around his fingers. She slumped against the wall, but he wasn't done with her yet. She needed him to convince her he found her attractive? How long did he have? How often could he get inside her?

He took care of their weapons then pushed her shirt and jacket off her shoulders. Then stripped her jeans down her legs, dealing with her boots first. She stood there naked, and he was on his knees in front of her, exactly where he could spend his whole life.

He could see her expression as he leaned forward and slid his tongue over her clit. The scent of her invaded his senses. The taste of her dissolved on his tongue.

Her eyes heated, and she widened her legs in invitation. He accepted. It felt like it had before. Like the only thing that mattered was making her come as often and as hard as possible—and not dying.

He wasn't sure he could last long enough for her to come again, but he'd passed SEAL training and Hostage Rescue Team selection, so he knew how to set small goals to keep going when the mission seemed impossible.

She whimpered. She'd always been extremely responsive—same way he was extremely responsive to her. To her scent, her looks, her smart brain and terrifying bravery.

She grabbed his hair and twisted it half out of his scalp. That was good. Pain was an excellent distraction from the searing hunger that had built up over the past five years. Once hadn't been enough. A thousand times would never be enough.

"Cas."

That was it. That was all she said, but it told him everything as her body shook and trembled around him.

Before she could collapse in a boneless heap, he turned her around and undid his pants, widening her stance from behind and pulling her hips back just enough to slip inside. She groaned as he found her breasts. He moved into her. Over and over, his perfect fantasy, not because of her ass or her breasts, but because this was Delilah and he was touching her again. He was in her life, who knew for how long, but if it was sex she wanted, he would do his best to provide.

Being close to her healed him. Made him feel whole in a way his amazing careers never had. He loved being an operator. Loved the adrenaline rush of fast-roping onto a high-rise or hitting a target at a thousand meters. But that didn't touch the vulnerable places deep inside him.

She did.

He withdrew and spun her around. Needing to look into her eyes. He lifted her up, and she wrapped her legs around him, as he pressed her into the wall, cradling her fantastic ass as he slid deep inside, over and over again.

"I love you, Delilah. I have always loved you." She met every thrust, every challenge.

As he held her gaze, he felt his control start to slip. He wondered if she'd ever say it back or if he'd lost that precious gift forever. He would spend a lifetime trying to win her back if she'd let him.

He saw on her face that she was close again. "Go over. Go over for me one more time, Lilah."

Her hands strained against his shoulders as her body pulsed around his. And then he came in a rush of light that made him feel as if he might pass out. He leaned against the wall, cradling the love of his life in his arms and praying they both survived the coming storm.

44

"Want more?" Delilah asked him as he poured over the images of the people who'd visited Joseph Scanlon in prison.

He let his gaze drift suggestively down the oversized FBI T-shirt she'd borrowed from him as she stood barefoot in the kitchen stirring a saucepan of freshly made chicken noodle soup. He'd picked it up from the store yesterday, as he'd remembered she used to like it because she said it reminded her of her mother.

It reminded him of her—like a thousand other things, including his treasured bone-handled balisong now hidden in a drawer in his apartment. He couldn't even look at it without painful memories rising up inside him.

"Always." He thrust aside thoughts of the past and deepened his voice suggestively. "You think you can handle it?"

"Soup." She swatted his calf with a tea towel but blushed a little.

This was a side of her he'd never seen before. They'd never been domestic in their relationship. They'd never been relaxed. They'd been too on edge. Too busy worrying about not blowing their covers and being diced into a thousand pieces of vulture bait.

Even the thought of anyone hurting this woman terrified him, but she wasn't about to give up her badge unless she was given no other choice. Even if she wasn't an FBI Agent, he figured she'd be in law enforcement somehow. It was in her blood. Being a beat cop would probably be a lot more dangerous than working white collar crime for the FBI.

"No, thank you." He needed to reconcile the fact she was as entitled as he was when it came to pursing her career goals and facing danger. "Regarding soup, I'm completely satisfied."

She shot him a look.

He grinned and held up his hands in defense. "It's not my fault I can't get enough of you."

"Well. Your knee certainly seems better. That's for sure." She tried to suppress a smile as she ladled another scoop into her bowl and sat down opposite.

"I have remarkable powers of recovery." He couldn't wipe the grin off his face. He couldn't remember the last time he'd been this happy. It was scary, but he refused to think that way. Because if this was all he got, he was going to damn well enjoy it for a change.

"You, sir, are incorrigible."

"Deprived."

"Depraved."

"You ain't seen nothing yet," he teased.

Her eyes latched onto the images he was looking through. "Anyone stand out to you?"

He sobered at the reminder of why they were here. "A few faces look vaguely familiar but..." He stared at one woman who looked like someone he should know, but it must be a coincidence because he didn't recognize her or her name. "I don't think I know them. Yael offered to do a deep dive into their backgrounds?"

"Anyone we flag for her."

He nodded and began to sort through them again setting aside the people who he suspected Scanlon could have used to help him set up and execute this bold revenge plan, including the woman who looked vaguely familiar but wasn't.

Delilah finished her food and put her dishes into the dishwasher. Dealt with the pan on the stove. Four nights ago, he'd thought he'd lost her forever, and today he'd been able to get close enough to make love to her. He knew she wasn't where he was in terms of where they might go from this. She'd given him no words. Made no promises, but he could hardly expect them. Assuming they caught Scanlon and whoever was working with him, Delilah still lived and worked on the other side of the country. He didn't know how they'd navigate that, but he was willing to try to figure it out this time. If she was.

He sent a quick encrypted email to Yael with a list of ten names to start digging deeper into. Then he stood behind Delilah as she sat working on her laptop. He massaged her tense shoulders. Leaned down to nip the tight muscles on her neck. "Did I persuade you yet that I find you the most desirable woman on the planet?"

She leaned her head to one side. And hummed. "Not a hundred percent…"

He spun her around on the stool and lifted her into his arms. "Well, I need to work on that then."

She reached over to flip the laptop closed and then got the kitchen light on the way to the bedroom.

Later, when they lay in bed, sated and tangled up in each other, she rested her head against his heart, and he felt as if it might burst from joy.

She traced a finger in a circle over his skin. It tickled but he refused to move in case she stopped.

"Will I ever get my life back, do you think?"

He thought about her burned down home and the loss of her friend and her partner. The fact she'd pretended to be dead rather than trust her colleagues.

Going backwards wouldn't be easy, but this was Delilah, so anything was possible.

He squeezed her and kissed the top of her head but didn't give her any false promises. And maybe he didn't want her to go back to that life. Maybe he selfishly wanted her to begin a new one, with him in it.

She called me *first.*

Even after everything he'd done to her, she'd called him first.

It gave him hope.

45

I t was still dark when early the next morning Delilah paced the satellite offices of Cramer, Parker & Gray, feeling amazing on one level and useless on another. Alex Parker had called her to apologize for being up in DC, but as he'd told her from the get-go, he had his best friend's wedding to deal with this weekend, and he'd basically given Delilah full-time access to one of his best analyst/hackers, so she couldn't complain. Other people's lives didn't stop because hers had crashed to a halt—not that the past few days had felt static. In fact, the opposite was true. She'd never felt more alive than since she'd been dead.

She crossed her arms on a huff.

She didn't appreciate the fact that feeling collided with the exact length of time Demarco had been back in her life.

He said he loved her, but he'd told her that before. And he'd still broken her heart. She felt his sincerity in the moment, especially after he'd confessed the abuse that he'd suffered as a child. But she didn't know what it meant for the two of them. And, like she'd told him, maybe worrying about tomorrow was a fool's game. Until she proved Scanlon was behind this string of murders, there was no tomorrow. Not for her. She'd always be looking over her shoulder or waiting for a bullet she'd never see coming.

Yael sent her a look.

"Sorry." She stopped pacing. "I'm not good at doing nothing."

"I can tell. It must be difficult. I kind of get it, although I can always find something to entertain myself with online."

"I'm going crazy not being able to work on the task force or know what's happening." She shook her head at Yael's silent offer because it could get her into serious trouble if she was caught or if Delilah let something slip she wasn't supposed to know. "I need to *do* something." She flung out her arms. "That sonofabitch is walking around on parole while people die. Five people in one week, and we have nothing to prove he's behind any of it yet— which isn't a reflection on you." She paused to assure the other woman. "We don't even know how he's getting around the country. Oh…" She walked to where Yael sat working on three different monitors at the same time. "Could it be possible he's flying himself? I mean, he doesn't have to file a flight plan if he keeps it below a certain altitude, right?"

"I'm not sure, but I can check." Yael nodded.

"And a lot of those military special forces type learn to fly different kinds of aircraft."

"Shane was a Green Beret, and I know he can fly a Cessna and is considering learning to fly a helicopter." Yael agreed. "I'll start a search for any licenses or ownership of any aircraft in the Scanlon family."

Delilah nodded. "Thank you."

A pop-up on Yael's screen pinged.

"Interesting." The woman leaned closer. "I have an alert on the name Scanlon for anyone booking commercial flights or train or ferry tickets. One Melody Scanlon just bought a ticket for late this afternoon, traveling from SeaTac to New Orleans. Isn't that his kid?"

"Yeah, she's like seven." Delilah froze. "What about the mother or stepdad. Name is Zimmerman. Nicole and Preston Zimmerman?"

Yael typed and then shook her head. "One ticket. Booked as an unaccompanied minor."

"She's sending her kid to stay with a convicted felon she barely knows?" Delilah couldn't believe it. "Is she out of her mind?"

Yael's eyes were wide. "Do you think Scanlon would hurt the kid?"

Delilah pressed her lips together. She was scaring the other woman and that wasn't fair. "According to Lincoln Frazer, no. But he also called him a psychopath, and I don't think Frazer had him as the primary caregiver when he gave that profile about him not being a danger to his own child." She began pacing again. "I get that some parents have to send their kids off alone but dammit."

If they knew the predators that lived among them, they'd never let their kids out of their sight.

"What time does her flight leave?"

Yael checked the screen. "Four-thirty p.m. PT."

Delilah checked her watch. "I'm going to call Trainer and see if the local agents can talk to the mother ASAP. Persuade her to change her mind." Although that might enrage Scanlon. "Do you need me here?"

It was obvious she was doing nothing useful except make tea.

"Nope. I can call if I have any updates on the searches I've set up."

Delilah picked up her jacket. "You get anywhere with that prison visitor deep dive?"

Yael popped the last piece of a blueberry muffin into her mouth. "I sent the first couple to both your and Demarco's emails. Working on the rest now." She checked her own watch. "I'm heading up to DC after work tonight with Shane, assuming he doesn't get called out on an op. We were going to make a weekend out of it as the wedding is on Sunday. But if you want me to stay here and work on this—"

The offer hit Delilah like a glancing blow to the nose and drew tears to her eyes. "No. Thank you. No." Not that it was up to her. She wasn't the boss. Yael was helping her out, and she was very grateful. "I assume if Joseph is planning to spend time with his kid, then he won't be busy killing people. You take the weekend with that man of yours. Make sure he spoils you."

Yael grinned. "You look happier today."

Delilah rolled her eyes. "That obvious, huh?"

Yael lifted her shoulders in a self-conscious shrug. "I recognize the glow. I hope he groveled appropriately."

Delilah thought of his words and actions from last night. "He did." She paused as she headed toward the door. "I honestly don't know if it'll be enough. Not because I don't care for him..." Her eyes went to the other woman. "Last time we broke up, it was the worst thing I've ever experienced, and I honestly thought I was going to die from grief, from the miscarriage, from losing him, losing my womb. It's all tangled up together inside like barbed wire, and I don't know if I can take that again."

Could they make it work this time when they'd failed so miserably in the past?

"I saw how he looked at you yesterday. I haven't ever seen him look at anyone like that. I asked Shane if Cas had been involved with anyone since he knew him, and he said no. He dated occasionally, but his heart wasn't in it."

Delilah smoothed her thumb over the key fob to the truck Killion had lent her. "I'm scared to get involved with him again."

"I can understand that." Yael pressed her lips together in a sympathetic line. "But it seems to me you already are."

———

Delilah went outside into the secure lot and climbed into the massive truck. She tried Nicole Zimmerman's home number first, but the phone rang without answer. She didn't know her cell number. She tried Greg Trainer's cell, but he didn't pick up. She tried him again, and the call answered but was immediately cut off.

Aghast, she stared at the screen for a full three seconds. He'd

TONI ANDERSON

hung up on her. She called him again because, dammit, this was important.

"Do you know what time this is?" He sounded as if he were growling through clenched teeth.

Had she woken him?

"This had better be good, Agent Quinn."

"I wanted to make sure you have agents talking to Scanlon's ex because—"

"I put in the request with the local SAC."

"But when for? Her kid is sched—"

"I *said* I dealt with it," he snapped. "You need to stop interfering with this investigation. I know your father used to be a big deal in the Bureau, but, trust me, he's not anymore. And *you* certainly are not."

He hung up again, and she couldn't decide if she was more humiliated or more furious. Probably a draw.

Goosebumps stole over her flesh even as she huddled inside her jacket. She thought about calling Cas, but he had his own job to do. She settled on Killion instead.

"BFJ Inc., how can I help you today?"

"BFJ Inc.?"

"Bad Frog Jokes. You had to be there. How can I help you, D?"

"Scanlon's kid is booked on a flight to New Orleans tonight. Unaccompanied minor."

"Shit."

So it wasn't just her. "I want to go out to Seattle. Talk to the mother. Persuade her it's a bad idea."

"No."

"Technically, I don't need your permission."

"What did Trainer say?"

Delilah gritted her teeth. "ASAC Trainer didn't even let me tell him about the kid being on the flight before he told me to butt out."

"Yeah, I thought so."

"He says that he put in a request for agents to contact the ex, but that could take a few days by which time the kid is already in danger."

"It's a bad idea."

"All it would take is a quick conversation. I can be back here by midnight. Trainer doesn't even need to know. It's not like I'm doing anything useful."

"What about Demarco?"

"What about him?"

"You telling him about this or going off on your own?"

"I'm simply going to meet Scanlon's ex. I'll talk to her, turn around, and get on the return flight home a couple of hours later."

"So you're going on your own."

Delilah wanted to scream in frustration. "I'm an FBI agent with seven years' experience, not some innocent civilian who needs someone else's protection."

"You go rogue now, you'll lose your career."

"I am *not* going rogue. And while I don't want to lose my career, I can't sit around doing nothing while I have a hope of talking Nicole out of sending her child to spend time with a man I believe has murdered five people in the past week. The worst that could happen is I spend the day on an airplane. At least I should be safe."

Killion released a heavy breath. "Look, I get it. I wish I could come with you, but I can't leave Audrey right now."

Emotion swamped her at that. At least she hadn't been totally abandoned by her friends.

"I'll call the airline and find you the next flight out as an undercover air marshal so you can keep your weapon. Go grab what you need, and I'll call you back in ten minutes with the airport and flight information. Use the false identity I gave you."

Satisfaction filled her. "Thank you."

He grunted. "Yeah, let's see if you thank me later."

46

C as was on the gun range when his cell vibrated in his pocket. He set down his long gun and moved away to call Killion back.

"How soon can you get to Dulles?"

Cas looked up at the lights of a commercial aircraft as it cruised high overhead leaving chem trails in the dawn sky. "Why?"

"Delilah is booked on a flight to SeaTac in two hours."

"Dammit." Emotions rushed through Cas. "Give me a second to collect my weapon, and fill me in as I head back to the compound."

———

Cas gained a grim satisfaction from being the last person on board the flight which Killion had had held for him. He'd grabbed a go-bag from work, rushed out of the HRT compound, and borrowed a work vehicle, saying he had to go to Washington for the case. He hadn't specified *which* Washington. The fact he'd lied to his bosses, his friends, sent a burning fire of regret through his system.

Hopefully, they never found out. If they did, he might lose his job. He would definitely be disciplined.

And still he couldn't regret his decision as he slid in beside this woman who never stopped challenging him. "Going somewhere?"

Her lips thinned. "Killion called you."

The words lit a fuse inside him. "The question is why didn't you?"

Her eyes sparked with anger, but she kept her voice to a quiet murmur as the cabin crew prepared for takeoff. "I'm a trained professional going to talk to a witness. And we both know the danger is currently in Louisiana."

Cas glanced at the young woman in the window seat who wore earbuds and had her eyes closed as she leaned against the fuselage.

He kept his voice so low Delilah had to lean toward him to hear. "We don't know for sure that's where *it* is. And," he interrupted as she opened her mouth to argue, "it seems obvious to me that he isn't working alone. What did Trainer say when you told him where you were going?"

"He told me he requested that local agents go talk to the ex, but even if they speak to her today, they don't know what we know. Only the taskforce does, and I don't think they're even totally on board that Scanlon is the killer." She held his gaze, her rich brown eyes earnest. "Trainer cut me off before I could tell him about the kid."

"So you took it upon yourself—"

"I already lost my best friend and a dear colleague," she shot back quietly. "I can't risk an innocent child dying too."

"What about your career? Doesn't that mean anything to you?"

Her stare turned stony. "My career is pretty much the only thing I have left in my life that I value, but I'm not sacrificing a seven-year-old girl for it."

Her words sliced deep. No. She wouldn't. Her bravery was one of the reasons he loved her, it was her recklessness that kept him up at night.

"Look, I know it doesn't make total sense to be the one who

talks to her, but no one else seems to be taking the danger seriously." She softened her tone. Touched his leg. "I appreciate the backup. I'm surprised your bosses allowed you to go so far from base."

Cas grunted as he pulled out his laptop as they'd reached cruising altitude. "I'm going to dive deeper into those background files Yael sent. Killion arranged a car for us at the other end."

"He's a good person."

"Don't tell anyone. He'll be mad if we ruin his image."

She smiled, and he felt something inside him ease. There was every chance being with Delilah when he should have been at Quantico would cost him his career, the reason he'd told himself he was leaving her five years ago.

And yet, there was no other choice he could make under the circumstances and nowhere he'd rather be.

47

C as drove, and Delilah took shotgun.

They'd arrived at SeaTac early but had had to wait for his bags, which included his weapons, to be offloaded. Cas refused to go anywhere without his equipment. That way if HRT did get a call out, he could still turn up prepared. Birdman and Sebastian Black would bring anything he forgot—assuming Payne Novak didn't cut him from the team.

It was a 25-minute drive to the Alki Beach area where Nicole and Preston Zimmerman lived with Nicole's daughter Melody. Thankfully, the time difference meant it was only two-thirty in the afternoon. Their return flight was scheduled for 5:10 p.m.

He couldn't afford to miss it.

He forced the anxiety about what would happen if his bosses found out about his little field excursion from his mind.

He was here now. With Delilah.

"You sure you don't want to wait in the car like the director wants you to?" he asked Delilah as he turned into the neighborhood where the Zimmermans lived.

"The director said no one was supposed to know I was still alive, not that I am under house arrest. Nicole won't recognize me." Delilah reached into her bag and pulled out a short, poorly cut, mouse-brown wig that presumably Alex Parker had provided her with and a pair of thick-framed reading glasses she'd picked up on the way through the airport.

She spent a moment fitting the wig and then slid the glasses up her nose. She added a wad of cotton inside each cheek. She wore the Navy blazer and a black turtleneck. Black pants and boots.

"What do you think?" Her voice sounded different.

She looked beautiful. She always looked beautiful. But she didn't look like Lacey Reed or Delilah Quinn.

"I'd be surprised if she made the connection."

They pulled up at a large modern-looking, gray-painted, single-family home with a double garage at the front. It was close to the Sound but too far away for a decent view of the ocean. The shrubs were all huddled neatly down for winter and rain dripped off the tree branches, which overhung the driveway.

He glanced around. It was a nice place, surrounded by lush greenery, but cold dampness clung to his skin, just like Virginia. He missed winter in Texas, but the summers were like living in a clothes dryer.

He could see a vehicle in the rearview on the next block over. Exhaust was running, so someone was in it. He adjusted his side mirror to get a closer look, but the person drove away.

He pushed open the door and led the way. There was no reason to think Nicole knew what he looked like, so they'd agreed he'd take point, as his FBI creds were legit should Nicole decide to question his identity. Of course, if she did so, then there'd be no way of hiding the fact he was standing in a Seattle neighborhood rather than in DC.

The doorbell echoed, and he could see through the clear glass at the side of the front door—attractive but a terrible security feature. Suitcases were packed in the hallway. They both held up their creds as they heard someone approaching.

The door opened to a woman he recognized from the trial. She blinked at him in confusion. She was on the phone.

"Someone is at the door, Mom. Yes, I'll remember sunscreen.

Melody will be fine. I mean, you're the one who told me a child needs a father. I have to go. I'll pick you up in forty-five minutes." She hung up on her mother and planted a fist on her hip. "What does the FBI want now?"

The hostility was clear.

"We wanted to talk to you for a moment about your ex-husband. Do you mind if we come in for a few minutes?" asked Cas.

She huffed a breath, and then her eyes swept the neighbors as if someone might be watching. "Like I have a choice. Come in. Take your shoes off." She headed back into the house, and they followed her into a brightly lit space that was open-plan kitchen, dining, and living room. The windows were huge, but the tall conifers edging the property provided plenty of privacy.

"You're going on a trip?"

Nicole Zimmerman wore yoga pants over a distended belly and a pretty blouse. Her hair was up in a loose ponytail, and her makeup was perfect. "A quick trip to Hawaii while I'm still able to fly."

Cas's mood sank. "May I ask if you have had any contact with your ex since he was released?"

"Why? What are the FBI trying to pin on him this time?"

Murder, attempted murder with a weapon of mass destruction, conspiracy to murder. "Nothing, but we are concerned with some incidents that raise a few questions."

"What incidents?" She pulled a crystal glass out of the mahogany cabinet and filled it with water out of the refrigerator door.

"You have a beautiful home," Delilah admired.

A look of pleasure filled Nicole's eyes. "Thank you."

"When is your baby due?"

Her hand went protectively over the bump. "May 15."

Cas glanced at Delilah, but there was nothing in her expression to give away any hurt she might feel when looking at a pregnant woman, knowing that was something she'd never experience.

Maybe she was okay with that. Maybe she didn't want kids. He frowned. Maybe he was the one with the hangups about children.

He got back to why he was here. "Are you aware that several of the people who were part of the case against your husband have recently died under suspicious circumstances?"

Nicole's eyes crinkled. "I wasn't, but if you had any proof Joseph was involved, you'd already have arrested him."

"It's early days in the investigation," he said quietly. "We understand he met your daughter on Tuesday."

"Yes. It went well apparently." She sipped the water and then wiped the corners of her lips.

"That was the first time he'd met her since his conviction?"

Nicole nodded. "I moved away after he went to prison. I grew up around here, and my mom lives about five miles away. She helped me with Melody when she was little. Joseph wanted me to bring Melody to the prison to visit, but it was such a horrible place I didn't want to expose her to that."

"So you came here and then met your second husband?"

"Yes." She nodded again. "We both went to the same high school, although we didn't really know each other back then."

"Do you mind if I ask if you were ever scared of your ex-husband, Nicole? Do you mind if I call you Nicole?" asked Delilah.

Nicole placed her glass on the counter, her fingers squeezed around it. "He could be pretty intense and had a temper if I didn't do what he wanted, but he never physically abused me."

As long as she behaved?

"Did he scare you?"

Nicole's eyes flashed before she looked away. "Like I said, he was an intense guy. All those guys were."

Cas felt the brush of the glance Delilah sent him. He'd been guilty back in the day. He liked to think he'd mellowed over the years.

"Is Melody desperate to reestablish a relationship with her daddy?"

Nicole pulled a face. "I wouldn't call her desperate, but it's important she gets to know him and his family. She's spending spring break down in Louisiana."

Cas wondered whose idea this really was and felt for the little girl. Perhaps Preston didn't want another man's kid around, reminding him constantly that his wife had been married before. "I'm sure it will be a good opportunity for you and your new husband to spend quality time together before the baby is born."

Nicole's gaze swung to him, and her eyes started to narrow in annoyance.

"I'm sure you would do everything you can to protect your children," Delilah inserted herself. "The FBI is genuinely concerned that Joseph Scanlon or his brother was involved in the murder of one of the FBI agents involved in the case against him—"

"That slut down in San Diego? I heard she died in a house fire."

Delilah flinched.

Cas clenched his fists.

"The admiral who stripped him of his trident was also murdered along with his wife yesterday morning."

Nicole shivered and hugged herself, a worried expression crossing her features. "I spoke to Joseph yesterday on a video call. He was at work in the garage in LaCroix. Are you saying he killed this admiral?"

"No, ma'am." Cas wished they had the evidence they needed to prove Joseph was involved when the guy was laying down all of his alibis with neatly slotted precision. "But it's possible he's working with someone—"

She threw up her hands. "So you have nothing. No evidence. Just a hunch that he might be involved in something whereas it could have been anyone. The FBI has a grudge against Joseph. He did his time. Paid his debt to society. Seems to me I'm the one who should hold the biggest grudge, but I've found it in my heart to forgive and move on."

How very gracious of her.

"Did you ever suspect him of any wrongdoing when the two of you were married?" asked Delilah.

Nicole crossed her arms. "Are you trying to implicate me now?"

"No, ma'am," Delilah assured her. "I'm suggesting that perhaps you're not that great at reading your ex, who is an expert manipulator."

Nicole's eyes bugged. "Wow. You came all this way to tell me I'm a lousy judge of character? Like I don't know that? He humiliated me in that courtroom. I stood by him, and then they played that video…I wanted to die from shame."

"I'm saying that perhaps he's still tricking you and maybe it would be worth waiting a little longer before Melody spends time alone with him…" Delilah was clearly searching for the right words, but Cas figured it was a hopeless cause. The woman had plans and obviously didn't want to change them without concrete proof her kid was in danger.

"Mrs. Zimmerman, I beg you—"

"Enough. I don't need you to tell me how to parent. You can both leave now." She held her arms out wide and herded them along like stray cows. "Out. We have to get to the airport. Melody," the woman shouted up the stairs and the sound of feet pounded down toward them.

A girl wearing deep pink leggings and a white top with sequins hesitated on the first landing, staring at them, a giant pink teddy bear clutched under one arm. Her sandy hair and blue eyes were identical to her father's.

Nicole opened a closet door and pulled out coats and boots. "Here, put this on."

"I don't want to go to Weisiana!"

Frustrated, Nicole shot them a glare. "You enjoyed spending time with your father on Tuesday, didn't you?"

The kid nodded reluctantly.

"He bought you that teddy and ice cream."

The bottom lip stuck out. Words mumbled. "I wanna stay with you and Papa."

"Papa and I are going away on a short break. You're going to meet the rest of your family."

No wonder the kid was confused.

"I wanna come with you!" The girl stamped her feet and looked furious.

When Cas had been her age, he'd have given anything to belong to a family, any family, but all too often it wasn't as wonderful as his young mind had envisioned.

Little Melody knew she was surplus to requirements and was soon going to be replaced with a younger model. Her survival instincts were screaming, but not because she was in fear of her father. She was terrified of losing her mother.

Cas leaned down and admired the girl's bright pink roller case with a unicorn on the front. "Is this your case? I love the horse."

"It's a unicorn."

"No kidding."

She nodded reluctantly. Then she started sniffling, but Nicole held up her hand in a silent signal that suggested her patience was at an end.

"We have to go now, or we'll be late. We have to pick up Grandma, and she's going to take you through to the gate. Get your coat on." She picked up her own jacket. "Everything you need is in your case. The flight attendant will help you put it on and take it off the luggage rack. You have your phone so you can text me when you arrive, a tablet for reading and watching movies, and coloring books plus something to eat on the journey in your backpack. You like flying, remember?" Nicole coaxed.

Melody shook her head vigorously.

Sympathy rose inside Cas, a desire to calm the kid. Because whether he and Delilah liked it, short of kidnapping Melody Scanlon, there wasn't much they could do to prevent her seeing her father. Frazer had said he didn't think Scanlon would harm the child. They had to hold onto that.

"Would you like me to put your luggage in the trunk of your car for you, Mrs. Zimmerman?"

Delilah's brows rose, but he could hardly watch a pregnant woman struggle with a heavy load, especially when she was already dealing with an understandably recalcitrant kid.

Nicole looked surprised. "Sure. Thanks."

They slipped their shoes on as she opened an interior door to the garage. There sat a Lexus RX and a fully electric Prius. "Melody. In." She popped the trunk on the Lexus, and Cas put both their suitcases and bags into the rear compartment. The kid climbed into the backseat with a mutinous expression.

"Thank you." Nicole opened the garage door. "You can leave through this way."

Delilah looked torn.

"I appreciate the concern, but Melody is going to be fine," she said firmly. "Next time call before you visit."

"Could we get your cell number?" he asked.

She gave it to them, and Delilah typed it into her phone.

"Have a nice vacation." Cas followed Delilah back to the rental car, wishing he believed the kid would be safe with a man who'd tried to blow him up two days ago.

48

Nicole felt frazzled and irritated as she pulled into traffic after dropping Melody at the gate with her mother, who would accompany her all the way to the aircraft. Someone on the other side would make sure she got to her father. She was no more unsupervised than when she went to school. Less so, considering the number of kids in each class.

Thanks to those FBI agents, Melody had kicked up a fuss and acted like she was on her way to her own execution.

At a red light, Nicole opened the center console and searched for some headache pills. Preston didn't like her taking medication while she was pregnant, but he wasn't the one in pain and what he didn't know wouldn't hurt him.

She hadn't figured out how to tell him she wouldn't be having a natural birth. She knew what childbirth felt like and had no intention of going through that without drugs. Coming up empty she dragged her purse onto her lap and dug around, closed her fingers around a bottle of Tylenol and thumbed the cap open.

She dry swallowed two tablets as the light changed.

She cursed the fact she'd left her travel mug at home because she'd been put off her game by the fact the Federal Bureau of Investigation had arrived on her doorstep.

That reminded her…

She called Joseph. It went to voicemail, which irritated her. He better get used to taking her calls if they were going to coparent.

"Calling to say Melody is at the airport, and you have her flight number. Call me as soon as she lands and you have her in your care. She has to text me every day, assuming you want this to become a regular occurrence." She sounded bitchy but whatever. This guy had cheated on her and then run drugs across the border. He'd destroyed their life together, not her.

She hesitated. "The FBI came to see me today. I hope for your sake they're mistaken about everything they think you've done." Distance made her brave enough to add, "Don't do anything stupid, Joseph."

Her fingers clamped around the steering wheel as she maneuvered through busy traffic onto I-5 N toward Harborview Medical Center where Preston worked as an administrator. It began to rain, and she turned on the wipers. Nicole felt sweaty and sticky and gross. Not how she wanted to greet her husband or start her vacation.

Why had the FBI ambushed her like that? Did they enjoy scaring the hell out of a pregnant woman? Or making her feel guilty for being a bad parent? Like either of those agents appreciated how difficult it was to raise a child? They'd made her feel like the criminal.

Even before Joseph had been arrested, he'd often been deployed. Military spouses deserved medals for being single parents, not to mention their own pension—although Joseph had lost all that after his conviction.

She bit her lip. Could he be behind these deaths? Had she made a terrible error in judgment letting Melody stay with him?

She'd lied to the FBI about Joseph scaring her, but prison had changed him. Humbled him. She could tell he was sincere in his desire to reconnect with his daughter.

It was Virgil who really frightened her.

She shuddered. The way he used to watch her, even with Joseph right there…

He gave her the creeps but Joseph had said his brother wasn't around that much, and he would surely protect his daughter from his brother.

Of course, he would.

Not that Virgil had ever tried to hurt her or behaved inappropriately. Staring wasn't a crime.

She got off on James Street and turned right on 9th. Another car followed her, probably heading to the emergency room.

Preston had an assigned space, so she pulled into it. He'd taken an Uber to work that morning, so they didn't have to leave both vehicles at the airport. It was dark now. She hoped she wasn't underdressed. He'd told her casual, but perhaps this was too casual?

She'd grab her long cardigan out of the case and dress the outfit up if needed.

She was excited to have a week in Hawaii where they could relax on the beach and enjoy some them time. Once this baby came along, things would be chaotic for a while. She doubted Preston would be any more hands-on than Joseph had been. What was it about men who prided themselves on being all the things that they couldn't even change a diaper?

She texted him that she was here and sat with the engine idling, even though Preston didn't like to pollute the atmosphere more than they had to. But she was cold. She huddled her shoulders on a shiver. Made her wonder why he didn't drive the Prius all the time, rather than her.

She shouldn't complain. He was a good husband who didn't go off for months at a time nor trick out the vehicles with bricks of cocaine—at least, she hoped not.

This was a busy spot. People going in and out of the hospital as the shifts changed over.

Preston texted that he was on his way down. She fixed her makeup, then got out, opening the cargo space and carefully easing her long gray cashmere coatigan out of her bag before zipping it closed again. She shrugged into the sleeves and then dashed around to the passenger side.

Preston liked to drive, and she honestly didn't mind avoiding Seattle traffic. She got in and, after a moment, turned off the engine.

She reapplied her lipstick in the vanity mirror and twisted to smile when he opened the driver's door.

Except it wasn't Preston. Someone she'd never seen before stood there wearing a black slicker with the hood pulled low over their face, aiming a long black pistol at her.

She opened her mouth to scream but no sound came out. They fired twice, each shot punching into her body, the noise making her flinch, although it didn't hurt. Not at first. Then the shock died away, and pain set in, slicing through her and lancing her with streaks of red-hot fire.

The person was gone before she could react. They closed the door, and she slumped back as the interior lights slowly faded.

The baby. Oh, my God. The baby.

Her hands searched for the wounds and pressed against the warm flow of blood. The lights of the hospital mocked her. Blood pumped out of her wounds, and she could feel herself fading too.

49

It was Murphy's Law that they'd ended up at the gate next to the one Melody Scanlon was flying out of, and that her flight was delayed. They'd separated as soon as they'd spotted the issue. Cas headed to a bar that overlooked the general area. Delilah nursed a coffee at the gate. She'd removed her wig and blazer before they'd gone through security.

Delilah caught the kid staring at her once and had forced herself not to smile or interact even though that was her instinct. The older woman beside her must be Nicole's mother. Grandma was reading the kid a book as she clutched the teddy to her chest.

After Melody's flight boarded and Grandma hurried away, Cas came over and sat next to her. He took her hand in his. Kissed her knuckles.

"She'll be okay."

"I hope so." Delilah swung to face him. She couldn't dwell on it. Not anymore. She'd done her best to get Nicole to change her mind, but it hadn't worked. "Any news on Holtz?"

Cas shook his head. "Not that I've heard."

Nothing was going the way they wanted it to.

His cell rang, and she watched him grimace before he

answered it. "I have to take this." He fished earbuds out of his pocket and slipped one in before answering. "What's up, boss?"

There was a short pause. "No, immediate updates. Nope. Pretty much status quo as this morning. Still waiting for the data searches to come up with something to place suspects near the murders and bombing. Awaiting DNA back on the Clarence Carpenter murder and anything they got off the IED. The Scanlon kid is on a flight to New Orleans to visit her dear old daddy. I assume that means Scanlon will stay put in his hometown for a few days, which is good news."

He covered his earbud and winced when the gate agent started the boarding process. Delilah saw him flick on the mute button until he spoke again.

"If you want me to come in to debrief, I can make it in about 90 minutes." He pressed mute again as whoever was on the other end of the call replied. "OK. Cool. I'll be in tomorrow. Oh, yeah, you're off to the wedding this weekend. I forgot. Have a good time. I'll call you if there are any developments."

Delilah felt her eyes getting wider and wider, but she held her tongue until he ended the call.

He took the earbud out of his ear and slipped it into the case in his pocket. "What?" he said without meeting her gaze.

"You said your boss gave you permission."

"No, I didn't."

"You let me assume…"

The gate agent was calling for every zone, and the gate was almost empty now.

Still, she stopped him joining the end of the line by catching his arm. "You risked your job to be here today." She wasn't sure how to feel about that. "This job means everything to you."

He gave her a soft, sad smile as they both stood. He cupped her face. "Not everything. You are not the only one willing to sacrifice the job for someone they love."

She followed him onboard unable to speak.

50

J oseph was leaving his meeting with his parole officer when his burner rang.

"It's done."

"Both packages?" Joseph glanced at his brother who was driving. They'd been sure to be seen in Thibodaux, even hitting the coffeeshop and flirting with a pretty little creole barista and her friend.

"Not both."

Fuck.

Virgil sent him a look and Joseph shook his head. "The deal was both."

"I'm not the only one who has failed to live up to the *deal,* partner."

They had to be careful what they said even on a burner phone. Neither trusted the other not to record it amongst other things.

Joseph growled at the censure. "A minor delay."

"Perhaps. But the second package is of no consequence. The location was busy, and I had to get it done before they headed off into the sunset. You're the one who initiated the timetable."

"Fine. Whatever." Joseph would deal with the motherfucker some other time. Maybe a couple of years down the line. When

Preston Zimmerman had relaxed and forgotten all about Joseph and the fact he'd stolen his wife. He wondered if the guy would fight for custody of his stepdaughter. If he did, Preston was going to meet his maker a hell of a lot sooner.

"I saw him, you know."

Scanlon froze. Questions tumbled through his brain, all too dangerous to ask.

"He was at the house before she left for the airport."

The fuck? "Did he see you?"

"No. I left as soon as they arrived."

"They?"

"Some other agent. At first, I thought it was her…"

"She's dead." Even if he never got Demarco, killing that bitch had been satisfying as hell.

"Yeah. This one wasn't as pretty." His partner in crime huffed out a breath. "When will you fulfill your end of the bargain?"

"Soon."

"When?"

"I said soon." *Motherfucker.* He didn't like to be questioned, but he couldn't upset this person. He rubbed his hand over his face. "The law will be all over me for the next few days. You know that. As soon as they verify my alibi, I'll plan the next move."

"Maybe I'll do it myself."

"You do and you'll be looking over your shoulder for the rest of your life." He wasn't giving up Casta Demarco. He wanted to watch him bleed out. Spill every drop into the dirt where he belonged. Prove which one of them was the better sniper, the better SEAL, the better man. "I'll live up to my part of the bargain. Now get off the phone and get rid of this burner. Switch to the next one. Can't risk anyone connecting the two of us. Not now. Not ever."

Joseph rolled down his window and tossed the cell into the depths of the bayou.

51

They drove back to Quentin Savage's townhouse in separate vehicles. She could see Cas's headlights as he followed her.

At the complex, she pulled on the long blonde wig and dashed through the incessant rain that seemed to have followed them from one coast to the other. She was getting heartily sick of the disguises and subterfuge, not to mention the weather. She wanted to bring Scanlon in for questioning or at least knock him off his game by confronting him and seeing what he did when he saw her alive. Force him to make a mistake.

But tugging a tiger's tail when they still didn't have any proof was a bad idea, especially when his seven-year-old daughter was the person who might be on the receiving end of any retaliation.

It was well after midnight as they headed inside the door.

They tossed their bags in the entranceway and closed the door on the wet night. Cas grabbed her hand and spun her up against the wall. Then he lowered his mouth slowly to hers, and she melted on impact.

His hands were undoing the buttons on her shirt when her cell rang.

She pulled away reluctantly. "I have to get that."

"Let them call back."

She laughed and considered it for a second. Then she dug into her pocket, and Cas rested his forehead against the wall and cursed in Spanish.

"It's Yael. Let me quickly see what she wants. Hello?"

"Delilah? Are you okay?"

"Yes, I'm fine. Why?"

"You haven't heard?"

At the other woman's tone Delilah straightened away from the wall. Cas watched her like a sparrowhawk. "Heard what?"

"Nicole Zimmerman was shot to death outside the hospital where her husband worked."

Delilah reached out for the wall and found herself being supported by Cas's strong arms. He maneuvered them to the couch, and she put the call on speaker. "When?"

"Around five. I know you were out there. I saw your cell signal data. What happened?"

Delilah looked at Cas, whose yellow eyes were shining with concern.

How she'd missed him.

"I went out there to try to talk her out of sending her daughter to Louisiana because I thought the kid might be in danger. I never imagined—" She covered her mouth as the horror of what had happened swept over her. "She was pregnant."

"I know." Yael sounded shocked.

"What about the husband?"

"He found her. Rushed her into the ER, which was only feet away, but it was already too late. What did she say to you?"

"She seemed to think we were overreacting, but we should have been more forceful. She didn't think Scanlon was a genuine threat. She was looking forward to her Hawaiian vacation too much to even stop and contemplate she might be in danger." Delilah squeezed her eyes shut.

"There's a task force meeting at 9 a.m. at SIOC to discuss this latest development."

She opened her eyes at that. "What about the little girl? A lot can happen overnight." Delilah could hear the noises of what sounded like a TV in the background of the call.

"We can't do anything about the kid. I have both Scanlon brothers on video at the airport picking her up when she arrived. He had a meeting with his parole officer before then, and his brother was with him the whole time. All very public and on camera in several places. I believe local cops plan to inform him about his ex-wife's death first thing in the morning."

"That sonofabitch is already well aware." Delilah knew it was him. Knew it as surely as she knew the color of Cas's unusual yellow eyes. "He set this up. He's collaborating with someone—"

"I agree. I'm working on it, I promise."

"I know, and I'm sorry." She cradled her forehead. "You should be enjoying your weekend."

"So should you. I'll call you in the morning. Alex wants me at the meeting as I'm in DC anyway."

"What about me?"

There were a few seconds of awkward silence. "Trainer didn't mention you. Right now, he doesn't know where you were today. Nor Demarco. You should both try to keep it that way."

Delilah sighed, her frustration audible.

"I'll keep you in the loop. You just promise me you won't do anything stupid."

"Define stupid?"

"You know exactly what I mean. Oh, one thing. Scanlon's brother has a pilot's license like you suspected. The family business has a Cessna 414A registered to it, but the plane didn't go out yesterday. I checked. I am looking into where it's been flown recently, but records aren't centralized. Shane thinks Scanlon could easily have learned to fly a plane like that in the Navy. Alex had me try to hack his Naval records, but I haven't managed yet."

"Don't we have access to them?"

"That's not the point," Yael said wryly.

It was scary how this group operated. Thank goodness they were on her side.

"Joseph has groomed his brother to be the perfect replica so that when he got out, he could easily move around while pretending to be Virgil."

"An identical twin would be a useful commodity for most would-be criminals," Yael agreed. There was a murmur of conversation in the background. "Shane says tell Demarco 'Hi' by the way."

"Tell Shane Demarco says he better treat you like a princess."

"Ha. Well, this princess needs some beauty sleep, which are not words I have ever uttered at this time of night before but, you know, coffee deprivation."

"Thanks again for the call."

"You betcha."

Yael hung up, and Delilah collapsed over her thighs, holding back tears. Nicole Zimmerman hadn't been a fan of hers and hadn't expressed a lot of empathy at her supposed death, but it didn't change the fact that Nicole shouldn't have died today. Nor her unborn baby.

The FBI had known about the potential danger. Now that little girl had lost her mother. Why hadn't Trainer put Nicole and the kid in protective custody?

Because Nicole wouldn't have gone willingly, and Scanlon had an alibi for every murder—except hers and David's.

"It's not your fault, Delilah." Cas rubbed his hand over her spine. "You tried. Even when other people didn't think Nicole was in danger and ordered you not to get involved, you went to her and tried to make her understand."

Her brain felt fuzzy with exhaustion and defeat. "He's running circles around us, and we're following the crumbs and failing to find any definitive proof."

"We'll get our proof. He's not infallible. He'll have made a mistake. But you know it takes time. We have to do it properly, so he goes to prison and stays there this time."

"He's smart enough to have a solid alibi every time someone

he has a grudge against dies. He hasn't even breeched the terms of his parole as far as the law is concerned."

"We'll find the holes in his alibi. The task force and Parker's company are going to find the evidence we need to make the case. We already know he's involved. We simply need to figure out who is working with him."

The wait was frustrating, especially now that a child was on the field of play.

"That poor little kid."

Cas's arms squeezed her. She knew he felt it too.

"Did we ever get the list of ex-cons who were tight with him in prison and were recently released?" she asked sitting up.

"I don't know, but right now you and I are going to get some sleep and regroup in the morning."

She shot to her feet and began pacing. "I can't sleep. I have so much energy racing through my system there's no way I can sleep."

"Fine." He climbed slowly to his feet, and she watched him stalk her like a predator hunted prey.

She narrowed her gaze at him. "What are you—?"

She yelped when he hoisted her over his shoulder and marched her into the bedroom and then dropped her carefully onto the bed.

"Are you serious, right—"

He grabbed her ankles and pulled her to the end of the bed. Tugged off her boots. Socks. Pants that he had to peel down her legs, along with her Glock 23, which he carefully placed on the bedside table. The fight went out of her. She lay there looking up at him. Quiet now. Staring at this beautiful man who'd risked his career for her today.

She knew what that meant to him.

He dragged the long sleeve T-shirt he wore over his head and tossed it aside. Then watched her eyes as his hands went to his pants buttons.

"You were saying?"

She couldn't remember what she'd been saying. She only knew she wanted to forget everything that had happened today.

"Nothing." She shook her head and watched him. She wanted to etch the memory of his face, his body, his passion on her soul in case he left her again. She blocked the thought. Like so many others right now, it was too unbearable.

"Make love to me, Cas."

His expression was sober as he came down over her. "I always do, Lilah." He kissed her lips. "I always do."

52

Cas cracked an eyelid and checked the clock. Four forty-five on a Saturday morning. He could hear the shower going, so hopefully Delilah hadn't snuck out when he'd been asleep. He wouldn't put it past her.

He sat up and realized it was a text ping that had woken him.

He checked the screen. Shit. He needed to go in. Looked like Gold Team were getting called out on an op. Was it related to the bombing on Wednesday? Or was it picking up some high value target from some trouble hot spot thousands of miles away?

He swore while climbing out of bed, digging for fresh underwear out of his bag.

Delilah came out of the bathroom with a towel wrapped around her head and a smile on her beautiful face. "Oh, you're awake. I hope I didn't wake you. I couldn't sleep."

"I have to go in. Emergency team briefing."

Her expression fell, so maybe he was rubbing off on her—or perhaps she was just enjoying the incredible sex.

The thought depressed him more than it should.

"I don't know how long I'm going to be. It could be an hour. It could be a month." This facet of his work had never bothered him before. Right now, he hated it.

"Oh." She crossed her arms over her towel-clad chest. "I understand, of course, I do." She looked around a little lost. "I'm not sure I'll still be here when you get back though."

That was not what he wanted to hear.

He pulled on his pants. "Savage said you could stay here until the end of the month. He's taking leave for his honeymoon." He found his keys and slipped one off the ring. "If you need somewhere else after that, here's the key to my apartment. I'll text you the address if this is going to take more than the day." He pressed it into her palm. "Stay as long as you want."

He held her gaze. *Stay forever.*

He was too cowardly to say it though. What if she said no?

He'd already pushed her a lot. He didn't want her to balk now by pushing too hard.

"Scanlon is unlikely to be watching my place right now, but keep your awareness up. You should be safe enough considering how many eyeballs are on him, especially as we can now monitor the aircraft, which is probably how he's getting around the country. And we have a good idea of the people he's likely working with."

She stared at the key like she didn't know what it meant.

It should have been a ring. A big fucking ruby or emerald because a diamond wasn't unique enough for this woman. Even if she threw it back in his face at least she'd know he was committed this time.

Willing to stick.

Desperate to stick.

He found a shirt and pulled it on. Grabbed his gear.

He quickly used the bathroom, and when he came out, he caught her hand. "Promise me you'll be careful."

She squeezed his fingers. "How much trouble can I get in between here and Alex Parker's office?"

"I'm not hearing the words, Delilah."

"I'll be careful." Her jaw firmed. "Now your turn."

"I promise I'll be very careful. I have something important to come back to now. I love you, Delilah Quinn. I never stopped."

He watched her throat convulse as she swallowed. He held his breath, hoping she might give him the words she'd used to say every time they parted. He'd never taken it for granted, not even back then.

She remained silent but her eyes were a different story entirely. He told himself it was enough. It had to be enough.

"Hopefully, I'll be back in an hour with breakfast."

She nodded.

"I have to go."

She nodded again. "I know."

He forced himself to walk out the door.

———

Cas rolled up to the HRT compound surprised to see Ryan Sullivan, Sebastian Black, Damian Crow, Seth Hopper, Aaron Nash, JJ Hersh, Ford Cadell with his K9 Hugo, and Grady Steel, waiting for him outside, despite the hour and the rain.

"What's up?" He hunched his shoulders against the rain as he strode toward them. "Is it Grace?"

Aaron Nash shook his head, and they turned as one to enter the building, heading to the briefing room. "Grace is fine. Scan went well on Wednesday. We got DNA results back from the incendiary device from the bombing."

Cas's gaze shot to his friend's. "And?"

"Matched a Navy SEAL down in Little Creek who I believe you interviewed?"

Cas nodded.

"The DOJ requested we escort Petty Officer Holtz up to DC for questioning." Nash's eyes gleamed darkly.

"NCIS are letting the feds have him?"

"For possible criminal prosecution regarding the bombing. They want their own piece of him for any military crimes, but obviously there's been some serious horse-trading going on in the upper echelons of power because the Bureau is getting first crack at him."

"Just Holtz's DNA?" asked Cas cautiously.

"Yeah." Nash gave him a look. "Who else were you hoping for?"

Cas slicked the rain off his forehead. He looked around at the guys and decided it was time to come clean with the rest of the team who didn't know all the facts about the case. "We suspect a guy called Joseph Scanlon who's a former Navy SEAL and good friend of Holtz's of setting the bomb. Task force is looking into him, but he has an alibi for the bombing."

Nash whistled. "I remember the case. I'd just gone through New Agent Training and watched the trial with interest. You were undercover on that one?"

Cas nodded.

"That was a hell of a bust. And the other undercover was the agent murdered on Monday night in San Diego?"

Cas thought of Delilah all soft and warm back at the house. "She survived. The killer accidentally murdered a friend of hers who was staying with her. This information is still need-to-know only." He looked around at his teammates to make sure they understood. "Once Scanlon figures out Delilah is alive, he's gonna lose his shit. Director ordered news of Delilah's survival to remain confidential even from her colleagues in San Diego."

The faces of the men around the table who hadn't already known looked appropriately surprised.

"You say this Scanlon guy has an alibi?" Sebastian Black crossed his arms.

Cas nodded. "He has an identical twin. The two of them have made themselves basically indistinguishable from one another down to matching scars and tattoos."

Aaron Nash lifted his chin. "That's going to be a challenge. Any image data might be called into question—plus eyewitness testimony is a bust... Fingerprints *will* differ though. And a deep dive into epigenetic profiles will likely show genetic differences, but they won't turn up on your standard DNA profiles and will cost big money—assuming we can find DNA samples to compare against."

"And that's why we call you The Professor," Ryan joked. "Smarter than the average bear."

"Everyone's smarter than you." Grady Steel cuffed Ryan on the back of the head. Good natured teasing rather than last month's drama. Cas was glad to see things getting back to normal.

Grady winced as he rubbed his leg, reminding Cas he'd been shot not that long ago.

"What's the plan?" Cas asked Nash.

"You tell me. Ackers put you in charge of this one." Aaron shifted his weight. "FNGs are on their way in. Half the rest of the team are in DC, for Savage's wedding."

FNGs were the Fucking New Guys and included the first-ever female to make it through HRT selection.

"My wedding invitation must have been lost in the mail," Ryan joked.

Cas thought about how to play it. "Let's take three armored SUVs. Hopper and Hersh with me and the suspect. Cowboy take point with the FNGs. Everyone else follow in the third car." He patted the Belgian Malinois then checked his watch. He didn't want to leave Delilah alone for any longer than necessary. "We leave in ten minutes with or without the FNGs."

53

Delilah presented herself to security at FBI HQ at 8:45 a.m. and was quickly waved through after they checked her identity and verified the fact she was expected. Security personnel weren't fellow agents. Hopefully, her name meant nothing to them.

Trainer had called her an hour ago and told her to get her ass here. He hadn't sounded happy. Perhaps the director had intervened on her behalf again. She hoped it meant she'd be able to sit in with the task force rather than twiddle her thumbs doing nothing.

She felt exposed as she headed across the open courtyard. She grabbed a coffee from the onsite Starbucks as she had a few minutes before the meeting started and the place was quiet. Then she hurried across to the elevators, got off on one floor and walked a mile of convoluted corridors to the next one. It was a maze. Another separate elevator got her to SIOC. Thankfully, she'd spent a lot of time in the building with her father back in the day and didn't get lost.

She headed into the briefing room and registered surprised glances from some of the other agents. Yael sat at the large conference table with her laptop open. Delilah sat beside her feeling decidedly unwanted and unwelcome.

"Hey, I wasn't expecting you."

"So I gather." Delilah pulled a face. "Trainer called me and told me to be here." She glanced around. Unease crept over her. "Given the warm reception, I'm a little worried about his motives now."

People filed in, and it was standing room only as ASAC Trainer stood at the front on the room sorting through his notes.

Delilah found herself staring at the clocks showing the different times around the world. They didn't have a clock for Louisiana, but she wondered if Joseph Scanlon had told his daughter about her mother's death yet. How would he spin it? What would happen to the kid? Would the grandmother take her in? Or was Joseph expecting to get away with his crimes and raise her himself?

Trainer began the meeting with a full-frontal assault. "Agent Quinn. I spoke to Seattle PD, and it turns out Nicole Scanlon left a phone message on her ex-husband's messaging service less than fifteen minutes before she died, telling him the FBI had just been to see her. But when I spoke to the SAC at the Seattle Field Office, she says no agents had so far managed to connect with Mrs. Scanlon."

"Zimmerman," Delilah corrected through gritted teeth. "She wasn't a Scanlon. She was a Zimmerman."

"Her name isn't the issue," Trainer ground out.

The hell it wasn't. And how come agents in the same city as her hadn't managed to talk to the woman, while she and Cas had flown across the country and found her at home without any issue?

"Do you have anything to tell me before I initiate a full investigation into your whereabouts yesterday?"

"That's not necessary, sir. And, if you'd let me talk to you yesterday, you'd have known we discovered Mrs. Zimmerman's daughter was catching a flight that afternoon to visit her father, solo." She wanted to drag her hands through her hair, but he'd see it as a weakness. "Without definitive feedback on this development I decided to act on my own initiative"—something FBI agents were supposed to do—"and go speak to her myself. Try to discourage her from letting her daughter stay with someone I believe is potentially dangerous."

"Let me get this straight. Even aside from the fact I had already specifically forbade you to contact the ex-wife, thanks to your actions Joseph Scanlon likely knows we're investigating him?"

Forbade?

"Joseph Scanlon knew we were going to investigate him before he committed any of the crimes. Hence the alibi for every damned minute."

Trainer looked smug. "What you seem to be missing from your own statement is he has solid alibis for all of the murders except Valerie Strauss and Agent Gonzales. We haven't even questioned Scanlon directly because we don't have enough probable cause."

Delilah stared at her coffee cup rather than reveal her true feelings regarding Trainer's investigative abilities.

"Your service weapon came back, and the only DNA on it is yours."

The agents around her shifted uneasily.

She looked up. "Of course my DNA and fingerprints are on my own weapon."

Trainer crossed his arms. "A defense attorney would suggest it is as viable a scenario that you killed your friend and set fire to your own townhouse to destroy evidence and then went to Agent Gonzales's home and shot him dead. Maybe there was a lover's tiff."

Anger had her tightening her jaw. "David was not my lover. He was a valued colleague and friend. And I would never have harmed Val." Tears blinded her for a second, but she blinked them away. She probably shouldn't be having this conversation without a lawyer but what the hell. "She's the best friend I ever had, and I did not hurt her in any way." Except for being the reason she died.

"Following this line of dubious logic, what exactly did Clarence Carpenter do to me?"

Trainer shrugged with a smug glint in his eye. "Perhaps that case is unrelated. Or perhaps you killed him to throw us off the scent. Perhaps his boss killed him when he heard he was working with the FBI. Frank Bannon has some criminal contacts and questionable business practices."

Delilah's mouth went dry because the guy had basically accused her of murder—exactly as Scanlon must have hoped when he'd taken her weapon and shot David.

"And all these other events?" She waved her hand in the air. "The bomb at the memorial service? The murder of the admiral and his wife? Nicole Zimmerman and her unborn child's shooting death?" She was incredulous. "Are they *coincidences*?"

"We don't have a shred of evidence to link Scanlon that isn't circumstantial, nor do we know for sure these incidents are connected."

Was he fucking kidding?

She looked around the room feeling helpless. Did these people genuinely believe they were sitting here with a desperate killer? An armed, desperate killer? Was this an elaborate setup and interrogation? She kept her hands visible on the table in front of her. "What about DNA? Is that back yet?"

Yael held her hand up like they were in school.

"We identified Petty Officer Kevin Holtz's DNA on parts of the device, and HRT have gone to pick him up." Trainer ignored Yael. "We'll be questioning him here in a few hours, but a good defense attorney could put the DNA down to something that happened in the course of his duties, a bit like you and your gun."

Nausea rose up inside her.

Yael turned her laptop to face the team leader. "We have Agent Quinn on camera going for a run after her house is ablaze."

"It's still possible for her to have committed the crimes." He raised his hand in a placatory gesture. "I'm not saying that's what happened, but I am saying we need to investigate the possibility, and Agent Quinn's continued presence and interference is a hindrance and conflict of interest to the case."

Lincoln Frazer entered the room and walked up to her. The agent on her left stood and offered him her chair. He took it.

Was he here to arrest her?

Yael spoke up again. "Did you all get the information on the light aircraft belonging to the Scanlons that I sent out early this morning?"

Trainer nodded. "We appreciate the help, but we can take over that part of the investigation now." Obviously, Yael had been tainted by association with her.

"Oh, so you're not interested in the fact I can place that aircraft at airfields thirty miles north of Norfolk early on Wednesday morning? And that it flew out of Renton Municipal Airport near Seattle on Tuesday evening? Or that it flew to Renton from Gillespie Field in California—a forty-minute drive from La Jolla—early Tuesday morning? Or that Virgil Scanlon was the pilot on record?"

"Not Virgil Scanlon who looks identical to his twin brother Joseph?" Delilah stage-whispered.

"Would be awful hard to tell them apart without a PCR machine in your pocket," Yael matched her tone.

"Damned good work. Did you get any sleep last night?"

Yael yawned. "Not a lot."

Trainer looked baffled. "If you can pass the details onto us, I'll have our analysts check and verify the information."

Yael smiled slightly and hit a button on her computer. "There you go. A hard copy. I'll email you the rest." A printer on the credenza behind Trainer began spitting out sheets of paper.

Trainer frowned. "I thought you needed a password to access that? How did you know it?"

Yael raised a quizzical brow. "I have no idea what you mean. It just popped up as an available machine. That's all the data I was able to assemble last night. No flight plans were logged, but each airport keeps their own records. You'll need to send agents out there with photographs of one of the Scanlon brothers for a definitive ID."

Trainer gave her a hard stare. "Are you telling me how to do my job?"

"No, sir." Yael shot him a blank smile as if she weren't twenty times more intelligent that the task force leader.

"Be that as it may," Trainer continued, undeterred, "it's still all circumstantial."

Delilah finished her coffee and stared down at the table in defeat. Trainer didn't care about facts. He just wanted rid of her.

"Look, Agent Quinn, we appreciate this is difficult for you, but I need to ask you to step back. In fact, I've asked that you be put on paid leave until this is all resolved. I'll need your weapon and your badge."

Delilah's gaze shot around the room. Humiliation pumped blood into her cheeks. She was being stripped of the job that meant so much to her in front of her colleagues. She pulled the black leather wallet where she kept her badge out of her blazer pocket. Joseph Scanlon would be very happy to discover this if he ever found out she was still alive. She didn't intend to give up her backup Glock, which technically belonged to her.

Lincoln Frazer closed his hand around hers. "Wait. I hardly think it's the wisest time to leave the target of a suspected serial killer defenseless." Lincoln Frazer raised his brows at Trainer like he thought he was an idiot.

They were in sync on that.

"Well, fortunately, you aren't in charge, are you?"

Delilah's eyes widened but the profiler looked unconcerned by the jab.

"That may be technically correct, however, more importantly, I spoke with the director before this meeting, and what you failed to mention was that she hadn't decided whether or not to suspend Agent Quinn. She said she'd taken your comments under advisement—the same way she would take my opposing opinions under advisement."

Trainer looked uncomfortable at being called out in front of everyone. "A criminal conviction is going to be a nightmare if Agent Quinn is involved—"

"And who invited her to this meeting?" Frazer wasn't bothering to hide his anger now. "When she could have been sitting at home, none the wiser about any of this?"

Trainer's face flushed. "I can't have her going off around the country interfering with this investigation."

"She tried to warn a woman she might be in danger, and that same woman is now dead!" Frazer's voice rang out in the small, overcrowded room.

"And from where I'm sitting, Quinn is as likely to be Nicole Scanlon's killer as Joseph Scanlon is."

Delilah felt her mouth drop open in shock.

Frazer reared back as if slapped. "What possible motive could she have for shooting a pregnant woman she barely knows?"

Trainer's gaze shot back to her. "Nicole Scanlon made multiple accusations against Agent Quinn in the past. Plus," he raised his voice when Frazer went to interrupt, "plus, there is the fact Agent Quinn could be jealous Nicole was pregnant." His stooped shoulders pulled back. "As she is unable to have children. Perhaps she snapped."

Delilah felt the blood drain from her head, and she had to fight the dizziness that crashed over her like a giant wave.

That Greg Trainer would splash her private medical information to everyone in the room, a secret she had guarded assiduously for the past five years, made her want to vomit. Rage filled her and tears burned the back of her eyes.

Frazer stared at the man aghast. "That was unforgivable. Agent Quinn will be making an official complaint, as will I."

She couldn't talk. Her lips and mouth felt numb. She stumbled to her feet. Fought for control of her tongue. "I assume I'm free to go? You're not making an *arrest* at this point?" Her voice dripped sarcasm.

Trainer shook his head. "Not at this point."

She stared at the black leather wallet on the table. Frowned. "Am I suspended or not?"

"Yes," said Trainer.

"No," said Frazer.

She scooped up the creds and put them in her pocket. She'd go with ASAC Frazer's decision as he was the same rank as Trainer and fuck him. "Let me know what the director decides."

All of a sudden Scanlon's attachment to his trident pin made a lot more sense.

"I assume I'm off the task force?"

Trainer jerked his chin down in a sharp nod.

She looked around the crowded room of her peers. "For the record. I went to warn Nicole *Zimmerman* that her ex-husband might be dangerous. I went to Seattle even though ASAC Trainer ordered me not to. I did it because the life of Nicole and that little girl, a child you have barely even mentioned, are worth more than my career. I hoped Nicole might listen to reason, but she didn't, and I am sick to my stomach she's dead now and that Melody is with a man who I know from personal experience is a violent misogynist. Nicole believed that prison had changed him, and he'd found religion. She refused to accept her ex might hold a grudge." She looked at the analyst who she knew was doing most of the work. "I don't know the exact time Nicole was shot, but I'll almost certainly be on the security cameras at SeaTac. Or on the plane. I'd get on verifying that as soon as possible if I were you." She pointed her finger at Trainer. "And rest assured, I will be making a formal complaint about your actions today. What you did here was inexcusable."

Trainer's face flamed in outrage and she wondered if he'd lash out.

"And another thing, ASAC Trainer," she reached the door and turned to stare him down, "next time you come for my badge, you better not miss."

54

Joseph opened the front door to the same deputy he'd spoken with two days ago at the garage. This time the lawman wasn't alone. A female deputy stood off to the side of the grand front porch looking wary.

She was right to be cautious. He could kill her before she even drew her weapon, but the same could be said of most people with the amount of training he had.

"Good morning, Deputy Herbert." He made sure to show his hands were empty as he leaned against the frame. "You working part time as a parole officer now? Checking my whereabouts?"

"No, sir. I'm afraid I've got some bad news to share."

Joseph frowned. "What kind of bad news?"

The deputy cleared his throat. "I believe your daughter is here with you?"

"Yes, sir. She's in bed. I have permission. Call her mama to check if you want." He managed to sound outraged and a little scared too. Scared of losing his kid.

He wasn't giving her back. She was his now.

"No, sir, it ain't that." The man cleared his throat again. "Is your daughter around?"

Joseph looked over his shoulder and then back. "Like I said, she's asleep. It took her a little while to settle down last night on account of it being a new place. Well, she was here as a baby, but she doesn't remember that." He stepped out onto the porch and closed the door keeping his voice low. "What's up? Is it the garage? Was there a break-in?"

"No, sir." The deputy's young face was creased with sincerity. "Your ex-wife was involved in a shooting last night."

Joseph sagged onto the front swing chair. "*Nicole*? Is she all right?"

"I'm afraid not." Deputy Herbert placed his hands on his heavy equipment belt. "Unfortunately, Mrs. Zimmerman died from her injuries."

Joseph let his mouth drop open and then covered his face with both hands. "I don't believe it. I just texted with her yesterday."

He'd texted her that Melody had arrived safely. She hadn't texted back.

"Oh, God. Who's going to tell little Melody? Who's going to tell my daughter that her mother is gone?"

"Deputy Châtel can help you with that." The deputy looked uncomfortable but happily passed the responsibility on to his partner even though it was part of the job—imparting bad news.

Joseph held the female deputy's gaze. "I'd appreciate that greatly because I don't think I could do it without breaking down. Oh, my Lord. If Melody hadn't come to stay here, she could have been shot too. Was it a drive by?"

The deputies exchanged a look.

Joseph frowned. "You don't suspect me, do you?" He blinked as if the thought had just occurred to him. "Me and Virgil went to the airport last evening to pick up Melody. Visited my parole officer in the afternoon like I told you I was gonna. I have witnesses for most of the day."

He'd made sure of it.

"We already done checked with Jim Jenkins. We know you were here." Hebert looked uncomfortable now. "Seattle PD requested it. I don't see how you could be in two places at once."

Joseph let his shoulders sag with relief. He knew Seattle cops would be looking to exclude him and make sure he had no involvement in Nicole's death. As long as his partner in crime didn't get caught, they'd never prove it. It was all part of the plan. The cops were going to do the work to clear him this time. They were going to be his defense against a DA even bothering to press charges.

"Thing is," Deputy Herbert cleared his throat, "the stepfather is insisting Melody catch the first flight back home."

"Home?" Joseph tucked his chin in and rose to his feet, shaking his head. "That's not going to happen. Firstly," he raised one finger, "Nicole and I share joint custody of our daughter upon my release. That was the only condition I set on our divorce. I was being polite by giving her a say in what happened because I didn't want to upset Melody unnecessarily. Secondly, Mr. Zimmerman has no legal authority over my daughter. He never adopted my child. No judge ever granted him any parental rights. He simply married Melody's mother."

The deputies exchanged another worried look as if scared he was going to turn violent.

"I can show you all the legal paperwork, although it'll take a few minutes to find it." On the top shelf of the safe in the study.

Again, the deputies exchanged a glance, but they finally relaxed a little. As if they believed him not to be a threat.

Letting their guard down.

His burner cell rang, and he checked the screen. *What does that sonofabitch want now?*

"Come inside. I'll put on coffee. We have donuts." Bought specially. "I'll find the documents, and after you've verified the legal information, I'll wake Melody, and you can tell her about her mother."

Because he didn't want that being her first real memory of their life together. Let the boys in blue take the hit. He'd be there to pick up the pieces.

55

The prisoner transfer went relatively quickly for the military, which meant they only had to cool their heels for an hour on base while paperwork was signed for Holtz.

Cas's old friend Senior Chief Terry Lopez had come over earlier and chatted with him and Seth Hopper for a while. The look in his eyes had been somber. This incident reflected badly on the entire SEAL community and on base security, which Cas assumed was being reviewed in minute detail. With the admiral's murder and possible connection between Holtz and Scanlon, everyone was going to be on edge wondering if there was another traitor in their midst. Because if you couldn't trust your brother-in-arms, who the hell could you trust?

It was not a good feeling. Another reason it had been so important to get enough evidence on Scanlon to convict.

Holtz appeared, hands cuffed behind his back, head hung low, eyes red—not from drinking this time—as he was marched across the parking lot.

Cas, who'd changed into a suit like a case agent, went over and took the man by the arm and led him to the middle vehicle. The team had assumed tactical positions, and operators climbed into their own transport as soon as he and Holtz were secure inside.

"Let me get your seatbelt for you." He leaned over and carefully strapped the guy in. He wasn't going to get anywhere with direct threats or intimidation tactics.

Never Opt Out Of The Fight wasn't a Navy SEAL motto for nothing.

The vehicles set off, fast, tight formation, lights activated. It was good training for the newbies and would shake this motherfucker up a little. Convince him he was in serious shit.

Cas said nothing. Just stared out the window.

"Well?" Holtz questioned after a couple of minutes of silence.

"Well, what?" Cas raised a quizzical brow.

"Why the fuck are the FBI hauling me off for questioning?"

"I can't say."

"Why not?"

"Petty Officer Holtz, you had your chance to make a deal yesterday. It's too late for any hope of leniency now."

Holtz's lip curled. "Bullshit."

"That's not what the evidence is telling us."

Holtz shifted in his seat. With his hands cuffed behind his back and his seatbelt pinning him in place, it wasn't impossible for the guy to try to do him some damage, but it was unlikely.

"Then the evidence is bullshit."

Cas let the silence grow. Holding his tongue was his superpower.

"What evidence do you have?" asked Holtz after another mile of travel.

"I assume your lawyer will tell you all about it. You do have a lawyer?"

Holtz's eyes widened, perhaps finally figuring out exactly how much trouble he was in.

"You hear about Admiral Sagal?"

"I had nothing to do with that." He licked his lips. "Guys are all looking at me sideways even though they know I was on base when Sagal was shot."

"And his wife, she was murdered too. Do you think it is a coincidence that whoever killed the admiral also took his Budweiser?"

Holtz rolled his shoulders. "Lot of people want the pin even if they don't have a right to wear it."

"That's right." Cas allowed a wide smile to stretch his lips.

"If you mean Joseph, then that's garbage. He earned it."

"So you said *repeatedly* yesterday. But Naval Command has the authority to take that right away. You think they'll take yours?"

Holtz's blue eyes flashed hot. "What do you mean?"

"You're implicated in the bombing of the memorial service of a serving FBI Hostage Rescue Team operator. You are implicated in the attempted murder of a federal agent and use of a weapon of mass destruction on US soil."

"Don't bullshit a bullshitter. You got nothing." Holtz looked away out of the window.

"Would you really be under armed escort to FBI Headquarters to be questioned if we had *nothing*? I'll let you in on a secret. You know the real shame? We've got nothing on Scanlon. Oh, we know it was him, but he's been very careful about setting this up. You're the one who's going to go down and from what I hear that's a pity. You were a damned good warfighter."

Holtz's expression soured at Cas's use of past tense.

"I haven't done anything."

"The only hope you've got is telling the whole truth and hoping the AG doesn't decide to make an example out of you. But I wouldn't hold your breath, even if you were a frogman."

Holtz stared out of the window. "I don't know what you're talking about."

"Sure," Hopper jeered from the front seat.

Cas made himself sympathetic. It was one of the things he did best. Empathize with killers and psychopaths. "This isn't some war game where you fail for cracking under interrogation. You already lost when you provided an ex-con with military explosives."

Holtz nervously chewed the inside of his cheek.

"We know about the plane. We can place one Scanlon brother in Virginia on Wednesday morning, but that's as close as we can get without access to the van he used to transport the bomb or some other evidence implicating him..."

Holtz shot him a look. "Again, I don't know what you're talking about."

This guy was trained not to give up details under interrogation. So was Scanlon. It wasn't making this case any easier.

Cas's cell buzzed and he checked the screen. Yael. Asking that he call her. He texted her back that he was unable to talk for the next three hours, making sure his screen wasn't visible to the man beside him. He couldn't risk the guy hearing or seeing anything about Delilah still being alive.

The text came back.

> Call me when you can. It's important.

———

It was just after noon when they arrived at HQ, having broken the speed limit most of the way. Cas hadn't gotten anywhere with Kevin Holtz on the rest of the journey and had largely let the guy sweat.

If he'd thought beating it out of him would do any good, he might have had the boys pull over. But physical pain fed the resilience of men like Holtz, the same way it worked for the members of the Hostage Rescue Team. That kind of challenge was easily faced.

It was the vulnerable emotional shit that the majority of them struggled with.

Or the prospect of life imprisonment or losing the job that defined you.

Four of them escorted Holtz from the underground parking garage up to the fourth floor into an official interview room. They transferred the cuffs so he was chained to a table that was bolted to the floor.

Cas spoke to one of the task force agents outside the room. "You need to have at least two agents in the room with him at all times. Do not undo his cuffs, and do not assume he can't get out of them."

The man gave him a plastic smile. "We've got this."

Cas hid his exasperation. He knew the training normal agents underwent, and he knew what SEALs were capable of.

"Don't underestimate him."

"We've got this, Agent Demarco."

"Operator," he corrected sharply. Because he needed to remind them he was part of the elite Hostage Rescue Team, and *he* still considered Holtz a threat. "Where's the task force set up?"

The agent pointed him upstairs toward SIOC. Hopper, Hersh, and Sebastian Black all fell in beside him and followed him up in the elevator.

Hopper looked around and shuddered. "I have some bad memories of this place."

Cas shot the guy a look. His girlfriend had been kidnapped off the street outside just a few weeks ago.

It gave Cas a bad feeling.

He found Yael in the main conference room. She began to pack up her things the moment she saw him.

"Sorry I couldn't call you earlier. I was in the back seat with Holtz—"

"She's gone." Her voice was a whisper.

A sharp hit to the chest made it difficult to breathe. "Gone how?"

Yael looked around as if worried about being overheard. "She left here about three hours ago and I haven't been able to reach her since."

Trainer entered the room, and Cas narrowed his eyes at the guy.

"She was upset when she left?"

"Very."

Trainer began heading toward them, but someone caught his attention. Cas's fingers began to curl.

"He suggested she may be responsible for Val's and David's deaths. She gave as good as she got, but then he told everyone about the fact she couldn't have kids. It was a low blow. He practically accused her of murdering Nicole Zimmerman because she was pregnant."

Hurt spread through him. Hurt and fury. "What's his beef?"

She lowered her voice further. "I dug a little. Apparently, Delilah's father was his SAC during his first office assignment. There were a few disciplinary incidents."

"Ah."

"I think we need to leave." Sebastian Black jostled him until he was headed to the door.

It was probably a good idea because Cas was feeling violent.

"Operator Demarco!" The salutation rang out over the bustle of the room, and everyone froze.

Cas looked over his shoulder. Raised a brow.

ASAC Trainer had his hands on his hips. "I need to question you."

Question him?

"Regarding?"

"Your statement to me the other day at Quantico."

Cas felt his heart slow down as if everything was happening in slow motion. He rarely lost his temper. He'd learned as a child that any show of negative emotion almost always backfired—so he'd channeled any anger into sport or the inherently violent nature of his work.

But he was about to lose his temper now, in front of all Trainer's cronies.

His cell dinged, as did Hopper's, Hersh's, and Black's. He checked the screen. "I'm afraid you're going to have to wait. We have urgent orders to return to Quantico."

Trainer looked as if he was rapidly losing his nerve. "Fine. Another time."

Cas narrowed his gaze even further and only moved when Sebastian physically pushed him from the room.

"What the hell was that about?" he asked, although no one answered him.

Yael hustled down the corridor. "Come on. This way."

They strode after her and piled into the elevator.

"Dammit. I'd hoped we were done for the day. Zoe's visiting for the weekend." Hopper sounded pissed.

"You met the parents yet?" Black asked.

"Not yet. Not gonna lie, I'm abso-fucking-lutely terrified."

Seth Hopper was dating the daughter of the Vice President, and Cas did not envy the other man.

It reminded him of Delilah's parents. Perhaps she'd gone to visit them?

Cas needed to figure out how to get out of whatever op they were supposed to go on next.

"You don't have to cancel any plans," Yael murmured.

Cas glanced at her sharply.

"I'm sure if you check, you'll find there was a glitch in the system."

"A glitch?" Black raised a brow.

"You hacked it." Hopper grinned.

"I have no idea what you are talking about." Yael looked pointedly at the security cameras. "Shane's picking me up out front, but I wanted a quick word with you first. Outside."

Cas was desperate to know what it was Yael didn't want to say where there was a chance of being overheard. "Tell him to come around to the side and meet us at the parking garage."

As soon as they got downstairs, Cas headed up the ramp into the frigid February wind. At least the rain had stopped. Yael followed him outside. Cas quickly tried Delilah, but she didn't pick up.

"Any idea where she went?"

Yael shook her head. "No airline tickets in her name."

"What about in the alias Killion gave her."

Yael shook her head again. "Maybe she went to visit her parents?"

"Why turn her cell off?"

"Breathing space?"

That was a possibility and calmed the internal panic a little. "Presumably there are no plans for the FBI to move on Scanlon today?"

"Not that I was allowed to know about. I was speaking to one of their analysts about the flight data I uncovered. Joseph could have definitely committed the bombing and the murders in San Diego. But not the admiral and his wife, or his ex."

"It's what? A fifteen-hour drive to New Orleans from here?"

"You don't seriously think she'd confront him alone?" Yael sounded shocked.

Cas pressed his lips together. "Knowing Delilah? Yeah, she'd definitely confront him alone if she thinks the kid is in danger."

He watched the HRT vehicles stream out and idle next to the sidewalk as Shane Livingstone's truck pulled up behind them. Shane got out and joined them.

"What's up?"

"Delilah's missing."

"You think she's gone after Scanlon?"

Cas nodded. "I can't let her confront him alone."

"And she might have just gone to the mall for some retail therapy," Yael suggested.

"Delilah is not *shopping*. And if she is, why isn't she answering her phone?" He put his hands on his head. "I can't believe I left her alone or that Trainer ambushed her that way."

"You could be fired if you take off again without permission," Shane warned.

"She means more to me than anything else in the world. Including my job."

"Don't do anything rash." Shane put his hand on his shoulder.

"Even if she's on her way down there we still have time to make a plan."

Cas blew out a big breath. Shane was right. Then he remembered the truck came from Killion. He called the spook. "Do you have a tracking beacon on that vehicle you gave Delilah?"

"Hello to you too."

"I need to find Delilah."

"You sure she wants you to find her?"

"What the fuck is that supposed to mean?"

"Well, she has a cell phone, and if she's not answering it maybe there's a reason."

"Patrick," he warned. "You are the last man in the world to take notice of 'reasons.'"

"Fine. The truck is at her mom and dad's home in Alexandria. What's going on?"

A huge weight lifted off his shoulders. "You didn't give her any identities I don't know about, did you? Something she may use to book a flight without me knowing."

"No. Should I be worried?"

Cas released a long breath. "No. No, I don't think so."

"Okay, good. Can I get back to my wife now? She's in labor."

Shit. "Yes, of course. God, I'm sorry."

"No, you're not, but that's okay. I care about Delilah too. Keep me in the loop."

"I'm truly sorry."

"That's normally my line. Don't worry. Childbirth is a piece of cake. Audrey has everything under control."

Cas heard cussing in the background.

"Text me if you need anything."

"Good luck. And keep me in the loop regarding Audrey and the baby when you get the chance."

"Will do."

Cas heard the worry and fear and excitement in Killion's voice and was overcome with the knowledge that would never be a

343

moment he experienced for himself—because if he couldn't have that with Delilah, he didn't want it with anyone.

Seth Hopper jumped out of one of the vehicles and hurried over.

"Hey, the media just linked these murders all together. I heard them speculating on the radio."

Cas exchanged a look with Yael. Had Delilah leaked information? Stirred up a hornets' nest? Or had a sharp reporter put together the recent attack and murders?

He checked his watch. "We should head back to Quantico. Let you guys get back to your weekend off."

Shane looked pensive as he watched Yael. "Perhaps we should head back too. We can drive up here tomorrow morning for the ceremony."

Yael nodded. "As much as I was looking forward to a weekend off, I can't rest knowing there might be something I could be doing to help Delilah."

A lump formed in his throat. "I appreciate that. See you back at Quantico."

56

Delilah had gone to a mall she'd hung out at as a teenager and wandered around in a bit of a daze before she'd picked up a few more supplies, including a decent winter coat. She'd turned her cell off because that way she didn't have to talk to anyone. Demarco was busy and, regardless, she refused to waste her life waiting for him to call her, especially if his job could take him away for months.

Months.

And, yet there was suddenly the possibility that they might have a chance of a future together. And being apart for a few months wasn't as daunting as losing him from her life forever. Not that he'd talked about a future together...

He kept saying he loved her. Perhaps, soon, she could get over her bone-deep fear and truly believe it.

She stood shivering on the doorstep of her parents' house in Alexandria. She wore her new beige wool coat, the long blonde wig, and dark glasses. She'd parked the truck on the next block over in case she needed to leave discreetly. Considering she'd sent an anonymous tip to newspapers in both San Diego and Lafayette suggesting Scanlon was linked to all the recent attacks across the country, it was prudent to give herself a little wiggle room. If a news van turned up to interview her parents, she could leave via the neighbor gate at the back of the garden and cut around. But they weren't likely to arrive anytime soon. The newspapers she'd contacted would need to verify facts first and talk to secondary victims like her parents only after they'd chased their primary sources for more details. She hoped they camped out on Scanlon's doorstep and made each move he took uncomfortable enough to not kill anyone else. Of course, there were still his co-conspirators to worry about. Someone else had definitely shot Nicole and killed the admiral and his wife.

She heard the latch, but the door opened to unexpectedly reveal a woman she'd never seen before. Her expression wasn't very pleased.

"Who is it, Gennita?" Her mother's familiar voice from the back of the house.

"Tell her it's Valerie." Her friend's name scratched in her throat, the loss hitting her afresh.

"Someone called Valerie," Gennita shouted back to her mom.

Delilah hadn't thought about the fact there would be strangers in the house. She knew the caregivers had been an enormous help to her mom, but the reality of having them in their home hadn't fully registered until now.

This was their reality now.

Her mother peeked through the door of the sitting room with wide eyes. "Oh. *Oh. Valerie.* Come in. Come in."

Delilah stepped into her parents' home feeling like a stranger.

"How lovely to see you again. Apologies. We've been getting a lot of reporters turning up on the doorstep, intruding on our grief. Gennita was guarding us. Come into the kitchen. Gennita, you head on home early. Stephen is sleeping. Get out while the getting's good."

"If you're sure, Esme?"

"Absolutely, Valerie and I will catch up over a cup of tea while I put on dinner. She was a dear friend of our daughter's, and we'll want some peace and quiet to reminisce." Her mother wiped a tear from beneath each eye.

They both watched Gennita head out the front door and down the driveway. Her mother closed the door, then Delilah found herself engulfed in a hug so tight it hurt.

"I'm so sorry, Mom." She hung on. "I didn't mean to make it difficult for you and Dad."

"You haven't." She sniffed without letting go. "The fact you're alive means you haven't at all. Only you being dead would make things difficult." Her mom laugh-sobbed. "Well, aside from Alzheimer's having no cure."

"I wish I had a cure." She rested her chin on her mother's shoulder. "I'm sorry I haven't been here for you."

"You were back at Christmas."

It seemed like a long time ago now.

"Can I poke my head in to see Dad?"

Her mother drew back, took her hand, and led her into the kitchen. "Wait until after we've had the chance to talk. If he gets upset or agitated, we might not get that opportunity, and I honestly never know how he's going to react."

"That bad?"

Her mother nodded. "That bad."

"That happened fast."

Her mom looked down and rubbed her hands together. "I guess we ignored a lot of the early symptoms. I feel now as if it's my fault. I should have made him go to the doctor sooner. There are meds…"

"Dad has never done anything he doesn't want to do. You know that better than anyone."

Her mother laughed a little. "Well, even now that hasn't changed. He's a terrible patient but, thankfully, he doesn't know it most of the time."

Her mother buried her stark reality under the guise of humor. Delilah tried not to crumble under the same weight. Her mom had always been the strongest person she knew. She didn't need a badge or a weapon when she had steel for a spine.

They went into the kitchen that they'd remodeled a few years ago. Even though it was light out, her mother drew all the blinds. "I'm assuming you still want the rest of the world to think you're not alive."

Delilah nodded. "For now. I feel wretched about Valerie's mother not knowing the truth, and my colleagues in San Diego." Acid ate at her sternum. Hopefully this would be over soon, and she could present the truth along with the person responsible.

"I do not believe you would have hidden this way unless you genuinely believed you were in danger and there was no reasonable alternative."

That was true. But she'd also hoped that Scanlon would have been arrested by now. Unfortunately, when her subterfuge was revealed, it would probably mean even more press on her parents' doorstep, but there was nothing to be done until the truth came out and the story died a natural death.

The landline rang.

"Ignore it." Her mom insisted and closed the door into the hall. "Your father won't hear it anyway. He never does."

"Still forgetting to put in his hearing aids?" Delilah winced at the way she'd phrased the question.

"He's been better at wearing them lately, but I think that's more a case of forgetting to take them out. I read some very interesting stats about hearing loss and dementia. Want a scone? I have cream and jam. I'll put the kettle on and throw a few things into the crockpot for dinner. I have another helper who comes in around seven p.m. and helps me get your father bathed and into his pajamas."

How he would hate the indignity of that.

"Can you stay for dinner?"

As much as she wanted to, she couldn't. "I'll take that tea and scone, but I need to get back." See if Yael had dug up any new data—assuming the analyst would still be willing to share information with her. Presumably that depended on Alex Parker and not ASAC Greg Trainer. "Why don't you put your feet up for a few minutes while I chop things for the crockpot," she offered.

She couldn't stay long but she desperately needed her mother's company for a little time.

———

Scanlon's burner cell rang, and he figured it must be urgent so he slipped into the backyard where the flowers his mother had planted years ago were starting to bud. The Spanish moss draped the old live oak and created shade from the sun that was hot today, even at this hour.

He answered. "Yeah?"

"She's alive."

Bullshit. "What the fuck is wrong with you?"

"Check the photo I sent."

Joseph opened the image despite his usual reservations when dealing with downloads from the internet. He'd ditch this cell ASAP.

"I flew to Virginia."

What the fuck?

"I wanted to see if I could figure out who was on the task force and maybe follow them home."

Bug them. Like Joseph had done with Agent Gonzales last weekend. Virgil had arranged for several listening/tracking devices to be sent to a mailbox using a stolen identity he'd bought off the dark web. It was virtually untraceable.

The photo showed a blonde knocking on a door in the rain.

It was grainy and indistinct and proved nothing.

"So I'm walking past the front entrance of the J. Edgar Hoover Building first thing this morning, and there she is. Plain as day. FBI Agent Delilah Quinn."

Bull. Shit.

"I figured out where she likely parked from the direction she'd come from and parked up near there a while. I didn't think I was going to get lucky before security got suspicious, but the Lady was with me. Quinn came out less than an hour later."

They'd have his partner's face on a camera somewhere now. He was a liability.

"This photo doesn't show me anything," Joseph said impatiently.

"Are you questioning my words or my eyesight?" The tone reminded Joseph this person wasn't some grunt in the prison system, and he needed to tread carefully. "She put on a wig in the vehicle. Then she went to a mall and bought some clothes and shit. While she was inside, I stuck the tracking device onto the truck she was driving."

He sent a photo of the license plate.

Government issue.

Interesting. But DC was full of government plates.

"And that house she's standing outside in the shitty photo I sent? That's Special Agent Delilah Quinn's parents' home."

Joseph stared at the photo of the woman harder. Could it really be her?

How?

How could it be true?

He pictured that night. The woman sitting on the recliner not even turning around when he came inside. It had been dark except for the TV.

He hadn't wasted time with gotcha speeches or given her the chance to pull a weapon. He'd brought that hammer down hard, and her skull had crumpled.

A blitz attack. He'd just wanted her dead.

She'd been wearing the FBI cap. She was the right size and shape as the Fed. She'd been in Quinn's apartment.

Was it possible she hadn't been Delilah Quinn after all?

And suddenly he knew it was true. He'd made a mistake. Made an assumption. He slumped onto a bench. His heart racing. His hands shaking. His veins felt as if his blood were on fire.

"You there?"

He pushed down the knot of rage. "Yeah."

"Shall I run her off the road? Shoot her?"

Joseph stared at the pitted, moss-stained statue of the Virgin Mary his mother had placed in the yard years ago.

The truck wouldn't be easy to run off the road, and Quinn had advanced training in evasive driving tactics. Plus, she'd be armed.

"Well?" The voice was impatient.

"I'm thinking," he snapped. "Is she staying at her parents' house?"

"I don't know. Way she knocked on the door was like she wasn't expected and wasn't sure of her welcome."

"Whatever you do, don't let her see you." Shit, this idiot was going to blow everything. "You have the tracker on the truck. Get the hell out of there. Use the tracker, and text me when she leaves. Use a new cell."

Scanlon heard a car engine start.

"I could knock on the door and shoot her right now."

"Watch what you say on the phone." *Idiot.* Unless he'd been caught and flipped in which case Joseph was already fucked, but he wouldn't go down easy. "There's a better way." And it would bring both the Quinn bitch and this moron close enough to deal with personally. Here. On his home turf. "Drive around the corner out of sight, and do exactly what I say."

57

C as stood in the doorway of Delilah's parents' home feeling like a damned fool. He rang the doorbell and turned and gave a thumbs up to the guys as they watched from the SUV. Delilah's truck was parked on the next block. Unless she slipped out the back, he should be able to catch a ride back to Quantico with her.

Hopper and Hersh both grinned at him manically from the front seats. This must be what it felt like to have parents who dropped you off on your first date. The guys gave him the thumbs up back and pulled away.

The door opened, and all of Cas's worst nightmares were realized, but at least there were no witnesses. He'd expected Delilah's mother but why would this part of his day be any easier than the rest?

Stephen Quinn's eyes crinkled in angry confusion. "Why are you here? I told you to leave Delilah alone. I told you what will happen if you don't. I'll make sure you never get into the Hostage Rescue Team." The guy looked haggard and old now, wearing plaid pajama pants, a white T-shirt, and a thick cardigan. The creases around his eyes and mouth were much deeper than they'd been the last time Cas had seen him. "Don't say I didn't warn you, young man."

The old man tried to push the door closed, but Cas heard Delilah's voice from inside, so he wedged his boot into the gap.

He wasn't leaving without her. Not this time.

"Daddy, what did you do?" She caught her father's arm and tried to open the door.

"Let me go! Who are you? Esme! Esme! Who's this person in our house?"

Delilah was wearing the long blonde wig, but the look in her brown eyes was stricken.

She pulled Cas inside, shutting the door firmly behind him.

"Sorry, I…"

She ignored him and followed her father into the living room.

Cas followed reluctantly.

She carefully pulled off the blonde wig and let her rich chocolate hair tumble. "Dad."

She moved so she stood to one side of her father's recliner.

"Daddy, what did you do?"

Stephen Quinn was arguing with his wife who was trying to make the man sit back down. "Delilah! Delilah." He grabbed her in a bear hug. "Darling girl. When did you get home?"

He looked so delighted. It hurt to watch.

"Just now." The words were throaty as if she were trying to rein in her emotions. "How are you feeling today?"

"Good. Good." He leaned closer. "Except your mother is trying to poison me with the number of pills she makes me swallow every day." He rubbed his hands over his face. "Makes my brain foggy, and I can't remember the things I need to."

"Mom isn't trying to poison you, Dad."

"What would you know? You're never here."

Delilah looked shocked by the sudden mood swing.

"Stephen Anthony Quinn," Delilah's mother cut in sharply. "One of these days someone is going to believe you about me poisoning you, and they'll lock me up in prison with all the criminals—is that what you want? What do you think will happen to you then? What do you think will happen?" The woman sounded fraught and exhausted and angry.

Cas could only imagine the anguish of losing someone you loved, incrementally, one memory at a time, even though they stood right in front of your eyes.

At first, Stephen's expression remained angry but it quickly crumpled, and he grabbed his wife's hand and sat back down on his recliner. "Don't leave me, Esme. You're the only one who matters. You're the only one who cares. Please don't leave me."

Esme crouched beside her shaking husband.

"I'm not going anywhere, you old goat. But tell me this, did you interfere with Delilah's personal life?"

His mouth frowned, and he turned away from his wife. "That's classified."

Esme Quinn rolled her eyes.

Cas didn't know if this was the right thing to do or not, but he held out his hand. "Assistant Director Quinn, it is an honor to meet you, sir. My name is Operator Casta Demarco."

Stephen straightened his spine and his eyes brightened. He shook his hand. "Nice to meet you." The grip tightened and the eyes crinkled in confusion. "Have we met before?"

Delilah's eyes were growing bigger and bigger.

Cas's mouth went dry. It felt important not to lie. "Yes, sir. Once. I was a lowly Special Agent at the time. It was a long time ago."

Stephen nodded and suddenly looked incredibly tired. "I remember."

He obviously did not. "Why don't you rest for a minute, sir? I'll fetch you a glass of water from the kitchen."

Esme nodded her thanks and Cas left the room. Delilah followed him.

A moment later, they both stood in the kitchen and stared at one another.

"He threatened you." Her voice wobbled.

"I wanted to join HRT." He shrugged. "You know that. It was

my dream for years. Your father threatened to take that away from me, but…" Cas closed his eyes. "But I already told you why we really broke up. It wasn't all on him… He was a convenient excuse I told myself at the time."

Delilah touched his face. "I don't believe you. Not anymore." A tear rolled down her cheek. "HRT was your dream, and he had no right to threaten you that way. His actions also stole your dreams of belonging to a loving family, and I'll never forgive him for that. You have to know I would have cut all ties with him to be with you if you'd only told me. You know I would have. And he wouldn't have gone through with his threats after I spoke to him."

He opened his eyes. "You love your parents, Delilah. I knew that from the way you spoke about them. The love. The pride. I couldn't take that from you. I would never destroy your family."

Family was everything.

She wrapped her arms around his waist and buried her head against his heart, and he held her tight. "I love you, Cas Demarco. I would have chosen you, and he would have come to love you too. He became very overprotective after my brother died, but that's no excuse. I'm sorry people have treated you so badly. They didn't know you or they'd have seen the true nature of your worth. They'd see the character of a man who'd willingly sacrifice himself rather than hurt others."

"I'm not a saint, Delilah." But her words warmed him and gave him hope. She loved him. That was enough.

"I want what we once had back again. It's not too late, is it?" She swiped away a tear. "Unless I'm arrested for murder."

He pulled back, both warmed and horrified. "You're joking?"

She grimaced. "Not really. Greg Trainer seems to consider me a viable suspect."

Cas ground his teeth together. "I should have punched him in the face earlier, that mother—"

He cut himself off as Delilah's mom entered the kitchen.

"I gave him one of his pills, so he'll sleep a little. Maybe he's right about me poisoning him because the only time I get any real rest is when he's sleeping. God knows I get to feel guilty about everything else, I may as well feel bad about that too."

She smiled through her tears and then held out her hand to shake his. "Esme Quinn. Delilah's terrible mother and Stephen's horrible wife."

"Mom," Delilah chastised softly.

"Casta Demarco, ma'am. People call me Cas. Pleasure to meet you."

Esme didn't let go of his hand, and her grip was too firm to pull away from gracefully. "I remember Delilah talking about you a couple of times, years ago, and then she stopped talking about you and she became sad. Is my husband the reason my daughter became so sad?"

Cas shook his head. "You can't blame your husband. It was my fault."

"Not true." Delilah took his other hand in hers. "But the fact we broke up isn't the only reason I was miserable. I miscarried, Mom, and had to have an emergency hysterectomy."

"When?" Her mother dropped his hand and picked up her daughter's.

"Five years ago."

Tears were bright in the woman's eyes. "And you never told me?"

"I never told anyone." She shot a look at him. "Only Val."

"Oh, Delilah. I'm so sorry." Her mother shook her head. "And I'm so sorry you didn't feel able to come to me. I would have been there for you, I promise."

"I know you would. I was unable to talk about it for a long time. And I didn't want to quash your hopes of having grandchildren."

Esme waved that away. "There are other ways to have kids if you decide you want them. And right now, I have enough to deal with."

She slapped her hand over her mouth. "Listen to me complain

when I'm not the one with some maniac after them or a horrible disease eating away at my faculties. I'm truly a horrible person."

Delilah hugged her mother. "You're not. And you need to be able to vent. It doesn't change how much you love him. Daddy was difficult even on his best day, but he loved you dearly exactly the way you are."

"Yes, well, we are a long way away from his best days I'm afraid, and it's only going to get worse."

The two women embraced, and Cas felt awkward and went to take a step back. "I'll wait outside."

Delilah reached out and grabbed his arm. Esme wrapped her arm around him and suddenly he was part of a group hug. It was the closest he'd come to being part of an extended family since he'd been that little kid kicked out of the foster family because an adult had abused him.

Fuck if he didn't want to cry. He managed to hold it together, grateful beyond measure and at the same time terrified it was all going to go wrong again, and being alone would be worse this time. A thousand times worse.

58

They'd made love when they'd gotten back to the townhouse, and then Delilah had showered and dressed and taken the files Yael had compiled about the prison visitors to sit on the couch and start over from the beginning. Scanlon had to have been communicating with someone to set up this complex plan, and as his SEAL buddies Holtz and Johnson both had alibis for Nicole's murder, it meant someone else was involved. Something nagged at her, but she couldn't pinpoint what it was.

It was only four p.m., but the storm clouds made it feel much later. Cas was at the other end of the couch, reading the Seattle Police reports on the shooting death of Nicole Zimmerman—thanks to Yael's magic skills. But no one had seen anything, just a shadowy figure, running away.

Cas's cell rang and his expression changed. "I have to go in."

"That's okay." Her eyes were gritty with fatigue. "I'm going to catch an early night."

He smiled and something melted inside her. "I'll call if I'm going to be long. Keep your phone close, and your guard up."

"Yes, sir." She yawned. She'd barely slept last night.

One side of Cas's mouth turned up. "Someone is waiting for me outside otherwise..." He leaned over and kissed her on the mouth. "This will be over soon, and we can figure out the future—together."

She nodded. She wasn't sure what that was going to look like, but knew she had some decisions to make.

Cas went out the door and locked it behind him.

Today had been traumatic and exhausting in a different way from the rest of the week. The fact her father had threatened Cas five years ago had blindsided her, and yet it made everything finally click into place and make sense.

And as much as he'd wanted to join HRT, had left the SEALs to do so, she knew that it would have been the family dynamic—the fear of not belonging—that had been the decider for him. That was the thing that had sent him running.

He didn't seem to understand that, as awkward as it would have been to start with, eventually her father would have come around. They would have fought and argued and still made up afterwards. Still figured out a way to fit into each other's lives because that was how most healthy families operated.

But how could he have known?

He couldn't.

And how could she stay angry with her father who was slipping so quickly away from her? She needed time to process her feelings for the man he was now, but also the man he'd been back then. She needed to untangle the complexities of love and family and betrayal, but she had so little time left with him...it might already be too late.

The question for her and Cas—and any chance of a future they might have together—was had they both learned from their past mistakes? Love wasn't the issue. It never had been. Communication was. Trust was.

But none of that mattered until they put Scanlon away.

She sat staring at a photo of one of the visitors and wondered why it made her senses tingle. The name wasn't familiar. The address raised no flags, but there was something about the eyes that tugged a memory...

Her cell rang and she answered it absently even though she didn't recognize the number. Various people from the task force plus Alex Parker and Killion all had this number. "Hello?"

There was a pause. "I honestly didn't believe it."

She instantly stood and leaned down to use the chat function on the laptop to message Yael who was the only person she'd messaged this way.

> Scanlon is calling my cell...

"Who is this?" If she could keep him on the line maybe Yael could trace it.

"Ha. Funny. Are you alone? And before you lie to me, you should know that I have something of yours you might care about so don't piss me off."

How did he get this number? Had he ambushed Cas outside? Alarmed, she picked up her Glock off the side table and went to the window, but there was no one out there.

"I'm alone."

She went back to the laptop to check Yael's reply.

> On it.

"How did you get this number?"

"Never mind. Listen up. I want you to go get in that truck of yours and start driving southwest."

She put the gun down to type.

> He knows I have a truck.

"I have no intention of doing anything you suggest unless it's to come watch the cops slap the cuffs on you after you confess to trying to kill me."

"You have five minutes to pack up your shit."

"Look, I didn't sleep last night, Joseph—"

As she spoke, she relayed his instructions to Yael.

"Hate to break it to you, princess, but you're not gonna sleep tonight either—and who is Joseph? Someone you're boning? Get in the fucking truck. You have four minutes and forty-five seconds to get whatever shit you need together for a long drive. Otherwise things will get real, fast."

"Why do you think for one minute I'd do as you say?"

"Because I have something you value."

Her mind raced with possibilities. "There's nothing I want that would be worth dying for, and you sure as hell aren't inviting me over so we can laugh about old times."

"I'll be sure to tell that to your parents."

She struggled to breathe.

"What do you mean? What have you done to my parents, you bastard?"

Ignoring the fear, she frantically typed into the chat box.

"Now, now, Delilah, no one likes a woman with a potty mouth."

"Fuck you. No one likes a man who kills innocents or kidnaps the old and infirm." Her mother would forgive her for talking about her this way. "And I'm not doing anything without proof of life, motherfucker."

His anger radiated over the line. "Get in your truck, bitch. Do as I say every step of the way, or they die. We see any cops or Feds with you, they die."

We?

Her heart started beating too hard. There was no amount of training in the world that could have prepared her for this.

She typed frantically.

> Says he has my parents. Kill them if law involved.
> Tell Cas.

She didn't know how he could help but she wasn't leaving him in the dark this time. Not now they'd finally found each other again.

> CIA has a tracker on the truck, and I have my cell, but I think Scanlon must have tagged my truck too.

How? Where?

"Proof of life or I'm not going anywhere," she insisted.

She grabbed her purse, her creds, her weapon. Made sure she had extra ammo.

An image downloaded of her parents' terrified eyes staring out over duct-taped mouths in what looked like the trunk of a vehicle.

Outrage roared through her. She started to shake. "I want to see a live stream otherwise there's no proof they are still alive."

"Do as I say or they won't be."

"You bastard."

"Keep the phone on. I'll call regularly with instructions, and you'll send me a photo of you every hour in the truck, so I know you're exactly where you say you'll be. You call anyone or screw with me, they're dead."

She typed madly on the screen to Yael.

> He sent a photo of my parents. I have to do as he says until we can figure this out. He wants a photo of me every hour. Not allowed to call anyone...

She didn't know if he was somehow monitoring her cell. But Yael could find out.

> Can he hear me on my cell?

> I'll figure it out. Drive very slowly. Stop for gas and supplies to slow it down. Say nothing about me or the FBI out loud for now. I'll get back to you with a plan as soon as I know your cell is secure. UR not alone. We'll get them back.

Delilah grabbed a bottle of water from the fridge, although, depending on how far she had to drive tonight, coffee might be a better idea.

The thought of anyone hurting her parents was unbearable. She already knew how ruthless Scanlon and his accomplices were. Rage burned through her alongside frustration. She needed to stop this sonofabitch before anyone else got hurt.

59

With the overcast sky it was almost fully dark by the time Cas got to the HRT compound with Cowboy and Sebastian Black. The streetlamps glowed sullenly in the damp dusk. Everyone was unusually quiet.

Grady Steel arrived at the same time. "What's going on?"

"Beats me."

They all headed into the briefing room and found Seth Hopper and JJ Hersh with Meghan Donnelly, Hunt Kincaid, and Will Griffin.

None of the higher ups were here. Cas frowned. "What's up?"

Hopper stood. "I heard something extremely disturbing from Zoe. She had lunch with a friend of hers who's a Forensic Anthropologist at the FBI National Laboratory. Apparently, this friend was surprised I was heading back home so soon. She thought we'd be heading off on an op."

Cas crossed his arms. "Why?"

"Zoe's friend was talking with a DNA analyst yesterday morning. Apparently, the DNA on the hair follicles from one of the murder scenes in San Diego matched one of the Scanlon brothers, although she said without better reference samples from both of them, they couldn't tell us which brother. Apparently, they were trying to brainstorm any other ways to figure out how to tell monozygotic twins apart more easily. She wasn't supposed to know where the case was from, but as this had been bumped to the front of the line because it was associated with the death of two FBI agents, it wasn't hard for her to guess."

"Wait," Cas interrupted. "They had this information *yesterday* morning? Why the hell didn't they send it to the task force? Scanlon could have been in custody by now."

Hopper shifted. "That's the problem. They did. They sent it to Trainer."

There was a beat of silence.

"You're saying Greg Trainer had this information yesterday?" Cas couldn't believe it. "That sonofabitch pulled that stunt with Delilah today to deflect attention away from the fact he failed to act on this evidence? If he had, Nicole Zimmerman and her unborn child might still be alive."

"It's possible the prosecutor quashed it. It remains impossible to prove which brother was at that scene without definitive samples, and they can't arrest them both." Hopper sat on one of the tables.

At this stage it might be difficult to prove beyond doubt which brother was which, period.

"Unless we can implicate them *both* in the murders," Ryan Sullivan added sagely.

Bone-deep fury seared Cas. The sort of anger that didn't die with time. He wanted to beat Greg Trainer until he lay bleeding on the floor, but that wasn't enough. He wanted his badge. "What Trainer did to Delilah earlier today was unforgivable."

"The question is, what are we going to do about it?" Hopper insisted. "We can't tell anyone we know about the DNA results without getting both the evidence techs into serious trouble, but we need this guy to be held accountable for what he did to your girl."

Emotion choked Cas at their unquestioning support and acceptance of Delilah because he'd vouched for her. These guys were his perfectly imperfect family. And he didn't need to be perfect either, he realized. He didn't need to prove his worth every damned day. Being part of a real family didn't require excellent grades or a flawless performance evaluation every single time. It just was.

He had weaknesses and foibles, but it didn't matter. These people didn't care.

He shook off the emotions that were trying to crowd him. Instead, he concentrated on the issue at hand. "Get the DNA tech to send the same info to Lincoln Frazer with apologies for the delay and earlier omission," he suggested. "He's on the task force, and it's legit to share that information with him as he's a ranking agent and the BAU's point person on the task force. More to the point, he stood up for Delilah at the meeting today. Otherwise she would have lost her badge then and there. If Frazer sees the evidence, he will hopefully ask why Trainer didn't pursue it sooner, and he can organize an arrest warrant for Scanlon."

Cas's cell rang. Yael. He answered, hoping she'd found something that would definitively nail Scanlon or identify his accomplice. "Hey—"

"We have a situation."

―――――

Thirty minutes later Cas sat in the back of Shane Livingstone's truck following Delilah's borrowed F-150 down I-95 toward Fredericksburg at a safe distance. Cowboy and Meghan were in another truck behind them. The rest of the team were getting the equipment together. The wedding festivities had been put on hold for the HRT gang and for FBI negotiator Charlotte Blood, who'd volunteered to join them on this hastily assembled plan to find Delilah's parents and keep them alive.

He'd informed Killion but hadn't heard back and had to assume his wife was still in labor.

It was a relief to have Delilah in sight though his fingers itched to hold her in his arms. Yael's news had been like a blow to the heart. That anyone would threaten a defenseless older woman and a man suffering from dementia made his stomach churn. That these were Delilah's parents made it a thousand times worse.

Delilah had already suffered enough. The thought of her losing her parents hit him the same way it had five years ago. It would devastate her. But he wasn't leaving this time. She wouldn't be alone.

Agents from the task force were en route to the house to discreetly search for evidence from the abduction.

Right now, he and his HRT colleagues had to be cautious in case Scanlon had an accomplice driving nearby who had eyes on Delilah. Thankfully, Kevin Holtz was still being questioned by the FBI—the question of the white van and missing explosives remained unanswered.

Cas had the horrible feeling that whoever had taken Delilah's parents was the same person who'd murdered the Admiral and his wife, the same person who'd shot and killed Nicole and her unborn baby.

Not someone who'd be swayed by guilt or empathy.

But maybe the FBI would get lucky, and the accomplice would get sloppy, and they'd spot them on the highway and pull them over and arrest them, and find Mr. and Mrs. Quinn in the trunk of their car, uncomfortable but otherwise whole.

Best case scenario.

The highway was relatively quiet on this dank Saturday evening, and they'd scoped out most of the nearby vehicles. The threat of surveillance was more likely a bluff to keep the target—in this case Delilah—under the control of the all-seeing, all-knowing bad guys.

"Okay. He's not in her phone," Yael confirmed. "I've spoofed the second tracker on the truck—which I had to be physically close enough to scan to distinguish it from the other one the CIA have on the vehicle. I can now make that signal appear wherever we want it to be."

"Can the tracker pick up audio do you know?" Cas asked.

"Great question. Unfortunately, I suspect this one can transmit audio, but unless it's in the cab it won't be able to hear what Delilah is saying to us."

"We can't assume it's not in the cab." So he couldn't call her yet as much as he wanted to.

"That truck has to keep driving regardless," Shane said. "Even if Yael fucks with the signal so we control it. We have to assume Scanlon's drawing your girl either to himself or to the partner in crime who presumably has the Quinns. Right now, we have no idea where that end point is, but we need to figure it out."

Analysts, including Alex Parker, were working to track vehicles that may have been used in the abduction. They'd be tearing apart that photograph of the Quinns sent to Delilah's phone pixel by pixel for clues.

"I'm not letting Delilah drive into anyone's clutches." He didn't care if it wasn't his call.

"I didn't say she had to." Shane looked over his shoulder. "We switch Donnelly into the driver's seat. She'll pass for Delilah in a pinch. Put someone in the backseat to watch Donnelly's six."

The truck had tinted back and side windows.

"We search for the tracker and make sure it's located outside the cab so we can communicate freely without the kidnapper hearing every word."

Cas stuck his fingers in his hair, pulling at the ends. He desperately wanted Delilah out of danger but wasn't keen on putting Donnelly in harm's way either. But Meghan Donnelly was a trained operator. She might be new, but she'd completed all the training and been a case agent before that, not to mention she'd been a soldier in the 82nd Airborne Division. "How do we deal with photos he says he wants? Can we just take a bunch with Delilah in the cab now?"

"Yael?" asked Shane.

"Firstly, I would be shocked if he actually follows through on the photo thing because he must know law enforcement can embed a tracking code into images and, even if he's cloaking his location, we can find him."

"But if he does ask?"

"Unfortunately, we can't simply feed him images of Delilah we take in advance because he might ask her to show him her watch with the time on it or see some kind of tourist attraction or sign or something on the side of the road she's supposed to be passing. Plus, there's the whole pesky sun coming up at daybreak thing." She rubbed her forehead. "And if he thinks she's talking to law enforcement, he'll know he's already lost control of the situation, and there's nothing to stop him or his associate killing the parents."

Cas felt sick. He needed to get Delilah out of danger and figure out where her parents were.

"Can we arrest the guy for probable cause?"

"We only have Delilah's word it was Joseph Scanlon on the call," Shane pointed out.

"And with voice spoofing technology available nowadays, we'd need more than that," Yael added.

"If we pick Scanlon up, it'll be all over the news. Plus, the Quinns would still likely be killed and dumped. We might never find out what happens to them." Shane glanced at his girlfriend and his expression softened in apology at his blunt appraisal of the situation.

Yael pressed her lips together clearly holding back emotions connected to her own trauma. "There is one thing I could try..."

"What?" Cas asked eagerly.

"I might be able to use a special filter superimposing Delilah's features on Donnelly's. It's not tested in the field yet. I'll need to take a bunch of photos of Delilah from different angles to model her head and neck." Yael bit her lip. "Donnelly would have to take a photo and send it to me. I'd add the filter, and Delilah would have to reply with the doctored image. We're screwed if he wants video." She dragged a hand through her hair. "But again, I think he's bluffing on the photo thing."

"How confident are you the technology will work?" asked Cas.

"I developed it for a virtual reality game I worked on last year to allow players to see themselves in the game in real time. They don't own the code I developed," she assured them.

Cas didn't care.

"I own it as long as I don't use it within the gaming industry. Alex and I've been playing with the idea of using it for government entities."

"Spies."

Yael shrugged. "Or FBI agents being forced to follow instructions against their will with lives at stake."

"Do you think it will work?" Cas asked again.

"If we can swap Donnelly for Delilah before the first image is sent? Ninety percent chance of success. We have the advantage of being able to double check the image to adjust the filter before we hit send. Unless there's a glitch in the software or signal or who the hell knows what."

"A glitch?" Fuck. He felt sick. The lives of Delilah's parents might depend on untested software and the skills of this brilliant but fallible hacker. It was a race against time and a test of nerves, and they didn't have any other choice if he wanted to protect the woman he loved. "Let's do this."

60

Delilah was on the highway when a large black truck drew level beside her. It was too dark to make out the face of the driver. Her heart hammered with apprehension. She had her Glock in her lap and braced herself between the wheel and the back of the seat, in case they tried to ram her off the road.

The back window slowly rolled down.

Cas.

She blew out a huge sigh of relief and let go of the tension that gripped her.

Thank God.

He put his finger to his lips to indicate she not say anything and jerked his finger toward the next exit. She nodded and put on her blinker, pulling up to the gas station to fill up because who knew how far she needed to drive tonight. Cas's truck rolled up on the opposite side of the pump and another truck blocked her in from the rear.

She slipped her Glock into her holster, popped the cover to the gas tank and got out. She prepaid using the credit card Killion had given her and stuck the nozzle into the tank to fill it up.

Cas kept his distance, gassing up the other vehicles, but two other men began surreptitiously and systematically searching her vehicle, presumably for the tracker. Cas jerked his head to show that she follow a dark-haired woman wearing a red, white and blue Nationals cap into the shop.

Delilah did as he indicated.

The woman held the restroom door for her into the single toilet.

"Hi, I'm Meghan Donnelly." She smiled and swept her over with a glance. "I need your shirt."

"Pardon?"

The other woman stripped off her black T-shirt and offered it to her.

"Because I'm going to be driving your vehicle from now on, and we want the kidnapper to believe you are still behind the wheel."

Delilah backed up a step. "If I don't do as he says, he's going to kill my parents."

The woman eyed her with sympathy. "You know how these things work, Agent Quinn. He's manipulating you so you can't think straight. Making you jump through hoops. Exhausting you."

Delilah shook her head. "It's working. I *can't* think straight."

Dark eyes much like her own latched on to her. "He doesn't want your parents, Delilah. He wants you. You know this. We're going to make sure he doesn't get you and we will do our utmost to get your parents home safe too. The entire FBI is about to be unleashed on these guys. They can't abduct a former Assistant Director without getting their asses kicked."

Delilah crossed her arms over her chest. "Dad has dementia. He'd hate that he couldn't protect my mother or himself."

"I'm sorry. I really am." Meghan Donnelly looked down for a second. "I recently lost my own father so I truly understand, but it doesn't change the plan."

Delilah reluctantly unbuttoned and shrugged out of the navy shirt she wore and pulled on Meghan's T-shirt. They both wore jeans and black boots, so the top half was good enough.

"The guys are doing a quick sweep of your vehicle to make

sure the bad guys can't hear whatever is being said inside the cab with their tracking device. One of my HRT colleagues will slip into the backseat to provide me with backup. We can manipulate the bad guys' beacon if we want to, so they won't know exactly where we are, but we'll be close. Hopefully, we'll see someone following us. In the meantime, you're going to put on my ball cap and climb into the back of the vehicle parked behind you."

"But you don't actually look like me..." Delilah pointed out. The woman was taller and broader across the shoulders, so her shirt was a bit snug. Her face was more girl next door, with freckles, her nose sharper than Delilah's own blunt one.

"Anyone who gets close enough to figure that out is going to be on my radar. These aren't high tech villains despite the tracker. They can't hack traffic cameras or security networks." She used two fingers to point to her eyes. "They lock onto me, I'll lock onto them." Her smile was cruel. "And we'll deal with them. We have signal blockers available, so if we spot them, they can't call anyone."

"How are you—"

Meghan put the cap on Delilah's head. "Yael will explain it all in the truck. I need to pee and get on the road."

Delilah found herself pushed out the door. She rolled her shoulders. She was an FBI agent, and she believed in this organization but, apparently, they didn't believe in her—otherwise why send this agent to replace her? But the Bureau had obviously pulled out all the stops because her father was a former Assistant Director and they took a poor view to anyone going rogue. She was already on thin ice in that department.

And while her job was not worth her parents' lives, she knew that the FBI had way more resources than she had on her own. She had to believe her parents were still alive and that they would get them home safe.

She headed straight to the truck and climbed into the backseat surprised to see Cas in the driver's seat and Yael in the passenger side with her laptop on her lap.

"Are you okay?" he asked gruffly.

She slipped her arm over the neck rest, pressed her hand to his heart, and squeezed as hard as she could. "I am now."

He picked up her hand and then kissed it.

"We'll get them back."

"Where was the tracker located?"

"In the rear passenger wheel well proving this isn't the work of some criminal genius. We should be able to talk to Cowboy and Donnelly without alerting the bad guys."

"How'd he find me? How'd he even know I was alive?"

They all pulled onto the highway, but the other two vehicles went west while they headed east along Highway 3. Delilah looked over her shoulder as the others drove away.

"Until we found the locator on the truck I wondered if he'd just decided to interrogate your parents on the off chance," Cas said. "Or maybe the kid recognized you from the airport and saw you on TV and mentioned it."

"Or he staked out the FBI National Lab, but considering security around the Marine Base that's high risk," Delilah suggested.

"What about this morning at HQ? See anyone watching you when you arrived?" asked Yael who had her head bowed over her industrial-looking laptop.

Delilah shook her head. "I wasn't paying attention. I was concentrating on what Trainer was going to say."

Yael and Cas exchanged a look.

"I'm going to ask to access footage and have you review it," Yael said.

Delilah nodded, although she wondered if they were just trying to keep her occupied, a little kid with coloring crayons.

"What happens next?" Anxiety for her parents gnawed along her nerves.

"Alex is looking for any cars near your parents' house that might have been used in the abduction."

"Ask him to crosscheck with any spotted near FBI HQ or in Quantico," Cas suggested.

"Good idea." Yael nodded and typed furiously. Less than thirty seconds passed before she sat up in excitement. "Hey, bingo. Alex got a hit on a vehicle…white Honda. Rental out of Ronald Reagan by one Richard Alonso."

"What the…?" Cas stared at the other woman.

"You have got to be kidding me," Delilah added.

Ricky Alonso. Cas's undercover name.

"Wait, wait. Alex patched me in. I have a driver's license photo ID." Yael swung her screen around. "Recognize him?"

Delilah felt dizzy as the blood drained from her head.

Cas's complexion turned ashen.

Yael pulled up another image this one from outside FBI HQ timestamped 8:45 a.m. that morning. "And look who was outside FBI HQ this morning around the time you arrived."

Pedro Alvarez walked along the street like he didn't have a care in the world. She hadn't even noticed him. She felt sick.

"Sonofabitch." Cas swore. "He's supposed to be dead."

Delilah's phone rang, and they all froze.

Yael held up her hand and set up something on her laptop, presumably a trace. Then she nodded to give the go-ahead.

Delilah answered. "Where are they?"

"Keep following orders like a good little girl, and you might find out."

Every word was being recorded, and the sonofabitch was going down—Delilah would make sure of it—but there was no guarantee as to her parents' welfare.

"Okay, Joseph, let's cut the bullshit. We both know that what you really want is me, so why don't you let them go, and we can meet somewhere and duke this out. Just the two of us. One on one."

"Who's this Joseph guy? You seem obsessed."

She rolled her eyes at his lame attempt to conceal his identity.

"You and me. That's what you want. It's what you always wanted."

"Don't flatter yourself, bitch."

"Aw, my heart is all aflutter at your sweet-talking ways. Reminds me, how's that kid of yours, now you murdered her mama?"

She could feel his rage pouring along the airwaves.

"If you want to see your parents again you shut your damn mouth. Why'd you stop a little while ago?"

The abrupt change of subject made her stumble for a moment. "Gas. Coffee. And a woman needs to pee regularly, but maybe it's been a while since you had to deal with anyone with two X chromosomes."

"Don't stop again until you need gas—which is about 500 miles in one of those rigs."

"I'll fall asleep at the wheel." She let her outrage shine through.

"Doesn't matter to me."

"Where am I going, or shall I set the GPS for your hometown?"

"You don't know where my hometown is, remember, sweetheart? And if you tell the cops about any of this, mom and pop won't be very happy."

"You want that photograph now because I've got one with my middle finger ready for you."

"I'll tell you what to do, when."

"Are you jerking off on this power trip? I guess you must be an expert at that by now."

"How long do you think your parents can survive in the trunk of a car without water?"

Her mouth went bone dry. "Don't hurt them. Please don't hurt them."

He hung up.

Delilah put her head between her knees. "Did you get a trace?" she mumbled.

"No," Yael said quickly. "He has some sort of VPN that I will break, but I need more time on the line with him. Alex pinged that rental car transponder though and it came up as being close to a private airfield." Yael looked up and pointed at a sign. "One we are about to pass."

Cas indicated to pull off the highway. They were headed to a small regional airport.

Her pulse raced. Delilah checked her weapon, glad she'd put a spare magazine in her back pocket.

"Dig around in the equipment bags. There should be ballistic vests and a couple of MP5s back there."

Delilah found the ballistics gear first and passed it forward.

She handed Yael one. "Don't want you getting shot again."

Cas pulled the vest on while he was driving. "You two stay in the SUV and lock the door. It's bulletproof."

Yael was visibly shaking.

"I'm not staying in the car. I'm not a civilian." Delilah dug into the back and found two MP5/10A3s. She made sure they were both locked and loaded.

Approaching the airfield, Cas cut his headlights. There were two large hangars, and the lights were all ablaze, but she didn't see a soul around.

"Think they're here?"

"Let's hope so."

Cas pulled up behind a hangar, and she passed him one of the HKs.

"If you're with me, you take orders from me because this is what I train for every day, understood?"

His tone was sharp with worry. She understood that better than most.

"Yes, sir." She wanted her parents safe, and these assholes contained.

"Keep behind me. Lock the doors and don't leave the vehicle for anything except us. Understood?" Cas addressed Yael with the same firmness. "Anything happens to you I'll never forgive myself, not to mention Shane would kill me."

"We could wait for backup," Yael suggested.

"And in the time it takes for them to arrive, they could be gone. Let's go, Agent Quinn."

They got out of the SUV, and Delilah slipped the strap over her shoulder and held the weapon, barrel down, pointed at the ground. They ran around from the back of the hangar and down the middle of the two main structures.

At the other end, Cas crouched and poked his head out to look left and right. "You stay here while I check this hangar." He pointed to his right. "Keep your eyes on that hangar door in case any bad guys come out in the meantime. Hold fire unless they aim a gun at you. Understood?"

She nodded and watched him melt into the shadows. She wished they'd thought to grab comms before they'd left the SUV.

She couldn't see anyone in the control tower, although the lights were on. She thought she could hear the sound of a plane overhead, but they were in a busy enough area that it could be going to one of several different airfields.

Maybe they were in the wrong place? Perhaps the kidnappers had dumped the rental and swapped it for another one that was right now waiting for her somewhere along the highway heading southwest, planning to pounce as soon as they thought she was tired or isolated enough.

Cas arrived soundlessly back at her side.

"Empty."

A shout cut through the night air, but she couldn't make out the words.

"Let's go."

Delilah had done many raids in her years with the FBI, but she'd never been this scared before. Everyone she loved was in jeopardy. She forced herself to push the emotion from her mind. To fall back on her training and follow Cas's lead. They'd always worked well as a team.

They arrived at the door, and he peeked inside. Drew back. "I see Pedro holding a weapon on a guy I don't recognize while he checks his plane. A white Honda is parked to one side."

Hope bloomed, and she shoved it aside.

"When he's not looking, I'm going to peel around this door and make my way to the far-right corner where there's cover.

You're going to wait ten seconds before checking to see if he is looking, and then do the same."

"Okay." She nodded, using her professionalism like a shield to prove she could do this even though her insides were jelly. Then he kissed her.

"I love you, Agent Quinn."

She could barely speak. "I love you too, Operator Demarco."

He pressed his lips together as if wrestling with himself. Nodded. Then he eased forward and peered inside.

And then he was gone, and she was huddled outside the hangar door clutching a sub-machine gun praying her parents were still alive. She double checked that the weapon was ready to fire and then took a quick glance inside the brightly lit hangar.

Cursed.

Pedro Alvarez was looking right at her.

61

C as crouched behind a white panel van that was covered with a blue tarp and watched Pedro raise his head and look toward the open hangar doors at the exact moment Delilah checked inside.

His heart stopped in his chest as Pedro started walking toward her, firing in quick succession before she even had time to raise her weapon.

Sonofabitch.

Cas squeezed off two shots, hitting center mass and ran forward as the man fell, ballerina-like, to the concrete floor. His gun fell from his hand and Cas kicked it away as he pulled a zip tie from his pocket, rolled the guy onto his front to secure his wrists together behind his back. Then he rolled him so he could see his face.

"Delilah!" Was she injured?

He heard footsteps as she ran across the open space, and he released a sigh of relief.

The man who'd been held at gunpoint came toward them. "He wanted me to fly him somewhere, and he was in a hell of a rush to get going. I didn't have anything to do with this. He shot Malcolm up in the control tower and grabbed me when I said I was a pilot."

The guy looked terrified. "I think he's dead. Malcolm. Helluva nice guy. Shot for no good reason except that asshole over there wanted to kill someone."

And didn't want any witnesses to tell the tale. Cas called 911 and requested ambulances on site.

"I appreciate that, sir," Delilah spoke quietly but firmly. She didn't lower her weapon. "We're with the FBI. Right now, I need you to lie face down on the floor and I will secure you for your own safety until we can verify your story. Was there anyone else with this man?"

"I only saw him."

Cas saw disappointment cross her features.

He held up another zip tie, and Delilah took it and went over to secure the confused-looking guy who was staring up at them both with huge, fearful eyes.

It was always best to contain witnesses because sometimes they turned out to be bad guys pretending to be witnesses. Cas was pretty sure after what he'd seen that this guy was genuine, but why take a risk?

Pedro wheezed, struggling for breath. His black eyes slitted then opened wide. "Ricky." He sounded happy to see him. "Long time no see, *compadre*. This is a surprise, no?"

Cas shook his head. "Why the fuck didn't you get out while you had the chance?"

Pedro's lips twisted. "Get out? How the hell would I get out? Where would I go? I went home to my family, and Felipe figured the cartel could use a man who was already dead. So they did."

"How did you survive?" All the culpability Cas had felt over the death of this man rose up in his mind. Years of guilt and self-recrimination.

"Ha. I didn't. The cops shot us without warning. We never had a chance. A little like you just did to me." Pedro looked down at the holes in his chest.

"You opened fire first."

Cas looked up at Delilah. Blood streaked one side of her head and ran down her neck. The realization that she'd come so close to death made him want to throw up.

"You survived."

"*La poli* believed I was dead." He coughed violently. "Took me to the morgue without even making sure. So many of us piled up on gurneys like trash." He laughed and blood bubbled between his lips. "It was funny—except for the fact all my friends were dead. When the workers left that night, I slipped out from the sheet they'd covered me with and stood there like a ghoul all covered in blood. I shook everyone to try to wake them up, but"— he pulled a face suppressing pain and emotion—"I was the only one alive. All the others were dead. I was really happy you weren't there too until I realized you were the one who betrayed us."

Pedro's black eyes burned with hatred. "I washed up, grabbed a lab coat, and walked out like I belonged."

He coughed and then let out another groan of pain.

"Your sister." The woman whose eyes had tugged on his memory. "She visited Scanlon in prison." She must have used a false identity.

Pedro's eyes turned hard. "Don't go blaming my sister for anything. She was told to pass messages, that's all."

"For you?"

"No one else cared about what you did. Only me. And the Cajun."

"So it's gonna be your fault when she goes to prison." Cas wasn't feeling very forgiving. Not with Delilah's blood dripping on to the concrete floor.

"Cas," Delilah interrupted and jerked her head toward the white Honda. "I'm going to open the trunk."

Pedro smiled. "Great to see you and Lacey back together. Ricky and Lacey. True love never dies."

Delilah started walking toward the Honda.

Pedro's smile grew wider. "I didn't hurt them. I was raised to respect my elders. They're fine."

Cas glanced toward the white panel van hidden under the tarp and a prickle of apprehension ran down his spine.

"Delilah. Stop."

Her fingers were on the catch.

"Goddammit, I said stop!"

She jerked back in surprise. "My parents might be in there."

Cas ran toward her and then carefully placed his ear to the cold metal of the Honda. "I think that's the van from the bombing the other day." He pointed to the corner of the hangar. "We need the bomb squad before we can open the trunk. I'm sorry."

Her whole face fell in denial, and she looked like she wanted to open it anyway.

The sound of sirens filled the air.

Pedro started laughing. "Too late. I'm so happy we're all together at the end."

Cas glanced at Pedro and then back at the rental car.

Shit.

"Run!" He yelled at Delilah and then grabbed the pilot off the floor and helped him stagger to the open door of the hangar. For the second time that week, the blast wave blew him off his feet.

As Delilah threw herself around the corner of the hangar door, the heat of the blast flashed across her, searing exposed skin.

She lay on the ground, winded and destroyed.

"No. No." The thought of her parents dying in such a horrific fashion… Her father, who'd served his country with long years of dedication, had deserved to be cared for in his hour of need. And her mom, her beautiful mom, who'd spent a lifetime arranging her life to the beat of his career. Who'd adored her role as wife and mother but had deserved so much more.

Delilah rolled onto her back and found Cas lying beside her. She shook him violently, terrified he was seriously injured before she remembered herself. She staggered to her knees and touched him gently.

The pilot sat up, dazed on the tarmac.

Cas shook himself and groaned as he reared up on his hands and knees. The flames had died down almost immediately, but thick smoke clogged the air. "That's getting old fast. Stay here."

"Careful," the pilot warned. "It's a miracle the av-gas didn't go up already."

The truck came careening around the corner. Yael screeched to a halt in front of them and lowered the window. "Are you okay?"

Delilah staggered to her feet. "I have to go see if my parents survived."

Cas's expression was incredulous. "Dammit, Delilah."

"I *have* to know."

She took a step toward the hangar, but he jerked her back.

"This is my op, remember. I call the shots, and you are not having that image in your head. Not ever." He ran to the side of the truck and thumped on the window to get Yael to unlock the door. He dragged out a bag and unzipped it and was suddenly climbing into a fire-retardant suit complete with a respirator.

Cop patrol vehicles were fast approaching.

"Talk to the cops and the fire department. Tell them this is an FBI-controlled scene. I'll be in and out in under a minute."

Before Delilah could argue, he was gone. All she could think was she didn't want to lose him too.

————

Cas ran into the smoke-filled hangar grateful to see that the explosion had been so fierce it had almost put itself out. But flames lingered around the building. Pedro was on fire, and Cas looked away from the gruesome sight of the obviously dead man. He tried to shut off his emotions as he braved the heat, grateful for the suit, forcing himself toward the open trunk of the still burning white Honda.

He got close enough to look inside, sweat running down his forehead and dripping into his eyes.

It was empty.

Relief hit him, followed by despair. Had Pedro killed them and dumped them already? Were they on the plane which was now starting to smolder?

He started that way when a weird banging vibration penetrated his pummelled eardrums and the respirator he wore.

He paused and looked around in confusion.

Shit.

He felt it again.

Where was it coming from?

The small plane was starting to burn, and Cas didn't like the proximity to the gas tank that sat in the far corner of the hangar.

Bang, bang, bang.

He whirled around. Worked his way to the white van. Touched the sides which vibrated as someone pounded on the inside.

He ripped away the flaming tarp. He didn't have a lot of time because the fire was heading inexorably toward the flammable fuel, so he ran around to the passenger side door and tried the handle. It was unlocked so he eased it open a quarter of an inch to peer inside, looking for wires of yet another bomb. He couldn't see anything and decided to risk it, saying a little prayer as he opened the door wide and checked inside.

Keys were in the ignition.

Delilah's parents lay trussed up in the back of the van like a couple of Sunday roasts. He climbed over the seat and ripped the duct tape off their mouths not that it would help much given the noxious fumes filling the air, but they both took deep breaths as if to draw in enough oxygen.

He spoke over their words of gratitude. "Do you know if there was a bomb planted in this vehicle?" He scanned the area for out of place wires or something that could hide explosives.

"I didn't see him plant a bomb, but he could have done something before he moved us out of the trunk," Esme told him worriedly. "He was a creepy little man who grabbed us." Her brows met. "He told us he had Delilah and he was taking us to her. Then he knocked poor Stephen out when he tried to jump him."

The former Assistant Director began, "I'll see you in prison for this—"

"Quiet, Stephen," Esme scolded the man who looked almost comically surprised. But it wasn't funny.

"He took a black sports bag out of here which he was very careful with," she said thoughtfully. "We were here for long enough that Stephen fell asleep—until the gunshots woke him. Is Delilah okay?"

Cas nodded but there was no time to chat. "Hold on tight if you can. We have to get out of here." The fire had grown and was now licking the tank of highly flammable aviation fuel. *Shit.* He climbed in the front seat and turned the key, praying it wasn't rigged. The engine rolled over.

It was impossible to leave the same way he'd come in because the small plane was now fully engulfed in flames and blocked the way. He reversed to give himself as big a run as possible. Cas built the revs, then aimed for a spot along the back wall and gunned it, just as the fuel ignited.

62

The fire department arrived and ordered them to pull back even though she'd flashed her badge and tried to explain an FBI Agent was inside and that it was a crime scene.

Apparently, they didn't care.

It was possible she was too fraught to make sense.

She moved the truck back another fifty feet while fire fighters began running hoses. She stared with growing horror at the increasing flames visible through the hangar doors. She couldn't see Cas anymore. Suddenly, an enormous fireball erupted out of the front entrance and Delilah covered her mouth with both hands, stifling a scream as her knees sagged.

Yael gripped her hard around the waist to keep her from falling, but she was staring open-mouthed too.

It was impossible to imagine Cas could have survived that blast, even wearing protective gear.

Delilah couldn't comprehend it.

She'd lost everything she cared about in the span of a few short hours—her parents. Cas. Every single thing she loved. And it was all her fault. It was all her fault because she'd made a mistake and dropped her guard for a few minutes. She didn't know how she'd be able to go on. Not this time.

Her heart throbbed painfully inside her otherwise empty chest.

There was a screech of tires as a white van came hurtling around the corner on two wheels, going so fast Delilah worried it might flip over. The van came straight for them, and the two patrol cops pulled their weapons.

But she recognized the weird figure behind the wheel. Stumbling forward, she ran out in front of the officers waving her FBI gold shield as her heart soared. "It's okay. He's FBI!"

Cas was alive.

The van pulled to a stop a few feet away and the passenger door was thrust open. Cas pulled off the respirator as she ran toward him. He jumped out, and she flung herself into his arms.

"I found them," he said against her shoulder. "I got them both out alive."

Oh my God, what?

He released her and strode over to the truck, searching through the bags and pulling out an evidence kit before coming back to take her hand.

"We need a medic!" he yelled, then more quietly to her. "I need to check for explosives before we open the rear doors, but they are alive and in one piece. I'll be quick."

Relief filled her. "I thought they were dead."

"Secure the vehicle until I open the doors. Keep everyone away. This van is part of a crime scene." He let go of her hand, and she hurried to the rear of the van, pulling her professional cloak around her shoulders as an ambulance pulled up.

It took a long minute and each second felt like an hour as she made people stand back and wait. Finally, the doors opened, and there were her parents looking ragged and scared, ruffled and dirty, but incredibly and amazingly alive.

She hugged them both tight after they clambered awkwardly down from the van's interior.

Inside the van, Cas carefully placed the duct tape which must have restrained them between plastic sheeting so it could be analyzed as evidence.

He finished what he was doing, always the consummate professional, and jumped down after her parents. For the second time that day he was dragged into a Quinn family hug.

Delilah couldn't believe they were all still here. All still alive. But the danger wasn't over.

Not yet.

———

Joseph could feel his plans unravelling all because that stupid Mexican prick had to improvise. He'd spent years meticulously planning how he'd get away with not one, but four separate murders in the space of a week, without anyone ever being able to prove a thing. Every detail had been thoroughly examined from every angle, every potential pitfall brainstormed until it was perfect. And then he'd set about putting his pawns in place and getting the details flawlessly aligned.

And while he was angry both Cas Demarco and Delilah Quinn had escaped retribution the first time around, he was confident enough in his abilities that he saw no reason to panic. There was always a backup plan for any op. And next time perhaps he could do all the things he'd promised to do.

But fucking Pedro...

The guy was so impatient he'd ruined everything.

Joseph had seen some online reports of a large fire at an airfield in Virginia—an airfield he'd flown out of on Wednesday morning, where he'd left the van Kevin Holtz had boosted for him a few days earlier. Holtz's father used the airfield to store his plane, so no one was likely to question it being there. They all revered the Navy SEAL "hero" who hung out with his dad whenever he had time.

The news stories had been quashed, but there had been a few social media posts, enough to realize Pedro had probably been tracked down because he was a goddamned amateur.

He'd said he could fly a plane. The plan was he'd borrow

Holtz's father's aircraft and fly down to Mexico with Delilah's parents onboard. As long as they had them, they had Delilah on a string. But now Joseph was pretty sure that Pedro had been lying about having a pilot's license. He'd been bullshitting, and now everything had gone to shit.

Was he dead? Or was he feeding the FBI everything they needed to put Joseph away again, this time for life?

He feared the latter.

The signal on the truck had also disappeared suggesting Delilah knew her parents had been found. Dead or alive, he wasn't sure. Didn't care.

Joseph wanted to beat the fuck out of something, but he had to hold onto the last of his control. He paced the floor, hands clasping his skull trying to ease the headache that had been building relentlessly.

Forcing the weakness away, he crouched down and struck a match to the old newspaper and kindling set in the hearth.

He needed to destroy the burner phone he'd used to talk to Delilah Quinn and Pedro Alvarez. It was the only physical link between them. The press had been camped outside his door for hours now and he felt almost as trapped as he had when he'd been locked inside that concrete box for five long years. At least the media provided him with an alibi for today's goatfuck.

"Brother?" Virgil stood in the massive doorway of the living room.

Joseph shook his head.

Virgil came inside and ran his thick fingers over the top of the baby grand piano no one had played since their mother had died a decade ago. He lifted the drapes to look outside at the news vans that appeared to be camped out for the night.

He closed both the blinds and the drapes. "Should we be worried?"

Joseph nodded reluctantly. "I might need to disappear."

Virgil's expression fell.

Joseph tossed the cell phone onto the spitting fire and piled more wood on top. Placed the guard in front of it and headed into the study where his father did the books for the business. He poured two glasses of good bourbon using his mother's heavy Waterford crystal tumblers. Passed one to his twin.

It was incongruous to have such a lavish setting for a mechanic's office, but his father had known what he was doing when he'd seduced and impregnated one of the richest spinsters in the district.

She'd always despised the gossips who'd whispered she'd married down. She'd been proud of her boys even if privately she and her husband's marriage had disintegrated to the point where they'd slept in separate rooms and barely spoke. She'd died before she'd gotten around to divorcing their father. Pity she wasn't alive now though. Melody could do with a woman's hand.

He glanced at the ceiling as he took a long swig of the amber liquid.

His daughter was sleeping now.

He'd had the local doctor prescribe some sleeping pills, so she'd stop crying. She'd get used to them eventually. Hopefully, sooner rather than later because the noise of her whining grated on his nerves.

Joseph finished his drink and poured them both another. "I could use a little time tomorrow—to *arrange* things."

Virgil's chin rose. "Don't do anything stupid."

Joseph shook his head. Frowned. Maybe he already had. His mind kept going back to Clarence Carpenter. Wrapping his bare arm around the man's scrawny neck and Clarence reaching back in panic and pulling at his hair, scratching at his arm. Joseph didn't think he'd left any other clues along the way, but DNA techniques were so sensitive nowadays. A few skin cells and strands of hair, they might be his downfall.

And Pedro fucking Alvarez. He was the weak link in this mission.

But he didn't think Pedro would betray him to the authorities, not immediately, anyway. He'd warned the guy what would happen to his sister if he did. Plus, Pedro had no love for the FBI and Cas Demarco in particular. Joseph was pretty sure the guy would rather die than tell Demarco anything about what they'd done.

"What are you thinking?" Virgil asked.

He stared at his brother, so like him now, it was like looking in a mirror. The only difference was Virgil was plagued with more of a conscience. "I was thinking I should take Melody out to the camp for a few days. If these bozos want to sit in a boat all day and watch me, let them." He jerked his head toward the media vans outside. "I figure they'll get bored after a little while or get cold or sunburned while *I* sit on the dock and teach my daughter to fish."

"You think the FBI will follow you out there?"

Joseph scratched his ear. "It would keep them occupied if they did."

Virgil nodded. "How long do you think you'd need to be out there?"

"Couple of days at most."

Virgil nodded again and finished his drink. "Hopefully, you'll bring home a few fish for dinner."

Joseph nodded. "Hopefully."

63

Delilah was standing beside her parents as paramedics assessed them. Aside from dehydration, cuts, bruises, and mental trauma they appeared unscathed. Agents from the satellite office in Fredericksburg had hastily answered the call for backup and were now securing the murder scene in the control tower and trying to contain the mayhem of the burning hangar. They needed statements from everyone.

Her father kept trying to give orders, eager to do what he thought was his job, but her mother thankfully managed to distract him.

The paramedic turned to her. "You need that gash looked at."

Delilah looked up in surprise and flinched when he dabbed at the side of her head with alcohol, cleaning the wound.

"Stick a Steri-Strip on it and give me a Tylenol, and I'll be fine."

The guy shook his head ruefully and did as she asked. She began cleaning the blood off her neck with a wipe he handed her. The bullet had whizzed so close she'd felt it melt her flesh. Cas had saved her life with his weapon skills—and she had his years of training with HRT to thank for that.

The man in question strode toward her. And took her elbows in his hands. "I have to go."

"What?" She frowned in confusion. "Go where?"

"Task force has been mobilized to head to Louisiana. Half of Gold Team are already en route, and the rest of us are joining them there."

She narrowed her eyes. "I'm coming too."

"What about your parents?" Cas looked toward them.

"They'll be okay. I have to go, Cas. I have to see him caught. I might be able to help. I know Trainer hates me, but I'll beg the director if I have to."

"Trainer's no longer the head of the task force."

"When did that happen?"

"About an hour ago. Turns out he sat on DNA evidence that proves one of the Scanlon brothers killed Clarence Carpenter, which was probably why he went after you so hard this morning. Deflect the attention away from himself."

"Why would he sit on it?"

Cas shook his head. "Possibly because it's still inconclusive as to which Scanlon the DNA belongs to and possibly because he has some sort of personal vendetta against your father and possibly wanted to use you to smear the family name. I guess he figured it wouldn't cost him much to delay by a day while making your life hell. Then Nicole Zimmerman was murdered and he was on damage control."

Delilah swore.

Yael came running toward them. "Alex said we can use the company jet. Shane and the others are going to meet us at Shannon Airport where the aircraft will be waiting for us."

"Give me two minutes to explain to my mom what's going on. You explain to the local agents we have to go. If they want to take statements, one of them can come with us."

Thirty minutes later, they were climbing onboard Cramer, Parker & Gray's private jet carrying all the gear that had been in the truck.

Cas whistled. "Fancy."

"This is how the other half lives." Delilah forced a smile. Her brows rose as she took in ASAC Lincoln Frazer frantically pecking away on his laptop. She hesitated because she hadn't officially been invited to this party. "Sir."

"Relax, Agent Quinn." He didn't bother to look up. "I hear you recovered your parents in good health?"

"Yes, sir, ASAC Frazer."

"Frazer will do. Take a seat. I want you to tell me everything."

———

As they sat down, Shane Livingstone, Ryan Sullivan, and Meghan Donnelly arrived, dragging with them even more gear which they secured at the back of the aircraft.

As soon as they clipped in, the flight crew set about preparing to take off.

Cas had listened quietly while Delilah told her side of events. She sounded tired, and the corners of her eyes crinkled as if she was in pain. The gash on the side of her head was vivid proof of how close to death she'd come tonight again, and he wasn't sure how much more of that he could take.

Cas took over, filling in a few of the gaps, giving Alex Parker and Yael most of the credit which the hacker brushed off.

"So who's in charge now?" Although Cas only took orders from the HRT chain of command, he wanted to know who was running the task force.

Frazer grunted. "They're appointing someone from HQ, but in the meantime"—his stare was disconcertingly direct and annoyed —"me."

"What do you think Scanlon will do next?"

"I honestly don't know, but I do know he won't confess or give himself up."

"How can we prove which Scanlon brother killed Clarence Carpenter?" asked Cas.

"We have means and motive for Joseph. We're going to arrest him and let the DA worry about how to prosecute. We need to contain this guy before anyone else dies." Frazer eyed him and Delilah pointedly.

Delilah covered a massive yawn.

"Why don't you get some sleep?" Cas urged Delilah. "There's a bedroom back there."

Her eyes flashed. "Don't treat me like the weak link."

"I'm not. I plan to get a few hours too, and I'm hoping you'll take pity on me and share."

Her gaze shot to Frazer, but Cas was done pretending.

Frazer packed away his laptop and silenced his phone. "I suggest we all get a little shut eye so we can face tomorrow refreshed. And"—he stretched a brow—"I'd grab the bed quick before I pull rank and claim it for myself."

With that, he turned off his overhead light, pushed back his plush chair until it was almost flat, and closed his eyes.

Cas waited. Holding his breath. Then Delilah took his hand and led him into the bedroom, closed the door.

———

When Cas slipped out a couple of hours later, it was still dark, but the others were awake and talking quietly.

"Delilah still asleep?" Yael sent him a grin.

He blushed a little even though all he'd done was hold her. He nodded and cleared his throat. "Any updates?"

"Both Scanlon brothers are believed to be home in LaCroix. Local PD had to deal with a disturbance last night when a news crew from New Orleans turned up to ask Joseph some questions about these murders. Apparently, the neighbors got pretty cranky with the press."

Cas rubbed his face. "Any new evidence?"

Frazer steepled his fingers under his chin. "We have the DNA profile that one of the Scanlons killed Clarence Carpenter— enough reason to interview and obtain a fresh DNA sample from Joseph. We have Pedro Alvarez on camera outside FBI HQ and a trail of evidence that suggests he abducted Delilah's parents, and most importantly, their testimony. Yael is working to isolate cell signal data that would tie Pedro and Joseph together, but presumably they've dumped those cell phones. We have Pedro on commercial flights that would allow for him to have committed some of the murders. We have eyewitnesses and airfield logs that show the Scanlon plane was in San Diego, Seattle, and Virginia. Once we get Pedro's DNA and fingerprints, we might be able to link him directly to one of the other crime scenes."

"Any idea what he's been doing these past five years?"

Yael answered, "Fell off the radar after he was declared dead."

Cas smiled slightly. "A bit like Delilah." He went over and helped himself to coffee from the Keurig. "Anyone want one?"

There was a pile of pods in the trash. He wasn't sure how much his fellow passengers had napped, but he was grateful he'd had the chance to hold Delilah close, if only for a little while.

"Yes, please." Yael held up her mug. "My caffeine ban has been lifted until this case is over."

"I'm sorry you're going to miss your boss's wedding."

"It sucks, but this is more important."

Frazer sent her a benevolent smile. "Maybe we'll be back in time for the reception."

Yael laughed. "Maybe."

"Team is planning to stage at the Sheriff's Office in Houma. Plan is to arrest good ol' Joseph on his way to church."

"Being born again has some advantages," Cas agreed.

"As good a place as any." Frazer nodded.

"Do we pick up the brother and father on conspiracy charges?"

"I'm waiting on a judge to sign a warrant, but so far he wants actual evidence both brothers are involved, and we don't have it."

"Yet." Cas took a sip of his coffee before handing Yael hers.

"Yet," Frazer agreed.

64

S canlon opened the front door of their century old home and watched the vultures stir.

"Wait here," he told Melody as she clutched her pink teddy bear under her arm and rubbed the sleep out of her eyes. Virgil stood beside her on the porch. "I'll be back in a moment. Don't say a word," he warned.

"I want to make a quick statement," he announced loudly as he walked down the front path.

Cameramen scrabbled for their equipment while reporters rushed toward him.

Once the first green light told him a camera was recording, he held up his hand for quiet and began reading a short statement he'd written as the sun had started to rise over the bayou.

"Good morning. I want to address the rumors swirling around the death of my ex-wife amongst others. I'm innocent. The Federal Government is pursuing a relentless vendetta against me, and leading the charge is the FBI. I have no knowledge of any of the murders they are suggesting I might be involved in and, indeed, haven't left the great state of Louisiana except for one sanctioned and supervised visit to reacquaint myself with my daughter after being unable to see her during the many years of my incarceration. I know what I did in the past was wrong, but I've paid the price and begged God's forgiveness. I have no desire to break one of the sacred commandments. I understand that I'm a public interest story but request, for the sake of my young daughter, to be left alone to deal with the grief associated with her momma's untimely passing." He held eye contact with the female reporter with the blonde hair and blood red lipstick. "Ma'am." He nodded to her and walked back to the house then herded the three of them back inside. He tossed the piece of paper onto the side table by the door.

"Ready to go out onto the swamp and see if we can spot any alligators?" he asked the kid.

She clutched the teddy tighter but nodded.

"You put on sunscreen?"

Melody shook her head.

"Go do it. And don't miss any spots because we aren't coming back just because you get burned, understand?"

She nodded again and dashed away.

Virgil watched her go and shook his head. "One of us should get ourselves a woman to help raise her."

Joseph smiled. "Maybe that pretty cop?"

Virgil grunted. "Nah, one who stays home and knows how to cook."

Joseph nodded again. Fair point. They both liked to eat.

————

They met up with the others in Houma, and Delilah found herself in a convoy of black SUVs and one armored personnel carrier, sitting with Yael, Frazer, and Livingstone with Cas driving.

The Sheriff had been informed and was sending the local SWAT team to assist.

"Well, that's irritating." Frazer checked his cell. "Scanlon isn't going to church this morning after all. Apparently, he and his kid got into a boat and drove away after doing a little piece for the news cameras."

"They have a cabin, a camp, I think they call it down here." Delilah leaned forward. "In the boonies on the lake. Location was in the case files."

"I have it." Yael pulled up the area on Google Maps. "Here." She pointed to an isolated shoreline, connected to the mainland but with such thick brush and swamp it could be impossible to approach from that direction.

"What about the brother?" Delilah asked.

"Headed to the garage with the father. Apparently, it's not uncommon for them to work on weekends."

"Think Scanlon's gonna make a break for it?" asked Cas.

Frazer inclined his head slowly. "He might. What are our options for an arrest?"

"We can wait for them to come back."

Frazer shook his head. "No guarantee he'll come back."

"We can insert via water or air. Parachutes won't do us a lot of good. Woods are too dense to land in, and if I'm going to have to fight an alligator, I'd rather do without a parachute holding me down."

"Readymade sushi rolls," Shane joked.

Delilah shuddered.

"Best bet," Cas said, "is to set up the snipers at various points around the lake—let's talk to Wildlife and Fisheries about the best places because they'll know the area. Once snipers are in position, we get the Little Birds in the air, and the assaulters can fast rope on the camp."

"Think he'll be armed?" Delilah asked.

"The local sheriff said that the Scanlons gave up all their weapons without any fuss when Joseph was due to be released as part of the parole conditions, but there's no way they don't have something hidden near the camp. Even for self-defense," said Frazer. "We need to prevent him from accessing a weapon before we have him under control."

"He's a Navy SEAL," Cas said ominously. "A pencil could be a deadly weapon."

Shane started laughing.

"There's a child involved," Delilah reminded everyone.

"We are aware," Frazer said testily. "Her safety is our priority. Scanlon's arrest is secondary. Think you can protect her?" he asked the two operators.

"Yes." Cas said.

"Yes," said Shane. "Even if he picks up a pencil."

Cas punched him in the shoulder, hard, and Shane yelped.

The kid was going to be scared after losing her mother. Delilah hated the idea of her being in danger, but what choice did they have?

"Okay, let's head to the nearest Louisiana Department of Wildlife and Fisheries building. Get the drones and helicopters in the air ASAP. We can't sit around waiting. The local grapevine will start wondering why two dozen special operators are camped out in town, and they're not going to believe we're all after fishing licenses."

"Yes, sir," Yael murmured with big eyes.

"Please," Frazer added. "I seem to have lost my usual assistants."

"Well, I'm not doing anything. I might not be a whizz on the computer like Yael, but I can make phone calls as needed," Delilah offered, wanting to be useful.

"I'll bear that in mind." Frazer's icy smile landed on her. "Let's get this done, people."

65

Two hours later, Cas lay cold and damp behind tall grass in a hide usually used by duck hunters about 800 yards away from the rustic cabin that had been in Scanlon's late mother's family for the past seventy years. Cas was dressed for the part in woodland camouflage jacket and brown pants one of the wildlife agents had lent him. They'd decided to hide in plain sight to the point they'd even brought a 12-gauge shotgun that they'd fired a couple of times, careful not to actually hit anything because they couldn't collect any game they brought down.

His olive drab GA Precision FBI HRT .308 sniper rifle fitted with a Leupold scope was probably a little beyond what a typical duck hunter might use. Sebastian Black lay beside him with his rifle, currently on the spotter's scope. Unlike the one Scanlon used during his unsuccessful attempt to kill Cas on Wednesday, their scopes were coated with anti-reflective material that cut down on glare.

Cas had dialed in elevation, windage, although the direction had shifted so Sebastian checked it again. Cas also adjusted for the mirage. At least they didn't need to worry about Coriolis effect at this distance of only about eight football fields.

With a cold bore shot and a child in the kill zone, there was no margin for error. Cas was praying Scanlon would surrender without a struggle when he realized he was facing overwhelming firepower. The guy did not have a death wish.

It felt strange simply to watch this man who'd tried to kill him and the woman he loved, not to mention all the other crimes he'd committed since he'd been released from prison, through the glass of his scope. It would be so easy to squeeze off a shot and end the threat of danger to Delilah and to his friends. Less than a second, and this could be all over, but so would his career and his chance of a future with Delilah, because he wouldn't allow her to sacrifice her own career to stand by him.

And wasn't that part of the problem the two of them always had—not allowing the other to put their relationship over their careers?

He pushed the thoughts aside and concentrated on the job itself. JJ Hersh and Damien Crow were set up to the west in another hide. And the other four snipers from Gold Team had slipped in covertly and were spread out in pairs at regular intervals to ensure someone should have a clean shot in the event Joseph Scanlon decided to attack the arresting officers or held his own child hostage.

Wildlife and Fisheries personnel had stopped boating traffic coming into the area, but they also had some agents out fishing in plain clothes so the area wasn't unnaturally quiet.

"We don't have to worry about lead," Sebastian Black stated on the personal comms that connected the team members in close proximity. "Joseph Scanlon is on the end of the pier with his fishing rod in hand. He doesn't look like he's going anywhere anytime soon."

Cas could see the shine of beer on the man's lips after he took a sip from a can in the cooler at his side.

The question was, *what else was in that cooler?*

The main thing about being a sniper people never really talked about was the bone calcifying boredom 99.99 percent of the time, followed by moments of intense pressure when actions had life-and-death consequences. Chances were they were going to be here all day. If things went south and this turned into a hostage situation, they could be here for weeks. And they couldn't afford to let their concentration slip.

"I think we're going about this wrong," Sebastian said suddenly. "Why don't we send in a couple of assaulters wearing Wildlife and Fisheries uniforms and ask to check his fishing license? It's normal and expected for them to be out here, and he likely wouldn't overreact."

The Little Birds were staging in a wildlife refuge about three miles west.

"That's a good idea," Cas agreed.

"Hey, what kind of snakes do they have in Louisiana?" JJ Hersh asked suddenly. "Because I think I just saw a cottonmouth swim past."

"I like Black's idea about inserting as wildlife agents," Birdman agreed. "And, yes, that was a water moccasin, and if you get bit again, I will kill you myself."

Cas grinned. "Hey, where's the kid gone?" She'd disappeared from Cas's field of view.

"She's in the grass to our left of the dock. She dipped her toes in the water."

"Aren't there alligators in these waters?" Birdman asked.

"And snakes," JJ agreed.

Cas kept his breathing nice and steady as he watched Scanlon take another sip of beer and turn to say something to the kid. She jumped back out of the water and ran up the bank, wide-eyed, to stand a few feet behind him.

Joseph had just reminded her about the gators.

Melody went over and sat on the steps to the deck of the cabin. Pulled a tablet from the backpack her mother had packed a few short days ago and tucked the pink teddy under one arm.

"Contact Frazer," Cas told Sebastian without looking away

from the crosshairs focused on Scanlon's center mass. "Tell him it's a better and safer plan to pretend to be Game Wardens. We can get two assaulters—"

The sound of a shot from a high-power rifle rang out and cracked off the surface of the lake. Half of Scanlon's head disappeared.

Sonofabitch.

He shifted his scope to the kid who stood frozen on the spot, her face twisted in a scream of horror he was too far away to hear. He flexed his finger to make sure he hadn't been the one to discharge his rifle. As tempting as it might be to get rid of Scanlon permanently, that wasn't who he was. That didn't show discipline or follow the rules.

"Who fired that shot?" JJ demanded over a litany of other people demanding the same thing.

"Is the kid okay?" Sebastian asked frantically.

Cas used the glass to scan her for wounds. "I don't see any injuries. From the direction of the blood spatter the shot came from the northeast."

Novak's voice came over the radio. "Scan the perimeter for any possible threats. Romano is checking out the area with the drones, but it's a vast space. I'm going to need everyone's weapon for forensic examination."

Fuck.

They were all going to be suspects in Scanlon's death. The eyes of the world would once again scrutinize every step they'd taken today. He and Sebastian exchanged a scowl.

"As soon as the drones clear the area, we're going to send in the assaulters to clear the camp and pick up the kid. After that, ERTs will work to find that bullet."

"You think one of us shot him." JJ sounded furious.

"No," Novak interrupted firmly. "No. I know none of you shot an unarmed suspect, and I'm doing everything by the book to make sure no one doubts my word, or the evidence."

Novak was protecting them all, but mainly him. Cas couldn't

have loved the guy more.

The question was, if they hadn't murdered Joseph Scanlon in cold blood, who had?

66

Delilah covered her mouth with her hand as the news of Joseph Scanlon's death was reported to the makeshift Incident Command center Frazer had established—an empty space above a bakery on Main Street, downtown LaCroix.

Killed in front of his seven-year-old daughter.

Delilah couldn't imagine how the past few days would shape that young child's life.

Who'd shot him?

Good thing she wasn't in the field, or she'd be the number one suspect.

Her pulse raced uncomfortably as a headache built. The sun poured through the windows. Relief filled her that Scanlon was no longer a threat. She wasn't even a little bit sorry he was dead, and that bothered her. When had she lost her empathy?

Perhaps when he'd killed her best friend and FBI partner? Or when he'd murdered Clarence simply to confuse the issue? Or perhaps after the first bomb had almost killed Cas? And she would bet that although Pedro had most likely murdered the admiral and his wife, and Nicole, and kidnapped Delilah's parents, it had all been Joseph's idea.

Conversations came in over the radio.

Scanlon was dead but no one knew who'd taken the shot. At least no one was admitting to it. She gnawed her lip. Would Cas have shot Scanlon in cold blood?

To protect her, maybe, but not without a direct threat.

And why bother when they were bringing him in anyway?

Either someone's finger had slipped on the trigger—unlikely as these guys fired a thousand rounds a week—or someone else had shot Scanlon.

Who?

Maybe someone he'd hurt? Or the cartel in revenge for Pedro Alvarez's death last night?

Or Pedro's sister perhaps?

Pressure built inside her skull and pain streaked through her temple. She grimaced as she pressed her fingers against her forehead.

"What's the situation on the brother and father?" Frazer demanded.

"As far as we can tell, they are both inside the garage. Cell phones haven't moved."

Yael had hacked into the feed of a security camera facing the front of the mechanic's workshop from a laundromat across the street, and no one had gone in or out for the past three hours. It had been Delilah's job to monitor the feed. It was stiflingly hot in this small office space with a broken AC unit and the inability to open the windows.

"I'm going to buy some painkillers. Anyone want anything?"

Frazer gave her a long assessing look but nodded. "Pick up some coffees and bottled water on the way back. And don't let the press see you."

Her survival had not yet been broadcast to the world, and she hoped she'd be allowed to talk to her SAC in San Diego before the information was publicly released. She nodded, relegated to coffee girl, but at least she was here. Still in the FBI.

She grabbed the Nationals ball cap she had yet to return to Meghan Donnelly and headed out the door. She had to wear her jacket to hide her weapon which didn't help the headache. On the street, she glanced inside the bakery and saw that the place was packed. The coffeeshop was adjacent, although she was pretty sure it was run by the same owner. She'd pick up the drinks Frazer had requested on the way back to save her carrying it too far.

The sun was hot on her skin, and she stood for a moment absorbing it, and the reality that this nightmare was finally over.

She hit the pharmacy and bought both ibuprofen and acetaminophen and washed down the first dose with some ice-cold Coke. Outside the store, she glanced around and realized the bayou flowed just a block over. She headed that way, curious as to what the river looked like and needing some fresh air while the meds kicked in. She gave herself permission to take a few minutes to process everything. She wished she could talk to Cas but didn't want to disturb him in what was likely to be a fraught and chaotic moment.

She was relieved to get her life back finally. First, she'd tell Val's mother about her daughter's tragic death and hopefully expedite the release of her remains so she could be buried. Then she could deal with the frustratingly mind-numbing details regarding the insurance claim on her condo and begin to smooth things over with her boss and colleagues in San Diego.

She stopped short.

Not that she wanted to stay in San Diego anymore, she realized. She wanted to be closer to her parents and, more importantly, she wanted to be close to Cas.

She passed a couple of shrimp boats and pressed her lips together in annoyance when two of the men started to wolf whistle at her. She wasn't in the mood to deal with them. She took a right at the muddy banks and followed a well-traveled path.

She picked her way past a boat shed, almost tripping over some chicken wire that had been left coiled up across the path.

She knew she was close to the Scanlons' workshop and didn't want to get too close. She wondered how they were going to react to the shooting. She wanted to know who'd murdered Scanlon, but that was for someone else to investigate this time.

The noise of a slowing outboard motor and then the sound of someone docking a boat floated over the air. She didn't want to be seen. She peeked around the corner and there, getting out of a powerboat was Virgil Scanlon.

Shit.

Had he heard about his brother? She didn't want to deal with him if he had. She didn't want a confrontation even though she was armed.

Where'd he been?

She hadn't realized the Scanlons had a boathouse down here. She scooted back and decided to cut through the small parking lot shaded by the massive live oaks whose branches snaked so low and wide she had to duck beneath the bows.

Her cell buzzed with a text, so she decided to give Virgil time to go back to the garage as she waited behind the massive trunk to read it.

Demarco, asking if she was okay.

She sent a thumb's up in reply. Her headache had started to ease.

You?

She tilted her head to listen to the noises around her. Birds singing. A squeaky old weather vane moving in the slight breeze.

She got another text.

I love you.

She smiled and took a step forward, about to text back but sucked in a shocked breath as she found herself grabbed from behind, a massive hand clamped over her mouth, silencing her scream before it released.

———

Cas wasn't allowed anywhere near the body of Joseph Scanlon. Instead, he found himself, along with the other snipers, on a boat driven by one of the Wildlife and Fisheries agents, staring across the water to where Novak and several other FBI and Fisheries agents were removing Melody Scanlon from the scene.

He frowned. "Hey, where are we going?"

"I'm taking you on a shortcut back to LaCroix. It's not on the map, and it's easy to get lost out here." The man glanced at the rifles that had all been put into their respective cases, but otherwise left loaded which was usually a no-no. The rifles themselves would prove HRT hadn't fired the fatal shot, and the presence of a third-party organization would help verify the chain of evidence.

But who the hell had shot Joseph Scanlon?

It made no sense.

He texted with Delilah. Told her he loved her. The three dots appeared to say she was texting him back, but nothing happened.

Shit.

He waited expectantly, but the dots disappeared.

"What's up?" Sebastian asked him.

He scowled. "Worried about Delilah."

"Why would you be worried about Delilah? Joseph Scanlon is dead."

Cas froze, and the thought that he hadn't fully been able to grasp finally came into sharp focus. "What if he isn't?"

"Dude, I saw his brains vaporize."

"What if the person we saw shot was Virgil? What if Virgil pretended to be Joseph to give his brother time to escape?"

"Cameras showed him giving the press conference then loading everything into his boat and leaving."

Cas shook his head. "They all went into the house first. What if the brothers switched T-shirts, and Virgil took on the role that he's probably been playing on and off his whole life?"

Sebastian leaned forward. "In that case who the hell shot Virgil?"

Cas stared hard at his teammate. His suspicions sounded farfetched and yet... "Joseph. He killed him. Steps into his brother's life, and we all believe the true villain is dead."

Cas looked at the dancing three dots of Delilah's text. She must have a lot to say.

But he couldn't quite shake the thought she might be in danger.

She was with the task force. She was fine. He was being paranoid.

He called Frazer.

"What if Joseph and Virgil swapped places this morning? And Joseph killed his brother to escape justice?"

There was silence on the other end but the listening kind.

"You didn't shoot him?"

"No, sir."

"And the other HRT snipers, they didn't shoot him either?"

"Definitely not."

"Then I'd say it's about time we had a chat with whichever brother is at the garage and his father. I was just waiting for Agent Quinn to return—"

"Return?" Even as Cas said it, he knew Delilah was in trouble. "Find her, Frazer. Get everyone on it and find her."

He hung up and leaned forward to address the Wildlife Agent. "Gun it."

"It's a no wake zone."

Cas shook his head. "This is life or death. If you don't want to take responsibility, then stand back because I will."

67

Delilah found herself lifted up off her feet and manhandled so she couldn't reach her weapon. He slammed her against the tree, winding her so bad she couldn't catch a breath. Then he snatched her Glock from the holster in her waistband and banded one arm around her waist, placing a meaty hand over her mouth, smothering her cries. He carried her into the dark garage as she struggled wildly. He closed the side door behind him with his foot, and she bit down on his palm hard enough to taste blood.

He pulled his hand away and punched her in the side of the head, the same place where the bullet had grazed her yesterday.

She grunted.

"Virgil?" A man's voice called through the dimly lit garage.

He clamped her jaw shut with a strength that felt like it might crush her bones. He stretched her neck back, and she had no problem believing he'd snap her in two if she uttered a sound.

"Yes, Pop?"

"I'm going to go grab a coffee. You want one?"

"Nah. I'm good. But lock up the front, huh? I need to do some paperwork."

The man's erection pressed into her ass, and a new brand of fear assailed her.

She began struggling again, but the other man had already left, and she found herself half carried, half dragged to the back room that served as an office. And the man who'd ambushed her pushed her inside and locked the door behind him with a quiet snick.

They stared at one another, breathing hard.

His eyes narrowed, and she suddenly knew this wasn't Virgil. This was Joseph. And she was trapped inside this small space with a man who hated her guts and had already tried to kill her once.

"You know, most people would be shocked at the idea you'd murder your own brother to switch places with him. But not me. I always knew you were a psychopath."

His eyes flared, and maybe the fact she'd told him she'd guessed his secret wasn't the smartest move on her part.

"You think I'm the only one who's gonna figure it out? You should run, now, while you still have a chance. Steal a boat and head to Mexico. The FBI is in town. But you knew that already."

"I probably should run, but I have waited too long and fantasized too hard about this moment, and they're still out there, chasing their tails. Now I'm gonna put your smart mouth to good use."

She snarled. "If you wanna risk it."

He grabbed her by the shirt and ripped the buttons apart. She remembered her self-defence training and brought her fists up and into his lower jaw, snapping his head back. But he caught her by a fistful of hair and yanked her around and slammed her into the desk, head first.

Her bones wanted to turn to jelly as he fought with the button on her pants. He was going to rape her—like he'd promised all those years ago. Her hands scrabbled across the desk, knocking off papers, searching for anything to use as a weapon. Her fingers closed around a pencil, and she gripped it firmly, hope and desperation surging in equal measure.

He got his hand inside her zipper, and she rolled on top of it, trapping it so he couldn't move.

Impatiently, he flipped her up and slammed her onto her back, once more knocking the wind out of her lungs. He dragged her jeans down her legs, and she kicked him in the face, relishing the yell of pain he released, but he grabbed on to her ankles and forced her legs apart. He unbuckled his pants and freed himself, then leaned down to leer at her.

"When I'm finished with you, I'm going to throw your body in the bayou where the fish will eat the rotting flesh off your bones and the gators will feast on what's left."

Her heart raced so fast in her chest she thought it might give out. Blood rushed through her ears in a steady whoosh. She smelled his sour breath in her face. Felt him hard between her thighs. His hand wrapped around her neck and squeezed hard enough to let her know exactly how he intended to kill her.

"Joseph," she whispered and licked her lips. She gripped the pencil tighter. She'd have one chance at this. He had more than a hundred pounds advantage, and it was all solid muscle. Plus, he was smart in the ways of killing and hadn't hesitated to bash in Val's skull or shoot his own brother.

He leaned closer to hear her words.

"You know I hate you." Without dropping his gaze, she drove the pencil into his left ear with her whole might.

He collapsed on top of her, unmoving, pinning her to the desk so completely she could barely draw breath.

She needed to get him off her, but she didn't have the strength. She didn't know what the father would do if he found them like this. The thought this battle might not be the end of the war had her trying to shift Joseph's bulk, but her arms were too weak.

Tears of frustration welled up.

And then sounds came. Sounds she craved. Sounds that filled her with joy and relief.

"FBI. Open up."

Sounds of agents making their way inside the garage.

"In here!"

Her whole body was shaking. She didn't want her colleagues to see her this way but the sooner she could get away from Scanlon's touch and smell the better.

"In here." Her voice was thin and scratchy.

The door crashed open, and there was the man she loved with her whole heart standing with a stricken look in his eyes. Two other men she didn't know flanked him.

"Joseph's dead. I killed him with a pencil."

She almost giggled at the absurdity of what she'd just said but that was the shock kicking in. Nothing about this was funny.

Cas dragged Scanlon off of her by the scruff of his sweatshirt and quickly shrugged out of the camouflage jacket he wore.

She still couldn't move.

The other men averted their eyes as Cas eased her gently upright and wrapped the jacket around her shoulders. He held her gaze, the deep yellow of his eyes reminding her of a haunted tiger.

"Are you...?"

She pulled up her pants with shaky hands. "He didn't rape me. He was going to. He planned to kill me and dump me in the river afterwards, but I grabbed a pencil off the desk and remembered what you guys said earlier in the SUV." She felt sick. "I didn't think it was going to work."

Tears filled her eyes then and flowed down her cheeks. "Thank you for finding me."

"Thank you for killing him." Cas zipped up the jacket and then picked her up in his arms and carried her out. And in that moment, she knew exactly how much she loved this man and how much she wanted to spend the rest of her days with him.

68

FEBRUARY 15

Mon., 7:30 p.m. Local Bar

It was only a day and a half since Joseph Scanlon had died a far too easy death. In his mind, Cas had replayed a thousand more satisfying scenarios to end him, but at least the man was no longer a threat to the woman he loved.

Cas sat in the bar and nursed his Dance of Days pale ale and wished he was with Delilah.

Yesterday, after she'd been checked out at the hospital and given the all-clear, she'd given her written statement and then insisted that she be allowed to fly out to the Bay Area to inform Valerie Strauss's mother about her daughter's death in person before she found out via the news media.

Cas had worried she was still in shock.

He'd wanted to go with her, had begged Novak and threatened to quit if he didn't get the time off. But, as Novak had forcefully pounded into him, he'd needed to write up reports and follow procedure if they didn't all want to be hounded by congressional committees looking to score political points off any perceived misdeeds for the next decade.

But he missed her.

The internet had gone into a frenzy over leaked details that one Scanlon brother had killed the other, and then a supposedly dead FBI Agent had taken down a former Navy SEAL with a pencil. The authorities hadn't found the sniper rifle that had been used to kill Virgil Scanlon, and it was likely Joseph had dropped it over the side of the boat on the ride home. They had discovered Virgil had purchased a sniper rifle in cash, belonged to a gun club, and had been seen practicing there in the weeks since Joseph had been released.

The whole identical twin and fake death thing, along with such high-profile and horrific crimes, meant there was no hope of the furor dying down any time soon.

Holtz had been charged with an array of offenses, and it was likely the man's days as a SEAL were numbered. They had little on Mark Johnson, but his actions over the past two years were being put under the microscope, and if there was anything to find, Cas was sure the analysts, including Yael, who refused to give up the search, would find it.

The admiral's gold trident pin had been found on the scorched body of Pedro Alvarez. His sister had been scooped up on conspiracy charges.

Melody Scanlon had been escorted back to Seattle to be with her stepfather and grandmother. The kid was probably traumatized for life, but hopefully the family members could get the therapy they all needed.

Greg Trainer had been put on paid leave while an investigation went on regarding the way he'd run the task force and the fact he'd released an agent's personal medical information during a meeting.

After making official statements and filling out reams of paperwork while still in Louisiana, Cas's and other team members' rifles had been sent to an independent lab for analysis. Then he'd flown back to Quantico with the guys. He'd cleaned up Quentin Savage's place, so it was neat and tidy with freshly laundered sheets. He'd gathered Delilah's belongings, along with his own, and taken everything to his apartment.

He was thinking about maybe making an offer on Savage's condo, except that all depended on what Delilah wanted.

He had no idea what shape the future might take. He just knew he needed her in it with him—assuming she still wanted anything to do with him…

What if she decided he wasn't worth the risk after all? Old fears and thoughts crowded into his mind.

Dionne Warwick sang, "I'll Never Love This Way Again," and Cas wondered miserably exactly how drunk he could get tonight without being fired in the morning. And maybe he needed to man up. Make the grand gesture and quit HRT, so Delilah knew exactly how committed he was to this thing between them. Every time he thought about what had nearly happened to her…

"Hey." Ryan Sullivan leaned against the bar beside him. "You okay?"

Cas grunted. Did he look okay?

"You heard from Lilah yet?"

He swung around to glare at his teammate. "Don't call her that."

Ryan quirked a brow. "What? Lilah? Why, is that your pet name during—"

Cas's elbow thrust sharply into Ryan's solar plexus. "Ryan, so help me God, if you say one more word, I will kill you."

Ryan pulled a face as he regained his breath. "Got it. My lips are sealed." He waited a beat. "So you haven't heard from *De-lilah* yet?"

Cas scowled into his beer glass. "Not really."

"She'll be here."

"Maybe she won't." That was his biggest fear. That she wouldn't have enough faith in him or his promises—because he'd failed her in the past.

"She loves you."

Cas took a sip of beer. "Maybe that isn't enough."

"What else is there?"

What else, indeed? Cas stared at the guy for a long assessing moment. Although he shouldn't be surprised. Ryan Sullivan was capable of great depth and insight, he just preferred to exist in the shallows whenever possible.

But love had never been the issue between him and Delilah. Communication, trust, and respect had been where they'd failed one another.

Laughter broke out and Ryan glanced over at the table near the jukebox that included Donnelly, Black, Griffin, and Crow.

"Is Birdman hitting on Donnelly?" Ryan's eyes narrowed.

"Donnelly can take care of herself."

"And I can take care of Birdman," Ryan muttered darkly.

Donnelly frowned over at them.

Sinead O'Connor's "Nothing Compares 2 U" started on the jukebox next.

Cas groaned and rested his head briefly on his forearms. "Who chose this playlist?"

As he sat back up, he saw Krychek via the mirror behind the bar, alone at his usual table. His expression didn't invite anyone to join him.

Ryan turned away from the others and slouched against the bar. "I hear the wedding went off without a hitch."

Cas grunted. He shouldn't feel resentful of other people's happiness, not when they'd worked so hard to get there. The other good news was Patrick Killion was now the proud father of a baby girl named Daphne, and Audrey was doing well.

He was happy for the man.

Truly.

He was just so fucking desperate for himself not to mess this up.

Ryan checked his watch as if he were expecting someone.

"Date?"

"What?" Ryan startled. "Oh, no, just thinking it's almost my bedtime."

"Losing your touch?" Cas hadn't seen the guy out with a woman since Christmas. Which for this guy was a world record.

Ryan huffed out an annoyed laugh. "What do you think?"

The notion was ridiculous. Women loved the guy.

The barkeep winked as she sent Ryan a flirty smile.

"I rest my case." Ryan dug into his pocket and pulled out four quarters. "Go put on a different song. This one makes me want to put my head in an oven."

Because he didn't trust Ryan's taste, he took the money and walked over to the jukebox and tried to find a song that wasn't about lost love. He chose Gloria Gaynor's, "I Will Survive," having forgotten the lyrics.

Resigning himself to the singalong that was sure to follow, he went back to finish his beer with the intention of heading home. His insurance company had provided him with a temporary replacement vehicle, which was a shitty sedan. Still, it would get him to and from work, which was all he needed this week.

Who knew what would happen next week or where he might be?

His teammates broke into song and Cas stood to leave.

"Have another beer." Ryan tried to get the barkeep's attention, but she was serving someone else.

Cas shook his head. "I'm gonna head back."

"Hey, I need to ask you something." Ryan sounded desperate.

"What is it?"

Ryan's eyes were huge, but then he glanced at the entry and his expression relaxed. "Nothing."

Shaking his head, Cas turned away and came to a dead stop. Delilah stood there with Yael and Shane behind her.

Her dark eyes were bright, and she wore an easy grin. The stress of the past week was gone from her face, though sadness lingered in the shadows of her eyes.

He had never seen anyone more beautiful in his life.

He strode over to her and lifted her up in his arms and swung her around. Then he placed her on her feet and kissed her like they were the only people in the room.

After a few moments, the whoops and hollers reminded him they weren't.

He pulled back, taking her hands in his. "Are you okay?"

She nodded. "Sorry I didn't let you know I was coming. I wanted to surprise you."

He shook his head. "It doesn't matter now that you're here."

"I love you, Cas."

"I love you. I'm going to spend every day proving it to you."

"You don't have to prove anything. I understand now why you did what you did."

He rested his forehead against hers. "Because I was an idiot who was too scared to have an adult conversation?"

She touched his face. "Because you didn't know how to accept unconditional love. Being on the Hostage Rescue Team, somehow, crazily, taught you that. Maybe it was the journey you needed to make so we could have this second chance."

His throat squeezed so tight he couldn't breathe. "I never wanted to hurt you. It still kills me to think about that, and how close Joseph Scanlon came to…"

"We don't have to worry about him anymore."

"Because you're a goddamned bona fide badass."

"I got lucky."

He didn't want to think it was only luck that had been at play two days ago. "You were trained and kept your cool under pressure. He underestimated you. I'll never make that mistake again."

"Neither will he."

They shared a relieved look.

Ryan came over and introduced himself, followed by all of his teammates. Delilah was hugged and kissed and treated like a long-lost member of the family. Even Krychek made an effort and actually smiled.

Some clown put on Rick Astley's "Never Gonna Give You Up," and everyone was singing and dancing around the two of them

---

like it was a party. But suddenly Delilah was in his arms again, and they stood there staring at each other as if time had stopped.

"Are you really okay?" he asked.

"I am now."

"Your parents?"

"They're fine. I'm going to see them tomorrow."

"I don't want to be apart from you anymore." He moved a strand of hair off her forehead. "I'm ready to resign from HRT and apply to be a case agent in San Diego." The Bureau was good about giving former HRT operators their choice of assignment. "I haven't done anything yet because I wanted to make sure that from now on, we make any important decisions about our future together. Last time, I didn't talk to you, and I should have. I should have trusted you."

"Oh, damn. Now I feel bad." She swallowed tightly but her eyes danced. "I spoke to the Director yesterday—she called me—and I requested, and was granted, a transfer to be the lead agent in the Fredericksburg satellite office as they currently have a vacancy."

His heart swelled to twice its normal size. "Truly?"

He had to wipe the tears from his eyes to see her nod.

"Lilah," he whispered. "I will never let you down again."

"I know, Cas. I know. That's why I asked for the transfer." She grinned and hugged him tight. He didn't think he'd ever been this happy before. Never in his thirty-four years of life.

She laughed. "We're going to figure out the happily ever after business, if only to spite Scanlon."

"I'd rather do it because you're the love of my life."

She sniffed and blinked away tears. "That too."

Over her shoulders, he saw the blonde from last week enter the bar. Montana's daughter.

She scanned the room and looked stricken as she took in the party atmosphere. It brought the loss of her father crashing back down around his shoulders, and he glanced around still holding tight to Delilah.

The music stopped abruptly. The blonde took a nervous step forward. She cleared her throat and swallowed.

Krychek stood and took a step toward her.

She sent him a look.

"Ah, hmm. Sorry to interrupt. My name is Daisy Montana, and I know many of you worked with my dad." She twisted her hands together, clearly nervous. "The thing is, I don't think he's dead. I think he's still alive."

Shock radiated around the room.

Cas took a step forward. "Why? Why do you think that?"

She never got the chance to answer. Jordan Krychek strode over and lifted her in a fireman's carry over his shoulder and headed straight out the door.

All hell broke loose.

———

Thank you for reading *Cold Spite*. I hope you enjoyed Cas's and Delilah's story. Ready for the next exciting installment of the Cold Justice® - Most Wanted series?

Pre-order *Cold Truth*...the next Romantic Thriller from *New York Times* and *USA Today* bestselling author Toni Anderson!

USEFUL ACRONYM DEFINITIONS FOR TONI'S BOOKS

ADA: Assistant District Attorney
AG: Attorney General
ASAC: Assistant Special-Agent-in-Charge
ASC: Assistant Section Chief
ATF: Alcohol, Tobacco, and Firearms
BAU: Behavioral Analysis Unit
BOLO: Be on the Lookout
BORTAC: US Border Patrol Tactical Unit
BUCAR: Bureau Car
CBP: US Customs and Border Patrol
CBT: Cognitive Behavioral Therapy
CD: Counterintelligence Division
CIRG: Critical Incident Response Group
CMU: Crisis Management Unit
CN: Crisis Negotiator
CNU: Crisis Negotiation Unit
CO: Commanding Officer
CODIS: Combined DNA Index System
CONUS: Contiguous United States

CP: Command Post
CQB: Close-Quarters Battle
DA: District Attorney
DEA: Drug Enforcement Administration
DEVGRU: Naval Special Warfare Development Group
DIA: Defense Intelligence Agency
DHS: Department of Homeland Security
DOB: Date of Birth
DOD: Department of Defense
DOJ: Department of Justice
DS: Diplomatic Security
DSS: US Diplomatic Security Service
DVI: Disaster Victim Identification
EMDR: Eye Movement Desensitization & Reprocessing
EMT: Emergency Medical Technician
ERT: Evidence Response Team
FOA: First-Office Assignment
FBI: Federal Bureau of Investigation
FNG: Fucking New Guy
FO: Field Office
FWO: Federal Wildlife Officer
IB: Intelligence Branch
IC: Incident Commander
IC: Intelligence Community
ICE: US Immigration and Customs Enforcement
HAHO: High Altitude High Opening (parachute jump)
HK: Heckler & Koch (a German firearms manufacturer)
HRT: Hostage Rescue Team
HT: Hostage-Taker
JEH: J. Edgar Hoover Building (FBI Headquarters)
K&R: Kidnap and Ransom
LAPD: Los Angeles Police Department
LEO: Law Enforcement Officer
LZ: Landing Zone
ME: Medical Examiner

MO: Modus Operandi
NAT: New Agent Trainee
NCAVC: National Center for Analysis of Violent Crime
NCIC: National Crime Information Center
NCIS: Naval Criminal Investigative Service
NFT: Non-Fungible Token
NOTS: New Operator Training School
NPS: National Park Service
NYFO: New York Field Office
OC: Organized Crime
OCONUS: Outside of the Contiguous United States
OCU: Organized Crime Unit
OPR: Office of Professional Responsibility
POTUS: President of the United States
PT: Physiology Technician
PTSD: Post-Traumatic Stress Disorder
RA: Resident Agency
RCMP: Royal Canadian Mounted Police
RPG: Rocket-Propelled Grenade
RSO: Senior Regional Security Officer from the US Diplomatic Service
SA: Special Agent
SAC: Special Agent-in-Charge
SANE: Sexual Assault Nurse Examiners
SAS: Special Air Squadron (British Special Forces unit)
SD: Secure Digital
SIOC: Strategic Information & Operations
SF: Special Forces
SSA: Supervisory Special Agent
SWAT: Special Weapons and Tactics
TC: Tactical Commander
TDY: Temporary Duty Yonder
TEDAC: Terrorist Explosive Device Analytical Center
TOD: Time of Death
UAF: University of Alaska, Fairbanks

UBC: Undocumented Border Crosser
UNSUB: Unknown Subject
USSS: United States Secret Service
ViCAP: Violent Criminal Apprehension Program
VIN: Vehicle Identification Number
WFO: Washington Field Office
WMD: Weapons of Mass Destruction

COLD JUSTICE WORLD OVERVIEW
ALL BOOKS CAN BE READ AS STANDALONE STORIES.

COLD JUSTICE® SERIES
A Cold Dark Place (Book #1)

Cold Pursuit (Book #2)

Cold Light of Day (Book #3)

Cold Fear (Book #4)

Cold in The Shadows (Book #5)

Cold Hearted (Book #6)

Cold Secrets (Book #7)

Cold Malice (Book #8)

A Cold Dark Promise (Book #9~A Wedding Novella)

Cold Blooded (Book #10)

COLD JUSTICE® – THE NEGOTIATORS
Cold & Deadly (Book #1)

Colder Than Sin (Book #2)

Cold Wicked Lies (Book #3)

Cold Cruel Kiss (Book #4)

Cold as Ice (Book #5)

COLD JUSTICE® – MOST WANTED
Cold Silence (Book #1)

Cold Deceit (Book #2)

Cold Snap (Book #3)

Cold Fury (Book #4)

Cold Spite (Book #5)

Cold Truth (Book #6) - Coming Next

The Cold Justice® series books are also available as audiobooks narrated by Eric G. Dove, and in various ebook box set compilations.

Check out all Toni's books on her website (www.toniandersonauthor.com) and find exclusive swag on her store.

ABOUT THE AUTHOR

Toni Anderson writes gritty, sexy, FBI Romantic Thrillers, and is a *New York Times* and a *USA Today* bestselling author. Her books have won the Daphne du Maurier Award for Excellence in Mystery and Suspense, Readers' Choice, Aspen Gold, Book Buyers' Best, Golden Quill, National Excellence in Story Telling Contest, and National Excellence in Romance Fiction awards. She's been a finalist in both the Vivian Contest and the RITA Award from the Romance Writers of America, and shortlisted for The Jackie Collins Award for Romantic Thrillers in the Romantic Novel Awards. Toni's books have been translated into five different languages and more than three million copies of her books have been downloaded.

Best known for her Cold Justice® books perhaps it's not surprising to discover Toni lives in one of the most extreme climates on earth —Manitoba, Canada. Formerly a Marine Biologist, Toni still misses the ocean, but is lucky enough to travel for research purposes. In late 2015, she visited FBI Headquarters in Washington DC, including a tour of the Strategic Information and Operations Center. She hopes not to get arrested for her Google searches.

Check out Toni Anderson's shop with exclusive merch and offers:
https://toniandersonshop.com
Sign up for Toni Anderson's newsletter:
www.toniandersonauthor.com/newsletter-signup

f facebook.com/toniandersonauthor

X x.com/toniannanderson

⊙ instagram.com/toni_anderson_author

♪ tiktok.com/@toni_anderson_author

ACKNOWLEDGMENTS

This is the twentieth Cold Justice® book!!! Kathy Altman deserves a lifetime achievement award for being the first person to read every single one of them. Thanks for always being there for me as a critique partner and a friend. And thanks to Rachel Grant for the excellent *beta* read and feedback (and also for being a wonderful friend). Appreciation to Tim Wheat for checking over and "roughing up" the Spanish in this novel. Any mistakes are mine.

Credit to my fabulous editorial team, Lindsey Faber, Joan Turner at JRT Editing, and proofreader, Pamela Clare (yes, *that* Pamela Clare!). What an amazing group of people I have to support me.

Eternal thanks to my assistant, Jill Glass, who is such a magnificent help in running the day-to-day business of being an author. Thanks also to my wonderful cover designer, Regina Wamba, for her gorgeous artwork. Kudos to Eric G. Dove for being the voice of the Cold Justice® books and for being such a lovely human being to work with.

Love and smooches to my husband—my personal hero—for doing *all* the things.

Made in the USA
Coppell, TX
10 October 2024

38454545R00259